122 RULES
Redemption

122 RULES
Redemption

Book Two in the 122 Rules Series

DEEK RHEW

Tenacious Books Publishing

Published by Tenacious Books Publishing

Copyright © 2019 Deek Rhew

Published by Tenacious Books Publishing in 2019
Tenacious@TenaciousBooksPublishing.com

This book is a work of fiction. Names, characters, places, and incidents are either the product of the author's imagination or are used fictitiously.

Library of Congress Cataloging-in-Publication Data
Rhew, Deek. First edition.
122 Rules - Redemption / Deek Rhew
ISBN 978-1-7338974-0-2 (print)
ISBN 978-0-9998978-9-8 (e-book)

Cover Image: © ShutterStock
Cover Design: Anita B. Carroll www.race-point.com

Printed in the United States of America

www.TenaciousBooksPublishing.com

Despite already having a cast of great characters and the opening scene set up like a meatball lobbed across home plate, this book took over three years—three!—to complete. I attribute my sluggish literary tempo to my inability to focus on a single task for more than five minutes without getting distracted by one of a million shiny objects that catch my atten... Oh, look! Squirrel!

Uh hem. Focus, Rhew. Focus.

Anyway, the simple truth of the matter is that on my way to writing this book, I got a little lost.

So, I dedicate this book to those who set out to do great things but often find themselves lost instead.

Chapter One

A cool saltwater breeze raised gooseflesh over the exposed scalp of the Redeemer's shaved head. The slumbering shadows behind the dark bedroom window remained motionless, yet he waited. Patience, just one of his many talents, and an infallible sense of timing kept him from making rash, rushed decisions and miscalculated movements.

Though his superior hearing would have alerted him to any approaching intruder, he nevertheless maintained his vigil, surveying the surroundings at regular intervals.

The clear sky allowed the moon to bathe the yard in a lunar glow. Trees and shrubs, which grew in utter randomness around the small plot of earth, cast deep pockets of shadow—just large enough to conceal him and his premeditations.

Discerning eyes, attuned to any inconsistencies or changes not attributable to the wary Pacific gusts, swept from potential hiding place to potential hiding place. Assessing and reassessing. Detecting no threats, he slid past the bush he'd used to obscure his form and glided forward, his footsteps no louder than a panther's paws on new-fallen snow.

The large overhang of the house's sloped roof shielded its side from the light in the sky. As he came in contact with the structure, he melded into the hodgepodge of nothingness, becoming just another subtle angle among the architecture.

He waited for a cry of alarm, but nothing disturbed the stillness except the rhythmical chant of crickets and the far-off pounding of the ocean in its eternal quest to grind rock into sand. He stood and poured half of a small vial onto the edge of the bedroom window frame. He moved to the other side and repeated the process. Crouching, he allowed the inkiness clinging to the building's foundation to consume him once again.

He counted, giving the lubricating oil time to penetrate, and upon reaching a predetermined number, he pushed against the wood frame. At his urging, it moved upward. The wood sliding against wood whispered like fine sandpaper over wet mahogany. Silent as the parting of a spider's silken web, he slinked over the lip of the sill, birthed through the thin drapes, and rolled to the floor.

The Redeemer closed the portal, sealing out the world that lay beyond. He stood and glanced around the simple living room.

Knickknacks and snapshots in cheap frames adorned the side tables of a deep couch. He quickly cataloged these details before he turned his gaze to the wall where three large paintings hung side by side.

The first depicted a small girl with startling sea-blue eyes and ragged clothing. She sat propped against a bleak stone wall, clutching a broken doll in her dirty hands. In the dis-

8

tance, a couple could be seen through a window, eating a lavish meal in a fine restaurant—a poignant commentary on the separation between the haves and have-nots.

In the second, a figure with the same enchanting eyes, only now a young woman, leaned against a tree. The forlorn, lost expression had been replaced by one of determination and survival.

His attention shifted to the third canvas, and his gorge threatened to rise in disgust and indignation.

Two women lay beneath a blanket in an embrace so complete, the couple appeared to be one. Foreheads pressed together, eyes—one brown, the other brilliant blue—locked in an expression of longing and contentment. Their affection poured out of the image in a filthy torrent.

The blue-eyed girl had shed her clothes and her dignity, and instead of continuing her ascension from rags to riches, she'd chosen to lie with another woman. After rising from a poverty-stricken street rat to a self-sustaining, potentially functioning citizen, she had chosen the path of the wicked, becoming nothing more than a common pervert. Typical. Without a father figure to guide her, she had discarded her sanctity and tarnished her purity, succumbing to licentious carnalities.

When the Redeemer had been a child, his father had beaten him and his mother—often until blood spilled and bones cracked—whenever either of them had wandered from the gray line of his version of divinity. An especially brutal schooling session had put his mother into the ground and him into foster care. But the lessons dealt at his father's righteous, unforgiving hand had taught the young Redeemer that pain and fear are great healers and the only true path of the holy. Through their proper application, deviant, freakish behaviors—such as a proclivity toward disgusting sexual hungers—could be driven out before taking root and claiming one's soul.

Perhaps the depictions in the paintings had been intended to show the fallibility and fragility of the human spirit? He examined the three pieces once again and then shook his head, tsking in disapproval. No. The brush had been wielded not in condemnation but in celebration of this abhorrent behavior.

His heart sank, not just at the grown woman's failure to withstand temptation but at the artist's poor choice to use perverts as the subject of the composition.

He had been guided to this artist, discovering her at the local gallery after several days of searching for a candidate worthy of his talents. Because she too took divine inspiration and created works of beauty and grace, she might be able to see the parallelisms between their hearts and minds.

Or so he had hoped.

He sneered at the disgusting painting and all it represented. Clearly, she lacked his ethics and moral compass. Without his natural gifts and heightened sense of morality, she had allowed herself to become impure.

Averting his eyes from the lewd sensuality, he glanced instead out the window while weighing the merits of leaving and finding another that hadn't wandered so far astray. But that would take longer than he had. His message needed to be delivered, and he didn't have months to decide on another courier. It would take extra time and effort—a lot of it actually—to cleanse the artist of her infatuation with this couple, but together, he and the artist could rid her of these repulsive fascinations.

Besides, by cleansing this vile creature of her wickedness, he could showcase the depth of his abilities and prove to the gods, once again, his resolution to stay the holy course.

The Redeemer pulled a knife from a hidden pocket and shred the third painting until nothing remained but tatters. He'd have burned it too, but the flames might have drawn attention and cut the evening's ceremony short. Though the removal of a single disgusting pornographic image would not change the destructive course of human devolution, his heart nevertheless felt cleaner. More at peace.

He returned his gaze once again to the first painting. Approving of this rendering of misery and heartache, he stared at it, looking beyond the store-bought acrylics and amateurish, though talented, brushstrokes.

The imprint of the artist's essence glowed within the canvas. He touched the image's surface and closed his eyes, absorbing its creator's energy, her vibrancy, her life. He cleared his thoughts of all distractions. Focusing and stretching his mind, he beckoned, mentally calling out and whisper-chanting the name of the other to join him.

The pressure in the small room shifted. The air grew heavy and chilled as though he'd stepped into a meat locker on a sultry August afternoon. His eyes popped open, and the last of the syllables died on his lips as a presence as hot and acrid as smoke from a burning tire filled his nostrils.

It swirled around his body, inspecting him. Phantom claws traced the curve of his spine, outlining the bald cap of his head. Though he couldn't see it, he sensed it coming to rest before him.

He smiled, encouraging it to join him. The other entered his body, and as it settled into his bones, muscles, and tendons, their molecules mingled and danced in an intimate ritual as the two beings coalesced into one.

He looked around, sharing the details of his feelings and visions with the creature. The other gazed in wonder, then urged him forward.

Though the Redeemer longed to find the woman and help her begin her journey to enlightenment, he allowed himself to be guided to a set of stairs, which ended in a second floor studio.

He wandered around the large, cluttered room, examining the various pieces of the artist's collection, but none of them held the same emotion, the same passion, as those in the living room.

Sitting on the stool before her easel, he tossed a half-finished work to the floor, propped a blank canvas in its place, and picked up her brush. Dipping the tip in a small jar of paint, he moved the bristles across the pristine surface. An extension of its owner, the little stick of wood and horse hair channeled her vitality. They splashed color and emotion across the canvas like a severed artery. Stroke after brutal stroke, their love of the woman flowed, creating a celebration of life and beginning the foreplay of her ascension.

When he finished, he set the brush aside and gazed at their creation. He—and the other—smiled.

Beautiful.

They gathered a small pile of blank canvases, descended the stairs, and followed the short hallway. He'd almost passed the entryway into the kitchen, but at the other's urging, he stopped. At first, he didn't know what had drawn its attention, but then a vision of the masterpiece they were about to create bloomed in his mind. Stunned by its graceful splendor and the addition of a final, perfect flourish, his heart cried out in rapture. The Redeemer stepped into the small space, carefully selected the perfect knife from the wooden block on the counter, and then continued making his way to the artist's bedroom.

A thin strip of moonlight sliced through the narrow space and spread across the figure lying beneath the blankets. He leaned the canvases against the wall and set the knife on the floor. They would be needed soon, and he wanted them within easy reach.

Pulling down the zipper of his body suit, the disengaging plastic teeth a feather's sigh in the stillness, the Redeemer disrobed. Preferring simplicity and practicality, he wore nothing beneath the garment and stood naked in anticipation.

He absently rubbed the scabbed, scarred flesh of his face, where a bullet had shredded skin and grazed bone a few weeks before, while his attention remained fixed on the sleeping figure. The reverberations of his heartbeat pulsed through his body like a warrior's drum calling soldiers to arms. A predator's thirst, a need as integral as the transfer of oxygen from lung to hemoglobin, began to take control.

He removed a small blade, a condom, four sets of padded handcuffs, and two small, silk sacks from a pouch of his suit. His body already excited and eager, he slipped the prophylactic on and ran his thumb over the knife's honed edge to verify its readiness.

His careful tableau of self-control began to unravel as he slid through the ray of light and loomed over the bed, watching the young woman sleep. Visions of him removing her flesh, one piece at a time, flooded his imagination. Premonitions of the beautiful experiences they were about to share brought tears of joy to his eyes and sent a mild anticipatory electric current flowing through the wires of his nerves. Each savored slice and sacrificial drop of blood fed his unquenched thirst as he cut away her flaws.

Her dark hair had been tied back, exposing a thin, graceful neck. With his superior vision, he could see her jugular pulse in the weak light, and he imagined the sensation under his fingertips as the beat tapered and then stopped altogether.

His gaze traveled to her bare shoulders, lingering on the delicate, pale skin covering her collar bones. He imagined the delicious sounds they would make when he crushed them.

He enjoyed every aspect of the process—the hunting and tracking, the watching and capturing, the purifying and cleansing.

Mostly though, he loved the begging.

First, they implored him to be left alone, and then they pleaded for him to stop. But in the end, they all begged. Begged him to take them. Begged him to help them ascend. That moment—the one where they truly began to understand the gifts he'd bestowed upon them, when he'd removed all of the flaws of their pitiful existence and they had become worthy of moving on—tasted as delectable and savory as a raw steak to a malnourished hound.

Perhaps even better though, the palpable anticipation before the first slice. The instant he took imperfection and began to make it better.

God, he loved his job.

He sat on the edge of the bed and leaned in close, inhaling her essence. Her hair smelled clean, with a hint of coconut. Both a chalky sweetness from her lotion and the bitter, insect repellent of a cosmetic remover drifted from her cheeks. A faint touch of lavender clung to her neck. He lingered, inhaling the sweat of her armpit, relishing the complex bouquet of raw femininity.

A single drop of saliva plummeted from the corner of his mouth, landing on the bare skin just above her heart.

The woman's eyes flew open, the combination of surprise and terror etched into their depths as he looked deep into her soul.

For an instant, he recognized the dark brown orbs, but he did not immediately know where he'd seen them.

Her breath hitched in a sudden intake of fear, and she prepared to scream.

Delicious.

"Don't." He shook his head. Leaning back, he punched her in the mouth, cutting off her first syllables in their infancy.

The combination of fright and the blow paralyzed her. She would remain impotent for only a few moments, so he used the time to secure his advantage.

Slipping the two cloth sacks over her hands, he cinched them tight. He didn't want any of her covered—every inch of flesh should be exposed—but prudence mandated this precaution. If she got loose, it wouldn't do for the police to be able to recover trace elements from under her fingernails. It wouldn't do at all.

A sharp stab of disappointment struck him as he removed the blankets. She slept in the nude. The foreplay of removing his partner's clothes would have heightened their intimacy.

But she had been exposed to sexual perversions and desires that contradicted nature and its elegant design. He could chastise her for these indiscretions, but the time required to correct her defects would be extensive and drawn out, and he didn't have the luxury of wasting precious minutes on the frivolities of lecturing her.

Besides, he had better, more convincing methods than mere words, ones that would guide her down the path of enlightenment.

He tethered her wrists and ankles to the bedframe with the handcuffs. He'd modified the chains to be adjustable and snugged them down. Everything had been staged properly.

His gaze roamed over the virgin landscape of her body. He couldn't just dive in and start willy-nilly slicing off parts of her—that would be barbaric.

The paintings that graced the walls of the Louvre and Smithsonian had been created by artists who were both scorned and misunderstood. Only in the unrelenting march of time had the mere mortal masses truly appreciated the greatness of their work. Like Edvard Munch and Vincent van Gogh, he would continue creating masterpieces on his medium of choice, at his own tempo, understanding that only long after his demise would his art and brilliance truly be adored by the ignorant populace.

Tracing the tip of the blade over the tops of her feet, he didn't cut her...yet. The first stroke of his version of a painter's brush would come soon, but for a moment longer, he would enjoy the sight of steel on bare skin.

As he walked around the side of the bed, he bumped something with his hip. A journal hung partially off the top of the nightstand.

Time pressed him for urgency, but since nothing increased the intimacy of their bond as much as knowing his lover's innermost thoughts and feelings, he picked the book up and flipped to the latest entry. The log chronicled a fight between her and someone named Kyme, complete with all the usual she said/she said of young adult drama.

Suddenly, it struck him why those brown eyes looked familiar. She'd been the other figure lying with the blue-eyed woman in the third painting.

His blood pulsed, and his vision turned red as he continued to read. Kyme, the woman in the paintings, and...her, the artist...her "partner."

Page after page, he read about the abomination that passed for a relationship. She hadn't just been exposed to the depravity of Kyme's sexuality; she had been part of it. Mired and bathed in it. Perhaps even its instigator.

He looked at the dazed woman in the bed. The purpose of her existence, the reason the gods had put her on this Earth, had been for him to use her to send the bitch a message. But this woman had tainted herself. Made herself unimaginably impure by succumbing to sins of the flesh.

It made his work so much more difficult when the tool had almost no redeeming qualities.

The woman had begun to moan. Pathetic little whines emanated from deep within her throat.

Unconcerned about fingerprints since he had seared those off with a torch years before, he returned the book to its perch. Taking a cup conveniently staged on her nightstand, he dumped water over her face.

She gasped awake.

Patience exhausted, he covered her mouth. "You will say nothing and do nothing unless I tell you to." In his free hand, he circled the wicked little blade in a figure eight above her face.

She pulled on the restraints while her wide, brown eyes followed the path of the knife.

He stared down on her like a vengeful god. "If you cry out, I'll cut you. If you don't answer my questions, I'll cut you. If you try and get away, I'll cut you. If you lie, I'll know it, and..." He lowered the blade and pressed the edge at a severe angle to her lips. "It will be the last thing you ever say. Do I make myself clear?"

She gave the slightest of nods.

He removed the knife from her mouth. "Let's start with something easy. First tell me your name."

She tried to speak, but her quivering voice made the words indecipherable. She swallowed hard and began again. "April. April Goodman."

"Is that you in the painting?"

Confusion clouded her terror-filled eyes. "What? What painting?"

Exasperated, he seethed. "In the living room. Fornicating with another woman."

She blinked. "I...fornicating? The one of me and Kyme? Yes... But we aren't fornicating. We're——"

He didn't let her finish. "Tell me, April..." Her name tasted like vinegar on his tongue. "Did you ever stop to think that maybe what you were doing was wrong? That maybe by whoring yourself out, you were destroying your chance at fulfilling your true destiny?"

"I...what? What destiny? Why are you doing this?" She tried to squirm away from him, but the restraints held her in place.

He started to wave the knife just inches above her face again, and she stilled. Around and around it went as he tried to soothe the beast within him that raged against her lies and denials, to keep it from doing something rash that he would later regret. He took a deep breath, and instead of screaming at her, he spoke with an icy voice. "Why? Why am I doing this?" He forced a smile onto his lips. "I'm doing this because it's *my* turn to ascend."

"Ascend? I...I don't understand."

"I know you don't because you're nothing but a common pervert. A tool. Let me see if I can simplify it so even someone like you can comprehend the magnitude of the events about to unfold. See, for me to ascend, for me to move beyond this place and claim my throne, I need someone special. But until a couple of months ago, even I didn't know who that someone was."

His simmering soul calmed as it became enraptured at the image forming in his mind. "When I almost lost my reward, when my life and my destiny came to a crossroads. When this," he pointed at his scabbed face, "happened and I lay in a pool of my own blood, I had a vision."

He swept his hand through the air as though he could show her the picture in his mind. "In it, I saw my own ascension. My destiny. More beautiful than anything on Earth. More beautiful than any human could imagine. And beside me, the channel to my divinity was a woman. She was my most perfect masterpiece. My final, flawless work of art."

April swallowed. "You think that's me?"

"Nooo," the Redeemer said, smirking as he waggled the blade above her eyes. "I can understand why you'd *wish* it were you. Who wouldn't want to stand beside me on a sacred altar, adored and worshiped by the unwashed masses? But a cosmic covenant cannot be fulfilled by just anyone. *You* are nothing. A nobody. Only *she* is the vessel worthy of birthing a new era, with me as the divine leader. *She's* the one. *She's* the womb. The bitch. Chosen by the gods to deliver me as their new king."

Longing, joy, and determination bloomed anew in his heart. "And that's why *she's* been so elusive, so hard to capture. The path of the deities is not an easy one. Otherwise, just anyone could do it. You see?"

Tears spilled down April's cheeks. "No. I don't see. I don't understand any of this. If I'm not the one that will help you...ascend or whatever, then you don't need me, and you can just leave me alone. I won't tell anyone you were here. Nobody has to——"

He shook his head and touched the tip of her nose with the pointed end of the blade. "Everyone has a part. Even you."

"No, I——"

"See, the gods put *you* here to be my messenger."

Though she spoke to him, her gaze fell to the blade in his hand. "What message? To who?"

Continuing in his cold, velvety voice. "My bitch. *The* bitch. Monica Sable."

She shook her head in little jerky movements. "Monica Sable? I...I think she left town. A while ago...for school or something."

He nodded. "Yes, that's right." He touched her chest with the knife. "And you're going to bring her to me."

"I...I can do that. Call her or something."

Ignoring her ignorant blathering, the Redeemer stroked the side of her face with the back of his hand. Traced the contours of her nose and brows with his fingertips. "Except you've been trying to ruin things. You've been trying to make yourself too vile. Too disgusting. Too unworthy. But not even you are beyond redemption."

21

"Let me go. I don't need to be redeemed. I'll call her right now. I'll—"

He tapped the tip of her nose with the point of the knife again and then resumed the figure eight pattern above her face. "I'm going to remove all of your flaws, all of your perversions, even if it takes the entire night. I've sliced up hundreds of little cunts like you, helping them rise up and move beyond this world. It's finally time for one of *you* to help *me*."

More tears streamed down her face, soaking her pillow. "Slice me? No, please. You don't need to do that."

Taking a long sorrowful breath, he said, "But you're a pervert. Sleeping with that woman is a blasphemy against nature and an insult to the universe. You've probably had sex with half the women in town. It makes me sick."

"What? No. I've never slept around...Kyme is the only person I've ever been with."

"Liar!" he screamed and backhanded her so hard only the restraints prevented her body from flying off the bed. He dropped the knife and wrapped his hands around her throat, squeezing until the veins popped in his forearms.

She struggled, trying to shove him away with her hip, but his large fingers dug into the soft tissue. The metal cuff binding her left wrist snapped the dowel in the headboard, and she tried to scratch his face, going for his eyes. But the silk mitten prevented her from using her fingernails.

She started beating her fist against his head and chest, but her efforts proved no more forceful than the fluttering of a sparrow's wings. As her punches weakened, her eyes rolled back.

The other spoke to him. Reminding him of his duty and calming the savagery and sorrow this disgusting woman had draped over his heart. He relaxed his grip, understanding the situation had come within a ghost's breath of getting out of control. He had almost let her provoke him into killing her, which was what she'd wanted.

It was what they all wanted.

By making a quick, neat exit, she would have denied him the ability to fulfill his destiny.

He would find Monica. His bitch would get this message and come back to town, and when she did, he would be waiting.

But first...he gazed down at the defenseless woman lying in her bed, dazed and vulnerable. He rebound the wrist that had come free in the struggle and picked his blade up from the floor.

The sun had set just a few hours before, and the Redeemer had a lot of work ahead of him.

He got up and retrieved the canvases he'd brought down from the studio, propping them up against the wall next to the bed.

Time to make some art.

Chapter Two

Tyron Erebus waded out into the dark ocean. He wanted to set his art free, and the sea served as the perfect easel for the world to admire his genius. He stood, watching in pure joy as his masterpiece floated away. The final adornment—and his message to the bitch and the mongrel—sparkled and glistened from the redeemed girl's finger as it caught the light of the full moon.

Anyone lucky enough to spot her should have held fast in wonder and envy, mesmerized by the purity that could be obtained when he made flawless that which God had botched.

With the waves breaking around his waist and the moon enraptured by the spectacle, April's body sailed out of sight. When he could no longer see her, he took a deep melancholy breath and trudged back to shore, returning to her home.

The hot spray of her shower cleansed his body of the salt and bits of bone and flesh the sea had not washed away. Though April no longer resided in this world, he inundated himself in the warmth of her lingering aura by using her body wash and soap.

When the water ran cold, he pulled open the curtain and ran his fingers over the threadbare Winnie the Pooh towel hanging on the rod. He pressed his face into the soft fabric and inhaled her aroma. Her essence felt as sweet and tender as the final, delicious kiss of a departing lover.

A surprising tear rolled down his cheek, and Erebus wiped it away. While overjoyed that she'd transcended, a profound longing to have her in his arms, to feel her heat, and to hear her cries of adoration struck his heart. With her gone, only loneliness and isolation remained to keep him company.

A sudden sob erupted from his throat, and he slid to the floor, weeping. Clutching the Winnie the Pooh towel to his chest, his heart wallowed in agony. If only their time together could have been more drawn out, or even better, if he could have gone with her. Moved beyond this place...as one. Their souls connected for eternity.

But he still had work to do. The humble servant, grinding away, doing his duty.

The heaving ebbed, and Erebus wiped at the wetness clinging to his cheeks. He slowly got to his feet, and as he dried the rest of his body, her essence coated his skin, providing him a small degree of comfort.

He replaced the towel with a fresh one and slogged down the hall to the washing machine, where he paused to lovingly touch the fabric one last time. The smiling face of the chubby bear winked at him as if to say, "Hang in there, kid. Your time is coming." With a deep pang of regret, he dropped the towel into the washer's barrel, followed by a capful of detergent, set the machine to hot, started it, and then returned to the bedroom to get his clothes.

Dressing, he gathered his few belongings. To keep from being spotted by the neighbors, he left through the same window he'd entered. Erebus prowled, stealthy as a lynx, through the slumbering town. Melding with backyard shadows and slinking down alleyways, he avoided overhead lights and the prying eyes of anyone who might be keeping watch in the middle of the night.

Though he contained an almost inexhaustible supply of energy, the evening's efforts had left him emotionally drained. When he'd traveled a safe distance from the site of April's redemption, he began searching for a suitable place to rest.

Erebus spotted an open, first floor window. The home's owners, comforted by the safety of the little town, must have wanted to let in the cool night air while they slept.

He silently pulled the screen out of its brackets and slipped inside. A single form lay, gently snoring, in the large four-poster bed.

Erebus closed his eyes, reciting a muted incantation, the whispered words lolling and comforting him as he offered up this sacrifice. Time lost substance as he fell into a communal trance, mentally beckoning in the darkness. The temperature fell, and a cool breeze danced over his hot skin as a warm presence touched his mind and nuzzled his heart.

For the second time in less than twenty-four hours, the other had arrived.

He slowly opened his eyes as he removed a thin wire from his pouch. Kneeling on the edge of the bed, he slipped the garrote around the sleeper's neck. Taking care to not pull too hard—he had once accidentally severed the head from a body when he'd overexerted the sharp cord—he snugged the wire tight.

The white-haired man's eyes flew open, and he clawed at the ligature. Blood spilled, staining the sheet and pooling on the mattress.

The instant before the man uttered his final gasp, the other slithered down Tyron's arms and into the dying man's body. The three of them, together, experienced the final beats of the man's heart, his final thoughts, and his exuberant joy at being selected by Erebus.

Tyron had to yank and goad the wire from deep within the man's soft flesh. It came out with a delicious slurp, and he wiped it with the bedspread, careful to remove all residue from its gleaming surface, and returned the simple weapon to a hidden pouch in his suit.

He searched the rest of the house, but no one else awaited him. Tyron perused through the pile of mail on the kitchen counter, all addressed to Elon Wick. Leaving the come-ons and bills where he'd found them, he padded back to the bedroom.

A minute later, he returned to the living room carrying the old man's body. He gently set him in what Erebus guessed to be his favorite recliner. But as soon as he let go, Elon slid forward. He fell from the chair, his head ricocheting off the coffee table, and landed face-first in the carpet.

Tyron cursed and tried again, but again, Elon hit his head and flopped onto the floor. Exhaustion beckoned for Erebus to go to bed, but it would have been rude to leave his host facedown in shag.

He wandered around the house searching for inspiration. Finally, he found it in the garage. Returning to the living room, he picked Elon up, set him in the chair, and, using an old, stained ratchet strap, bound the man in place. When Erebus hesitantly let go, his host leaned forward slightly, but otherwise he stayed upright.

Erebus moved about the room to see how Elon looked from different angles. In almost all of them, it appeared as though the gentleman sat watching television. Just a retiree spending a well-earned lazy time in his favorite armchair after a career of hard work.

Erebus nodded, satisfied with his handiwork, and practically stumbled back to the bedroom.

So tired he could hardly move, Tyron disrobed and slipped into Elon's bed, naked. The still-warm sheets, saturated in blood, welcomed him like a womb. Sighing, he fell into a contented sleep—the deep coppery scent of the thickening ooze tantalizing his olfactory senses the same way another man might enjoy the smell of baking chocolate chip cookies.

He remained in Elon's home, ignoring the phone when it rang and the police when they pounded on the door the next afternoon, canvassing the neighborhood about "Monica's" death no doubt. Poor, misguided souls.

Chapter Three

Sam's apartment looked as though a frat house demolition crew had declared war against housekeeping. The blaring television bathed the room in a mindless daytime melodrama. Empty bottles of beer, half-crushed soda cans, and smashed potato chips littered the carpet like confetti after a New Year's party.

Lying in a heap on the couch, Sam lounged in a warm ray of sunshine partially filtered by half-drawn blinds. A green and yellow Ducks ball cap hung low on his forehead, blocking out the worst of the harsh afternoon light. His slit-eyed gaze drifted from the laundry on the floor, to the dirty dishes piled in the sink, to the overflowing trashcan.

The maid's weekly two-hour cleaning sessions had become an invasion of his privacy and broke the groove of monotonized inertia, forged through weeks of disciplined lethargy.

Though the little cleaning woman had never once openly expressed her opinions, disapproval lingered in her judgmental eyes and dour expression as she'd dusted shelves and vacuumed the carpet. Often while bagging stale beer cans, she'd muttered incoherent blasphemies her profession didn't allow her to openly say to him.

He believed that she'd have burned his ears and shamed his soul with her fiery, raging scorn if given the opportunity. So instead of relieving her of her duties face-to-face, Sam had called The Agency and asked that she not return.

He looked around at the carnage that passed for his apartment. Perhaps he should have reconsidered their offer to send someone else.

Shrugging, he dismissed the chaos. His gaze wandered back to the soap opera.

The show had returned to the story of a stern-looking man, Mark, and his heart-torn fiancée, Janet. Just before the commercial break, Mark had informed Janet that they "needed to talk."

"That's an understatement, Mark," Sam told the TV characters. "Go on, tell her. Tell her how you *accidentally* slept with her sister. Oh, and don't forget to mention that your bride-to-be's twin is now pregnant."

This particular show had been one of his ex-wife's favorites. In the ten-plus years since they'd watched it together, little had changed. He took solace in the familiarity of the players and the stakes of their affairs. Hooked on the drama's daily contract to deliver sinful helpings of greed, lust, backstabbing, and heartache, he'd become a recommitted viewer.

From someplace deep in the recesses of the fluffy pillows, the couch began to buzz. Sam reached between the cushions, rooting around for his phone. His fingers slithered through something sticky and then meandered into something crunchy until they finally happened upon the little device.

Pulling it out, Sam wiped it and its crusty goo across the front of his sweatshirt. The screen displayed the caller's identification as *Blocked*. Not that he'd actually needed to check since only a handful of people had the number and even fewer had any interest in him.

He sighed. The call he'd been anticipating had finally arrived.

You don't want to answer that, Sparky, Chet said.

His inner conscience's warning surprised him. During the war, Chet—the personification of what most people would refer to as their "gut instinct"—had warned him of danger long before his physical senses had detected anything. Listening to his gut had saved Sam's life, as well as the lives of the men he'd commanded. And since the beginning of his involuntary vacation—with neither a case to solve nor imminent threats to caution against—his inner conscience had been silent.

But, oddly, Chet had woken up for what was probably a routine check-in from Sam's handler.

Sam looked at the phone again, perplexed. Chet had never warned Sam about communicating with Josha. Not a single time.

We've got a good thing going here, Chet continued. *Let it go. We can get back to Mark and Janet, and you can keep on gorging until Little China runs out of kung pao chicken and the taps of Corona and Bud run dry. The morphing process from mediocre to portly cretin is nearly complete. Why break your momentum?*

Though Sam hadn't assassinated the president or embezzled funds, from a certain perspective, his actions during the Monica Sable case could have been construed as going rogue. *Moderately* rogue. Roguish.

31

Unfortunately, The Agency didn't have a sin sliding scale, and if the hammer fell, there would be no leniency for years of dedicated service. No pass for slight—perceived or otherwise—indiscretions. The Agency's regulations, especially the ones about following orders without question, were unambiguous. The punishment for breaking rank—aka treason—crystal clear.

Sam stared at the phone but still didn't answer. *You know I wouldn't even be in this position if I'd avoided your advice to "think for myself" and "do the right thing." If they get it in their heads that I've disobeyed, I could go to prison, or worse.*

His inner conscience shrugged. *I'm more of a moralistic guidance counselor than a legal one.*

Sam rolled his eyes as the phone buzzed again.

Counselor Chet continued, *Here's my advice—take the battery out and throw the phone into the dumpster.* He indicated toward the TV. *A couple's future hangs in the balance. We have to be there to help pick up the pieces if Mark and Janet's relationship doesn't survive. The stakes have never been so high.*

What the hell? Sam groused. *You used to bust my chops when I watched this show. You said, "It's drivel and mindless." Now you're telling me to ignore a call from my boss so I can keep watching it?*

Chet sighed, long and deep as though his Neanderthal of a student had at last trampled the final bits of his overtaxed patience. *What I said was, "It's a mind suck on the deflated assbrain of society."*

But now you're advocating for it?

Chet shrugged again. *What can I say? It's kinda grown on me.*

The little device beckoned once more, and Sam's attention returned to the pending phone call. *If I don't take it, they'll send someone to "check" on me and that will lead to all sorts of unpleasantness.* He punched the answer button.

"Sam." He sat up while trying to use the remains of a half-shredded, dirty napkin to wipe away the rest of the goo and crumbs from the back of his fingers.

"How's the vacation going?" Josha's familiar voice squawked through the receiver.

The question caught Sam off guard. He'd expected a direct, pull-no-punches accusation from his no-nonsense boss. Well, if Josha wanted to play coy pleasantries, Sam would roll with it.

Giving up trying to clean his hands, he tossed the napkin to the floor. "Splendid. Seems that Mark and Janet are back together after having been split up for a while. Only he's more into her sister, Chelsea, and of course, Janet had the baby with Rick. And even though she—the baby, I mean—was born two months ago, she just celebrated her sixteenth birthday. You know how these things go."

Josha hesitated for a second. "Well, it sounds like you're making good use of your time."

Sam brushed cookie crumbs from his dingy sweatshirt. "I'm your top agent and a taxpaying, contributing member of society just enjoying a little well-earned R and R. What do you need?"

"I don't need anything," Josha replied. "Just checking in to see if you're enjoying your time off."

Chet piped in. *Or he's seeing if you're home so a dozen guys in black can come get you.*

No, I don't think so. They wouldn't need him to call me to know that.

Right, Chet said. *Just like the world's all-time, number one stalker and Peeping Tom, they see you when you're sleeping, and they know when you're awake.*

Sam tried to hide the exasperation and impatience in his voice as he turned his attention once again to his handler. "That's not like you. Besides, is it really a vacation if you make me take it? You know I'm good. I can come back now. I'm sure there are some dregs of society that need to be chased down. You really want me to relax? Send me someplace exotic where I can kill bad guys at a resort."

A rare smile came through Josha's voice. "Like Chicago?"

Sam grimaced. "Okay, maybe not Chicago. I hate that city."

"Sounds like you're still a bit tense. Are you sure you've been resting?"

I'm surrounded by comedians. Sam rolled his eyes. "Yes."

The rare joviality dropped from his handler's voice. "Well, that would mean that you actually took some time off like I told you to."

Sam fumbled among the debris on the floor until he found the remote, then muted the TV. "I've been here as *ordered.* Drinking margaritas and indulging the twenty-somethings with daddy issues. It's been grand."

All business now, Josha continued, "As much as I'm sure the local ladies would appreciate having someone so experienced show them a good time, I doubt you've made the effort to school anyone in the art of romance or Kama Sutra."

34

Here we go, Sam thought.

"Don't suppose you know anything about what happened in New York?" Josha asked.

Sam brushed at his sweatshirt. More broken chips and cookie crumbs tumbled onto the cushions. "There's always excitement in the Big Apple, but I'm guessing you have something specific in mind."

Josha took a deep breath. "Seems former mob boss Laven Michaels, whom you are somewhat acquainted with, suffered a rather sudden demise."

Deflecting the implied accusation, he answered ambiguously, "I've never met the man."

"No, I know you haven't, but you do know of him." Josha's voice had a derogatory edge to it that Sam did not enjoy.

While Sam hadn't directly been involved in the destruction of Laven's organization, he'd used back channels to get intel to the right people, who were more than happy to do it for him. But he should have known he'd never be able to fly below The Agency's radar, no matter how careful he thought he'd been. They always knew everything. Always.

They see you when you're sleeping... Chet sang quietly.

Ignoring Chet, Sam said, "I see the news and read the internet, so for argument's sake, let's say I do."

Josha huffed. "Then you would know that his lawyers pulled a Hail Mary and got him out of prison, but about five minutes after his release, he was gunned down on the steps of the courthouse. Then, his entire organization got taken apart by his competition."

Sam did know this. He hadn't even bothered to pull the police records; the internet reports had done a splendid job of describing, in intricate detail, the death of one of the most notorious mobsters in New York's history. "A murdering drug lord got murdered? I'd call that justice served."

Josha's voice went cold. "And it went down right after *you* just happen to be on a case involving his organization. I would call that a coincidence, only I don't believe in coincidences."

"Josha, I didn't kill Mr. Michaels. He was playing a dangerous game, and no matter how big a fish you are, there's always someone bigger."

"Yes, but someone served him up to a school of piranha," his handler bit back. "Someone provided intel that led them to that very moment of his release, and they also provided intricate details of his organization. Laven and his entire drug operation got devoured in a feeding frenzy."

Sam shrugged. "It sounds like a win-win to me."

The cold in Josha's voice turned to ice. "On the surface it would, but the FBI and NYPD are not exactly throwing a party. They had people infiltrated in that organization. It had taken years to set up, and it had provided a steady stream of intel. Shipments, suppliers, dealers, all of it. The new family wasn't interested in mergers and acquisitions, and our friends lost a lot of good people."

The agents and officers had known the stakes when they'd signed on. The brave men and women who went undercover, sacrificing their lives for months and years at a time, had understood what could happen. If they hadn't wanted to take the risk, they would have stayed behind their desks. Josha knew all of this but had insinuated that their deaths had been Sam's fault.

Anger flared deep and hot in his blood. "So, they—the police and the FBI—are our friends now? What happened to compartmentalization?"

"Things change. We're all one happy, dysfunctional family."

Sam snorted.

"Blow it off all you want," Josha snapped. "But there's a storm coming, and it promises to rain down buckets and barrels of shit. What I need to know is if any of that is going to fall onto us."

Sam gritted his teeth to keep himself from making a career destroying comment. Josha fretted over political fallout and the loss of police lives, yet he hadn't seemed bothered at all that Sam's last assignment had been to kill Monica Sable—an innocent whose only crime was being in Witness Protection so she could testify and put Laven Michaels away for life. Josha had probably never even taken the time to speculate on why someone high up in The Agency had lied about her identity, provided a list of false allegations, and assigned Sam to remove her from society. Permanently.

Sam seethed at his handler's hypocrisy and lack of concern over corruption within the organization and the hierarchy. Had he followed Josha's directive, had he not questioned his orders, an innocent woman would have died, and Laven would have been freed from jail to continue controlling the New York City streets.

Someone with access to The Agency's resources had been on Laven's payroll, or the powers that be had *wanted* the mob boss to remain in control of the streets. In either case, Monica would have been murdered to keep Laven out of jail. Unfortunately, aside from Sam's intuition and a slew of circumstantial evidence, he didn't have any physical proof.

He ground his teeth together, frustrated Josha couldn't see the truth even as it stared him in the face. Sam resisted the urge to tell him that the storm hadn't begun the day Laven died, but the instant someone started giving out handshakes instead of handcuffs to drug lords. "Even if I'd had anything to do with it, it's my job to remain invisible and leave no trail. No one would have known it was me."

"If you were the one who leaked the information, you weren't doing *your* job."

A flood of anger cascaded through his heart. "Are you charging me with breaking command?"

Josha's accusatory tone softened a little. "No. Like I've said in the past, you're one of my best. I can't afford to lose someone just because they push the boundaries of ethics. If I did that, I'd have no one left on my team. But I've purposely not dug too deep because I don't want to officially know about it."

Intentional ignorance? Sam wondered. *That's Josha's defense? Fine. Whatever. It serves me as well as it does whomever Laven paid off.*

Ultimately, it didn't matter...this time. Laven had been killed, his operation dismantled, and Monica saved. "Okay, well then, what do you need?"

"What I need," Josha said, "is information. Laven had a lot of employees, but I need the specifics on his special tasks man, a wet works specialist by the name of Tyron Erebus. Also someone that you may be acquainted with."

A knot as large as a river stone formed in the pit of Sam's stomach. "I've heard rumors of such a person, but I'd also heard he died."

A staccato rap of a keyboard echoed from the phone, then paused. "Someone tried to kill him in St. Louis."

"Tried?" The stone grew larger, filling his gut with its solid density.

Josha typed and then paused again. "Yes, 'someone' blew half of his face off, but you know how certain perps have a way of *not* dying. And now he's killed someone in your girlfriend's hometown."

Sam jumped to his feet. A chip that had been on his shoulder sailed through the air and disappeared in the forest of carpet fibers. "What? Are you sure? Are we supposed to chase this down?"

"Yes, I'm sure, but no, we're leaving this alone," he replied firmly. "It's outside the scope of our responsibility. It belongs to the feds and the locals."

Sam's trigger finger itched at the memory of Erebus' furious expression as the madman charged, knife in hand and murder in his eyes. Sam could still feel the recoil of the gun as he pulled the trigger, see the side of the murdering psychopath's face explode and the blood splatter in an arch across the wall as the bullet found its mark.

Only it seemed it hadn't. Not entirely.

With sirens wailing in the distance and his chest sliced open from Erebus' blade, Sam hadn't taken the time to verify Erebus' demise. He'd spent his whole professional life priding himself on minding the details. The one time that it had really mattered—maybe more than any other—he'd failed.

Sam returned his attention to the phone call. "Aren't we also part of federal government? Shouldn't *we* be involved in this?"

"Things aren't *that* different," Josha scoffed. "I said we're dysfunctional and happy, not cooperative. Besides, this isn't our case. Whoever catches him will be a hero. That's not us. We aren't heroes. We aren't anyone."

Josha paused for a heartbeat. "My team was someplace we shouldn't have been, doing something we shouldn't have been doing. I've been tasked with damage control. So as part of interagency relations, the FBI's providing assistance to the county boys, and I'm providing assistance to the FBI...if I can."

Though his boss had made it sound like the collective would take the responsibility, Sam knew that someday he'd be held personally accountable. A sharp stab of failure jabbed his heart. Desperate to be put on the case, he searched for an argument. "I thought we, The Agency, didn't exist. That's what you just said."

"We do, but we don't."

Sam threw up his hand in exasperation. "Josha, I've never known what that means."

"And you don't need to. But let me reiterate. This isn't our case."

Sam sighed. "Okay, fine. If you aren't going to let me clean the mess up, then why are you even talking to me?"

"Because," Josha said, "even though I don't officially know if you've had up close and personal experience with this guy, I want you to take a quick look at the evidence and give me your insights, and anything else that I can pass along to help our people stop him."

Sam cocked his head. "Our people?"

"We're all on the same side here."

Round and round we go.

"Of course," Sam said, shaking his head as he tried to clear it of the doublespeak. "Give me the details on what he's done."

More typing as Josha pulled up the case file. "The victim was a female, early to mid-twenties, severely lacerated and almost entirely skinned. Very little blood remained in her system."

"Meaning the perp kept her alive as long as possible. Letting her bleed," Sam surmised.

"Cause of death isn't certain given the extent of the injuries," Josha said. "Nearly half of her bones were broken, she'd been raped, and her heart was missing."

Sam blinked in surprise. "That's new." No victim in Erebus' extensive dossier had ever had an internal organ removed.

"Yes," Josha said. "It is. He's escalating. Could have been a near-death experience changed his perspective. Made him realize some of the joys in life he was missing out on."

Sam ignored the not-so-subtle insinuation and shoved aside the queasiness gripping his stomach. "Trace evidence?"

If the information bothered Josha, his voice gave no indication. "No fluids or anything under the fingernails. Unless something new turns up, there's no possibility of a DNA match. The FBI found no fingerprints, hairs, or fibers that did not belong to the victim."

Sam stood and began to pace the room. "There was a waitress in Colorado who'd been killed a couple of months ago in a similar fashion. Same lack of evidence."

Josha paused much longer this time as he clicked and typed. "According to the records, a man with a description matching Erebus' had been at the diner about that time. Police have no leads."

Sam stopped walking. "Do you have the reports on this latest killing?"

"I've already sent them to you."

Sam rummaged around under a pile of discarded pizza and Chinese takeout boxes, pulling out his laptop. He started the machine and logged onto his email. Scanning the attached documents, he started clicking through the gruesome images.

According to the police, the body of the woman had washed up on shore the morning before, after having spent at least several days at sea. Very little of the tattered flesh remained, exposing the gray, salt-bleached bones, many of which had not just been broken but crushed. The woman's sternum had been cut down the middle. A gaping hole remained where her heart had been. Faded strips of material had been wrapped around each limb near the torso.

The eyeless skull stared out of the pictures while the woman's jaw hung open in an eternal scream of suffering. An image swam through his mind of her begging, pleading for the pain to stop. For mercy. But no savior had come, no cavalry had arrived with trumpets blowing and steeds snorting in the nick of time to save this lost creature.

The flesh appeared ravaged beyond the effects of decomposition and scavenging by crab and shrimp. Thousands of cuts permeated the remaining epidermis and parted the soft tissue beneath. The bones themselves, the ones that weren't broken, looked as though they had been mauled by a pack of lions fighting over the spoils of the hunt.

"What's that wrapped around the arms and legs?" Sam asked.

"Tourniquets," Josha replied quickly, as though anticipating the question.

Sam paused, the ill feeling graduating to mild nausea. "This is Erebus' MO. Who is she?" Though he'd asked the question, he feared the answer.

"Look at the next couple of photos."

Clicking through one bloody image after the other, Sam froze. His blood chilled. The headline, MURDER IN THE COVE, screamed in glaring newspaper font. The image of a high school girl hung under the accusatory words. Her hair had been longer then, but the smile, the shape of her nose, the Marilyn Monroe mole...he knew them well. Sam read the supporting paragraph.

The mutilated body of Monica Sable washed up on shore this morning...

"No..." Sam shook his head. Incredulousness, sadness, and a deep sense of failure assailed him. The overwhelming emotions decimated the unfamiliar, though welcomed, peace that had taken up a hesitant residence in his heart. "He got her. After all that, he still got her. I don't know how he even knew where to look..." His body sagged under the weight of guilt.

Sam's vision swam, and he buried his face in his hands. He'd followed his conscience, risking everything to save her. He wagered his life, freedom, and career to fight Laven's assassin, Tyron Erebus. He'd even managed to put a bullet in the murderer's brain...or so he'd believed. But all he'd risked and all he'd fought to achieve had been for nothing.

Sam had been a fool. He couldn't have saved her. He couldn't save anyone.

"Go back and read the supplemental to the coroner's report," Josha instructed.

Lifting his gaze once again to the damning headlines, Sam flopped a leaded hand onto the computer's trackpad and scrolled to the official coroner's reports. "These are dated today." He checked his watch. "In fact, just a few hours ago."

"They're waiting for test results," Josha said. "The reports won't actually be official and released to the police until tomorrow night at the earliest."

Sam took a deep breath and continued reading the horrific details.

...though many of the teeth had been removed, a partial match of dental records identified the victim as April Goodman...

He reeled from the emotional whiplash. "Monica's not dead?"

"No. Height, weight, hair color, gender, age, all a match. But what really threw everyone off was the class ring she wore. It had Monica's name engraved on the inside of it."

"Monica used to wear a ring," Sam said, frowning, "but it was a skull and heart balanced on the Scale of Justice. It didn't look anything like this. If this isn't her, then why did the girl have her class ring?"

"We don't know that yet. They both graduated from the same school, though in different years. Other than that, there doesn't seem to be a connection between them. The police on the scene made a preliminary identification and the newspaper ran with it. It's a case of small-town incompetence. Check the last page."

Sam clicked through the images to a headshot of a young woman. "They look somewhat alike," he said, "but clearly this is not Monica. Plus, this woman is a painter; Monica wanted to be a lawyer. They couldn't be more different. So other than physical similarities, they're not connected in any way?"

Josha let out a short breath. "Besides being from the same town, just one thing—Erebus. He's killed at least one of them, but so far, no other bodies have been discovered that could be your girl."

Sam mulled this over. Erebus went to Alabaster Cove, slaughtered a lookalike, then tried to make it look like he'd killed Monica. But why? Why go through the effort?

"They found her at sea... As far as I know, he's never killed anyone on a boat before. That's way outside of his norm."

As soon as the words left his lips, the voice of Dr. Wergent, Sam's psychology instructor from his academy days, floated up through his memories. "Sam, you're making an assumption. What do the *Rules* say about that?"

Rule #38:
Making assumptions is the quickest way to mislead yourself.

Unsubstantiated leaps of logic are the most assured way of leading yourself down the wrong path of action. Following misguided reasoning and invalid information is a waste of resources, time, and energy. Question the validity of every fact by verifying its source. Turn over all intel, looking for holes. Only once thoroughly vetted do you trust a fact to be a fact.

——*122 Rules of Psychology*

Sam considered the methodical, personal way Erebus dismembered his victims. Everything he did had a meaning. A purpose.

"He didn't kill her on a boat," Sam said. "It's too sterile, too void of...her. He wants the death to be slow—hence the tourniquets—but it also has to be intimate. Unless she lived on the ocean, he would have killed her in her house, most likely in her bedroom. The police are looking in the wrong places. They aren't going to find anything by searching Monica's old home, and they certainly won't find any evidence in the local watercraft."

Josha stopped him. "If he didn't use a boat, then how did he dump her body in the ocean? Did he just throw her off the pier?"

Sam considered. "Everyone needs to stop thinking of this guy as your run-of-the-mill slasher. He didn't *dump* her body. That's too barbaric. He set her adrift. He let the tide take her away."

Skepticism tinged his boss' voice. "Not to question your kinship with an insane, murdering psychopath, but why would he do that?"

The various pieces began to fall into place, clarifying the images and chain of events. "He's sending a message. That may be why he took her heart. He may be trying to get everyone's attention. Read the reports for his last murder; no other identifying marks were found on the waitress. Look at his previous work; you'll find nothing in any of those either."

Josha didn't reply while he clicked and typed, presumably verifying Sam's suspicions. "Okay. Yes, that's true. But I'm still not convinced. The heart's new, and I guess the ring does seem intentional. Maybe he just got too cocky and decided to start using a calling card. Taking credit for what he's done."

Sam sorted through the images. The pictures made his gorge rise. "No, this was a deliberate detail he added. He wanted Monica's name in the papers. Do we know where she is?"

"She's been on vacation," Josha said. "My sources tell me that she'd been abroad but came back not long ago because she has plans to return to school. She's going to resume her pre-Laven life. Also, her friend Angel is with her."

Sam said, "She's going to have to put those plans on hold. Erebus is still looking for her." He shook his head. "I can't believe he's still alive. And with half his face shot off, I can't believe no one has noticed him."

"Nobody matching his description was ever recovered, and there are no hospital records of anyone coming in with such an injury. He either wasn't as hurt as you thought, or he went somewhere else for medical help."

Something nagged at the back of Sam's mind. "I'm confused. Laven's dead, and without its head, his organization was decimated. The contract on Monica must have been cancelled. So, either Erebus has one hell of a work ethic or he's still after her because of some other reason we don't know about. The question is, why? Why is he still after her?"

"That's the reason I'm talking to you about this at all. You're the expert. You tell me."

Sam massaged his temples; pain had begun to radiate from his forehead. "I don't know."

"Think it over," Josha said. "I want you to write a report on everything you know about this guy. I want to know your impressions on what motivates him, besides being a knife for hire—why he does what he does to his victims and why you think he might still be after Monica. More importantly, I want to know where you think he'll go next and what he's got planned. Get it to me tonight or tomorrow morning at the latest so I can vet it for the Bureau. They will vet it further and pass it on to the county boys."

"I thought we weren't involved. We weren't there," Sam said.

"I'll tell them that in the interest of interdepartmental cooperation, we've created a full psychological profile on this guy."

Sam frowned. "You said we were a happy, dysfunctional, *non*-cooperative family."

Irritation laced Josha's words. "You knew what I meant."

Sam didn't, but he also didn't want to press the point and snap what little patience his boss had left. He still had a chance to right a wrong. He could still save Monica. "Since *we* started this, shouldn't *we* finish it? As you said, I know this guy better than anyone. I——"

"No."

Sam tried again. "But the FBI is having the police search for the wrong person. They think they're just looking for a random killer. They don't understand that she needs to be protected. I can——"

Josha stopped him again. "I said no." He took a deep breath. "Sam, since there seemed to be some confusion before, I'm telling you explicitly. You are *not* to follow up on this. I think I can make the stink of our part in it go away, but the case now belongs to the police and the FBI. Being involved any further will draw a huge target, not just on you but on The Agency itself. Once you've written your report, drop it. Do I make myself clear?"

Sam scowled, frustration and anger roiling in his gut. His urge to argue almost overwhelmed his need to toe the line for the greater cause. "Crystal."

"Good."

Sam clenched his jaw. "Will you at least keep me up-to-date on what happens?"

Josha paused. When he spoke again, impatience and finality tinged his words. "When the tests come back, the FBI will officially release the report to the police. *They* will solve this and bring Erebus down. You do not need more information because as soon as you email me, you will delete the files I sent and forget all about this case. Now, finish the report, stay home, take your vacation as I told you to, and do *not* get involved."

The line went dead.

Chapter Four

Midnight loomed as the light from the Triumph motorcycle flashed on the small sign marking Cove Alley Avenue. The narrow road, which Sam had passed—twice—jutted off the highway in a copse of vegetation. He steered the bike down the isolated, ribbon-thin turnpike that wove through the dense forest up and down the coastal mountain ridge.

The further southwest he traveled, the thicker the trees grew until only the occasional wisp of moonglow penetrated the thick canopy. Amongst the undergrowth of scrubs and twisted saplings, glowering eyes watched as he sailed through their world, not on a ship of splinter and tattered canvas but on one of steel and polished chrome.

Sam paid these phantoms no mind. His thoughts instead lingered on the dark and morose images of death and a growing string of corpses.

He had stuffed printed copies of the documents and pictures Josha had sent him, as well as a couple of changes of clothes, into the big bike's saddle bags. Thirty hours and several hundred miles after his boss' call, Sam had just begun reviewing the information in his head for the umpteenth time when Pocahontas, the bike's dash-mounted navigation system, signaled a turn ahead.

He squinted into the darkness, trying to corroborate her instructions with the mishmash of vegetation lining the highway. At the last second, he found the turn and guided the bike down the narrow offshoot.

After a few miles, the GPS changed its mind and redirected him back the way he'd come. It then decided it had been correct after all and tried to reroute him to the same dark street.

Sam swore at the little computer and cursed himself for trying to finish this leg of the journey in the dead of night instead of holing up in a hotel someplace. But he'd pushed on. Afraid that the longer he waited, the more time Erebus had to find Monica.

Pocahontas made one last effort, telling him to turn down a street that didn't exist. Finally, the technical marvel gave up and flashed "signal lost" across her neon green display.

Sam took a guess at what she'd meant by her last instruction, but the road he picked turned from asphalt to gravel, then from gravel to dirt. He brought the bike to a stop in front of a white and red candy cane striped gate, marking the end of the civilized world and the beginning of the primitive one.

Swearing again, he doubled back, this time finding the turn he'd missed. After driving all day, exhaustion egged on his "getting lost" irritation.

Where the hell is this place, and why would anyone want to live out in the middle of Nothingsville? Chet groused.

Sam looked deep into the darkness that didn't so much surround them as consume them. *Supposedly there's a city out here. Somewhere.*

Josha figured you'd go all Maverick and try to track down Erebus on your own, so maybe he sent you bad intel hoping you'd fall off the edge of the Earth. It turns out Columbus was wrong. The planet's flat after all.

Sam shook his head. *Uh-uh. No way. I already knew about Monica's hometown; it was in her case file. That's high-level corruption conspiracy theory crap you're talking about. Next you'll be telling me to make a hat out of tinfoil and dig a bunker in the middle of North Dakota.*

I'm just saying that we need to be aware that it's not just the perps that lie to us anymore. Chet paused for dramatic effect. *Everything we think we know needs to be reexamined. Everyone we think we can trust, we can't.*

Sam's head swam at the implication of Josha succumbing to greed or other ulterior motives besides the greater good of the country. Sam had let himself believe that his handler had been duped into putting a hit on an innocent. Of course, The Agency—or whoever controlled it—probably had a few people taking bribes for services. However, if Josha himself had allowed—or worse yet, had instigated—the Monica case, then Sam's entire foundation would crumble out from underneath him.

His inner conscience's voice continued to plague him. *Also, the ranks aren't the only ones subject to corruption. This is at least the third time you've violated a direct order.*

His decision to save Monica's life instead of end it, had been based more on intuition than on the facts—or lack thereof—of the case and because of his damned inner conscience's grinding day after day to stop blindly following orders and think for himself. Ironically, now Chet seemed to have switched sides, berating Sam for *not* obeying his commander.

While Sam chastised those within The Agency for corruption, here he was, once again, breaking rank and order. With no way to defend himself, he conceded Chet's point. *Touché.*

The motorcycle's light flashed on the sign, announcing he had reached the city limits. Relief flooded Sam's veins. Not just because they'd finally found the elusive little town but also because he could change the subject.

Chet let the conversation drop...for now. *Mr. Columbus, I believe we have stumbled upon the promised land.*

☆☆☆☆

At the precipice of the final peak before the decent into Alabaster Cove, Sam stopped the bike and shut the engine off. The road wove down a steep-sloped ridge that lined the coast.

The city—twinkling with lights and nestled in a deep bowl between the mountains and the sea—lay before him like an inverted star-filled sky. Surrounded on three sides by mile-high Earth and the fourth by the ocean, it had only a single lane in or out.

Thunder rumbled as a thick layer of cheesecloth clouds draped the moon, and an electric current charged the air, giving it the weight and substance of a wet wool blanket.

He needed to get moving before the storm arrived. First, though, he wanted a quick, high-level view of the land.

Sam dismounted and pulled his helmet off. The liner, soaked with his sweat, slid against his skin like a wet tongue. A cool, salty breeze graced the hairs on the nape of his neck, bringing them to attention.

He turned in a slow circle. Besides the city, he could see no other indications of civilization in any direction.

Returning his attention to the west, his gaze roamed over the isolated community. He'd been to tiny cities before, where everyone knew everyone else. Their small-town mindset could either help him or hinder him, depending on whether or not its people accepted him into the fold or rejected him as an outsider.

Thunder rumbled again, this time much closer. He needed to go. Sam started the bike and began weaving his way down the mountains toward Alabaster Cove.

Though the streets were well lit, the late-night darkness shrouded the town like a forgotten cemetery. The gurgle of the Triumph's hefty engine echoed off the slumbering storefront windows.

He guided the bike down the street and came to a stop, with the slightest squeak of brakes, at the town's only traffic light.

Really, a red light? Do you think your luck could get any better? Chet seemed even more irritable now that they'd arrived.

Sam used the time to survey his surroundings. A gas station, two motels—one seedy, the other more upscale—a grocery outlet, a thrift store, a surf shop, and a couple of tourist trap gift boutiques. Further on, a belt of suburban houses and apartment complexes separated the downtown from the surrounding pine-covered coastal range.

Perplexity rang through Chet's voice. *Why would anyone live so far removed from the rest of the world?*

Sam shrugged. *Different strokes and all that. I suppose I can see the appeal. A simple life, far away from everything and everyone. Nothing to do all day but hang out at the beach and surf. I could get into it.*

You're right, the world would be a better place if you stayed as far from the rest of society as possible.

Sam ignored Chet and turned his attention back to the light. He'd been waiting for several minutes. Though the blacktop looked freshly laid, and the equipment shiny and new, there had to be an old-fashioned relay timer running the system.

Feeling foolish, but not wanting to break the law within the first two minutes of arriving in town, he remained behind the white line of the deserted crosswalk. Sam looked left and right. Several parked cars had been nestled alongside the road, but nothing moved.

Screw it. Sam gunned the engine and drove against the red. He had almost made it across the intersection when the signal mockingly turned green. *Of course.*

Halfway down the block, a police car materialized in his side mirror, turning the world into a blistering disco as the cruiser's flashers came to life. *Are you kidding me?*

Chet rolled on the ground, clutching his side in laughter. *Ha-ha-ha! It seems your luck has sunk to new depths.*

Just watch. We'll have a good laugh over incompetent street maintenance, shake hands, and then we'll on our way.

Chet continued to chuckle. *I think your delusional over-confidence is adorable. Let me know how that works for you.*

Sam pulled to the side of the road and shut the bike off. *You'll see.*

He removed his helmet. Other than the ticking of the cooling motor and the burble of the sheriff's car, only the crashing of distant waves and the slight rumble of thunder broke the silence. Though the ocean lay a mile or so off, its gentle cadence and the tang of sea-soaked air added to the relaxed, oddly familiar vibe of the town.

He glanced around as a cool measure of peace settled over his nerves while a disquieting tremor reverberated through his heart. The epicenter of his sudden emotional earthquake came from a strange conviction that he had been here before.

Puzzled, he tried to recall having lived or visited anywhere remotely similar to Alabaster Cove. Maybe it only reminded him of someplace else? The Agency had sent him all over the globe, but each place and each face had been nothing more than an assignment. A temporary means to a larger goal, under an assumed identity and a fake persona. Nothing real. Nothing of substance.

Like him.

The source of the sensation had to be from his childhood. A ghost of the past wisped through his mental fingers. Filaments of images flashed, and tendrils of feelings haunted him—weighty and nearby, but all just out of reach. When the emotional phenomena began to fade, it left longing and the sadness of loss in its wake, though for what or whom Sam could not begin to fathom.

He tried again, but if the memories existed, they continued to elude him. Perhaps these recollections would prove to be false, nothing more than a touch of déjà vu from an overtired, overactive imagination. Or perhaps these nebulous spirits were real, and it would be Sam himself that turned out to be the phantom.

The sharp click of shoes on concrete broke his sudden melancholy. He looked up as the policeman approached. Sam nodded. "Good evening, officer."

Fiftyish, broad and bear-like, with *Sheriff Austin* stamped into his shiny badge, the peace officer aimed a small but powerful flashlight in Sam's face. "Evening. In a hurry to get somewhere?"

Sam held up a hand to block the light from blinding him. "I think something is wrong with the signal. I waited for it to turn green, but it didn't." He gave his most endearing smile and shrugged. "City maintenance. What can you do?"

The officer stared down into Sam's face, then gave a slight shake of his head. "I beg to differ. I just happened to be coming around the corner as you skipped through that intersection. Looked to me like you didn't want to wait. The law is designed to keep folks safe." The sheriff narrowed his eyes. "You don't think you're above the law now, do you?"

You have no idea, Chet said, laughing.

Sam dismissed his inner conscience's slight. *Quiet. Did you notice?*

Chet grinned. *You mean the Panama Red on his breath? Yeah. Seems the good officer has a taste for exotic marijuana and a relaxed approach for keeping the peace. Maybe you could ask for a hit? It might give you some personality. Probably not, but I'll cross my fingers.*

Sam sighed, turning his full attention back to the face glaring down at him. What could he say? The cop had him dead to rights. Sam could argue the point, but getting into a petty dispute with the local fuzz—even if the officer in question might be stoned—seemed like the wrong way to introduce himself to the people of Alabaster Cove. Besides, he wanted this man on his side since he might need the good sheriff's help at some point.

Sam gave him a sheepish smile. "You're right. I should have waited a few more seconds." He reached into his jacket. Slipping his fingers past the gun in the inside pocket, he pulled out the driver's license, registration, and insurance card.

The sheriff aimed his flashlight at Sam's California driver's license. "Mr. Bradford, please wait here." He turned and walked back to his car.

Rule #4:

Whenever possible avoid trivial law infractions and interactions with law enforcement.

Staying within the law, especially the basic rules that apply to everyone every day, will help you keep a low profile and make blending into the herd easier. Acting as though you are above the rules will not only make your presence more obvious but will make you memorable. Police officers are trained to pay attention to details and have a greater ability to recall people and situations. By avoiding them, you avoid leaving a paper and witness trail.

—*122 Rules of Psychology*

Just blew that, didn't you? Chet's mood had improved dramatically since his earlier grousing about getting lost.

Thunder rumbled again, louder and more insistent. A faint whiff of sulfur drifted on the electrified breeze as the barometric pressure dropped and Mother Nature prepared to assert her pissy side.

Sam had briefly considered using one of his many fake personas; however, that would have made his "I went away for a surfing vacation" explanation that much more difficult to sell to his handler.

Chet's good-spirited voice continued to ring in Sam's ears. *You're kidding right? You think that Josha and his firing squad won't see right through your BS story?*

I'll think of something else then, Sam snapped.

Chet shook his head. *Chances are fifty-fifty that Josha already knows you're here and has put an APB out on your butt.*

Sam had wondered about that possibility and had discounted it as paranoia. But, as he sat alongside the road in the middle of the night, he realized the notion of getting arrested for disobeying his superior's orders didn't seem as preposterous as it had when he'd thought it up back in his apartment. Trying to appear casual, Sam set his helmet aside and un-straddled the bike. This whole thing could go south before it even began, all because he had been too impatient to wait for a stupid traffic light.

As Sheriff Austin returned, every muscle in Sam's body tensed.

The sheriff handed him an old-fashioned ticket book. "Alright, Mr. Bradford, please sign here."

Sam relaxed. Internally, he breathed a sigh of relief as he scrawled his name on the line marked The Accused.

The sheriff ripped off the white copy and handed it to him. "You have ninety days to either pay the fine or go to court and contest it. In either case, please try to remember the laws are in place to protect everyone."

Sam folded the ticket and stuffed it into his pocket. "I will. Thank you, officer."

The policeman gave him a nod and then walked toward his car, but he stopped and turned back as if something had just occurred to him. "Oh, and Mr. Bradford."

Sam looked up. "Yes, Sheriff?"

"Welcome to Alabaster Cove." The peace officer got into his patrol car and pulled away. The shiny cruiser glided down the street, turned right, and vanished from view.

The looming storm chose that moment to make its grand entrance. The clouds opened up, and a sheet of rain, as thick and cold as a glacier-fed waterfall descended upon Sam—the deluge so heavy it instantly penetrated his water-resistant bike suit and soaked him to the skin.

Much to Sam's irritation, Chet resumed his maniacal cackling.

Things had to turn around...didn't they? *I'm going to need a vacation from this vacation.* Sam started the bike and headed toward the nicer of the two hotels.

Chapter Five

Sam woke to brilliant light forcing its way around the sliding door curtains. In his sleep-laden fog, the dark center and mystical glowing edges reminded him of a solar eclipse.

His gaze drifted to the nightstand clock. Eight fifteen—in the morning, he assumed.

Swinging his feet out of bed, Sam stretched his back, the muscles stiff and tired from the long ride. He pulled the drapes aside but had to shield his eyes from the blinding brilliance that assaulted his dilated pupils.

He slipped open the patio door and stepped out onto the third-floor balcony. The warm sea air greeted him. After raging all night, the storm had exhausted itself, allowing the sun to wink over the pine-covered cliffs from an unblemished sky. In the distance, seagulls bickered and squawked to the cadence and gentle rumble of waves expending the last of their kinetic energy against the American coast.

Breathing deep, he relaxed against the railing, enjoying the sun's warmth on his skin. To the west lay an unobscured view of the deep rolling Pacific. From his vantage point, the town appeared to fall off into the sea, as though half of it lay beneath ocean.

He closed his eyes and mentally cycled through the files Josha had sent to him. The Agency knew who had slain this innocent. But since The Agency technically didn't exist...

Or did it? Josha never cleared up that particular point during their conversation. Neither his boss, nor anyone else for that matter, had ever stepped forward to clarify that little detail.

Sam would not let April's death go unanswered, and he would not allow the madman to get his hands on Monica. No matter how many times the investigators bungled this case, Sam would guide them along the right path.

The police hadn't yet looked in April's home because they hadn't known to do so. If they did, they most likely wouldn't find any trace, and thus they wouldn't be able to connect this case with any of Erebus' other murders.

Both the sheriff's office and the FBI believed the dead girl was Monica. It struck him that the FBI had grown so large that the Crimes division didn't know the WITSEC division had paid for her to travel abroad. In fact, Monica may not have even been in the US when the girl's murder took place.

Breaking his reverie, he opened his eyes and glanced around again. He needed to get to April's home before anyone else did. He might be able to find evidence that would otherwise get trampled by the half dozen deputies that would soon be trudging through the crime scene.

Taking one last look out over the city, he went inside to change clothes.

☆☆☆☆

Since only five miles separated the town's widest points, Sam elected to walk to April's instead of taking his bike. He wanted to get a feel for the land and its people. The more he knew, the easier the mysteries and intricacies of the case would be to unravel.

Unlike when he'd rolled in and things had been buttoned up tight, the city now thrived with life. People went about setting up shop, sweeping away the beach's chronic sand, removing storm debris off their front steps, and preparing for the day.

Several old VW buses with surfboards poking out open tailgates headed toward the beach, their drivers shifting gears on engines that made the "ba-ba-ba" sound unique to vehicles designed by German engineering the first couple of decades after World War II.

Chet piped up after having been quiet for most of the morning. *Hello, 1960.*

No kidding.

Sam had researched the town before he'd left his takeout-box-laden apartment. Renowned for quaint entrepreneurship and outdoor sports, many websites claimed Alabaster Cove to be the go-to for world-class surfing. Though just a blip on the map, it ranked higher among a lot of professionals than Australia or Hawaii.

The last time he'd gone surfing had been with his brother, Jake, at Venice Beach, a decade and a half or more ago. The two of them had spent all day on the water, then drank beer and flirted with bikini-clad, half-drunk sorority girls all night.

His mind drifted through the warm recollections, lingering on his brother's infectious laugh, his easy philandering charm, and the bright light in his eyes. *I wish you were here, Jake. You'd love this place.*

The nostalgic images and feelings so captured his attention that Sam had almost forgotten why he'd come. But then dark swirls invaded as the past marched forward. Pain, regret, longing, and death shoved their way to the forefront of his imagination, leaving him hollow and guilt-ridden.

Sam shook his head, waking himself from the daydream that would have turned into a nightmare had he allowed it to continue. Disgusted that his emotions had led him astray, he tried to clear his thoughts of these distracting ghosts from his youth. Sweep them away before he got swept away in them.

Chet sighed. *Okay, what's the point here, Chief? Jake is long gone, and there is no use dredging up those old memories.*

I'm not dredging up anything, Sam grumbled.

Chet stared, his eyes blazing. *Really? Because from where I sit, it seems like you aren't doing shit to stop them. You need to focus. We've got a murderer who fancies himself a sous chef. So, unless you do something about it, and soon, this sonofabitch is going to be serving us up a big plate of Monica tartare.*

Sam turned away from his inner conscience. *Yeah, whatever. I've got it.*

Do you?

Enough. I said I've got it.

Sam had never allowed himself to linger on the past. Being able to separate and compartmentalize his feelings had made it possible for him to do his job and still sleep at night. He didn't have to weigh his actions against his own moral compass or second-guess the orders handed to him. Being cold, meticulous, and emotionally void had made him one of The Agency's best field operatives, but that hard, protective shell had cracked the moment he'd hesitated to pull the trigger on Monica.

He needed to control these rogue thoughts from interfering with his mission and distracting him.

Chet remained quiet, though his inner conscience could have justifiably continued beating the point. Instead of blasting Sam into the next universe, Chet let it go. *So, what the hell is up with this place?*

As Sam made his way down the main avenue, people waved at him and said "good morning." Unnerving. He lived in LA, and no one smiled in LA. For any reason. Ever.

Relieved he didn't have to continue the argument or reevaluate his own motivations, Sam relaxed. *I don't know.*

You had a bit of trouble finding it. Maybe you turned down Mayberry Lane instead? Zigged when you should have zagged?

Sam shook his head. *Can't argue with that. Pocahontas was acting like we'd wandered into the Bermuda Triangle.*

He walked along the half-mile comprising the main thoroughfare, past the intersection where Sheriff Austin had "welcomed" him to town. The traffic light appeared to be functioning just fine now.

Turning down another street, he passed a series of small restaurants—a diner, a hole-in-the-wall Italian place, and a fifties style burger joint, which boasted to be the home of the original Fat Rubi.

In an isolated town like this—where no apparent incoming revenue streamed, combined with the decaying nature of the salt air—the businesses tended to be run-down and dowdy. But for the most part, the paint looked fresh, and the storefronts had a well-loved, young entrepreneurial vibe.

As he made his way toward suburbia, he found himself returning waves and the "good mornings" as they were tossed his way, like a father and son throwing a baseball in the backyard.

The first time he returned one of these greetings, Chet raised his eyebrows.

Sam shrugged. *When in Rome...* He turned down an innocuous-looking road, following it until it ended at a modest sea-bleached split-level.

He had arrived at April Goodman's house.

Chapter Six

Tyron ground his teeth as he reread the article in the local news rag. The front page was a pile of conjecture, theory, and wild speculatory sensationalism. Aside from the caption, GIRL WASHED UP ON SHORE, beneath a blurry photo, nothing—nothing!—had been accurate.

In a town as small as Alabaster Cove, someone *should* have realized that one of their own had disappeared. But no one had made a missing persons report. No one thought to question the police's faulty reasoning or their shortsighted conclusions. These blundering morons couldn't even get the identity of the body right.

If just one of the idiots down at the sheriff's office contained an ounce of competency, they'd have realized their mistake and sent the investigative team swarming over April's house like roaches in a bag of week-old trash. By now the gifts Erebus had left for them should have made national news and become the world's largest calling card, ferreting out Monica and leading her right to his doorstep.

Had they done *anything* right.

But these incompetent blowhards had no idea who'd *transformed* April. Who'd redeemed such an unworthy creature. With no leads, no information, and no clues, they expected the medical examiner to do their jobs for them by wringing facts out of a corpse.

Here's a hint: You won't find anything on the girl. You thought you were the shit because up until now, you've only had to deal with amateurs. But these are the big leagues. The police academy never prepared you for anyone like me.

His disappointment in the ineptitude that passed as the protectors of society did not detract from the admiration he held for the beauty and exquisiteness of his own handiwork.

Tyron Erebus had created the perfect masterpiece. It had turned out better, more breathtaking and more brilliant, than even he could have imagined. His ability to take something so hopelessly flawed and transform it to an object of beauty should have astounded and enchanted those lucky enough to gaze upon her.

He glared at the newsprint and shook his head. Instead of calling his creation "the hideous and merciless slaughter of an innocent victim," the small-minded media should have referred to it as "a merciful miracle, created by the hand of the divine."

What Erebus created, what he'd shared, had been nothing less than perfect. Those bigots should have been defending his art. They should have been bathing him in adoration and wonder.

While he didn't know for certain, he suspected there must have been others evolved enough, wise enough, to see him as a prophet and virtuoso of his medium. They would view his work not as something to be shunned or disdained but as the perfect realization of peace and harmony—a masterpiece created by the removal of wickedness, one piece at a time, until nothing remained but purity.

But these visionaries had to stifle their own voices and hide their true passions or the misguided—like the police and the media—would seek them out and destroy them.

He looked down at the paper again. ...*hideous and merciless slaughter...*

Glancing at the byline, Erebus curled his lip. "Maybe I should pay you a visit, Rexton Miller, idiotic 'journalist' for *The Cove Gazette*, and show you what a 'merciless slaughter' really is. You won't get it wrong again," he seethed. "I promise."

Tyron glared at the article as if he could change the contents by willing the pixels of ink to rearrange themselves. But he wasn't that powerful...yet.

Growling in disgust, he tossed the newspaper across the room. Its pages fluttered and objected as the rag fell into a heap at the feet of the elderly gentleman sitting opposite him.

The man didn't move to gather them, nor did he bother to glance down. His adoring gaze never wavered from Erebus' face.

"There. Look at that crap." Erebus gestured at the fishwrap as he jumped up and marched across the room. He placed his hands on either armrest of his companion's chair and stared deeply into the man's wide pupils. "No one understands what we are doing. No one gets it. If only they could begin to comprehend the complex beauty we are creating. But those radicals don't appreciate us, Elon."

He reached up and stroked the gentleman's cheek. His soft touch did not elicit a reaction as the dry, milky-blue irises gazed at him in rapt attention.

Erebus traced the man's face with the back of his fingers. "But you do. You appreciate what I...what *we* are building. You understand, and I love you for it." Erebus touched the tip of the gentleman's nose and sighed. "Now if only you could tell the world."

Sighing resignedly, he kissed the man's wrinkled cheek, sidled across the floor, and flopped into his seat, staring at his companion across the living room.

Love and urgency filled Elon's cataract-crusted eyes. *You must find her. Find her now.*

Erebus frowned. "But how, Elon? She's not—"

Elon cut him off. *Stop. Just stop. I welcomed you into my home because you were born for greatness. You were born to cleanse the world of impurities. You were born to ascend, and eventually, you will rule the heavens. Act like it.*

As Elon continued to whisper, Erebus leaned forward, listening intently. A slow smile slinked across his scarred face.

When the old man finished, Erebus leaned back, processing the information. He had to stop getting distracted by all the undeserving rodents who didn't appreciate him. He needed to remain focused on looking for *her*. He'd been guided to April, who, in addition to being a messenger, had been a practice exercise—a warm-up of sorts—for the bitch.

Instead of temporarily satiating his thirst though, April had only whetted his appetite. Priming the bloodthirsty pump for the main meal.

Elon was right. While Erebus walked the Earth, he would never gain the appreciation he so rightfully deserved. *They* were jealous. *They* could never understand him. *They* would eventually fall, and he, Tyron Erebus, would punish them all. He would crush every last one of the pathetic, weak-minded, filthy-souled cretins who had ever dared to sin against him. Their cries would gain them no mercy. Their pleading would garner no favor.

The day of reckoning would come.

Until that day arrived, however, he would do as the truly gifted and misunderstood have done for centuries and trudge on.

He pulled Elon's computer onto his lap and opened a fresh browser window. The storm must have taken out the external internet connection, limiting access to the local town. All other sites returned an irritating *Site Not Found* message.

He took a long breath, understanding that this too must be guidance from the gods. After pausing to think for a second, he pulled up the city's homepage. *Welcome*, written in sand, greeted him. He typed a new entry into the screen's *Search* box and clicked the magnifying glass.

Tyron Erebus began to hunt.

Chapter Seven

S am rapped on April's front door and waited. When no one answered, he knocked again. Leaning in, he listened for footsteps or other signs of life, but only the muted burble of crashing waves disturbed the morning quiet.

He glanced around the deserted street. Empty porch swings swayed lazily in the cool breeze. Ocean-themed homes—adorned with ship anchors, driftwood, and a slew of random beach paraphernalia—lined the cul-de-sac. No cars drove past, and nothing moved on the other side of curtained windows. Instead of being quaint and peaceful, the neighborhood gave off a postapocalyptic vibe.

Maybe Erebus got them all? Chet mused.

Sam didn't reply as he descended the creaking porch steps to the yard. Only a few scraggly bushes and some beach grass eked out a meager existence in the sandy soil.

He started around the property, stopping at the first ground floor window. Sam cupped his hands to the wavy glass, but drapes blocked his view of what lay beyond. He stepped back. Old fashioned wood frames often got sealed shut by years of disuse and layers of paint. However, this one looked as though it might still function.

The latch had been left unlocked, so he pulled on a thick pair of latex gloves and tried to open it. But the window only slid up an inch before seizing. He slipped his fingers under the sash and yanked. Groaning and protesting, it jolted open another inch but refused to move further.

Sam shook his head. *I wondered if this was how our perp got in, but there's just no way. This thing is making such a racket, April would have heard him a mile away. Besides, he'd have to have nearly broken the damned thing to get it open. There must be another one in better condition.*

Hold on, Chet replied. *Take a closer look at the track. What's that stain?*

Sam leaned in. Something other than water had darkened the inside of the wooden slot. He touched it. His gloved fingers came away slick. He sniffed the oily substance. *It's a lubricant of some kind.*

That would have made the window quiet and functional, but only for a while. The frame looks like old untreated pine, and this salt air has dried it out. The oil might have made it easy to open. But after the wood soaked it up, the frame may have swelled.

Sam gripped the top of the glass enclosure and pulled down, but it didn't budge. *So, this must be where our perp got in.* He put all of his weight into the effort, and the window dropped back into place. Just before it sealed though, a whiff of something raw and rancid struck him in the face.

Chet waved a hand in front of his nose. *And by my estimation of the layout, this would be her living room.*

Sam nodded and moved on, continuing his investigation of the property while trying to shove aside the implications of that awful smell. He found nothing else out of the ordinary and no other signs of forced entry. Returning to the porch, he pulled out a small toolkit and made short work of the front door lock. Sam slipped inside.

Closing the door behind him, he withdrew his gun and stood in the entryway. The stifling odor—which he'd sampled outside the window but hadn't fully appreciated until now—seemed to have removed most of the oxygen from the air. "Hello. Anyone home?"

Only silence answered his greeting.

More than just the smell filled the space though; death lingered within these walls. Its presence clung to every surface and hung thick in the air.

He started to slide past a closed door when a spot on the floor caught his attention. He knelt, examining it closer.

Blood. A few inches away, another thick drop blotted the hardwood. The trail led down the hallway and stopped at the back door.

Sam stood and slipped around the corner into the kitchen. No threats awaited, but inwardly, he cringed as the tired linoleum creaked and groaned with each footstep. He moved past the stove and refrigerator, around the thrift store dining table, and ducked into the small adjoining bathroom.

He peeked around the doorjamb into the living room. Though the space was a mess, and globs of blood coated the knob on the back door, no psychopaths waited to cut him to ribbons.

Sam turned and started up the staircase. Old wood and nails popped and protested as he rounded the mid-floor landing. When Sam stopped just short of the top, the squeaking floorboards announced his presence as loudly as a band of trumpets.

Chet observed Sam's movements with detached curiosity. *Hopefully our perp is deaf.*

Sam hesitated before cresting the last few steps, keeping below the line of sight. *Do you think he's still here?*

I do not. But I understand your need to be melodramatic, so carry on.

Sam took a deep breath, then sprang up and rolled to the side. No gun shots sounded, no menacing words threatened, no homicidal maniacs attacked. The huge open space proved to be as empty as the rest of the house.

I told you, Chet said, though he sounded disinterested.

Sam shouldered his weapon. *Am I boring you?*

Chet shook his head. *There's just a lot to do, and I want you to get on with it.*

Arrays of paintings, next to an assortment of blank canvases, leaned against the wall immediately to his left. The images, all duplicates of one of several beach scenes, were each in a different stage of completion. The prints pleased his eye, though he didn't have the training nor the natural aptitude to judge the composer's talent and skills.

So much for creativity, Chet mocked.

Sam continued to flip through the art. *This is pretty typical. She made a few that sell well, then mass-produced them to pay the bills. I'm sure she does...did some originals too, but I doubt that an artist from here would be rolling in dough.*

There was a gallery downtown. She must have a booth or something. We need to talk to the owner.

Sam leaned the images back into place. A large picture window overlooking a rocky stretch of coastline took up most of the west-facing wall. He walked over to the easel parked in the center of the room.

The canvas perched upon the tripod looked as though it had gotten caught in a paint store explosion. Angry splashes of color didn't so much cover the surface as much as saturate it. A few feet away, another painting lay face-down on the floor.

After snapping a picture of each, he swapped the two paintings. Instead of the disaster of randomness, old sailing warships battled it out on a rough and forbidding sea.

Nearby, an empty glass and several bottles of wine stood like bowling pins at the ready. They looked prepared to serve at a moment's notice, as if belonging in an alcoholic's version of a fantasy cartoon where cups and plates ask you to be their guest.

Curly wires from a paint-splattered sound system ran to speakers on either side of the window, a CD simply labeled *Kyme in Tuscany* on the spindle. He clicked the *play* button and a female's husky alto, quiet and subdued, wisped like dusty smoke through the open space. The song—about a sweet, funny Valentine—ended, followed by a small setting applause. "That was for you, April. Honey, I love you." She began another somber ballad.

Sam sat down on the stool, envisioning himself as this artist who lived in this house. Alone. Creating duplicates of her best work, drinking gallons of wine, and listening to her lover sing to her from afar. Though he doubted April's flame had anything to do with the murder, he nevertheless made a mental note to follow up.

He got up, took detailed pictures of everything, swapped his gloves for a new pair, then went downstairs, returning to the living room. Among the mild assortment of cheap furniture, two paintings hung on the wall, while a third had been shredded. Fractured frame and bits of canvas lay strewn across the floor as if ravaged by a wolverine.

He photographed the carnage, gathered the strips of cloth, and, crouching, pieced them back together. The resulting image—two women in bed under heavy blankets, foreheads pressed together—didn't perplex him as much as the rage that had decimated it.

Chet studied the couple. *Based on the files Josha sent, the one woman looks like she could be April. If so, I'd bet my left nut the other woman is Kyme.*

Sam snapped a picture of the remains of the painting, then slipped his phone into his pocket.

Please don't wager with my body parts.

Chet pretended indignation. *What? You doubt my deductive reasoning capabilities? Besides, if we won, you'd have a third testicle. At long last, you'd have something women might find mildly interesting about you.*

Ignoring his inner conscience, he briefly toyed with the idea that Erebus had targeted April because she'd had a girlfriend, but he immediately dismissed the notion. It all came back to the ring. She'd had on Monica's ring. That wasn't divergent. That wasn't to mislead.

That was a message.

Time to see what Erebus had to say. Sam stood, scattered the painting's remnants back to the way he'd found them, and made his way to the bedroom.

Sam didn't bother with the cloak and dagger of busting in with his gun drawn. Stepping over a trail of blood, he turned the knob and pushed open the door. Though no one physically attacked him, the smell of rot plowed into him like an enraged linebacker. Light from the entryway spilled in, providing just enough illumination to highlight the worst details of the scene.

He averted his eyes from the showpiece, which had been elaborately crafted for the largest possible impact.

Rule #33:
Never follow the path that has been staged for you.

If a scene has been staged, purposefully choose not to follow the obvious trail. Examine everything else first. Get a feel for and assess the situation. Gather supporting data and minutiae before turning your attention to the big picture. The perpetrator's intention is to mislead you. Take away their power by not playing their game.

—122 Rules of Psychology

By not looking where Erebus wanted him to, Sam remained in control. He forced his eyes to take in everything except the bloody bed and the morose images on the wall, turning his attention instead to the dresser.

Aside from April's evident preference for camouflage, he didn't find anything hidden or unusual about the contents of the drawers. Likewise, the closet continued, though did not expand upon, the woman's clothing repertoire.

Sam got down on his knees and peered across the floor. His gaze drifted past a wide pool of blood beneath the bed and locked onto something small tucked under a gap in the molding. Crossing the space, he bent down and, with a pair of tweezers, retrieved the item.

A prophylactic envelope glinted in the weak light.

According to the reports supplied to him by Josha, the medical examiner believed that the perpetrator had brutally raped the victim, either during death or immediately postmortem. But no foreign fluids had been found within her. Unless April had been bisexual, she would have had no need for a condom. Sam bagged the aluminum-lined pouch and tucked it into a pocket.

Moving on to study the nightstand, he rifled through each drawer before picking up the small, blood-spattered book sitting on top. Opening it, he discovered April's diary. After reading a few of the entries, he took pictures of each page and then returned it to the exact position he'd found it.

Sam turned his attention to the bed. The blankets and sheets lay in a bundle, spilling out onto the hardwood. They were stiff with fluid, and he had to pry them apart to complete his inspection.

Only a single corner of the mattress had escaped saturation. Except, the stew of fluids was more than just blood. A lot more. Chunks of skin, bone, and other fleshy materials Sam didn't want to think about covered the blanket.

One of the headboard dowels had been broken while the rest had been coated in smatters of dark red and black droplets. Two of the remaining spindles, one on each side, had been scratched to the point of being ravaged.

Tyron must have used handcuffs to secure the girl, and during the melee, she'd snapped one of the wooden tethers. The pressure needed to break a dowel at that angle attested to the severe violence that had preceded the end of the artist's life.

Sam forced his eyes to travel to the six canvases stuck to the wall above the headboard. Five images surrounding a center one had been arranged in a star pattern, with a fat dripping line of dark burgundy encircling the morose tableau.

When he'd been in the military, Sam had seen men die painful, horrific deaths at the hands of extremists. Over the years at The Agency, he'd been exposed to the worst of humanity's depravity. But the aberration before him made his stomach lurch and heave.

Sam choked down the bile threatening to spill from his throat. Covering his nose and mouth with his jacket sleeve, he breathed through the cotton while his world swam in and out of focus.

He wanted to shred the canvases. Rip them apart and slash the message sent by the worst madman Sam had ever encountered. He shoved down the guilt trying to claw its way through the tarnished, emotional wasteland of his soul. If only he'd actually completed the job and killed Erebus, April would still be alive, and Monica wouldn't be in danger.

Sam wouldn't make that mistake again. The next time they met, the madman would die.

But there would be a time to answer violence with violence. He had to get in control of his raging emotions before he did something rash. Sam swallowed hard and mentally detached himself from the scene. Pulling out his phone, he focused its camera at the center canvas and snapped a picture. The vile digital representation coalesced in high-definition pixilated form on the small device's screen.

Sam tried to keep his breaths shallow as he further isolated himself—zeroing in on methodology and detail. In a day or so, the police would discover the body's true identity. This would be his only chance at an unobstructed view of the crime scene. He had to be sure to get everything he needed in one pass.

As he worked, it got easier to center himself, focusing on process instead of humanity. Intelligence instead of emotion. Fact instead of injustice. He took the last picture and then returned to the entryway. Just before closing the door, he looked around once again.

For a moment, he allowed his feelings to return. Revulsion fled as hot, searing rage chased it away like an alpha dog resuming control of the pack.

Erebus wanted to deliver a message. In this, he had succeeded. But the reply wouldn't be what the psychopath expected. Not in the slightest.

Sam closed the bedroom door and left.

Chapter Eight

The diner smelled of hamburgers, fried onions, and greasy potatoes. Black-and-white checked tiles covered the floor, silver sparkle stools stood at the counter, and deep red leather booths lined the front window. An old-fashioned jukebox, which glowed like Las Vegas, played "Johnny B. Good." Enough flashing neon signs, chrome Chevy busts, and glitzy tin posters of slick greaser duck butt styled hair hung on the walls to make an epileptic plead for mercy.

Sam settled into a booth. He ordered, flipped on his tablet, and got lost in a world of murder and mayhem as he reviewed the images of April's home.

The woman's journal had contained little in the way of fact. Instead, it had served as an emotional dumping ground for her on-again, off-again relationship with Kyme. He'd been correct in assuming that she'd been longing for the musician. But Kyme had stormed out three months ago, after a screaming match, and never returned. Though he still had her on the list of people to talk to, it seemed unlikely she would know anything that would help his investigation.

His food arrived and he ate absently as he scrolled through the bedroom pictures until the star shaped collage of canvases materialized on his tablet. The memory of noxious rancidity attacked him again, as vividly as if he still stood among the gore and death. What little appetite Sam did have vanished, and he pushed the plate of the half-eaten Fat Rubi special aside.

He looked away, taking a deep breath. After he'd calmed his troubled stomach, he turned his attention back to the small screen, studying the gruesome images one at a time.

Other than Erebus being a vicious murdering asshole, and the notes scrolled across and below the canvases, Sam could find no other hidden messages in the killer's gruesome artwork.

He clicked on the first picture of April's studio and began the entire sequence over again. An answer hid among the everyday mishmash and the terror-laden artifacts of the dead girl's house, but he could not coax it out. Whatever the elusive detail, it remained just out of his grasp.

It's in the bedroom. There's something there you need to pay attention to. Chet, as usual, gave him a blurry map and some vague directions but kept the mysterious specifics to himself. His inner conscience either didn't know or wanted Sam to find the clues and solve the mystery on his own, like some sort of corporation's personal growth seminar.

Sam needed information, not more riddles, but Chet didn't always work like that.

Pushing away his frustrations and zeroing in on the details, he looked deep into the images—grouping, categorizing, and cataloging the nuances—assuming nothing and reexamining everything. Camouflage clothing. Kyme on the CD player. A journal full of entries about a lost love...

The niggling sensation of being about to uncover something consequential nipped at him. He returned to the pictures of her room and the feeling got stronger, as though the clue played the child's game of Hot and Cold with him. He sat on the edge of discovery, and just as his mental fingers began to wrap around it...

"Anything else I can get you?"

...it dissolved into vapor once again. Sam tried to grasp at the thought one last time before giving up.

Sighing, he looked up into the face of the black-haired waitress smiling at him. She had *Triniti* printed on a name tag tacked to a way too tight blue blouse. She glanced at his half-eaten food but made no comment.

Sam tried to return her smile, but he couldn't quite conquer the irritation of being interrupted. *Damn. So close.* He considered offering her a chair so they could review the pictures together. *You could also take me around and help me interrogate the townsfolk...*

Though he'd been mentally grousing sarcasm, the idea had merit. People, especially men—the sheriff and his deputies, for instance—showed off to and flirted with waitresses, especially pretty ones with big smiles and even bigger endowments. Someone from the police office—a secretary, a spouse, a dispatcher—might have come in feeling talkative. Gossip was a small town's major stock-in-trade.

Chet piped up. *Finally, a good idea. Milk the waitress...for information. But don't dawdle, we need to get this done as quickly as possible.*

Sam glanced up at her. *Okay. I'll do the best I can, but I can't just break out the hot lights and start interrogating her with a million questions.*

So, turn on the charm, Casanova, Chet said, waving a hand in her direction. *Pretend to have a personality and maybe she'll give us something useful. If you don't have an opening line, you could mention that you won a third testicle in an office bet.*

Sam rolled his eyes at his inner conscience and then focused on the woman, his smile growing from half-hearted to mischievous. "How about a little insider information?"

She placed her hand on her hip. "Hmmm...I guess it depends on what it is."

"Is there any place around here to catch some live music?"

She scrunched up her face for a second, then bit her lip. "Well, we do have a few local groups. *The Drift Knots,* a kind of new-agey band, plays at the tavern on Friday and Saturday nights. *The Beach Bum* are a bunch of locals that sing...well, you can probably tell what they sing from their name. They do the occasional gig down at the park for school events, charities, that sort of thing."

Triniti tapped her lip with one well-manicured fingernail. "Let's see... There's about a dozen random guitar players around—some decent, some not—none of them really serious. Oh, except for Kyme DeNaught, who's kinda soulish-folkish-jazzish. She's away so much I almost forgot her."

Pay dirt. Sam shrugged as if his taste in music embarrassed him. "Oh, that sounds just my speed. Kyme DeNight you said?"

Triniti grimaced. "DeNaught. Ugh. To each his own, I suppose."

He raised his eyebrows. "Not your thing?"

"Hardly," she said, shaking her head. "I like my music to have a little grit to it. Something you can sink your teeth into that gets you out on the dance floor. It's gotta have a beat, ya know? Anyway, I'm not one to pass judgement. If you like slow and depressing, then who am I to say that sounds about as fun as a root canal?"

Sam laughed. "Yep, somber and reflective, that's me. Where can I find Ms. DeNaught?"

She shifted her weight to her other foot. "If you want to catch her, you're gonna have to do some driving. She plays the West Coast circuit. From here all the way up to Pier 66 in Seattle. I have no idea where she's at right now. Though if you wait for a few days, she might come back for the funeral. Sometimes she plays at those sorts of events. Like I said, slow and depressing."

"What funeral?"

"Oh, you're not from around here, so you must not have heard."

Sam shook his head and gave her his best puzzled but curious expression.

Triniti's voice dropped to a whisper. "A girl was murdered here last week." While her tone and grimace conveyed the somber mood appropriate for such horrific news, her eyes lit up with the excitement of being able to reveal one of the town's hottest topics to someone new. "According to the rumor mill, almost all her...um...skin and stuff...was cut off, and she was dumped into the ocean."

"Oh, that," he said, matching her quiet tone. "Yeah, I read about that in the paper. I didn't pay a lot of attention because where I come from murder is, sadly, an everyday occurrence."

"Well, around here, it's big news." She crouched down so they were eye-to-eye. "And what wasn't in the papers was that she was tortured. And I don't mean like what they show on TV, with being tied up in a chair and slapped around a bit. I'm talking mutilated and mauled and kept alive for as long as possible. A deputy, who was one of the first ones to arrive at the beach after the call came in, said her body was so mangled he thought she'd been attacked by a shark."

Sam widened his eyes. "Seriously?"

"Yeah." She nodded. "But then the doctor checked her over and said she'd been cut like a thousand times with a knife or something. He also said that her heart was missing, but that *wasn't* what killed her."

"It wasn't?" Sam tried to appear surprised and baffled.

She shook her head, looking both horrified and conspiratorial at the same time. "Uh-uh. The deputy told me that based on the amount of blood in her body, she most likely bled to death. In fact, they think it took *hours* for her to die." Triniti shuddered and wrapped her arms around herself.

Sam shook his head, feigning shock. "What? No way. Did you know her?"

Triniti nodded again. "In a little town like the Cove, everyone knows everyone and their business. Only..."

Sam leaned in closer. "Only?"

Triniti slid into the booth opposite him. She glanced around. "Only they said it was this girl named Monica, but I think they're wrong."

Sam frowned. "I don't remember who they said had died, but there didn't seem to be any dispute over her identity. Pretty sure the article even quoted the police. Why don't you think it's who they say it is?"

His intuition had been right. This girl knew stuff, and from the light in her eyes, she liked to talk about it.

"See, Monica left town for New York U a long time ago. She isn't like some of the others who leave and come back."

"Why not?"

Triniti leaned in a little closer. "After her dad died, her mom went completely off the rails. She turned from Plain Jane boring into one of the meanest town drunks in Cove history. So, no one was surprised when Monica packed up all her stuff and took off the day after she turned eighteen. She's not been back since... That is, until a few days ago. A friend of mine told me he saw her and her friend, Angel, drive into town the day before the storm hit."

"Someone saw her?" Sam's heart skipped a beat. The last he'd heard, Monica had been out of town for an extended vacation. Unfortunately, The Agency hadn't exactly been keeping him in the loop on her where-abouts, and good to his word, Josha had not provided any updates. "But doesn't that make it *more* likely that she's the one who got killed?"

Triniti frowned. "No, no. See that's what the police think too. Only...the timing's all wrong. They found that girl's body *before* Monica came back. The sheriff was in here a couple days ago, but he blew me off when I tried to tell him."

"I don't understand why he wouldn't at least listen," Sam said. "If you're right, that means they've seriously messed this thing up. The sheriff sounds like an amateur."

"Don't get me wrong," she said. "He's an okay guy. He can be a little handsy, if you know what I mean, but at least he takes care of the drunks who want to bust up the place. And overall, he does a decent job at keeping the peace. But at his core, he's lazy. That's why he's here and not in a city with *real* crime. I can tell you, he sure wasn't interested in me messing up a part of his case that he thought was a no-brainer."

"Wasn't the body wearing a ring that had a name engraved on it though? I'm no detective, but I can see why he'd think that part of the case was closed."

Triniti shook her head. "Yes. But a ring is just a ring. It's not anything special. I could go down to the pawn shop and find a dozen just like it. Doesn't mean I'm the person whose name's on the inside."

Sam frowned. "But if it's not Monica, then who is it?"

Triniti pointed her ruby red fingernail at him. "That's the sixty-four-thousand-dollar question, isn't it? I don't have any idea."

"So, if Monica is here and not dead, then why hasn't she just come out and said so?"

"Look at it from her point of view. There's a murderer on the loose, and *our* sheriff is heading up the investigation." She shook her head. "Even though the county boys are involved now, I'd stay hidden too."

He studied the waitress' face. If her source could be trusted and Monica had come back to town, what did that mean? Had Erebus already found her, and even as Sam searched, her body floated somewhere out at sea? Or was the psychopath still hunting her?

"I got to meet the good sheriff on the night I rolled into town," Sam said, giving her a half-smile. "It was my honor to contribute to the town fund by way of a moving violation."

Triniti rolled her eyes. "Stupid traffic light."

Sam let the grin slip away. He wanted to ask her what she'd meant about the light, but it seemed less important than keeping her focused on the case. "So, have they got any suspects?"

She shook her head. "Not that I've heard, and they aren't going to for a while."

"Why not?"

"Cause ain't nobody getting into town," she said, sitting back in her seat. "The county fuzz left right before the storm blew in. It rained like that story from the Bible and caused a slide in the east. A bunch of trees came down the Kinick River and wiped out the bridge. Apparently, the phone and internet lines run along the base of the bridge, so when that went, those did too. 'Til that's fixed, we're completely isolated."

"There's no other way in or out?" Sam frowned. "No back roads?"

"Go outside and take a good look around." Triniti pointed out the window. "You can't get over those cliffs unless you're a pro climber or you've sprouted wings and learned to fly. Even then, what are you going to do when you get to the top? The next closest town is eighty miles away."

"How long do they think it'll be before it's fixed?"

She folded her hands on the table. "Word is it'll take at least a week. They've got a crew on it, but the works department leaves a little to be desired."

By now, the investigation should have led them to April's house. He should have had to wade through police, forensics, and news crews, who, in normal circumstances, would have been leeching such a sensational story like ticks on a dog. But her neighborhood had been quiet and serene, as though nothing had happened.

Sam couldn't leave even if the case led him to do so. But if he couldn't leave, then neither could Erebus. Maybe Sam could make this work in his favor. Track the bastard down and deal with him.

Unfortunately, Monica had probably been trapped here too, giving the sonofabitch the chance to not only turn more locals into minced meat casserole but also get to her...if he hadn't already.

Logically, Erebus should have gotten his rocks off and beat feet looking for new and exciting opportunities to maim and kill in lands far away from the heat of an investigation. That was what people in Tyron's line of work normally did, since prison or the electric chair would seriously dampen their style. Except that Erebus had gone to a lot of effort to set the stage, which meant he'd gone into hiding and waited to wrap up whatever unfinished business he had with Monica.

His inner conscience's voice broke his reverie. *You need more information. This waitress is connected. Stay with her. You can't keep on interrogating her at work. Ask her out. Get a couple of drinks into her and see what else she has to say.*

Sam returned his attention to Triniti and smiled. "Well, it seems like I'm going to be in town for longer than I thought. Maybe I'll try my hand at the local surf. What's the best place for a board and wetsuit?"

Triniti stood. Relief and maybe a little disappointment at war on her face. "Oh, you don't need a suit. The water's like seventy degrees."

"Seriously?"

She returned his grin. "Yeah, the ocean's like a huge bathtub. Do you surf much?" She gave him the once over. Her gaze returned to his, lingering a little too long.

She's going to ask me out, Sam informed his inner conscience.

Chet snorted. *In your dreams.*

"Well, I used to go all the time," Sam said. "But I haven't been in a while because I've been traveling."

Triniti pointed toward the street in front of the diner. "Well, the best place to get your gear is *The Board Wake,* just 'round the corner on Third. It's my friend Max's shop. When you get there, tell him I sent you."

"Do you get a kickback from the sales?"

She laughed. "No, but if he knows you know me, you'll get a discount."

"Ahhh," he said. "Got it. Thanks for the tip."

Sam turned his grin to his inner conscience. *Here it comes.*

Chet rolled his eyes. *I do my best to keep your ego in check, but the damned thing is like Whack a Mole.*

Triniti turned to go and then spun back around. "My friends and I are going out tomorrow afternoon. Afterward, there'll be a barbeque, music, and lots of beer. Sorry, the tunes won't be depressing, but maybe you'll still dig them. We'll be about six miles down south, under the big tent that looks like a Hawaiian shirt. You should stop in."

Sam mocked his inner voice. *There it is!*

That's not exactly the same thing as a date.

Sam continued his internal victory dance. *You just can't stand it when you're wrong. Talk about ego.*

He focused once again on the woman waiting for his reply. He had no idea what "six miles down south" meant, but she interrupted him before he could ask.

The waitress offered her hand. "By the way, my name's Triniti."

He studied her as his large fingers enveloped her slim ones. Dark eyes, flawless skin, slim waist, and a chest way too big for her narrow frame. Hailing from the capital of plastic surgery, he could spot artificial enhancements a mile away. Her shirt, tied in a knot at the small of her back, allowed sculpted abs to peek out just above the waist of her black slacks.

Speaking of mountains... Chet started.

Sam shook her hand. "Sam Bradford, from LA."

"Nice to meet you, Sam Bradford from LA. So, will I see you tomorrow?" Her eyes sparkled as she zeroed in on him.

This was the type of girl who knew nothing of rejection, at least being on the receiving end of it, and he would not be the one to begin such an education. Not right now, anyway. Besides, a group of locals would be exactly what he needed. Someone knew something; he just had to find the right person.

He gave her his best lopsided grin. "Sounds like fun."

She checked her watch. "Great. Tell ya what, I get off at two tomorrow. Be here, and I'll show you around. Then we can go meet my friends."

He stood and dropped some money on the table. "Sounds like a plan. Oh, and thanks for the lead on the shop. I'll head over and check it out." He started toward the door.

She called after him. "Don't forget to tell Max that Triniti sent you."

He turned back to her. "Oh, I'll drop your name wherever I go and see what it gets me." Sam gave her a little wink.

She blushed and went back to work.

Chapter Nine

Monica stared down at the copy of *The Cove Gazette* lying in her lap.

MURDER IN THE COVE.

The mutilated body of Monica Sable washed up on shore this morning. She had been brutally killed in what police are calling a crime of passion...

Awkward, tight-lipped smile with an over-the-top teenage makeup job, her senior high school yearbook picture stared back at her from the newsprint. Monica traced the outline of her teenage cheeks, her forehead, her eyes. She remembered the fierce determination in the gaze of the girl who'd gotten straight As, spent the evenings and weekends waiting tables and washing dishes, and received a full ride to NYU.

This same girl—the one who'd had only one real friend and went home to an empty house every night—had made great efforts to hide from the world the sadness that lurked in her soul. But her pain and loneliness shone like a spotlight in the exhausted depths of her eyes, visible to anyone who'd wanted to look. Though almost no one had ever bothered.

The image blurred. Monica swiped at a tear that threatened to betray her swirling emotions and twirling thoughts. She took a deep breath and gazed through the windshield at the brilliant blue sky. "This whole thing perplexes me."

Angel glanced over and then returned her attention to the road as she navigated the suburban streets. "What *exactly* don't you understand? Killers kill."

Monica sighed. "The man who did this is Erebus, right? We both agree on that?"

"Except that the FBI told us your boyfriend, Peter, killed him in St. Louis." Angel kept her eyes on the road as she spoke.

"Well, I have a feeling that the person who washed up on the beach might disagree with you." Monica held up the picture in the paper.

"I didn't say I agreed with the FBI." Angel shook her head. "They either got their facts wrong, or Erebus has come back from the grave. One way or the other, we can't do anything for *her,*" Angel said, pointing at the girl's picture. "I'm all about the living, so *we're...*" She gestured back and forth with her thumb, indicating the two of them. "...getting out of town. I don't know about you, but I'm done with the Cove."

Monica set the paper in her lap. "I don't care if I never come back, but even if we leave, does it matter? He'll just follow us."

Irritation flashed briefly through Angel's eyes. "It's not us he's after; it's you."

"Nice. Well, just so you know, no matter where we go, he'll just keep on coming after *me*. I can't run away forever." Monica shrugged. "Maybe it's lawyer's intuition, but I'm certain he'll eventually find and kill me."

"Maybe it's lawyer's intuition," Angel mocked, then rolled her eyes. "Me. Me. Me. Don't you think maybe this guy has something better to do besides sit around all day thinking about ways to kill *you*? Gawd, Mon. Sometimes you're such an egomaniac—though I guess that's a requirement for being a lawyer—and it does give you something to gripe about. Most egomaniacs love complaining."

"I'm not an egomaniac," Monica said, folding her arms. "And I'm not complaining!" She searched for just the right way to say it. "I'm being a sensible pragmatist."

Angel laughed. "I love you dearly, but you're no prag-matist. You're a worrywart, the tightest anal retentive that's ever lived, and a pessimist of the highest order."

Monica huffed. "I'm not a worrywart or a pessimist...or an anal retentive."

Angel laughed again. "Honey, if you went for a proc-tology exam, your butt would yank the doctor's finger right off. Pop!" She held up her hand, with the middle finger folded so it looked like one was missing. "For the record, three fingered proctologists are *not* in high de-mand. So not only do you bring the mood down at par-ties, but you've got the potential to put a perfectly good butt doctor out on the street."

Monica tried to hide the smile that tugged at her lips. "Okay, maybe I'm a little wound up. But I'm also being sensible."

"Sensible?" Angel scoffed. "Hardly. You've gone all pessimist, egomaniac, complainer, anal retentive, downer on the subject. Admit it...of the two of us, *I'm* the pragmatist."

"Alright, Ms. Pragmatist. What's your plan? How are you planning to keep me alive?"

"Simple," Angel said, shrugging. "We take the FBI up on their offer to give us new identities, then fade into oblivion. If Erebus can't find us, he can't kill us."

Monica studied her friend's profile. They saw the world from opposing points of view, agreeing on almost nothing and yet everything at the same time. Angel, the straightforward simple girl, often saw clarity when Monica only saw murk. "I don't know. Maybe."

Angel cocked an eyebrow. "No 'maybe' about it. It's a simple, bulletproof plan. No need to make it more complicated."

Monica allowed a smidge of hope to seep into her heart. Perhaps for once she should accept her friend's opinion. Perhaps she needed to give optimism a chance. "So, while everyone else thinks I'm dead, maybe Erebus doesn't know we came back, or that even if we did, this..." She held up the paper again. "...scared us away?"

Angel gave her a half-smile. "That's a girl. We came to town so I could quit my job and empty the apartment, but we decided instead to get the hell out of Dodge."

The pieces seemed to fit. Monica could almost visualize the path Angel had blazed out of this predicament. "You're pretty smart, ya know?"

"That's my secret super power," Angel said, her smile widening. "I'm more than just stunning good looks and a dazzling personality."

"Let's not forget your humility."

Angel cut her eyes to Monica before returning them to the road. "Right? Mother Theresa could learn a thing or two from me."

As the women fell silent, Monica stared out the windshield trying not to think, but her efforts proved futile. Her mind lingered on a point that she could not let go.

Angel glanced at her. "No, Mon. Stop. Stop thinking. Stop it right now."

"How do you do that?"

"I'm frigging Nostradamus and Freud rolled up into one. You're not exactly difficult to figure out." She huffed a breath, glanced back over, then slapped the steering wheel. "Oh, fine. What? What is it?"

"I keep coming back to the ring." Monica rubbed her forehead. "Why was she wearing it and where did he get it?"

Instead of answering, Angel's face fell for a split second before she cleared it of expression.

Monica sat up straight, leaning in close. "Ang, you know something. What? What is it?"

Angel scowled. "Who's Nostrada-Freud now?"

"Spill," Monica demanded.

Angel sighed. "Okay, fine. I think I *might* know where he got it."

Monica's heart tripped. "You do? Where?"

"Me."

Monica had to blink away her surprise. "What are you talking about? You? You gave my ring to Erebus? What, did you take him to prom or something?"

"Well," Angel said, taking a deep breath. "Obviously I didn't just hand it over to him."

"Okay, then how?"

"Remember right before you left town to go to New York and we boxed up all the stuff from your mom's place? I kept asking you what you wanted to keep, and you told me to stop asking and just throw it all away?"

Monica nodded. "Yeah. You know how much I hated my home life. There wasn't anything I wanted aside from some of the pictures of me and my dad."

"Well, I mighta sorta have kept some of the stuff, and one of the things *might* have been your ring." Angel glanced at her and cringed.

Monica dropped her arms to her lap. "You kept my ring? We've been holed up in your apartment for two days talking about this and you just *now* mention it?"

Angel hunched her shoulders. "I kinda forgot about it until just a few minutes ago."

Monica stared at her friend. Anger, frustration, betrayal all warring in her heart. "Are you saying you did or you *think* you did?"

"Look, it was a long time ago and we were in a hurry. You kept saying 'Throw it away. Throw everything away.' You can be very insistent and hardheaded when you want to be, but I thought you would eventually regret getting rid of all your stuff. So, I stashed a few things in my mom's attic."

Angel let out a sigh and continued, "I didn't create a detailed list or anything. I was trying to be fast and had to sneak it past you. But that ring might have been one of the things I kept."

With an almost audible pop, the building bubble of anger burst and drained away. Angel, as always, had tried to come to her rescue. Saving her from her own bullish impulsiveness. "Are you saying he went after your mom? We should go check on her. Wait, didn't your mom move?"

"She did, but we don't need to go check on her. She's fine."

Confused, Monica tried to put the incongruent pieces together. "I don't understand."

"On the morning before she moved," Angel began, "she called to tell me that she had some stuff to bring over. I told her that since she had a key, she could just stick the boxes or whatever in my spare room..."

"...and you never went through them," Monica finished for her.

"Yes. I forgot all about it, but when that bastard ransacked my apartment, he must have found them."

Like everywhere else, Angel's spare bedroom had been torn apart.

"'Ransacked' is a civilized way of describing that disaster," Monica said. "'Decimated' would be more accurate. 'Total annihilation.' 'Guerra de bandas en su casa.' You've never been the best of housekeepers, but even for you, the place was a wreck. I don't think there was a piece of glass he didn't break. Your couch looked like it had been ripped apart by a pack of coyotes on LSD. He even shredded your carpet. Who does that? And the knives and blood in your bed..." Monica shuddered.

Angel signaled and turned down a side street. "I don't think I'm going to get my cleaning deposit back."

"That's for sure." Monica snickered, and then a thought struck her. "That only proves my point though."

"What point?" The guarded tone had returned to her friend's voice.

Monica rubbed the back of her neck. "You said yourself he found the ring in your apartment."

"That's only a theory," Angel replied. "I don't know for sure."

"Come on. There's no other explanation." Monica motioned toward the picture in her lap. "It's not like this girl was just walking along and he noticed she was wearing my ring."

Angel snapped the turn signal a little too hard. Braked for a stop sign a little too quickly. "Fine, counselor. It's all circumstantial evidence, but let's say he did find the ring in my apartment. What about it?"

Monica's head spun as the fragmented puzzle floating around in her mind fell into place. Then understanding dawned. "It's a message. He's saying he's going to get me. You too for that matter."

"Oooohhhh no," Angel said. "We already had this discussion. He's only got eyes for you, sister."

Monica shook her head. "I wouldn't be so sure. When he tried to grab us back in St. Louis, you completely humiliated him."

"Me? What did I do?" Angel asked as a sly grin graced her lips.

"What did you do?" Monica laughed. "Well, for starters you jabbed him in the eye with a lit cigarette, damn near knocked him unconscious with an old tree branch, kicked him in the groin, and stomped on his wrist so hard I'm surprised you didn't break it."

Angel laughed. "Oh, yeah. That."

"Yes, that," Monica replied, her tone growing serious. "I'm just saying we need to face the truth. Sooner or later, he's going to catch up to us, and when he does—"

Angel slammed on the brakes, rocking them both forward in their seats. Monica barely kept her head from hitting the dashboard before Angel turned, her eyes blazing. "So that's it then, huh? I keep saying we need to fight, and you keep saying we may as well give up." Angel leaned over, unlatched Monica's door, and flung it open. "Fine. There you go then. Get out and start walking. Be sure to announce yourself wherever you go so that any psychopaths within a three-mile radius are sure to hear you."

Monica stared at her but didn't move.

Angel glared. "What are you waiting for? Get out and get this thing done with. Might as well help Erebus get his jollies off. Who knows, maybe he'll even let me watch before he does me. I swear, sometimes you drive me so crazy that I want to skin you myself."

"Ang, I—"

She held up a finger, pointing it only inches from Monica's face. "No. No more. You either come around or I swear to God I'm going to go through town with a bullhorn and a sandwich board telling everyone not only that you're here but that you lost your virginity to Bobby Dugas."

Monica did a double take. "Bobby Dugas? The dork from high school that wet the bed and had all the acne? That Bobby Dugas?"

"He doesn't wet the bed; he has urinary incontinence disease. And before you say it, no, it isn't the same thing. But yes, *that* Bobby Dugas."

"Isn't he the one that purportedly got a boner in the locker room?"

Angel scowled and shook her head. "'Purportedly.' You can take the girl out of law school... Anyway, yes. Even though you said you were just doing your civic duty to prove he's not gay, we all know that the real reason you slept with him was because no one else was willing to sleep with you."

Monica sat up straight, putting her hands on her hips. "What? There were lots of guys willing to sleep with me!"

Angel raised her eyebrows. "So, your defense is that you're a ho?"

"What? No. I... You know I never slept with Bobby Dugas."

"Who are they going to believe?" Angel asked, pointing at Monica. "The slut that begged the biggest geek in town to ride her like a hobbyhorse or the girl with the megaphone and the sandwich board? Let me tell ya what, there's no putting that genie back in the bottle. You can deny it on a stack of Bibles, but the biddies of this town will never let the slut-dork duo borking in daddy's wood panel station wagon legend die. It's simply too delicious not to believe."

"You're going to wear a sandwich board too?" Monica asked, trying not to smile.

Her friend furrowed her brow. "I'm trying to make a point. You're a slut with a death wish. You need to be dealt with."

Angel must have let up on the brake pedal because the car started to move. She made no effort to stop nor steer.

"The car's rolling," Monica said.

Angel shrugged. "So what, dead slut girl?"

Monica reached over and slipped the transmission into park, then closed her door. She took Angel's hand. "I'm sorry. You're right. We need to keep fighting. I just saw my old picture with the headline and it got to me."

Angel relaxed her face and gripped Monica's hand. "That's not you."

Monica stared into Angel's love-filled eyes. "Yeah, I know. But everyone thinks it is, and no matter how hard we try, it still might be."

"No, it will never be, but that isn't what I mean." Angel took the newspaper and held it up.

"This picture is you, but it's you in the past," she said. "You've changed so much. Even you said it. All that stuff you went through transformed this timid girl, who didn't know anything but studying and keeping her head down, into a kick-ass warrior. You're strong, but together we're stronger. That bastard doesn't dare come within a mile of us or we'll take him down. We've done it before; we'll do it again."

Monica regarded the tenderness of her friend's expression and the determination of her tone. "If you really believe that, shouldn't we be hell-bent on getting out of town and as far away from here as possible?"

A grin spread across Angel's face. "I'll fight him if I have to, but there are people who do this sort of dirty work. That's what we pay our taxes for. We'll stop in at the police station, drop our bomb about you being alive, and get out. Simple. Wham. Bam. Thank you, ma'am."

"Actually, the government has been footing the bill for my expenses for a long time now. And since you don't have a job, you don't pay taxes."

Angel dropped the car into gear and accelerated down the road. "Details. Details. I can't talk about this anymore. Death-wishing sluts are exhausting. You wouldn't understand."

A few minutes passed in silence before Angel announced, "I have a headache. We haven't eaten in hours. Let's grab something on the way."

"Really? You're hungry? Now?"

"Yes, now," Angel said, nodding. "Look, there isn't anything outside of the city for miles and miles, and once we pop into the sheriff's office and say howdy do, we're headed straight out."

Monica took a deep breath. "Okay, fine."

Angel changed course, guiding the car toward the center of town.

Chapter Ten

Sam followed Triniti's directions down Third Street, passing *The Spin Cycle—Bike Sales and Rentals* and stopping at the next glass door entrance. A miniature surfboard jutted out over the entryway. *The Board Wake, Epic Fayl Designs* had been scripted across its smooth surface in a large, flowing font.

As Sam pushed through the door, a small bell jingled.

The simple interior, with a sawdust floor and an exposed beam ceiling, smelled of fresh cut wood and hot wax. A huge flat screen TV gleamed behind a surfboard countertop desk. Silently, boardhead Bodhi and FBI agent Johnny Utah—played by Patrick Swayze and Keanu Reeves in *Point Break*—argued in the rain. On another screen, *Endless Summer* glimmered in all its 1966 cult movie glory.

Sam very much approved of each choice.

His gaze moved on to the series of posters starring a man with long blond dreadlocks and an impossibly defined physique. The first was titled *Faylure is the Only Option.* In it, the photographer had captured the blond man sailing out of a tube of frothy water as large and round as the interior of a grain silo. The board, save the final few inches of the tail, seemed to be flying over the turbulent white and blue ocean. The man's face bore an amused half-grin, as if he and the sea shared some off-color secret.

In the next, titled *Faylure to Thrive*, the same man stood on the beach, a sleek longboard with *Epic Fayl* scrolled across its belly laying at his feet. His confident smile radiated from the paper while his arms hung around the waists of two raving beauties in micro bikinis. If aliens had abducted the trio, subsequent kidnappings would only yield disappointment as the world's most perfect specimens would have already been bagged, tagged, and cataloged.

Sam studied the poster closer. Ms. Bikini on the left looked familiar, but at first, he couldn't place the dazzling smile, black hair, and exuberant bosom. Then he recognized her as the woman from the diner—Triniti.

Chet leered. *Aren't you glad you listened to me for once? Because of me, you've got a date with a smoking hot waitress and her twins.*

Sam couldn't tear his eyes away from her barely-clothed chest. *It's like they're watching me. Staring. This is not an attractive picture. In fact, it's a little disconcerting. It feels like they're sizing me up so they can mug me in some dark alley.*

At gunpoint. Well, maybe not "gun." Chet pointed his two index fingers away from his chest. *Drop your pants; this is a stick up!*

Sam chuckled under his breath. *Those suckers aren't going to hold up anyone. They're as fake as a politician's soul. Admit it, touching her would be like fondling a Ken doll.*

Chet shrugged. *Just saying that if I were the doctor that had done the work, I'd put a picture of those babies on my desk right next to the wife and kids.*

Didn't you tell me to not get carried away earlier? Sam asked. *I think your focus is drifting from the task at hand.*

Chet sighed. *Okay, fine. But tomorrow, when you're spending the afternoon in the shade of those magnificent Tetons, you need to remember that it was my idea to ask her out.*

As part of the case...

Chet waved his hand in dismissal. *Sometimes you have to mix a little pleasure with business.*

Sam turned his attention away from his inner conscience and its incessant ramblings. He glanced at Triniti's counterpart and froze. The other young woman brashly displayed the generous, though non-modified, gifts nature had bestowed upon her. At first, he hadn't recognized her. But when he looked past the fake tan, bleached hair, and fake smile and studied the curve of the woman's nose, the set of her mouth, the shape of her face, she almost looked like... *Is that...?*

Chet stared too. *This* is *a small town, isn't it?*

Sam peered deep into the picture. In her near-nakedness, April Goodman peered back.

Chet pretended to hold a microphone as a huge cheesy grin graced his lips. *Sam, I'd like you to meet April. Local artist. The recently deceased enjoys painting, long walks on the sand, and floating naked and fleshless in the ocean. Before her untimely demise, she used to pose for posters wearing nothing more than a little bit of butt floss and a pair of quarter-sized bandages over her areolas.*

A voice from across the room interrupted dating game host Chet. "Hey! What's up?"

The man from the posters sauntered toward Sam in worn flip flops and faded plaid shorts. His long, sandy dreads had been tied back in a thick ponytail. Tanned skin and a ripped, polished physique gleamed from under the shirt's ragged shoulder straps.

Eyes bright, he smiled as he approached, and Sam grasped the offered hand. The man's *Maximum Faylure* tattooed forearm flexed as he shook with a grip as strong and sure as a farmer's. His rough palm and fingers belonged to a working man. "Max Fayl," he said.

"Sam. Good to meet you."

"Same here." Max tipped his chin toward the poster. "Studying the local art, I see."

Sam pointed to the image of Triniti and her thousand-watt smile. "I just met her at the diner. In fact, she told me this was the best place in town to get a board."

Max's grin broadened. "Ah, you've met our local celebrity."

"She didn't mention she was a celebrity," Sam said.

Max chuckled. "Hmmm, that doesn't sound like her. Well, she is the female regional champ. So, as far as local celebs go, she's about the most famous around."

Sam turned his eyes back to the poster. "Surfing champ, model, and waitress. Quite a resume. Are everyone's occupations so...diverse?"

"Myself withstanding." He patted his chest. "It's hard to support yourself on surfing, no matter how many trophies you've won. Most of us bottom feeders do a little of this and a little of that to make ends meet."

Sam pointed to April's picture. "What about her? She looks familiar. Surfer too?"

Max's expression brightened even more. "That's my younger sister, April."

Oh shit. Sam's heart began knocking in his chest while anger surged through his veins.

Because of shoddy, sloppy police work, the investigative team had allowed themselves to be duped into making the wrong conclusions based on weak, circumstantial evidence. Instead of cleaning up their mess and moving the case forward, they'd announced their idiocy to the world.

Max and anyone connected to his sister might have begun to wonder why April hadn't been returning phone calls. Perhaps they thought she'd gone to Seattle to find Kyme or that maybe she was just being an artistic flake. But a bomb had been dropped on Max's life, and whether he knew it or not, he was about to be torn apart by a shit ton of emotional shrapnel.

As if he needed another reason, Sam doubled his resolve to take Erebus down. *That bastard is going to answer for this. He will pay.*

While rage lingered in Chet's eyes, he still remained focused. *But if you blow your cover, he'll get away with it. If you let your emotions take over, he'll get away with it. If you don't think clearly, if you let him get to you, he'll get away with it. There will be a time for revenge. Keep going. Keep your happy face and don't let on.*

Rule #51:
Do not allow emotions to cloud your judgement.

Emotions can not only get in the way of clear, concise thinking but also blind you to facts, hinder your deductive reasoning, and prevent you from making logical decisions. They are also one of the fastest ways of losing control of a situation. Never allow your emotions control. You must always remain in control of them.

—122 Rules of Psychology

Sam shoved his rage and frustration to the very depth of his being, calming his pounding pulse and boiling blood.

Max continued, oblivious to the impending disaster in his life. "Her 'little of this' is art and her 'little of that' is part-time modeling. And even though she's on the posters and looks like she could tame a wave just by sneering at it, she can't ride. Not even a little. I've tried coaxing her, cajoling her, and bribing her, but it's like trying to convince a cat to jump in the pool and learn to backstroke."

He crossed his arms and leaned against the wall. "I've offered her free lessons, and while I think part of her wants to, she just can't make herself do it. It's weird because she spends most of her free time on the beach. Hell, even her studio has a huge picture window overlooking the ocean.

Though, I guess that makes sense since it's usually the topic of her paintings."

Sam put on his best poker face. "So, she just doesn't like to surf?"

"Nope," Max said. "She's aquaphobic. Always has been."

Sam frowned. "This seems like an odd place to live when you're afraid of the water." His internal thermostat began to lower as he separated himself from the glowing ball of anger.

"Right?" Max said. "Well, we grew up here and neither of us wanted to leave. I guess no place is perfect." He glanced at the poster again. "I've always told her that she looks great in print. That if she really wanted to make a living outside of the Cove, she could go to LA or New York. I've got a few friends with connections. We could make it happen. But she's a small-town girl, and this is our home." He shrugged as if to say, "What can you do?"

"Anyway," Max continued, "I doubt you stopped by to talk about my family or the local art scene."

Au contraire, mon frère, Chet said.

Sam returned the smile. "I can appreciate art, but I don't claim to understand it. To be honest, the stuff at IKEA looks as good to me as the million-dollar stuff hanging on the walls in the Louvre. Maybe even better."

Max laughed. "Same here. But don't ever let April hear you say that. She'll give you a lecture that'll make your ears bleed."

"I'll remember that if I ever meet her," Sam said. Though he should have probed deeper into April's life, he really didn't want to talk to Max about his dead sister anymore, so he changed the subject. "I'm looking for a longboard. Something easier to control, at least for now. It's been a few years since I've been out on the water."

Max held up a finger. "Come with me. I know exactly what you need."

Sam followed the sandy-haired man to the front of the store.

Max waltzed up to a wall covered in a plethora of brightly-colored boards, each with *Epic Fayl Custom Surf Design* printed on its underbelly. He started flipping through them and talking excitedly at the same time. "You'll pick it back up before you know it. No problem. The body remembers what the mind forgets. And, since you're new to my boards, you should check several of them out. No rental fees."

Sam raised an eyebrow, surprised. He'd anticipated having to spend a small fortune. "I don't understand."

Max stopped. "Here's the deal. You try a couple on for size, and I guarantee one of them will call to you. When you find the right one, it'll be like having the woman of your dreams in your arms. Even when you try to hold another, *she* will haunt you at night. Eventually you'll realize you can't live without *her* and you'll be back to make the relationship permanent."

Sam chuckled. "Maybe."

Max slapped him on the back and smiled. "I don't know how many times I've heard 'maybe' before. Hundreds, maybe thousands."

Sam didn't want to mislead the proprietor. Surfing was just another angle for him to pursue on the case. He wouldn't be buying anything, and he didn't want to cheat Max out of any potential rental money. "Besides, I don't know how long I'm going to be in town."

Max's smile grew as though he'd heard that a thousand times before too. "Not to worry, mate. Even if you don't find 'the one,' even if you don't come back, at least you'll get in a good ride. You'll be another brother living the lifestyle of sun, ocean, and the great surfer way."

"Besides," he said conspiratorially, "if the topic comes up, you'll tell your friends you were treated fairly and that these boards are the best you've ever tried. They will be intrigued, and..." He pointed at Sam's chest. "There is no emotion more powerful than human intrigue. It's what helped us evolve from monkeys, and if curiosity can turn apes into men, it can get people through the door of my shop."

While Sam found emotion-driven marketing to be an odd way of running things, the business looked healthy. He could think of no rebuttal, so he nodded.

Max's smile broadened. He began thumbing through the boards again. "Excellent. So tell me, where do you call home?"

"LA. Born and raised."

Max clucked and shook his head in mock shame. "Well, since Triniti sent you, I won't charge extra for the wet suit in spite of that. I guess I can't really hold it against you. We don't get to choose where we spend our childhood. Then life happens, and we end up in places we never expected. Am I right?"

Sam nodded again.

"Anyway," Max continued, "the important thing is that you got out of that rat hole, even if it's only for a little while."

"It *is* a rat hole," Sam admitted. "We had to drive two hours just to get to the beach when I was growing up. But with traffic, it's even worse now. I loved Malibu as a kid, but Triniti made the Cove sound like the end-all be-all."

Max glanced back, and his easy smile returned. "It's all true, mate. You have no idea." He wrapped his arm around Sam's shoulders and pointed, as if gazing out over the ocean. "Wait till you get out there. You'll think you've died and gone to heaven." His smile turned to a smirk and he gestured at the boards. "The surf is fantastic, but these make it feel like you are gliding over melted butter. I make each one by hand."

He reached over, slipped one from the shelf, and held it out. Sam took it, running his fingers over the custom paint and lacquered finish, which gleamed and shimmered in the low light. "You made this?"

Max folded his arms and smiled. "Every one of them. My workshop's in the back."

Sam looked it up and down, impressed by the clean lines and stunning craftsmanship.

Max pulled out three more, jamming them into the sawdust floor. "Try out one or all of these." He launched into a short spiel about the pros and cons of each design. Sam only understood a fraction of the lecture, which contained a lot of words like "lift," "drag," "thrust," and "flow." He'd come for help with a case, but somehow he'd ended up in a physics class on water dynamics.

After the proprietor finished, Sam pointed to one with a smiling hula girl on it. "I'll take that one."

Max lit up like a kid on Christmas morning. "Good choice. She's one of my favorites. I'll get her ready. You can stop by anytime to pick her up. Come on up to the desk; I need your John Hancock."

Sam followed the almost-skipping Max to the counter in the back corner of the store. He dreaded hurting this man's spirit but knew he eventually might have to. Perhaps Sam could enact a little revenge on the surfer's behalf. It wouldn't bring April back or help fill in the massive hole that would be punched through Max's heart when he found out what had happened, but it might help him feel like a little bit of justice had been served.

Sam looked forward to delivering that justice.

Chapter Eleven

Tyron had more patience than a herd of monks on a thousand-mile pilgrimage to Rome, but even he'd grown weary of the tedious research. The town already had little in the way of an internet presence, and days after whatever broke went down, he still could not reach any websites outside of its minuscule borders. Clearly these fools had no interest in anything or anyone else in the world, so they probably hadn't even bothered to begin working on restoring access.

Being so cut off made his searching that much more frustrating.

He sighed as he returned to the city's home page, then clicked the next in the series of local businesses. *The Board Wake's* website, complete with the sound of crashing waves and gentle music, came to life in all its ridiculous simple-tonness. It centered around the owner, a smiling blond man with long dreadlocks, who boasted he made the best custom gear for diehard surf fans.

Erebus scanned through the irrelevant text and clicked the *Promotions* page. His eyes widened as the first image materialized on the little screen. The man in dreads,

Max Fayl, stood on the beach with his arms around two nearly-nude women.

He had to fight to keep from vomiting up his own pancreas as his gaze landed on the first female. She had a chest so large and a frame so demure she looked like a caricature drawn by a hormonal teenage boy. Tyron sneered at the screen as another wave of repulsion attacked his gorge. Unable to contain his anger, he screamed, jumped up from the desk, and began to pace the room.

As he marched, he once again glanced at the lewd image on the computer and decided that he'd done enough research for the day.

But just before he slammed the lid of the laptop shut, he paused as a different scene formed in his mind's eye. In it, the website had morphed into a collage of images of this woman after he—Tyron Erebus, a prophet, redeemer, and maker of beauty—had transformed her. Turning her from disgusting freak into a seraph with a thousand flicks of his blade.

His rage cooled and his sneer turned into a smirk as he sat back down. He swallowed a thick glob of indignation as he forced himself to look again, studying the shape of her body, the tilt of her head, and the width of her come-hither smile.

Erebus imagined removing her flaws one after the other. The flow of her blood over his hands, the melodious dissonant chords in the harmony of her screams, the rapid tempo of her heart, and her searing heat. Then that final delicious crescendo as he injected his fire, releasing her from this world and jettisoning her into the next.

Yes, he would mold her into a masterpiece. He would redeem this lost soul.

He looked again with fresh, plotting eyes and nodded. The first thing he'd do was remove those grotesque monstrosities on her chest, slice them up, and force-feed them to her, one silicone bite at a time. He might even take pictures and send them to Max Fayl, who could post them on the website.

As the idea transformed from vision to premonition, it became so clear, so sumptuous, he could already hear her begging.

Having made a plan, his vital organs no longer threatened to expel themselves in moralistic protest, so he allowed his gaze to travel to the second woman. Cocking his head, he looked closer. The artist, while still in her impure and imperfect state, smiled up from beside the blond man. It seemed that in addition to peddling second-rate paintings, Ms. Goodman had also turned a profit by showing a great deal of her skin.

Erebus smiled and sat back. The skank had no skin to show now.

The grin melted, and he frowned as understanding dawned. The same woman whom he thought he'd randomly chosen as the harbinger of his message now just happened to show up in this picture. No way was that a mere coincidence. Fate had led him to her. But why? What did Fate want him to know?

He thought it over for a moment and then, on a hunch, opened a new browser window and began to type. Logging into the town library, he selected the *Local Genealogy* link he'd previously ignored, entered *April Goodman*, and clicked *Show Family Tree*.

Though she had switched to her mother's maiden name of Goodman, April's birth name had been Fayl. He chose the link for siblings and an image of a smiling blond man with dreadlocks popped up.

While Erebus stared at the picture, the temperature in the room suddenly dropped, rolling across his skin as if he'd opened the door to a meat locker on a hot summer afternoon. Cool fingers gently grazed Erebus' scalp. He froze as they traced his neck and caressed his face.

At first, he had mistaken the loving touch as that of the other, but then April's voice, soft and grateful for the redemption he'd bestowed upon her, whispered in his ear. *Follow this. Go to my brother. As you did for me, he will lead you to your destiny.*

Gooseflesh broke out over every inch of Tyron's body. Though he'd helped many women ascend, none had ever come back. No one else had ever shown gratitude from beyond the other side.

His journey, his path, had been lonesome. He'd been sought by the police and persecuted in the media. But the saving of souls and cleansing of spirits could not be measured in popularity polls. And April Goodman had just reassured him that the gods blessed his sacred mission.

Heavy with the burdens and expectations weighing upon him, Erebus printed the advertisement and laid it on the desk next to the computer. He would visit the surf shop's owner and get the answers to his questions.

His gaze returned to the image of Max Fayl's sister.

Her reassuring words had confirmed that he'd done the world a favor by turning a whore into art. Not only had he created something breathtaking to behold, but he had removed yet one more leg-spreader from society. It would be an impossible, insurmountable task to rid the planet of all such scourges. But upon his exit, his lifetime of effort would leave the world a better, more beautiful, more pure place than when he'd entered it.

Nothing in April's diary indicated that she'd slept with anyone other than Kyme, so Erebus reasoned that she'd simply chosen to not document the fathomless depths of her sexual depravities. For the right price, she'd probably have slept with most anyone—including her own brother.

He studied the picture in detail. Based on their indecent apparel and their obvious hyper hormonal state, the photograph must have been taken as part in the trio's foreplay, and immediately thereafter, they'd fornicated right there in the sand for all to watch.

Exhibitionism gave him the trots, and no matter how mainstream it became, he would never condone the practice. Magazines and online media outlets dripped with articles about racy, raunchy sex, each publication pushing the limits of acceptability as they tried to outdo one another. It had gotten so bad, so prolific, that he'd found it almost impossible to browse the internet without some woman trying to shove her body onto him.

April had atoned for the mistakes she'd made. The perversions and temptations she'd succumbed to had contaminated her soul, leaving it as black and malignant as a smoker's lungs. The big breasted woman needed to be taught modesty and humility or face an eternity of damnation.

Females were designed to be the gatekeepers of a pure society and only allow the strongest, most virile males past the barricade of their tightly-closed legs. At all times, women should have their bodies covered, their mouths shut, and their behavior virtuous. When they failed to uphold their obligations, society suffered. Promiscuous, licentious behavior diluted and polluted the entire human genetic pool because they allowed weaker, feeble-minded males to procreate.

He turned his attention to the blond man. Tyron did not hold Max Fayl accountable for the urge to copulate. In fact, he applauded the man's desire to propagate the species. As a male, his primary purpose and responsibility was to ensure his lineage by injecting his seed into as many viable wombs as possible.

Erebus shook his head. The women had wandered from the path of righteousness, but Max Fayl could not be held accountable for their faults. He had only been following the instincts written into the human genome millenniums ago. Unlike them, he'd been upholding his obligation to better the human species.

Though Max Fayl might be blameless in the females' debauchery, Erebus saw no need to *not* kill him either.

He had questions to answer, and after fulfilling that obligation, Max Fayl would be a witness. In the big scheme of things, the owner of the surf shop served no more importance than a cockroach, and like all insects, Erebus would crush him.

That wasn't murder; that was his job.

In a little town where everyone knew everything about everyone else, Max Fayl knew something, and he *would* talk. Maybe he knew the bitch or the mongrel. Or perhaps they'd dated or been in contact.

After leaving Arizona, the bitch had traveled across the country back to New York. But beyond that, the trail hadn't just gone cold; it had ended completely. She had to have gone someplace. If that someplace turned out to not be here, he needed to stop wasting time in this backwards part of the country and go to her.

At the very least, Erebus would get a lead on the other slut in the picture. Maybe she'd even be enough to quench his thirst and help keep his needs at bay. At least for a while.

He couldn't stay in Elon's house forever. At some point, the old man would be missed and someone would come looking. So in addition to gathering information, he'd have to find a new place to hide.

He checked the time. Most of the local businesses folded up their welcome mats by five. He needed to leave soon to catch Max Fayl before he clocked out for the day.

Erebus tucked the picture into his pocket and headed toward the door.

☆☆☆☆

Tyron pulled the ball cap down low, trying to get the bill's shadow to hide the scars on his face. But no matter how hard he pulled, the damned blinding sun made it impossible to completely conceal the damage to his cheek and the side of his head.

He wished for the thousandth time he could have waited until after dusk for this sojourn.

As a creature of the night, he loved the darkness. It understood him and he it. The brilliance and chaos of the day left him overwhelmed and exhausted, his energy drained as fast as a cheap car battery a month past its warranty. The brightness burned his skin and, even through heavy sunglasses, scorched his retinas.

The shop lay just a mile from his hideout. As he traveled, he kept his head tucked and his pace brisk but casual. Up ahead, the surfboard from the website jutted out over a storefront.

Eyes down, he focused on the sidewalk as he traversed its rough-hewn surface. He didn't dare look up for more than an occasional brief glance. Otherwise, he risked revealing his face to one of the many passersby. A man in a cap, jeans, and t-shirt would go unnoticed, but the scars would be memorable.

If someone recognized him, he could quietly silence them. But despite his remarkable skill set, not even he could nab people in a crowded city in broad daylight. Too risky. Besides, since the shop closed soon, he simply didn't have the time to kill everyone. His best option would be to remain as incognito as possible.

He stopped outside the large window, just shy of the door. Shading his eyes against the glare, he removed his sunglasses and peered through the dark glass. At first, the place looked deserted, but when his eyes adjusted, he spotted a large man studying the same Max Fayl and two naked bimbos poster Erebus had printed out earlier.

Sex sells.

The big man looked up as someone approached. This newcomer had long dreadlocks tied back into a pony-tail. The two shook hands and then talked for a while before walking to the side of the store. Max Fayl yammered some more before pulling out several surfboards. The other man, *of course*, pointed to the one with the half-naked Polynesian girl on its belly.

Then, yet more talking. What could possibly be so interesting? People wasted barrels of time on mundane and unimportant topics. Tyron stared at the men, willing them to finish.

After the customer finally left, he would walk in, lock the door, drag Max Fayl into the back, and extract whatever information he possessed by whatever means necessary. He would then kill the shop owner and leave by the rear entrance. Simple and neat.

He needed to be inside, not standing out on the side-walk like a traveling carnival show. Perhaps he should go in, capture, and tie up *both* men?

While the idea of getting to torture two people sound-ed like a delightful way to pass the evening, he thought overpowering a second person added complexity and uncertainty. Besides, as satisfying as it would be, he hadn't actually come to kill these men. He needed to focus on getting the information from Max Fayl.

But this conversation was taking forever.

Perhaps he should waltz in and shoot the customer. Once he'd dragged the body back behind the counter, he could get on with his business.

But after Erebus subtly glanced around, he dismissed the idea. Too many potential witnesses with too many cell phones to call the police.

Finally, their prattle seemed to be dwindling, and the drawn out jabber session ended. Just as Erebus tensed, preparing himself for a little fun with the shop owner, the two men turned and marched to the back desk where they began yet *another* conversation.

Erebus' shoulders slumped, and he sighed. He could be here all night if these two ladies didn't stop gossiping.

As the customer filled out some paperwork on a clipboard, he turned around, leaning back against the counter.

For the first time, Erebus got an unobstructed view of the man's face.

A tremor ran through his body as fear slithered inside his gut and coiled around his heart. His hand flew to his cheek, rubbing the scabbed, scarred flesh. His pulse rocketed as he recalled an image of this same man bringing a gun around and pulling the trigger. The shot, louder and more eternal than the singularity explosion that had formed the cosmos, played out in slow motion. Erebus charging in a rage. His foot slipping on a spot of grease on the floor. The projectile that should have blown his skull into fragments, ripping and searing his flesh like a red-hot branding iron.

Two months ago, he had glimpsed into the darkness of eternity. Two months ago, this man had introduced Erebus to fear. Two months ago, Tyron's sleep had gone from blissful and silent to cursed and chaotic. This man, this demon, had unleashed a plague upon Erebus' life.

He looked again at the man's face. The chill slinked from his gut up his back, as though the icy talon of a dragon traced the stack of vertebrae. He began to shake.

Erebus closed his eyes, trying not to get sick. Fear. In his world of control, the emotion felt as foreign as an ancient language and as unsettling as sudden blindness in a crowded square.

But the coldness inside him began to boil. Raging anger burned in his core and radiated out to his extremities. How dare this man introduce terror and trepidation into his emotional repertoire.

Erebus had never hated anyone before. But the feeling bubbled up, floating on a wave of pain and anger, and broke the surface with an audible pop. "You!" He hissed. The man's audacity to think he could hurt him, defeat him, and scar him fanned the flames of indignation, turning rage into loathing.

He now understood why he'd been led to the surf shop. Not only did Max Fayl have information he needed, but Tyron had been given the chance to even the score. He'd been handed a gift and an opportunity.

He'd find out what Max Fayl knew and kill him. If the bitch never returned, he'd leave town before someone noticed him. But before he did, he had some business to conduct, a little debt that needed to be settled.

He would wait until the man completed whatever eternal transaction they had started, then follow him. Once alone, he'd do what he should have done a long time ago. This time he'd have the upper hand. Nothing quick like a knife to the throat or a blade between the ribs either. He'd slice open this man's guts and leave him in an alley, holding his own intestines as he bled to death. Then Erebus would get what he'd come for from Max Fayl.

Tyron Erebus waited as the sun began its slow descent into the west and darkness crept in on the little town.

Chapter Twelve

Monica watched out the window as Angel guided the car into one of the parking spaces in front of the 1950s style diner. Her friend put the vehicle into park and shut the engine off.

Instead of opening her door though, Angel looked down the street one way and then up the other direction. She peered through the windshield and into the restaurant in front of them.

Monica followed her gaze, but nothing out of the ordinary caught her attention.

Angel frowned, slowly opened her door, and got out.

Monica followed, perplexed by her friend's sudden apprehension. "Change your mind?"

Instead of replying, Angel stood in the doorframe and stared at the surf shop behind them.

The Board Wake had opened during Monica's junior year of high school. Though she had never been inside, she'd seen the owner—Mark, or Max, or something—a few times. Many of her classmates had gushed over him, but to Monica, he'd always seemed arrogant.

She glanced back at Angel. Her friend's focus seemed to have shifted from the shop to the pedestrians flowing down the sidewalk.

At first Monica didn't see anything wrong, but then her gaze shifted to a man, his hands cupped around his face as he looked through the window. Though she couldn't explain why, her heart stuttered and then began to thump in her chest. Something about the set of his shoulders, or his stance, struck her as familiar.

"Mon, get back in the car." Angel's whispered words didn't penetrate at first.

Monica looked her. "What? Why?"

Angel's face had turned vampire pale. "Now!"

Monica didn't question her a second time. She slid into the car, shut the door, and slinked down in her seat. "What is it? You look as white as a ghost."

"That man. Does he look familiar to you?"

Monica nodded. "Yes, but I don't know why."

"Take a good look."

They craned their necks, gazing out the back window.

☆☆☆☆

Sam handed over his driver's license. "Just use the Alabaster Inn as my address," he said, glancing around the sales floor. "So, when did you open your shop?"

Max nodded, took the license, and quickly filled out the rental receipt. He yanked out the carbon copy, then paused. "Well, that's complicated. See, my old man taught me everything I know about working with wood. My mom was an artist, and she taught me to draw and paint. In high school, I made my first few boards in my dad's shop and sold them to the locals. The money was decent but not enough to live on, so I did odd jobs and designed in the evenings and on weekends. I eventually found an investment partner who loved my work so much she helped me get this place set up. To answer your question, it didn't so much have a grand opening as it evolved into this."

"It's really lucky you found someone to help you get things running," Sam said. "Getting investors that believe in you can be a bitch."

"I totally lucked out," Max replied, smiling. "But we worked out a deal, and I've got everything paid back. It helps that I have really low overhead. The shop's inexpensive, and I do all the work myself."

Sam touched the smiling hula girl on his board. "This is really fantastic. I figured your sister, being an artist, did the graphics."

Max laughed and shook his head. "Nah. Mom taught us both, but April really ran with it. She's the gifted one. I'm a glorified hack. But it works for me, and it works for my customers."

"I'll admit, I might already be in love with my hula girl."

"I told ya." Max's infectious laughter reverberated around the room. "See," he said pointing, "you haven't even been out yet and you're already thinking of *her*."

Sam shook his head. "Maybe you're right. So, is Fayl your actual name? It's a little exotic. And it works so well with the promotions, it makes me wonder if you made it up, like an author's pen name."

Max set the clipboard down and leaned against the counter. "Nope. It's the real thing. Fayl's a family name. It's French or something." He handed Sam a copy of the paperwork. "Looks like we're good to go."

They shook hands. Sam thanked him and turned to leave but then spun back around. "Is April married?"

Max cocked his head, a half-smile playing on his lips. "Why? Are you thinking of asking her out?"

"No. You said her last name was Goodman."

A shadow passed over Max's face. "Oh, yeah, I can see why you'd think that. No. Our folks died a few years ago. Mom and April were tight, so she took Mom's name. You know, to honor her and keep it going."

"Oh, I'm sorry. My condolences."

Max took a deep breath and gave him a sad smile. "Thanks. But no condolences are necessary. It was a long time ago. Sis and I have always had each other. So, even if everything else is gone, at least we'll have that."

Sam faked a bright smile. "I'm glad. Thanks again." He put on his sunglasses and headed toward the door.

☆☆☆☆

Erebus tensed as the big man strolled to the front of the shop. Unwilling to be caught off guard again, he assessed his prey for weapons but could see none.

Tyron reached into his pocket, his fingers grasping the blade concealed there. He would sidle up behind the bastard, slip the razor under the man's shirt, slice him open, and then blend into the crowd, leaving the man to bleed to death on the sidewalk.

Clean and neat. The ensuing chaos would cover his retreat.

He had only peripherally registered the arrival of a car among the steady flow of pedestrian traffic, but since it had not been of consequence, he'd not paid attention. However, the slamming doors behind him broke his concentration. He'd been diligent and covert, so he didn't think anyone had identified him. But he also didn't want to be caught off guard in case the police had arrived, so he tore his eyes away from the window and risked a quick peek over his shoulder.

The two women continued to stare out the rear window when the man in the baseball cap glanced back. He narrowed his eyes as he studied them, perplexity tinging his scarred face.

Monica gasped. "Oh, shit! We need to get to the police and get out. Now."

Angel tried inserting the key. For several seconds, she fumbled and jabbed. Finally, it slid in smoothly and she cranked it so hard her knuckles turned white. Just as the man took a step toward them, the engine roared to life.

Angel dropped the car into gear. "Yeah, I think you're right." The car lurched backward, and they screeched to a stop in the middle of the street.

☆☆☆☆

Erebus stared. Because of the sun's reflected brilliance off the vehicle's trunk and rear window, he couldn't see into the car, but something about it intrigued him, lured him in to look closer.

He had just taken a step forward when the car came to life. It screamed out of the parking space and skidded to a stop in the center of the road.

Surprised, he froze, expecting it to tear away.

Instead, the engine randomly revved and clunked from gear to gear as if the driver had never operated a motor vehicle before. A shadow descended over the scene. Erebus glanced up to see the only cloud in an otherwise perfectly blue sky filter out some of the sun's intensity. His gaze returned to the spectacle playing out in the middle of the business district.

Now that no blinding glare prevented him from seeing past the glass, Erebus found himself staring into the wide eyes of the bitch. The universe transformed from chaos to order as randomness coalesced and fell into place.

For a moment, no one and nothing except the two of them—Erebus and his bitch—existed. Calm serenity washed over Erebus' soul, like the cleansing blood from a freshly pierced artery. He smiled. The gods had delivered her to him.

His mission, his holy mission, could now be completed.

Monica would have been thrown into the dashboard had she not been holding on. She glanced at her friend.

Angel dropped the gearshift into *neutral*, swore as she fumbled with the knob, flipped it up past *drive* and into *park*.

Monica turned her attention back to the man on the sidewalk, certain he would be approaching with his gun drawn and revenge in his eyes. But he remained rooted in place, staring through the window...at her.

As they locked eyes, the world—Angel, the crowds, everyone and everything—faded away and she stood alone, naked and defenseless against the madman. Erebus' yellow eyes bore into hers, and a slight grin played at the corners of his lips.

He had come for her. He had found her. He *would* kill her.

Somewhere a thousand miles away, Angel swore and cursed as the engine revved, but the vehicle did not move.

Monica waited. They'd become easy prey sitting in the road, but since they'd also become a bit of spectacle, a few of the pedestrians had stopped to gawk.

She'd had just enough time to think that she probably should have locked the doors when a loud clunk resonated from somewhere deep in the engine compartment. Angel whooped, and the car screamed in protest as they tore away. The murdering psychopath dwindled in the distance, though he never stopped staring at her.

Rubber skidded as Angel maneuvered around a corner. The caterwauling tires slammed into the curb. Angel jerked the wheel, tossing the vehicle violently to the side. Monica's head smacked into the passenger window and broke her gaze with the killer.

Angel regained control and accelerated, leaving the madman and his lunacy behind.

☆☆☆☆

The automobile thunked and clunked, then leapt forward. But even as it sped away, Erebus continued to watch the bitch. Savoring her aura and basking in her fear.

The car tore down the street and whipped around a corner so fast it smacked up against the curb. It screeched against the impediment but didn't slow.

He remained so mesmerized by the fleeing vehicle that he only peripherally registered someone exiting the surf shop. Tyron glanced at the big man as he blended into the pedestrian traffic flowing toward the center of town.

Max Fayl appeared in the doorway of *The Board Wake*. He flipped the welcome sign to *Closed* and turned the deadbolt.

Erebus' attention skipped between the trifecta of intersecting events. He looked in the direction the car had gone, glanced at the crowd where the big man had disappeared, then turned back to Max Fayl's store.

Just as he had been guided to April, he had been led to this spot to bear witness to this moment. The gods had very high expectations of him. But they had also promised him a good and faithful servant's reward. Grateful for the burden and the chance, he would earn his worthiness of the proffered gift. He would not disappoint those who had bestowed the honor and opportunity upon him.

Erebus' smile grew. He turned on his heels and walked back to Elon's. He had work to do. A lot of it.

Chapter Thirteen

Angel didn't slow in school zones or pause for yield signs, nor did she stop for the red light along Main Street. She ripped around corners and zipped through residential neighborhoods toward the police station at the edge of town.

Monica held on as Angel barreled over a speed bump on a quiet suburban street. Asphalt slammed against the undercarriage, and Monica looked out the back window to see if they'd left an oil slick or pieces of the car behind. Fortunately, the road appeared free of vehicular debris, but if Angel didn't let up soon, she'd destroy their getaway car.

Turning to her, Monica said, "You can slow down, you know?"

"I'm just putting some distance between us and him," Angel replied, without taking her eyes off the road.

The car bounced through a pothole and Monica's teeth snapped together. "He can't catch us. Not even Usain Bolt could keep up with your crazy driving."

Angel revved the engine harder. The side mirror of a parked car blurred past, within inches of the passenger window.

Angel had always been a fighter, so this response baffled Monica. It would have been much more in line with her friend's character to have gotten out of the car and faced the psychopath in front of God and the world. "Why are we running?"

Not tearing her eyes from the road, Angel swerved around obstacles, continuing to endanger everyone and everything. "Because he can't catch us if we're doing a hundred."

"But you always say to fight."

Smacking the wheel, Angel said, "Because we had a plan. This guy is supposed to be dead, or at least not here, and he tracked us down. He was waiting for us. We tried to kill him, Peter tried to kill him, the FBI and police have tried to kill him, but he keeps on coming. It's like some awful horror movie where a Freddy/Jason hybrid refuses to die. Fighting him on his terms doesn't work. I love you, and I'm keeping you safe. For now, that means getting the hell out of here."

Even as Monica got tossed around like an old rag in a clothes dryer, a warm bubble of affection swelled in her chest.

Angel glanced over and rolled her eyes. "Don't get all mushy on me now. We have work to do."

"That was just so sweet. I love you too," Monica said, touching her shoulder.

She scowled and shrugged off Monica's hand. "You pick the strangest times to get sentimental."

Angel yanked the steering wheel. The tires howled in protest and spit gravel. As she straightened the vehicle's trajectory, the cinderblock police station materialized in the windshield. Angel didn't slow as they approached, and Monica wondered if they would just fly past.

At the last second, Angel spun the wheel and applied a generous dollop of brakes, sending the car into a long, screeching slide. Just before they slammed into the side of the building, the vehicle thumped up against the curb and stopped in a dramatic spray of dust and unhappy rubber.

Angel jammed the shift lever into *park*. "Okay, we go in, tell our tale, and then get the hell out. No meandering. No time wasted time for niceties. We let these people take down the bad guy; that's what we pay our taxes for. Agreed?"

Monica nodded. "Let's go."

They exited the car and headed up a walkway flanked by manicured grass and shrubbery. The new sidewalks, landscaping, decorative light posts, and fancy ironworks gave the public building an old town, turn of the century vibe. "Wow. Well, at least if you're going to jail, you'll go in style," Monica remarked.

Monica followed as Angel marched up the walkway, flung open the door, and charged inside.

Decorated with thick carpeting, still life paintings, and lush potted plants, the office had been designed more like a New York penthouse apartment than a municipality on a budget. A receptionist filing her nails at a large oak desk did not acknowledge them as they approached. A small gold sign identified her as Mrs. Templeton.

Angel stormed up to the desk. "Mrs. Templeton, we need to see the sheriff."

The receptionist remained focused on perfecting the edge to her fingertip. She neither looked up nor replied.

Angel leaned in closer. "Now."

Mrs. Templeton sighed and set her file down. She put on a pair of half-glasses and turned to her computer.

Angel tapped her foot while she waited.

After a minute of staring at the screen, the receptionist peered up at them over the top of her spectacles. "Sorry, the sheriff is busy."

Angel threw her arms up and looked around the otherwise deserted office. "Doing what? Nothing ever happens in this town."

Mrs. Templeton removed her glasses, letting them dangle by the silver chain around her neck. She sniffed as though vermin had scurried onto her dinner table and interrupted her meal. "He has duties, miss. He has responsibilities to keep this town safe. I'll book you an appointment."

Monica sighed. "You always bring out the best in people, Ang. We don't have time to play these games." She glanced around and grabbed Angel's hand. "Come on." She led her friend down the hall.

The receptionist leapt to her feet, yelling as they stormed away. "You can't go back there."

Monica didn't bother to look back as they made a beeline for the glass door with *Sheriff Buford Austin* stenciled on its frosted surface. "Come and arrest us." She twisted the handle and ushered Angel inside.

Mrs. Templeton came running behind them. "Sheriff. Sheriff. I tried to stop them. I told them that—"

Monica slammed the door in the receptionist's face, cutting her protests off mid-sentence. She locked the handle as the receptionist tried to get in. The two women turned around.

A thick man in a khaki-colored officer's uniform reclined in his chair, feet and hat propped up on his desk. He chewed on an unlit stogie while a magazine covered his generous lap. He didn't budge but instead continued to gnaw his cigar as though frantic women barged into his office every day.

Bloodshot eyes, nuzzled deep in pudgy pouches of skin, flicked back and forth between the two of them. He stopped to linger on Monica's face. The phone rang, but he continued to stare at her as it yowled like a pissed off dachshund. The big man sighed and tossed the magazine onto the desk before picking up the handset.

"It's fine," he barked into the receiver. Without waiting for a reply, he returned the phone to its cradle and rubbed his forehead as if he'd suddenly developed a headache. "So, the rumor is true. It really wasn't your body that washed up on the beach. Well, shit. That's gonna make it so I have a ton of paperwork to file."

Monica put her hands on her hips and scowled. "Sorry my being alive is such an inconvenience."

Sheriff Austin dropped his feet to the floor, picked up his hat, and set it on a thick wave of salt-and-pepper executive hair. "Well, these things happen. Don't you worry about it."

Monica took a step closer to his desk. "I'm not worried about it. But you've got a lot more problems than just paperwork, Sheriff. There's a killer on the loose. He's ruthless and murders without provocation and without mercy."

He peered up at her from under the brim of his hat. "What I've got is exactly what I'd suspected all along, a body that hitched a ride on the California Current. It came down from LA or San Francisco, put there by one of the lunatics that trolls those cities. We don't have those sorts of problems here." He tapped the desk with a thick finger.

"You most certainly do—" Monica began.

He cut her off. "Part of why we live in the Cove is because none of us wants to deal with the crazies up north. I run a safe town, ladies. Now why don't you take your drama and scoot." He waggled his fingers toward the door. "I have work to do." He reached for the magazine.

Angel grabbed it just as his fingers grazed its gun-covered surface. She glanced at the cover, rolled her eyes, then threw it in the trash.

She leaned on the lawman's desk, her eyes locking with his. "Look. We've dealt with this lunatic before. He chased us across the country and tried to blow Monica up in her own house. He murders anyone who gets in his way. In fact, he's almost killed us about a half a dozen times. That girl in the newspaper, what happened to her is him in a *good* mood. You don't even want to see him pissed off."

Angel glared down at him with enough fire to flash fry a rabbit. "I don't know who you found, but she was from *here*. This guy isn't thousands, or even hundreds, of miles away like you want to believe. He's here, Sheriff. We just saw him in the middle of town. Now you may be too old, too fat, and too lazy to do anything about it. But you need to get your fingers on the phone and get some people, *competent* people, in here working on this, or the bodies are going to start stacking up like your daily morning pile of pancakes."

The sheriff stared at her. He didn't react, nor did he flinch, but he slid his hand over to a notebook on his desk. He flipped it open and picked up a pencil. "Okay, so tell me about this supposed lunatic that, though you've survived multiple attacks and being blown up, is the terror of my town. What's his name? What's he look like?"

Monica held her hand just above her head. "Medium height. Medium build. Jeans, long-sleeved shirt, and a baseball cap. His name is Tyron Erebus, though he might be under an alias."

The sheriff shifted his gaze to Monica. "Because you *think* he's under an assumed name, I suppose you want me to arrest every man in town that fits this description?"

She folded her arms. "He also has scars on his face from where Peter shot him while we were in St. Louis."

He raised his eyebrows. "Who's Peter?"

"He's a spy with the FBI or CIA or something."

The little space between the sheriff's eyes crinkled as he jotted in his notebook. "But you don't know who he is?"

"Who?" Monica asked. "Peter or Erebus?"

The peace officer sighed. "Let's start with this Peter character."

Angel shook her head. "No, not really. He and Mon were going out, but she broke it off. Then one night, not long after they stopped seeing each other, we—Monica and me, I mean—were eating dinner at this pizza place in St. Louis when Erebus showed up and killed everyone that worked there. He was about to kidnap us, but then Peter shot his way through the front window and started blasting the place apart. Then he and Erebus got into a fight." Angel pretended to punch an invisible foe in the face and gut.

"When did this Peter fella shoot...um, what's his name? Ear bus? In the face?"

"Erebus," Angel said. She shrugged. "I'm not completely sure. I think it was after they started fighting." She gestured to Monica and then back to herself. "Peter told us to run, and since they both had guns, we did."

Monica held her hand in the shape of a pistol. "Peter even shot my laptop because he said Erebus was using it to track me." She dropped her thumb like the hammer of a gun. "Bam!"

The sheriff blinked, and his face turned red. He snapped his notebook closed. "Let me see if I've got this straight. A madman from St. Louis, who's already been shot in the face by your boyfriend—who incidentally also shot your computer—has risen from the dead? In my world, people who eat a bullet don't just get up and start walking around, ladies. Bullets kill, and once you're dead, you're dead. So, this ghost has come back *and* traveled across the country to...what? Kill everyone here? Really, try and look at it from my perspective."

Angel stiffened. "I don't care how crazy it sounds. You've got a real problem, Sheriff."

Sheriff Austin pointed at thin stack of folders on his desk. "Do you see this? These are my open cases. The entire lot consists of a DUI, two possessions, and a disturbing the peace. That's it."

Angel shrugged. "Am I supposed to be impressed?"

"Do you know what isn't in here?" He tapped the pile. "Missing persons reports. If your madman was killing people, don't you think someone would have noticed? Even if no more bodies wash up on shore, people don't keep quiet when someone they love suddenly stops answering their phone."

"Sheriff, he's here," Monica said. "We just saw him. Maybe he hasn't killed anyone else yet. Maybe that's why you don't have any reports."

He shifted his gaze to her. "You said you saw him in the middle of town?"

She nodded.

He pointed to his cheek. "You also say the side of his face is shot off?"

"A lot of it," she said, nodding again.

The sheriff took a deep breath. "I'm as tied to the rumor tree as anyone, probably more so because of my position. Say your theory is right and he's just hanging out. He's checking out the sights and getting drinks down at one of the taverns. But someone with those kinds of scars would have gotten noticed. I would have heard about it. The only people here in the Cove are surfers, old people, and pretty girls. Not thieves. Not vandals. And sure as hell not deformed cold-blooded killers."

Monica threw her hands up in frustration. "I don't care about rumors, or reports, or any of it."

Sheriff Austin glanced at the ceiling as if praying for patience. After a moment, he took a deep breath and pulled a thick pad of legal documents out of a desk drawer. "I'll tell you what; I'll file a report. That way we'll have a record of this conversation. I don't doubt that you *think* you saw what you saw, but I also think you're excited and a little hysterical over an isolated incident from St. Louis. What I do believe in is due diligence, verifiable facts, and the process."

"Great," Angel snapped. "Thanks for the vote of confidence. Let me know how the process does at protecting people from this asshole. You go right on filling out your little forms, or ignoring the whole thing, or whatever you're planning to do. We did our civic duty and gave you the information. What you do with it is your business. Our business is keeping ourselves alive, and we intend to do just that, far, far away from this little berg."

She turned to Monica. "Come on, love. It's time to get."

The sheriff held up a finger. "Now hold on just a minute."

Monica glared at him. "You can't stop us. We haven't done anything."

When Sheriff Austin leaned back, the chair protested and squawked as it dealt with his bulk. "I don't intend to stop you. In fact, I'd love it if you left town. I'm really not in the mood to deal with this nonsense."

"Good," Angel said. "Then we're going."

"Now, hold on," he said. "Before you go, there's something you need to be made aware of."

Angel raised her eyebrows but didn't reply.

He looked at each of them in turn. "I run a peaceful town. I spent years in the big cities dealing with nutballs and lunatics, and I don't need anyone creating a bunch of rumors and disturbing the quiet."

Monica glared at him. "What does that mean?"

The sheriff folded his hands on his desk. "It means that I don't want you two running all over town flapping your gums. We just survived a flood, and before that, a body washed up on shore. Folks are spooked and have more than enough to deal with. The town is a dry bed of kindle and you two with your wild accusations are kerosene and lit cigarettes. The town ordinances allow me to detain anyone who is a danger to the public."

"Perhaps you should try catching this guy then," Angel snapped. "I can guarantee you he's a 'danger to the public.'" She did air quotes with her middle fingers.

The sheriff started to say something, but Angel cut him off. "Don't worry, Sheriff. We won't disturb the peace. In fact, we won't even be here. We're headed out."

She turned to leave, but again, the sheriff stopped her. "You might want to hold off on your plans for a bit."

Angel spun back around. "I don't think so. *You* can play with the murdering psychopath. We've got a plane to catch."

The sheriff shook his head. "I hope you got refundable tickets."

As Angel glared down at him, angry heat radiated off of her in waves.

Sheriff Austin answered her look with the slightest of smiles. "See, the storm the other night took out a good chunk of the bridge. Since phone lines and the external network run along the base, we lost those too."

Angel pulled out her mobile phone and held it up. "The tower's still standing. I saw this afternoon."

"Yep," he conceded. "That it is. Unfortunately, the line connecting it to the main system was bundled with the internet and whatnot. The only things working right now are power, water, and local, in town internet."

A knot, thick like a lump of cold molasses, formed in the pit of Monica's stomach. She shuddered. "No, that can't be."

He shifted his gaze to her. "Afraid it is. Our guys are working on the bridge, but there was a lot of damage, and not just to us but to this part of the state in general. The network crews are working overtime. Unfortunately, we're lower in the priority list than higher populated areas, so it's going to be at least another few days before they get things connected back up again. In the meantime, you're just gonna have to cut down on your conspiracy drama and chill."

"What are we supposed to do?" Monica asked.

"That's easy," he said. "Relax. Go lay on the beach. Take in the sights. I don't know what you think you saw, but it isn't a homicidal maniac hell-bent on killing the fine, upstanding citizens of our fair community."

Monica started to protest, but Angel touched her hand. "Come on; let's go. There isn't anything more to be done here."

Though she wanted to argue, Monica realized the futility of it. They turned and headed to the office door. She glanced one last time at the sheriff, who sat watching them.

They navigated the hallway—almost getting second-degree burns from the receptionist's glare—and left through the front door. After climbing into the car, they sat staring out the window.

Monica already knew the answer to her own question, but she couldn't stop it from forming on her lips. "Do you suppose he was making that stuff up about the bridge?"

"No, I really think he'd love it if we left town. Also, I don't think he believed us. Correction, I don't think he *wanted* to believe us, so he chose not to."

Monica dropped her gaze to her hands. "Seems like we might have had a little more credibility considering he thought I was dead and all."

"To a lot of people, facts are often inconvenient," Angel replied, shaking her head. "We proved him wrong, and he didn't like it. Then we gave him information, which he also didn't like."

"He has no idea the shitstorm that's about to rain down around his ears," Monica said. "Erebus saw us. I stared at him while you were messing around with the gas pedal or whatever. He recognized me; I could feel it. He's here for me, or maybe both of us. But we can't leave town. We can't call for help. The FBI isn't here. Hell, at this point, I'd even take Peter's help, but we are alone. So, what do you think we should do?"

Angel remained quiet for a minute, and then she looked up with steely-eyed resolve. "We fight."

Chapter Fourteen

After leaving Max's shop, Sam headed to the art gallery where April sold her mass-produced paintings. He'd expected it to be closed like everything else in town, but to his surprise, a small *Open* sign hung in the window. He pushed through the door, pausing just past the threshold until his eyes adjusted to the low lighting.

The windows, covered in lush curtains, made the store as dark as the inside of a pyramid. Small torch-like spotlights embedded in the wall under each painting lit a path, as if to guide lost souls deep into the heart of the tomb. Crypt silent, the ambiance didn't so much resemble a sophisticated museum in a big city as that of a haunted mortuary from a B budget movie.

Sam stepped up to the first painting and squinted at the artist's signature. He had to lean in so close his nose almost touched the canvas. Unfortunately, the dull yellow light bleached the scribbles into a blurry muck, making it impossible to read.

"That is an original Mont Black." The half-whisper came from near Sam's shoulder as a man materialized from the darkness.

Every muscle in Sam's body went rigid as he fought the almost overwhelming instinct to punch—and incapacitate—this persona non grata. No one had ever caught him off guard the way this man just had. No one.

He took a deep breath and forced himself to ease his mental finger off the kick-ass-first-ask-questions-later trigger. And while getting surprised had unnerved him, it also pissed him off that his inner conscience hadn't warned him about someone sneaking up behind him. *You could have given me a heads-up he was coming. I thought you had my flank.*

Chet shrugged. *Sorry, he never even pinged my radar.*

Calming his heart and taut nerves, Sam assumed his best poker face. "I haven't heard of Mont Black before."

The short, willowy man—evidently unaware of how close he'd come to taking a blow to the schnoz—peered through glasses perched half-down his nose at the painting. "He is, as with all of the talent represented on these walls, a local artist. His style is not of my personal preference, but many find his contrasting imagery to their liking."

Chet pretended to look through imaginary glasses perched half-down his nose. *Would it be your personal preferences for us to kick his pompous little ass?*

Why yes. I find that is my personal preference, Sam replied. But instead of shoving one of his size twelves up the man's rectum, he extended his hand. "Sam."

The bespectacled man looked as though Sam had offered him a flopping trout. "I do not shake hands; it is uncivilized and unsanitary." He bent at the waist in a half-bow. "Mr. Renard."

Chet laughed. *I'll give you a million dollars if you start pummeling this guy right here, right now.*

I can't go around beating up all the people you don't like. There wouldn't be anyone left in the world.

The little man flared one of his nostrils as he sniffed.

Granted, Sam mused, *there should be exceptions to the rule.*

Fine, Mr. Congeniality. Go. Do what you need to do.

Sam turned his attention back to the proprietor. "Please, tell me about your gallery and what you have to offer."

Mr. Renard pivoted and began making his way down the first corridor. "As I said, we only house pieces created by local artists. Though we invite every experience level to submit to us, we are very selective. We only allow the most talented of the talented to display their works in our gallery."

Sam nodded as though he approved of the man's stuffed-shirt self-importance and the ridiculous prints on the wall. "I see. What happens to those whom you do not feel are talented enough?"

Jolting to a stop, the proprietor shuddered slightly as he stared at Sam with the same earnestness a doctor would use to inform his patient he had Stage Four cancer. "I don't really concern myself with such details, though I suppose there are flea markets and novelty gift stores for such...um, work."

After flaring the same nostril yet again, the curator resumed his silent march and smooth spiel. "A lot of the town's more sophisticated visitors enjoy taking a little piece of the Cove back with them. And why wouldn't they?" He stopped and indicated toward an abstract painting that could have been a family portrait, a bowl of fruit, or dogs playing poker. "Take this Martin for instance. Many reviewers compare it to..."

Chet put a make-believe gun to his head. *Please, can we leave now? If I don't drown in pomposity, I may just have to end my life.*

Sam smiled at his inner conscience. *I know this is painful, but we need to let him do his thing so we can guide him to our topic.*

Chet pulled the trigger and fell back. He lay on the floor, arms and legs splayed. He twitched once. Twice. Then he lifted his head and grimaced. *Damn. I must be in Hell. I can still hear him talking.*

As Mr. Renard moved on, he pointed at various prints and remarked on brush stroke techniques, settings, and backgrounds. Sam followed, letting the man babble.

They had almost finished the tour when they came upon an image of old-world warships battling it out on a rough and forbidding sea. Sam stopped. "Oh, this I like."

The curator paused. "Ahhh, yes. *The Orient Under Fire.* This is a rendering of the famous clipper during the Battle of the Nile, a confrontation, I'm afraid, she would not survive. This battle had raged across the Mediterranean—"

"Who is the artist?" Sam did not let Mr. Renard get another good head of steam going, nor did he want a history lesson.

The proprietor shifted gears from lecturer to salesman. "Ms. April Goodman." Pride etched his voice as though his own daughter had created the image. "I recall the hours of study that went into making this one of a kind—"

Sam interrupted him again. "So, you know her?"

The little man gave a single, sharp nod. "Most certainly. I make it a point to know all the artists in my gallery."

Seriously? Chet scoffed, shaking his head. *How well can you possibly know her if you don't even know she's dead? Not to mention, there are like ten copies of this "one of a kind."*

The curator looked deep into Sam's eyes. "I introduce a potential heir to not only the work itself but also to the hand that created it."

"Okay. Introduce me."

"Ms. Goodman is a twenty-four-year-old native," Mr. Renard said, smiling. "Her mother was a talented artist in her own right and taught her from a young age. Ms. Goodman continued her classical training from two other local artists—Helen Michem and her husband, Lincoln Michem—both of whom are still very active in the scene and have collections here as well. We passed some of their pieces earlier. I could show you, if you are interested." He turned to lead Sam back into the bowels of the gallery.

Sam did not follow and shook his head. "No, thank you. Please continue."

The proprietor returned to his spot. "Very well." He gazed affectionately at the painting once more. "Ms. Goodman's artistic voice has clearly been influenced by Mr. and Mrs. Michem. However, there are stylistic flares similar to that of Philip Plisson and Montague Dawson. While drawing upon these influences, she has developed her own tone and timbre that many in the art world admire. Some say her compositions are reminiscent of a glass of pinot noir and a side of decadent brie..."

He paused, looked Sam up and down, and muttered, "Or, in some cases, a PBR and basket of chili fries."

Please, please, please kick this guy's ass, Chet begged.

If only... Sam replied. *Maybe later.*

Mr. Renard's left nostril flared ever so slightly as he resumed his speech. "I like to think of her work as..."

Rule #64:
Sometimes you have to wade through a mountain of worthless white noise to find a single sliver of useful information.

Exercise patience and diligence when listening to someone who is loquacious in nature. Also, pay close attention. They will often divulge information you need during their ramblings. Guide them to the facts you need; however, it is often necessary to let a rambler ramble. Usually they are so impressed with themselves, they don't even notice they are providing you with valuable intel.

——122 Rules of Psychology

Sam let the gallery owner babble on about the deep meditation and early morning walks that had inspired April's creativity. The small man described—in nauseating detail—the types of acrylics she liked to use and, depending on the subject of the painting, her preferred texture of canvas.

Chet ground his teeth and began to pace. *If you don't cut this guy off, I'm going to jab a brush through my temple. Killing myself would be less painful than letting this guy melt my brain with insane minutia.*

Sam smiled and shook his head. *You can't kill yourself. You don't have a body. You're stuck, dude.*

Chet continued to pace. *Great. Just great. Tell me, what did I ever do to deserve this?*

Sam chuckled at his inner conscience's consternation. *You did let this guy sneak up on us.*

"...hopefully, Ms. Goodman will be back in full swing soon. Though that 'stalker' put a crimp in her productivity, I think that's done now. She has plans to unveil a new—"

Sam started. "Wait. What?"

Mr. Renard paused and smiled. "I know, I'm excited too. Ms. Goodman has been invited to display some of her work at a symposium next month. She always does well. The San Franciscans appreciate her flare for capturing the essence of the ocean and its eternal turmoil. She has several new and exciting pieces she's been—"

Sam put a hand on the man's shoulder. "No, not that. What did you say about a stalker?"

Mr. Renard cleared his throat and pursed his lips, embarrassment etched in his expression. He glanced at the hand on his shoulder but, to his credit, didn't shrug it away. "Well, yes. She hasn't been as productive lately...actually that's an understatement. To be quite frank, she hasn't created a new piece in almost a month. She believes someone is watching her. I know it sounds crazy. Ms. Goodman is normally one of our more stable artists, but creative types can sometimes be..." He cleared his throat again. "Eccentric. All part of the vibrancy of imagination, I suppose."

As he stepped out of Sam's reach and began to walk down the hall, relief filled his eyes. "Here, let me show you a piece by——"

Sam remained rooted in place. "Why did she think someone was following her?"

The curator stopped, his shoulders drooping, and turned back. "You really want to know this?" He let out a long, exasperated breath.

"She says," Mr. Renard began, "that she had seen a man with a scarred face several times around town. The last time I saw her, she'd been terrified that he'd followed her to the gallery. I ran outside and would have called the police, but no one was there."

Sam almost laughed. The pretentious prick versus Tyron Erebus. Now *that* would have been something to witness.

"We live in a safe town," the curator said, "so I don't believe it's anything to worry about. She wanted to call the sheriff, but I convinced her that it was nothing more than an overzealous fan." He hesitated. "To be honest, I'm starting to wonder if she's coming down with a case of paranoia. Talents, such as her, who find themselves in the public eye can do that. Get a little obsessed with their own popularity. I personally never witnessed anything, and she came here several times a week. I recommended that she consider talking to a psychiatrist or a counselor."

Sam nodded. "I see. And when was the last time you saw Ms. Goodman?"

Mr. Renard tapped his chin. "Oh, it's been at least a week. Two probably. I've tried calling, but she almost never answers her phone."

"You don't think that's unusual? Maybe you should have reported her missing."

The little man put his hands behind his back. "I do business dealings with Ms. Goodman, but I'm not her caretaker."

Chet laughed. *Oh snap. Look at Mr. Retentive getting all feisty on your ass.*

Sam took a step closer. "But you also said you make it a point to know all your artists personally. I assume that means you make it your business to know quite a bit about their personal lives. Maybe you even provide a little coddling? You know, some one-on-one time with Ms. Goodman."

Chet pretended to hold a microphone. *And he goes for the throat. But how will the opposition respond? The crowd holds its collective breath.*

"This is sounding more like an interrogation." Mr. Renard narrowed his eyes in suspicion. "In fact, I'm beginning to believe you came here under false pretenses, Mr. Sam. I don't even know your whole name."

The man scanned Sam from head to foot. "If I didn't know better, I'd say you were a cop or something. And if that's the case, I don't need to talk to you."

Chet applauded. *And the prissy dude spikes it with the Fifth Amendment! Things take a turn for the worse as Mr. Tactless fumbles with the subtle art of conversation and leading questions. Maybe you should consider a new line of work.*

Sam pulled out his wallet and flashed a fake, though authentic looking, badge. "Mr. Renard, I'm here to investigate the death of one of the citizens in this town."

The little man's face blanched, and his eyes grew large and round until he looked like a giant squid. "Are you talking about that poor girl that washed up on shore?" The man shivered. "I didn't know her personally, but I can assure you that neither I nor Ms. Goodman had anything to do with it."

Sam tucked his wallet back into his pocket. "Right now, I'm just gathering information. I'm not suggesting that April was involved, but there is a tie between the two of them."

Chet snorted. *That's the understatement of the century.*

"What I'm trying to do," Sam continued in his best authoritative voice, "is explore every avenue of the victim's life and pare down my *suspect* list. If you'd feel more comfortable, I could question you formally. Of course, that would mean that your customers would see you leaving your business in the back seat of a police cruiser."

The man's pallid skin stretched and pulled as his jaw bobbed up and down, though no retort came from his pale lips. He stopped, cleared his throat, and tried again. "I...I...don't...understand. What does this have to do with me or with Ms. Goodman? Am I a suspect? You don't have anything on me."

Chet leaned in closer to his imaginary microphone. *Uh-oh, sports fans. Looks like Team Pompous is on the ropes. Can he recover? Can he defend his title?*

Sam gave the man his most withering glare. "You don't need to understand. That's *my* job." He jerked his thumb back to his chest. "And right now, everyone is a suspect," Sam said, thumping Mr. Renard's sternum. "I'm a busy man, and what I want to do is sort my list so I know where to focus my efforts. Those who cooperate and have nothing to hide get moved to the bottom of the list. Those who hinder a federal investigation...well, let's just say we keep the spotlight on them."

Mr. Renard's eyes had gotten so wide they looked as though they were about to fall out of their sockets. He held up his hands in surrender. "Look, I display her paintings and help bolster her when she's down. I believe that you are suggesting we may have more than a business relationship—maybe even sexual—but she isn't interested in men, if you catch my drift. My guess is that she went up north to be with her girlfriend, a singer who tours the West Coast. Kyme something or other. That's why I didn't report her missing. She's left for a month or more without telling anyone. Besides, this isn't the first time she's thought she was being followed, and I don't think it'll be the last."

"She thought she'd been followed before?" Sam asked, frowning.

He nodded. "Yes. Overzealous fans, she says. Overzealous imagination, I say."

"So, you never saw the man who was following her?"

Mr. Renard shook his head. "No. Like I told you, I don't think he actually exists. I think it was all in her head."

Sam handed him a business card. "Thank you, Mr. Renard. You have been most helpful. I might be back. Please call me if you think of anything else."

The curator looked the card over and then tucked it primly in his breast pocket. "I will, and I will call you when Ms. Goodman returns. I'm sure she will have more work done soon."

Chet sighed. I *seriously* doubt that.

Sam stepped out of the gloomy store and back into the sunshine.

Chapter Fifteen

Sam wandered down the boardwalk until it ended at a sand bluff. He stared out over the twinkling ocean as the sun began to dip into the dark blue water. A slight breeze played with his hair and brushed against his cheeks. After the heat of the day, the coolness refreshed his skin while the crashing waves settled his nerves, enticing him forward onto the beach.

He needed a calm, quiet place to digest the information he'd gathered. The jumble of facts and disconnected pieces had to be sorted and cataloged before they could be placed into any semblance of order.

After cresting the small hill, he paused. Below him lay miles of sand and brilliant light reflecting off the water. Immediately past the bluff stood a sign resembling a milepost marker. *Mile 2* glinted in white, sparkled paint on a reflective green background. He stared at it for a moment, trying to fathom its purpose, but he came up short. Dismissing it, Sam moved on.

He shaded his eyes, studying the breakers. Both Triniti and Max had bragged about the town's epic surf conditions, yet these two and three footers wouldn't challenge a newbie.

He frowned, perplexed by the ease with which he'd disproved their boasting. *So much for major waves and epic rides.*

Except, Max made a living selling surfboards. So that lent credence to the claim, only... Unable to make sense out of the incongruent facts, Sam shrugged and let his mind wander even further.

At one time, Sam and his brother, Jake, had practically lived on the water, drifting on boards of fiberglass and wood. The intricacies of a surfer's relationship with the ocean were both deep and complex. The sea was a force. A fling. A lover. And no matter how many years had slipped by since last dancing with his old betrothed, the romance still permeated every bone of his body. Even hundreds of miles inland, she still shaped his perspective and beckoned for him to come to her.

But lurking just beneath her beautiful smile, jewel-crusted crown, and inviting embrace lay a nasty, merciless temper. Complex and unpredictable, she could choose to grind him into a reef, smash him with debris, or pulverize him against the rocks. But such was the price when dancing with this princess.

While Sam had respected the sea, Jake hadn't feared her. Jake hadn't feared anything.

As Sam strolled, he did nothing to stop his mind from following this new, random path of thought. Ebenezer Scrooge had been visited by the Ghost of Christmas Past. Like the misguided businessman, Sam too faced a relentless spirit that would not be ignored. Only it seemed that his phantom's arrival hadn't been marked by a bell that tolled midnight but by this little seaside town perched on the edge of oblivion.

For just a moment, the years melted away and Jake's laughing voice rang in his ears as it floated above the sound of the surf. "Come on, little bro! You'll never be as good as me. Maybe it's time for you to give up. Tell ya what, why don't you just go back to shore with the rest of the kooks and let an expert show you how it's done?"

His fraternal twin—born at 11:45 p.m. on June third to Sam's 12:13 a.m. on the fourth—had always treated Sam as though he'd been years younger instead of less than thirty minutes.

Goading him over beers one evening, Jake, with his arm draped around a sun-bleached blonde, had smiled his relaxed, infuriatingly confident smile. "I got to drive first. Vote first. Drink first. Got laid first."

This last item had made the blonde giggle and blush.

His brother had poked a finger toward Sam's chest. "Have you ever even *been* kissed? Well, little bro, if you ever need advice, you can always come to me. You know what they say about wisdom coming with age."

Sam, having tagged along stag on his brother's date and gotten several beers deep into the evening, had leapt across the table at his leering twin. The ensuing brawl had proven to be the detriment to both the people and the objects around them; it had also gotten them ejected from the bar. Permanently.

Sam smiled at the memory but then sighed, exasperated with himself.

What the hell? Why was he even thinking about Jake? Nothing except pain could be gained replaying those old memories. He needed to put his personal thoughts and feelings away and focus on the job at hand.

He tried to envision April's house, the gallery, the facts, but the echoes of his brother's laughter fragmented the images.

No matter how much he wanted to, no matter how many mind control or thought compartmentalization techniques he used, Sam, like old Ebenezer, couldn't chase the ghosts away. They—especially Jake—sometimes got up to a good chase of chain rattling and cupboard slamming and refused to stay in the vault with the memories of his ex-wife, his folks, and everyone else he'd hurt or let down.

Chet, in full-on military mode, glared at him. *Okay, Bradford, you've had your little pity party. Dredged up some old memories so touching Oprah wants to invite you on to her show. You girls can spend your "special" time together drying your tears with monogramed hankies and blubbering into each other's skirts. Someone pass me a bucket; I think I'm gonna hurl.*

Look, Sam said, shaking his head at his inner conscience. *I came out here to think. I need to sort through the facts of the case. Yeah, yeah, Jake's come up a couple times, but so what?*

Chet continued to look down on him. *What do you mean, "So what?" While you've been building mental sandcastles with your dead brother and getting ready for your Hallmark Hall of Fame documentary, Erebus is out there slicing and dicing like he's auditioning for a Ginsu commercial. You don't know what he's doing or who he's planning to turn into veal cutlets next. You said you wanted to come out here to think, so get to work.*

Sam closed his eyes and concentrated. He gathered the thoughts and feelings of his brother, sweeping them out of the corners and recesses of his mind and into a neat pile.

Scooping them up, he funneled the disorganized jumble into a little glass cube and snapped the lid shut.

Whirling eddies of color and images pressed themselves to its transparent surfaces, trying to escape the prison, but Sam refused to let them out. He placed the block in the mental vault among a million others, sealed the thick, gleaming steel entrance, and gave the lock an enthusiastic spin. As the clicking of the combination dial slowed and then stopped, his world became silent and ordered once more.

He sat down in the sand and focused, placing himself back in April's house. Standing in the central hallway, he turned, looking in every direction, taking the time to linger on the details. The killer's aura draped over his skin like a cold slab of calf's liver. Even warmed by the salt air and comforted by the familiar sounds of the beach, frigidity crept over Sam's soul, raising the hairs on the nape of his neck and chilling the marrow in his bones.

Physically, he shivered, but mentally, he walked down the hall to the kitchen. He logged the missing knife in the wood block on the counter, but otherwise, nothing new caught his attention. Sam moved through the dining room, noting the creak of the floor and smell of death and mildew, and stepped into the living room.

His gaze lingered on the wood-framed windows where he suspected the killer had entered. The wavy glass overlooked the beach...

He popped open his eyes and pulled out his tablet. Cycling through the pictures, he stopped on the ones of the living area and zoomed in on the floor. Along the hardwood beneath the windows lay a smattering of sand.

There's no way for sand to get that far inside the house, Chet said. *We were right, he must have slipped inside through the window and had sand clinging to his shoes. What's next?*

Sam thought it over. *He had to have gone upstairs to the studio first. By the time he was done with April, he would have been covered in blood. I can't see him killing her, taking her body out to the ocean, cleaning up, and then going upstairs. That doesn't feel right.*

Besides, he had to get the canvases.

Sam's stomach twisted into a hard knot. *Yes, the paintings. He would have made those as he did his thing.*

Gritting his teeth, Sam closed his eyes and forced his mind back into April's house. He stood where Erebus must have stood, watching the girl sleep. Her last peaceful moments on Earth. The scene moved forward. The knot in Sam's stomach grew like a tumor as Erebus worked on his "paintings" and hummed along to the tune of April's wails of agony no human being should have known existed.

When Erebus finally put April out of her misery and silence descended, Sam turned his attention to the gruesome images arranged in a star pattern above the bed. The flesh from April's body had been plastered to the stark white fabric, forming abstracts not dissimilar to the ones he'd seen in the gallery. Satan's imitation of a Picasso—feet, hands, torso, scalp all spliced together to form the vague recollection of a human form.

Taking a deep breath, Sam forced his gaze to the pinnacle of the arrangement. Erebus had wrapped the girl's face around the canvas at the star's peak. Her mouth hung open as if the madman had first captured and then caged her soul, dooming the woman's spirit to spend eternity drowning in a red sea of pain and suffering. A trail of blood poured from her lips, spilling down her chin in a waterfall, to the epicenter of the morose tableau where her heart hung by a lacerated aorta. A knife, presumably the one missing from the kitchen, pinned it to the wall.

Beneath the severed organ the madman had written: *With this sacrifice, I give redemption.*

The dark crimson sentence—shaped like a crooked smile—somehow felt more vulgar, more invasive, and more abhorrent than the woman's death itself. As if Erebus had tried to somehow justify not only her slaying but the repulsive manner in which he'd carried it out.

Even Chet had gone pale.

Sam did his best to ignore his nausea, mentally trying to remain detached and objective. He stared at each canvas individually, searching the details and nuances of Erebus' "art." Finally, he dropped his gaze to the parting message scrawled in blood underneath the bottom image. *You're next, bitch.*

He moved back, studying the arrangement as a whole. *Aside from the bitch part, there's a primitive, savage sort of vibe to this arrangement. As if he's worshiping an ancient demon or something.*

Chet, who'd turned a lovely shade of green, began to pace. *Okay, so he went all Aztec priest and then what? Rode off into the sunset like the Lone Ranger? Or did he stay, hoping to find more people to sacrifice to his lizard god?*

Sam shook his head. *No. It's more than that; he wrote the word "redemption." Like somehow he'd saved her or something. And my gut says he's still here. In fact, maybe he's...*

"Hey! How's it going?"

Sam glanced up, broken out of his reverie as a dark-haired girl approached.

Chet rolled his eyes. *Ah, shit. Just what we need, another distraction.*

Chapter Sixteen

Angel's eyes glinted with determination as she drove the car out of the police station parking lot and back toward the center of town. Monica loved her friend's fortitude but wondered if all of their efforts would be in vain. The sheriff wouldn't help them. He had, in a not so roundabout way, called them liars and drama queens. They had to protect themselves, but she had no idea how.

Monica remained quiet, though her nerves continued to ratchet up tighter and tighter as Angel guided the car through town, cruising slowly past the place they'd last seen the murdering psychopath. Erebus no longer waited for them, but Monica sensed his presence just the same.

Only sheer force of will kept her from flinging open the door and running down the street, screaming her fool head off. Rationally, she knew that would only make it more likely they'd get killed, but still...

Angel pulled into a space in front of the hardware store, shut off the engine, and began to get out.

Monica grabbed her arm. "Love," she said, trying to keep the sarcasm and panic out of her voice. "Why are we here? Now seems like a really bad time to try and fix up your apartment."

Angel paused. "I told you, we're going to fight."

Monica cocked her head. "Yes, but..."

"Trust me." Angel pried Monica's death grip off her forearm and crawled out of the car. Slamming the door behind her, Angel strutted through the entrance of the hardware store.

Monica hesitated but followed. She pushed through the door and stepped up next to her friend, who waited on the store's landing. "So, what exactly are we looking for?"

Angel narrowed her eyes to rock hard flints. "Something to take the bastard down."

Monica gazed around the large, two-story building. Arbitrary labels marked the end of each aisle. "Yeah, okay, but with what?"

Angel picked up a small hand rake from a nearby turnstile, studying the evil-looking tines. "Anything sharp and pointy." She swiped the tool through the air as if it were the claws of a tiger. "Get whatever looks like it will hurt him."

Monica continued to gawk, her already diminished confidence whittling away until it cried for mercy. "Maybe we should try and find a gun instead?"

Angel put her hands on her hips and turned to Monica. "Really? Us with a gun? Could you imagine? Erebus would be out of a job because we'd probably end up killing each other. I don't know about you, but my subscription to *Guns and Ammo* magazine expired a long time ago. Besides, do you think you can just go into any convenience store and say, 'I want two candy bars, a bag of chips, a large diet, and, oh yeah, a bazooka with extra bullets, please?'"

"Okay, okay." Monica held up her hands. "Point taken. But I really have no idea what I'm looking for. It's not like I go into one of these places every day. The last time was with you, and that didn't go very well. Remember?"

"Why are you always such a pessimist?" Angel scoffed. "It went just fine. As I recall, we got the chain on your handcuffs cut."

"Yes," Monica said slowly. "But to do it, you had to tell the guy that worked there that you were my master and I was your sex slave."

Angel shrugged. "That was nothing more than a creative means to an end." She grinned. "I'll bet he's still dreaming about us." She turned her attention to the gray-haired gentleman sporting a red checkered vest ambling toward them.

The clerk, whose name tag identified him as *Bert*, smiled at Angel as he approached. "Can I help you ladies find any..." When his gaze locked onto Monica's face, his jaw fell open. It bobbed up and down several times as he fumbled his words.

Monica silently cursed the sheriff and his lazy ass ineptitude. Being "dead" would turn every random interaction—going to the hardware store, for instance—into a three-ring circus.

The man's complexion had turned pallid. "Isn't that... Aren't you..."

"I'm not—" Monica began.

"Um, Bert?" Angel stepped in front of the clerk.

He blinked as if seeing her for the first time. "Huh?"

"Is something the matter?" she asked, as though she had no clue what had boggled his brain.

176

Bert's gaze narrowed as he looked at Angel closer. "Wait. I know you. You used to harass my daughter in high school."

Internally, Monica sighed as she recognized the father of Angel's high school archrival, Lucy. The girl had been everything Angel wasn't—popular, rich, confident—and she'd made sure Angel knew it. Not that Angel had been, well, an angel. She'd given back as good as she'd taken, maybe even better because she'd sent Lucy home in tears on many a splendid occasion.

"I what?" Angel touched her chest as though feigning innocence. "No. That can't be. I don't even *know* your daughter."

He placed his hands on his hips. "Yes, you do. You and everyone else called her Loosey Lucy so much that it ended up being the name they used for her senior yearbook picture." Bert turned and looked at Monica. "And you're the girl from the paper." He swallowed. "Except you're..."

Dead girl or victimized daughter. Pick a focus, Bert. We need to own up to being dead or apologize about your kid. Either way, hurry up and decide.

Angel placed her palm over his cheek, dragging his attention back to her. "Bert, honey. Pay attention. Do I have your attention?"

He gave a slight nod.

"First of all, now that you say it, your daughter's name does ring a bell. But I'm not the one that started the rumors that she'd slept with the entire football team, including the mascot."

Oh, Angel, don't. This isn't going to end well.

He stared at her. "The mascot? I didn't say she slept with the football team. She was the head cheerleader and prom queen, not a——"

Angel cut him off. "And it's not my fault if *someone* thought she was a complete and utter bitch and decided to get revenge on the little princess with a few unsubstantiated and innocent rumors. Besides, that was years ago. I'm sure she's a saint now. It's time to get over it and let the past go."

Despite the strenuous circumstances, Monica had to stifle a giggle over Bert's incredulous expression. Like father, like daughter—Angel could run circles around them both.

"Innocent rumors? Who would even——"

"Second," Angel interrupted again. "You're the third person today to accuse my friend of being that poor girl from the paper." Tsking, she shook her head sadly and then wrapped her arm around Monica's shoulder. "This is Susan, from Walberg, Arizona. She came with me to help pack up my apartment, but everyone in town is treating her like she's a zombie. Does she look like a zombie to you, Bert?"

Though Monica loathed using her old Witness Protection alias, she shrugged and nodded to confirm Angel's lie.

Bert blinked again. He glanced back and forth between them. "No. No. Of course not. But she looks just like——"

"I know," Angel said, as if the idea baffled her. "There is a slight resemblance, I suppose. But *that* girl is dead, and Susan here," she squeezed Monica a little too hard, "is clearly alive."

He shook his head slowly. "Now that you say it, I guess they don't look *that* much alike." Bert hesitated. "Sorry," he said to Monica. Except his voice came out in a squeak. He cleared his throat and tried again. "Sorry. My mistake."

Playing her part of the misidentified stranger, Monica gave a single nod but didn't reply.

He looked over at Angel. "For the record, my daughter did *not* sleep around."

Angel furrowed her brow in mock indignation. "Of course she didn't. And whoever said otherwise should have their head examined."

He looked like he had more to say on the subject, but instead, he huffed a breath. Before he turned to leave, he studied Monica's face one last time, suspicion lingering in his eyes. "Okay, well, if there's anything I can help you find, just let me know."

"We're just looking. Thanks," Angel replied, smiling sweetly.

He glanced back as he wandered off to do whatever hardware clerks did when they weren't solving a stopped up toilet crisis.

Pulling herself out from under Angel's arm, Monica whispered, "Why did you tell him that? He's not stupid. He has to at least suspect you were the one that changed his kid's name in the yearbook to Loosey Lucy, and——"

"Um, excuse me." Angel batted her eyes and cupped her ear as though she hadn't heard correctly. "*Who* did you say changed her name in the yearbook?"

Monica sighed. "Fine. It was me, but I only did it because *you* convinced me to." She waved a hand through the air.

"That's not the point. I'm pretty sure he knows you were lying about his kid, and I'm pretty sure he knows you're lying about me. Why not just tell him who I am and be done with it?"

"Think about it," Angel whispered. "Monica Sable's 'murder' is the biggest news to hit the town in fifty years. And you being *alive* only throws gasoline on the gossip flames. *Everybody's* going to be talking about where they saw you, who you were with, and what you were doing. The more people that talk, the easier it will be for Erebus to find us."

"Okay, but do you honestly think he," Monica pointed in the direction Bert had gone, "believed you? You don't think he's not already on the phone with his wife telling her that the mean girl from Lucy's high school days and the dead girl from the paper just strolled through the front door of his shop? Word's going to spread like wildfire."

Angel shrugged. "I don't know. Maybe he is and maybe he isn't. You weren't exactly helping, so I had to improvise." She let out a long breath. "Look, the longer we stand here arguing, the longer he has to watch you and figure out who you really are. Let's do what we came to do and beat feet."

"Finally, something we agree on." Monica turned and once again studied the signs hanging above the end of the aisles. "I really have no idea where to begin."

Angel nodded and marched down the center walkway. "Let's start at the back of the store and work our way forward."

Monica trailed after her friend who turned down *Yard and Garden*.

They stopped at the end of the row, and Angel picked up a bag of grass fertilizer. "I saw in a movie once that you can make bombs from this stuff. I think we need some pipe or something." She looked around as though she expected how-to-make-an-explosive instructions on a shelf someplace nearby.

"Really?" Monica rolled her eyes. "That's what you're thinking? I don't know anything about that sort of stuff and neither do you. Maybe you should go ask Bert if he knows how to make a homemade bomb out of lawn food?"

Angel dropped the bag back onto the shelf. "Fine. Whatever. If you're so smart, then what do you think we should be looking for?"

Monica scanned the tall stack of shelves. "Anything that will hurt him and that we can operate without a degree in chemical engineering."

Angel pulled a machete from a display rack. "Like this?" The blade flashed as light ricocheted off its wicked edge. She swung it around like a samurai sword. "Wha cha cha." She sliced an imaginary Erebus in two. "Take that!"

Monica smiled and nodded. "I'll go get us a cart."

☆☆☆☆

They continued up and down the aisles, adding items to their haul. Angel found a pitchfork and a pair of hedge clippers. She chopped at the air and jabbed, looking about as menacing as a baby velociraptor in a pink bunny suit.

Monica found a sharp spade and a bundle of wooden stakes.

Angel glanced down at the stakes. "Well, that would be great...if he were a vampire. Do you plan to attack him when he's lying in his coffin? Let's look for holy water and garlic while we're at it."

Monica rolled her eyes but left the bundle in the cart. The sticks were long and pointy. That was good enough for her.

They wandered into the tool section. Electric saws and sanders hung from the shelves, and although they looked as though they could inflict great damage, Monica had no idea how to use them. Plus, the need for electricity would dampen their effectiveness if they weren't near an outlet.

Monica picked up a battery powered saw, examining its serrated teeth. While portable, she couldn't imagine how she'd be able to get Erebus to hold still long enough for her to use it on him, so she put it back.

Angel picked up an odd-looking hammer, inspecting it from all sides as though she'd discovered a new and fascinating breed of insect. "What about this?"

Monica looked at the tool's tag and frowned. "What's a ball-peen?"

"Maybe that means psycho buster," Angel replied, rapping the round part of the hammer into her palm. "Regardless of what it means, I'll bet this would hurt if you got hit with it."

For the first time since leaving the police station, Monica's spirits lifted, and she nodded. "Let's get two then."

Angel picked up a second, smaller one in her free hand.

Monica selected a pair as well.

The two women began to wave them around as though conking a herd of would-be assassins on the head.

Monica brought her hammers around and down. "Whack!"

"Whi-cha!" Angel yelled in a stage-whisper as she arched hers through the air. "Take that, you stupid frog!"

Monica laughed and prepared for another attack when movement at the end of the row caught her eye.

"Everything okay here, ladies?" Bert had returned. His forced smile morphed into one of inquisitive concern, bordering on a scowl.

Angel still held the tool at a skull-crushing level and fluttered her lashes, giving the man one of her most innocent expressions. "Yep, everything's just fine."

His brow furrowed as his gaze lingered on the wielded makeshift weapon. "Okay, well, let me know if I can help you."

Angel dropped the tool in the cart and winked at the store clerk. "We will."

His scowl turned to distrust as he turned and shuffled away, staring over his shoulder at Monica as he disappeared around the corner.

Monica added one of her hammers to the growing hodgepodge. "This seems about the right size."

Angel tossed in her second one. "Yep, I think this one has the perfect balance of malice and kick-ass-itude."

Monica picked up a large screw driver. "This looks like it could hurt someone."

Angel added a box knife to their collection. "So does this." She grabbed an extra box of blades and tossed them into the cart. "Just in case. Hey, what if we tie one of the knives to the end of one of your vampire stakes? It's not an electric shark rod like in those documentaries on TV, but I suppose it's better than nothing."

"How do we do that?"

Angel shrugged. "I dunno. We could ask Bert?"

Monica shook her head. "He's too busy trying to figure out how come I'm not dead. I don't think we could actually ask him any questions and expect reasonable answers. And, even if that weren't the case, I have no idea how I'd broach that subject."

"True, true. Besides, he'd probably toss a monkey if we asked," Angel said, grinning.

Monica chuckled. "What does that even mean?"

Angel started to laugh. "I don't know. Maybe we should ask Bert?"

Monica laughed harder. She held up her arms and ran in a circle, mimicking a monkey. "Woo woo woo, ha ha ha haaa." She cried out as she pretended an invisible prankster had tossed her across the room.

Angel continued the charade by falling to the floor. "Heee....splat!"

A tear rolled down Monica's cheek, and she doubled over laughing, clutching the potentially weaponized-screwdriver to her stomach. "Hey, Bert! We don't want to see you tossing your monkey. That's for private time."

Angel stifled her giggles as she put a hand on her hip and wagged a finger. "Yeah. Don't you know you'll go blind?"

Monica howled with laughter. "And grow hair on your palm?"

"Umm-hem." Someone cleared their throat.

Monica looked up into the disapproving face of Bert. She stopped for a heartbeat and then erupted with laughter.

The man glared and stomped off.

After a few minutes, Monica regained control of herself. She wiped her eyes with her sleeve. "We still need a way to tie the cutter to the end of the vampire stake. Some string or something might work."

Angel held up a role of tape. "What about this?"

"That would work," Monica said, nodding. "I once had a boyfriend that used duck tape to fix everything."

Angel handed it to her. "It's duct, with a T. Not duck as in *quack*."

"Are you sure?" Monica frowned. "I don't think so. I'm pretty sure it's duck as in *quack*."

Angel shook her head. "What? That doesn't make any sense. Why would anyone use tape on a duck?"

"I dunno." Monica shrugged. "I'm not a carpenter. But I don't know what a ball-peen is either, or why you need a special hammer for one. What's a duct anyway? Sounds like getting out of the way of a baseball or something."

Angel stared at her. "Huh?"

Monica bobbed her head as though dodging an invisible ball. "You know. He ducked out of the way."

Her friend continued to stare at her. "Really? *You* graduated top of our class? Really?"

"We went to a small school," Monica said quietly.

Angel shook her head.

Monica held up her hands. "What?"

Angel took the tape back and tossed it into the cart. "It's *duct*. Trust me on this."

"Aaanywaaay, will it work?"

"Probably," Angel said, guiding the cart to the front of the store.

Bert and another red-vested man glanced up as the women approached the checkout register. The clerks quickly slipped something—which looked suspiciously like a newspaper—under the counter.

When Angel parked the cart, the two men peered down at the assorted randomness.

"Did you find everything you were looking for?" Bert the friendly salesman had long since vacated the premises. Surly, suspicious Bert had taken his place.

Angel smiled at him as she dropped the stakes onto the counter. "Yes. Thank you. Your store has a variety of products which we found to our liking. I plan to leave your establishment a glowing review on your website."

Rodger, the store manager according to his name badge, stepped back as his coworker began ringing up the items. The manager didn't say anything, but he stared at Monica as though trying to telepathically read her innermost secrets.

Surly Bert's frown deepened.

Trying her best to ignore the manager's undivided attention, Monica began to unload items onto the checkout counter conveyor. "It was a very educational experience. You must learn new things all the time."

Angel added the ball-peen hammers. "Like going to college every day."

Surly Bert's frown graduated to a full-on glower.

The expression reminded Monica of the hateful glare his daughter had used all those years ago. *Oh, yes. Now I remember why we changed her name in the yearbook. Looks like she came by her bitchiness honestly.* Instead of commenting on apples not falling far from their parental trees, she said, "You guys are really lucky. I never learned anything in Arizona like I did today."

Surly's hands flew over the register as he entered their purchases. "I can only imagine," he muttered. He finished ringing them up in silence and informed them the total would be $360.98. "How would you like to pay for this?"

Angel cocked her head and batted her eyelashes. "With our good looks and dazzling smiles."

When Surly started to speak, Angel cut him off. "But since the good ole US of A doesn't accept beauty as a form of currency, we'll pay with cash." She opened her wallet.

"It's such a shame," Monica said, shaking her head. "We'd really clean up."

Angel handed Bert a wad of twenties. "Wealthy beyond imagination. Don't you agree, Bert?"

Surly peeled off one of the bills and held it up to the light. He studied the money, then swiped a pen across its surface. The frown returned, growing as he repeated the process with the remaining bills.

"Is there a problem?" Rodger asked.

Monica turned to the manager. "Bert is just making sure no one tries to take advantage of this fine establishment by verifying the authenticity of our currency."

Angel smiled. "He is a model employee and should receive a raise and a promotion."

Monica nodded.

Surly grunted and crammed the money into the cash register. He counted out the change and tried to give it to Angel, who held up her hand. "No, no. You keep the change. You are a prince among men. You single-handedly have restored my faith in the hardware industry."

The two men stood shoulder to shoulder, watching as Monica and Angel pushed their overloaded cart out the door.

Angel glanced back and whispered. "What's Bert's problem?"

"I have no idea," Monica replied, shrugging. "You even gave him a tip."

She sighed. "Right? I thought I was more than polite." They maneuvered the cart down the sidewalk ramp and loaded their purchases into the car. Monica took the cart back inside, but the men had disappeared into their lair.

She returned to the car, and they drove back to Angel's apartment.

☆☆☆☆

Angel stormed around the small living room. "Are you crazy?"

Monica sat on the couch, watching her friend pace. "Why? It's going to be a beautiful night. Besides, there isn't anything else to do, and I could really use the walk. My nerves are totally on edge."

"What do you mean, 'Why?'" Angel turned to her, waving her hand toward the front window. "Erebus is out there!"

"But you're the one that said we needed to fight." Monica cocked her head. "How can we do that if our heads are cloudy?"

Angel rolled her eyes. "Obviously your head is cloudy, but mine is crystal clear. I said we'd fight him, not deliver ourselves on a silver platter. He doesn't know where we are, and almost everyone thinks you're dead. Don't you think it's going to cause a ruckus when people see you? Talk about a good way to get noticed."

"We told the sheriff I was alive, and you didn't fool Bert for a minute. By now half the town probably knows," Monica replied. "I hate to break it to you, but the word is out."

She looked around the devastation of Angel's apartment. "Clearly, he knows where you live, so I don't see how hanging out here is any safer. The best thing we can do is be unpredictable. Besides, in a couple of hours, it'll be pitch black out. It's not like we're going to wander around the center of town on karaoke night. If I had my druthers, we'd be out of here so fast you'd get whiplash. But that's not a choice we can make right now."

Angel resumed her pacing. "There isn't anywhere else to go. My apartment—*not* parading around the beach—is the safest place to be."

Monica tried to catch her friend's gaze. "Why do you think that? Do you not remember what happened in Arizona? Even though I was in Witness Protection, the bastard was still able to track me down. He blew up my house and my friend. Had I been thirty seconds earlier, I'd have been charcoal too. For all we know, he's stacked up crates of dynamite in one of the other apartments and is just waiting to be sure we're here before he lights the fuse. Until we can get out of town or take the sonofabitch down, the more we stay on the move, the safer we'll be."

Angel stopped, staring at her for several heartbeats. At last, she slumped her shoulders and exhaled a long slow breath. "Fine. We'll do it your way." She picked up a long screwdriver and a hammer. "But I, for one, do not intend to go down without inflicting a whole heap of damage on a certain killer's head." Angel whipped a ball-peen hammer through the air.

Monica smiled. "That's the spirit."

The two women began to gather their supplies.

Chapter Seventeen

S am stood, brushing off the back of his pants as the woman and her formidable bosom approached. "Hey, Triniti."

She'd traded her waitress' uniform for a bikini top, sheer wrap, and tight shorts. A pair of flip flops dangled from slender, manicure-tipped fingers as she lilted across the sand. Hanging from a thin shoulder strap, a small purse hugged her waist. The sway of her hips and her coquettish smile looked more predatory than flirtatious.

"What are you doing out here?" he asked.

She looked him up and down. "I think that's *my* question, Mr. 'At the Beach in Chinos and a Button Up Shirt.'"

Since he hadn't gone back to his hotel to change after leaving the gallery, he still wore his long sleeve shirt, cotton pants, and work shoes. The semi-casual attire coordinated with the swimsuits and board shorts about as well as black socks and sandals.

"I suppose that's fair," he replied, chuckling. "I haven't gotten around to buying something less formal."

She tsked at him. "Well, you've missed your chance. Everything's locked up tight for the evening. Don't worry,

I'll tell anyone that sees us that you're my colorblind cousin from Canada."

"Canada?" Sam glanced down at his outfit. "This isn't *that* bad."

She peered at him over the top her huge sunglasses. "It would be impossible to pass you off as an unaware genius, no offense, so I gotta come up with something plausible." She slipped her glasses back on. "I need to keep the ill-dressed from tarnishing my reputation as a fashionista."

Chet smiled. *I like this girl.*

That's enough out of you.

Chet's grin grew. *Just sayin', I think we could really hit it off. Maybe you should step aside and let the master take over?* He cracked his knuckles and shook out his arms as if getting ready to go a couple of rounds.

Sam rolled his eyes at his inner conscience. "Anyway, I'm just taking in the sunset. It's been years since I've seen one on the coast. You?"

"Got off work just a bit ago and am shaking off the stress of the day." She gave an overly enthusiastic yawn and reached her hands up in a long cat-like stretch. The arch in her back thrust out her chest, pushing the limits of the bikini top's harnessing capacity.

"I usually come here for a walk in the evening." She nodded toward the ocean. "If I'm not out there."

"Yeah, I heard you were a big shot regional champion," he said, making a Herculean effort to keep his focus from dropping below her eyes. Even in his peripheral vision, a canyon of cleavage beckoned. "Saw your posters up on Max's wall. He seemed surprised you hadn't mentioned it."

As she finished her stretch, she lifted her sunglasses and winked. "Girl's gotta have a few secrets. How else can she maintain an air of mystery?"

"Well, your secret's out."

Triniti raised her eyebrows. "Not all of them." She let the glasses fall back into place and put a hand on her hip. "Time for you to clear up a few of yours. Why did you come here?"

Gotta love small-town curiosity, Chet said.

Right?

Alright, time for you to start dancin'.

Sam slipped off his shoes and socks, rolled up his pant legs to mid-calf, and began to walk. Triniti fell in step beside him. "Well, I haven't been surfing in a long time."

She glanced at him. "Yeah, you mentioned that. But why come *here*? Malibu is just down the street from LA."

They crossed to the firmer wet sand and strolled along the ocean, just out of reach of the breakers. The coolness radiated through his feet, taking the edge off the difficult day. "The long and short of it is I've been working nonstop for over four years. No holidays, no vacations, no nothing."

Picking up a shell, she rubbed it with her thumb. "Ahhhh, the classic workaholic."

"Yes. And my boss told me to take some time off. He said, 'Get away. Go meet a girl. Go surfing. Go relax.' I came here because Malibu just doesn't feel the same as it did when I was kid."

"Hmmm," she purred. "And why not?"

It's haunted. My brother whispers here, but he's practically a poltergeist there, he thought.

But instead of unloading his sordid past onto her, he said, "It's gotten too commercial." When she didn't comment, he continued. "Anyway, I did a little research to see just how far away I could go and still be stateside and on the West Coast. Found this place and hopped on my bike. Really it's as simple as that."

Rule #73:
Blend some elements of truth into your background. It increases believability.

Stories are, by definition, fiction. Trying to formulate a past on the fly while making it sound believable is difficult unless great thought and planning has gone into the structure and background. However, blending elements of truth, no matter how trivial the details, into the tale lends it credence to the ear and can get it past the most honed of bullshit detectors.

—122 Rules of Psychology

Though she seemed to be looking in his direction, she hid whatever expression lingered in her eyes behind the dark lenses of her sunglasses. "So far you're doing pretty well with your boss' list. Got away and met a girl. No surfing yet though. I'd give you a four out of ten on the effectiveness of your plan and an eleven out of ten on the girl."

Sam laughed. "Humble. I've only been in town a couple of days; I'll get there. I've got the board and plans to go out."

"Plans are just plans. Besides, you don't *exactly* have the board if it's still at Max's."

He nodded. "True. But I'll get it tomorrow. So, you know my story. What's yours? Are you from here? Folks? Siblings? Kids?"

She laughed. "I wouldn't exactly say I *know* your story."

Sam didn't reply. He kept walking and let the silence spin out.

"No. No kids. No husband." She reached down and scooped up a small shell, suddenly very interested in brushing sand from within its intricate crevices. "I'm an only child and small-town second generation. Born and bred right here in the Cove. My dad was a champion surfer who spent more time on the water than off. He taught me everything I know about cars and surfing. Mom could surf, but she was really just a groupie."

Surprised, Sam stopped. "Cars? Are you saying you're a grease monkey?"

"Yep. You need to meet Charlie, my van," she said, a note of pride in her voice. "I fixed him up myself."

"I'd have never guessed."

She began to walk again. "Never judge a book, Mr. LA. I'm full of surprises."

"No doubt," he mumbled as he walked faster to catch up to her. "Your folks must be very proud of you. Regional champ is a big deal here in Cali."

A shadow passed over her face. "Yeah, well, they were. At least my dad was."

"Was?" He frowned. "I sense a story coming. Does your dad still board?"

She hesitated. "You're really good at this."

"At what?"

She seemed to be staring at him from behind her large dark sunglasses. "Diverting the subject. I wanted to know about you, but now we're diving into *my* family history."

"There's really not much to my story." He gave a slight shrug. "As you said, I'm a workaholic. We workaholics are a boring lot. It's not a diversion; I'm just curious. So, your dad. Does he still board?"

The shadow he'd seen earlier darkened. "No. He's dead."

"Oh, I'm sorry. What happened, if you don't mind my prying?"

She nodded as she continued to meander. When she didn't say anything for a minute, Sam gave her time to work through her thoughts and emotions. "I don't mind. It's been, mmm, about twelve years now. The short version is he was running a tube at *Mile 9* and went over the falls. His board came out, but he didn't. Later, after they found him, the doc said that he'd hit his head on the reef. Everyone knows that's one of the risks riding so far south. Everyone talks about it. Jokes about it...or at least they used to. Not with me though. No one makes a crack about riding that far south to me anymore."

Sam still had no idea what it meant to ride "that far south." He wondered if it had anything to do with the milepost sign he'd seen earlier.

Her voice had gone quiet, a stark contrast to the brash girl who'd chatted him up in the restaurant. "It almost killed mom. She stayed for few years, but everywhere she looked, she saw his ghost. Not long after my twentieth birthday, she decided I was old enough to take care of myself and moved to Kansas to live near her brother. Apparently, he was more of a comfort than her own daughter."

"Ouch," Sam said, grimacing.

Triniti threw the shell into the ocean. "Right? Whatever. It's not a big deal. As they say, it's water under the bridge."

The shell bounced off an incoming wave and then disappeared beneath the surface. He wondered just how many times she'd told this story. "Do you ever get to see her?"

She picked up another shell and threw it too. "We talk on the phone occasionally. But I have no interest in corn and tornados, and she has no interest in walking with her dead husband. So, we're at a stalemate." She turned to him. "I didn't mean to bring the mood down with my family drama."

"Well, I asked."

She gave him an unenthusiastic smile. "Be careful what you ask for and all that, I suppose."

Sam couldn't fault her for dwelling on the past since he'd just taken a stroll with the lingering dead, who either didn't want to move on or whom he simply wouldn't *let* move on. Either way, it resulted in the same thing.

Triniti pointed into the distance. "Hey, look. Some of my friends have a little party going on. Come on, I'll introduce you." Without waiting for an answer, she took his hand and led him toward the small crowd gathered around a beach fire.

As they drew near, a guy's voice called out. "Hey! Hey! Hey! Look what washed up on shore, and she brought yet another tagalong."

Triniti ran up to a dark-haired man with an impossibly perfect physique and gave him a half-hug. "Dios! What's going on? I thought the party wasn't 'til tomorrow?"

"What? This?" He wrapped her in his muscular arms and smiled. "We aren't having a party, just a little impromptu get-together."

She pulled back and looked at him over the rims of her glasses. "Uh-huh. I see how it is."

"Trin, it wouldn't be a party until the best-looking lady arrived, now would it?"

She wriggled out of his grasp and punched him in the arm. "Save it. Your flattery doesn't work on me."

He laughed. "Sure it does. You just don't want to admit it." The man turned to Sam, offering a handshake and a large smile. "I'm Dios."

Sam grasped the man's hand, and they shook. "Good to meet you. I'm Sam."

Triniti draped an arm around Sam's shoulders. "He's a workaholic from LA."

"Oh, one of those." Dios shook his head sadly. "The town's crawling with them. Are you coming to retire or for the surf?"

"Pardon?"

"Well, there are only two reasons people come here. One, because they're old and looking for a place to spend their golden years, or two, they come to surf."

Sam nodded. "I see. Well, I'm a little young and way too poor to retire. I was practically born on the water and have tasted waves from Malibu to the Florida Keys, but I've never been here."

Dios appraised him and turned to Triniti. "Overly dressed. Poor. A bit cocky. I'd say the two of you are a match made in heaven." He glanced at Sam. "Though you need to watch out for this one." He dropped his voice to a stage whisper. "She's fine as long as you don't mind a girl with a few, um..." He paused as though searching for just the right word. "Idiosyncrasies."

Triniti slugged him in the shoulder again. "Whatever." She took Sam's hand, dragging him behind her. "Come on. Let me introduce you around."

Chapter Eighteen

Erebus stared out the window of Elon's humble dwelling as he waited for darkness to chase away the sunlight. The businesses of the shitty little town closed at the first sign of dusk and, with the exception of the restaurant strip, the streets had mostly cleared of pedestrians.

As the ocean snuffed out the last few embers of day, he slipped into the night. Slinking along alleyways and skulking through the gloom between street lamps, he made his way across the sleepy city.

After hopping a fence at the rear of the surf shop, he paused, waiting for cries of alarm and challenges to his presence. Nothing broke the stillness except the occasional trundling of a car down the street and the annoying, relentless crashing of waves on the beach.

The beach and surfing. Surfing and partying. Partying and drinking. Drinking and sex. *Ugh.* These beatniks rankled him with their laid-back, frivolous lifestyles and their inconsequential existences.

Most of the population—case in point, the rodents of Alabaster Cove—had disregarded the moralistic intuition embedded in their genetic blueprints. The resulting human debris polluted the species and diluted the genetic pool with licentious behavior, weak spirits, and even weaker minds.

As improbable as it seemed, the souls of these heathens could still be redeemed. It just took someone willing and capable to step up and do the intricate wet work that no one else wanted to do. But a legion of Erebuses couldn't cleanse them all. And every day, he faced the staggering task of shouldering a workload intended for hundreds.

Sighing over the injustice of his overwhelming burdens, he slid along the wall and stopped to press his ear against the door. Inside, a machine yowled like a pack of coyotes.

He grasped the knob and twisted. He'd expected it to be locked, but it turned easily in his grip. As he cracked the entrance open, a jaundiced blade of light sliced through the black of evening.

Erebus opened the door a little further, and the ruckus—maybe a sander or industrial vacuum—blasted his eardrums like an armada of trumpet players. He peered through the crack. Cans of paint and assorted chemicals lined the opposite wall, but a haphazard pile of woodworking materials blocked his view of the larger space.

Slipping inside, he closed the door and crouched behind a stack of lumber. His nerves itched, and his muscles tensed as he prepared to disable anyone who noticed him. But the machine kept running and no one called out.

He glanced around the corner and down the length of the workshop. Recognizable from the back by his long blond dreadlocks, tied tight in a thick ponytail, Max Fayl ran a large disk sander over a long plank of wood. He wore a heavy-duty pair of ear protectors and some sort of filter mask.

The scream of the tool reverberated through Erebus' skull and vibrated the fillings in his teeth. Ignoring the discomfort, he scanned the rest of the workshop. The hippie surfer seemed to be working alone this evening.

Tyron scuttled around the corner, creeping up behind the shop owner. When he felt something thin and hard under his shoe, he paused and glanced down. The sander's long power cord wound through cans of lacquer and paint.

Crouching, he wrapped some of the cord's extra length around his hand and picked up a narrow board from the floor. He slowly stood and began moving forward again, carrying the wood like a baseball bat. Each of his footfalls stirred up little plumes of sawdust as he narrowed the distance.

He raised the wood to strike, but either his movement or his shadow must have caught Max Fayl's attention. The man wheeled around just as Erebus brought down the plank. The air mask, even larger than Erebus had expected, caught the brunt of the blow, deflecting it.

Max Fayl—suddenly looking less like a hippie surfer and more like an enraged gargoyle—shook his head while his eyes flared from behind protective goggles.

Max raised the sander, clearly intending to use it as a weapon. Having anticipated and prepared for this possibility, Erebus smirked as he yanked the electrical cord. His grin faltered when, instead of coming free from the wall socket, the cord snugged up tight and the sander failed to stop growling.

Back to Plan A.

As Erebus began to raise the stick again, Max charged. He backed away from the raging shop owner and the whirling, angry disk. Tyron hadn't managed more than a few steps when his feet tangled, and he fell to the floor. Landing in a heap, the board flew from his hand and out of reach.

The furious hippie loomed over him, the sander snarling like a demented chupacabra just inches from Erebus' face. His pulse pounding, Tyron lay flat against the floor, holding his hands up in surrender.

The sander fell silent, though it remained in attack position. Sawdust rained down from the hateful machine onto Tyron's face and heat from the motor warmed his skin.

With his free hand, Max tore off the headset, goggles, and mask, tossing them aside. "Been meaning to get that lock fixed. Figured eventually someone would break in. Give me one good reason why I shouldn't reshape your face."

Erebus' gaze flicked between Max's blazing eyes and the disk's rough, rock-hewed surface. "I...I just need some money. I've got problems, and I need a little dough to tide me over."

Max's nostrils flared, and his eyes bore into Erebus'. "Yeah, well, don't we all? So, you thought you'd just break in here and take what you wanted. Maybe give me a lump or two for my troubles."

Erebus stammered. "Loo... Look, I'm sorry. I'll just go." He started to turn over, but the sander roared to life right next to his ear. As the sound exploded through his head, he dropped back to the floor, trying to create as much space between him and the infernal machine as possible.

The monstrous tool fell silent once again. More dust sprinkled down onto Tyron's bald head and onto his cheeks.

Max shook his head. "I don't think so. I'm not going to kill you, unless you give me no choice. I'm sure the world would be a much better place with one less sneaky sonofabitch, but I have to face myself in the mirror every day. Self-defense? Oh, hell yes. I'd grind you to powder in an instant. But defenseless on the floor, I can't do. But just because I'm not a cold-blooded killer doesn't mean you get to go free."

He released the sander with one hand and reached into his back pocket, pulling out a cell phone. The small device slipped from his fingers and fell to the floor.

As Max glanced in its direction, Erebus swiped the surfer's feet, taking his legs out from underneath him. The hippie fell to the side, landing in a cloud of dust while the sander bounced out of his hands.

Erebus leapt up and kicked Max in the stomach. The man doubled over, and Erebus countered by kicking him in the face.

Tyron picked up an industrial-sized nail gun that lay on a nearby bench. He stomped his foot down on Max's arm, pinching it in place. Erebus put the head of the tool into the surfer's open palm and pulled the trigger. A satisfying thwack emanated from the gun, and Max screamed.

He tried to roll over and grab for his hand, but Erebus kicked him in the face again, splaying him back onto the floor. Erebus stepped over him and stomped down on his other arm.

Tyron's skin prickled with happy gooseflesh and his penis grew hard as he placed the head of the gun into the man's other palm and pulled the trigger.

Thwack. Max screamed again.

Erebus stood, smirking. "I like this thing." He tugged experimentally at the air hose. "Though it's a bit clunky and not very portable." He glanced down at Max. "Do they make a smaller version?"

Max sneered at him, his eyes watering. "I'll kill you."

Erebus tossed the gun aside and then swung his foot like a soccer star shooting for the net. The hard rubber of his boot connected solidly with Max's face, hurling the man's head back against the floor. The store owner's eyes rolled deep into their sockets and he stopped struggling.

Tyron made his way to the far end of the shop. Pushing through a heavy door, he moved across the sales floor to the desk where the two men had been talking earlier in the day.

He yanked out the drawers, rifling through each and tossing them to the floor. In the last one, he found a receipt book. Flipping open the cover, he turned to what must have been the final sale of the day and read the signature scrawled at the top, confirming the customer's identity. Samuel Bradford.

His gaze dropped to the address at the bottom, and he smiled as he tore out the page.

Stuffing the carbon paper into his back pocket, Tyron retraced his steps and paused by Max's side. He picked up a hammer from a nearby bench and stared down at the dazed man nailed to the floor. Erebus could already feel the satisfying crack of the man's skull, hear the delicious crunch as his bones shattered. The bland floor would glimmer and shine in a fresh coat of blood.

But the nail gun lying in the pile of sawdust caught his eye, and he tossed the hammer aside.

Retrieving the pneumatic tool, he knelt, digging his fingers into the shop owner's thick ponytail. When he yanked the man's head up, Max's eyes flew open. His gaze found Tyron's and he glowered.

Erebus shook his head. "Pathetic. Just pathetic. You had a chance to take me down. You could have left here the victor, but you failed because you're stupid and weak." He leaned his face into Max's. "The Fates don't tolerate weakness. They have no use for it, and neither do I."

He placed the tip of the gun against Max's forehead. "You may have been able to skate through life being feeble and worthless, but this time, your ineptitude is going to cost you."

Max's eyes simmered with hatred. "You will pay for this. I promise."

He laughed. "Go meet your maker, hippie. Maybe he'll listen to your pitiful whining." Erebus pulled the trigger.

☆☆☆☆

After finishing with Max Fayl, Erebus had slipped out and, keeping to the shadows, made his way to a nearby dock. Stepping out onto the rough wood surface, he began sifting through the dark and deserted boats. He rejected one after the other, seeking just the right combination of size and technology.

He'd already worked out every detail of his next move, almost feeling bad for the authority simpletons trying to find him. They had no chance of capturing him. None. He would, as always, stay a dozen steps ahead.

Not even Sam Bradford—who had shot him in the face—had been successful at stopping him.

While many claimed to be able to do what he did, most of those overweening fools were either doing time in the clink or had found themselves a cozy coffin apartment six feet below ground.

Yet Erebus remained free. His skills in high demand.

Unlike others in his profession, he maintained an infallible work ethic. He had a professional responsibility to give his customers the best return on their investment—even if, as in the case of his last employer, they no longer lived. Regardless of that inconsequentiality, he would still complete the assignment.

He had a reputation to uphold after all.

Granted, this particular job had a personal element to it also. But that in no way interfered with his duty or the objective. Not really.

As he stepped on board a dory loaded with nets and fishing gear, he froze when a metallic click emanated from nearby.

Keeping his breathing slow and shallow, he listened intently, trying to discern which direction the noise had come from. Another clunk followed by the unmistakable flick of a butane lighter. He leaned to the side, staring along the middle of the boat where a mild glow illuminated a hole in the deck.

Erebus cleared his throat and walked forward, allowing his footfalls to squeak on the sea-bleached wood floor. A mop of curly gray hair and two eyes reflecting the glowing end of a cigarette popped up out of the engine compartment. A withered hand raised a lantern, setting it on the deck. "Can I help you?"

Tyron smiled. "I'm sorry to bother you. I've got a faulty starter and am trying to replace it, but I need a second pair of hands to hold the blower while I get under the damn thing. Saw your light and wondered if you'd be willing to help. I know it's late, but since I've got a charter first thing in the morning, I need to get it fixed tonight." Erebus glanced about. "I don't think there's anyone else around."

The grizzled old seadog scratched his head. "Yep. I'm the only one here tonight." As he spoke, the cigarette bobbed and weaved like an amateur prize fighter. "Sure. I can help." He wiped his hands on a dirty rag, then wrestled his lengthy frame out of the tight engine compartment.

As the man passed, Tyron slipped the garrote out of its pouch. Wrapping the ends around his hands, he passed the ligature over the old guy's head, cinching it tight against his throat. The man gasped. He clawed at the wire, but his struggles quickly weakened. Finally, he crumpled into a heap.

Tyron started to pick the body up, intent on throwing it overboard, but paused as a better idea occurred to him.

Erebus entered the boat's cabin and pressed the ignition button. The engine started with a quiet burble and the navigation system came to life. He nodded. *Perfect.*

Hopping out onto the dock, he ran back to shore and retrieved an overloaded little red wagon he'd lifted from a suburbanite's back yard. Rusty wheels squeaked and objected to the heavy load in its overflowing hull as he guided it down the dock. Tyron enjoyed the irony of the purportedly safe child's toy containing such deadly cargo.

Under the cover of darkness, he loaded his newly acquired boat with equipment and set to work.

After everything had been staged, Tyron released the mooring and hopped back on board, rocking the boat gently in the calm ocean. He verified the systems had been prepared to his satisfaction and steered the boat away from the small pier.

Keeping the running lights off, he navigated using the built-in GPS. Half a mile out, he turned the vessel until it ran parallel with the shore and clicked the *Maintain Course* option on the computer.

He exited the cabin and made his way to the bow. Kneeling, Erebus flipped the starter switch on the timer he'd rigged earlier. He smirked at his little "getting acquainted" package, then stood and headed to the rear of the vessel, where he'd attached a dinghy. After he climbed aboard, he cut the tie-line, leaving him bobbing like a rubber ducky in the wake of the larger boat as it continued on its journey.

He started the engine and guided the craft back toward the dock. Now he just needed to wait.

Chapter Nineteen

Triniti continued to grow more animated, embellishing Sam's story with each retelling as she half-dragged him from person to person. He couldn't have orchestrated a better exposure to the residents of the Cove, except he almost never got to speak. Once she'd made the introductions, the conversations remained wholly about Triniti herself.

At first, Sam had been able to squeeze in a few words here or there. But a couple of beers turned his companion's tongue from speed walker to roadrunner. Finally, he gave up trying and relegated himself to observer status.

Sam shook the hand of a pretty brunette in a one-piece and slip-on skirt, but he couldn't absorb the barrage of the brunette's bio Triniti machine-gunned at him. He would have asked, but Triniti's circular breathing prevented a break in the torrent of words.

The pretty woman smiled at him. He'd hoped her name would have come back up during the conversation, but if it had, he'd missed it. Triniti's verbal torrent stumbled when a man called out to her, giving the brunette a chance to speak to Sam. "What brings you down from LA?"

Sam opened his mouth to answer, but Triniti turned back, wrapped her arm around his neck, and cut him off before he could formulate the first syllable. "Well, he's a classic workaholic. Eighty-hour weeks. Money and power are his life. But when you're a mover and shaker, spending that much time in the office just comes with the territory. Big clients and even bigger money. You know how those things go. Fortunately, his boss forced him to take a break." She laughed. "He had to practically run Sam out the door..."

The poor brunette's expression melted from politely interested to deer-in-the-headlights as his date pelted her with words. The woman's eyes flicked to Sam's, the now-familiar, Triniti-induced desperation lurking in their depths.

Sam smiled back at her, trying to be reassuring, but he was unable to vocalize any sort of comfort. He wished he could have begun advocating for the poor woman's release. However, to do that, he'd need to be able to interject more than a grunt here or a nod there. Though thorough, The Agency's Hostage Negotiation classes simply hadn't prepared him for this situation. *Maybe they should bring Triniti in as a consultant?*

Triniti continued to ramble in spite of the anguish of her audience. "So, next week is the regency surfing finals. I was thinking I'd..."

He sighed. He'd already heard this same litany about ten times. Sam considered tuning out and reviewing the case in his head, but he needed to stay focused. Kernels of information lay in the bushels of conversations at social gatherings. He would just have to weed them out.

Triniti began her wrap-up. "Anyway, we have more people to meet. Have fun, Chelsea." For the first time since he'd met her, the brunette's eyes lit with hope. She glanced back as she sidled away, pity for him as well as relief for herself mixed in her expression.

Triniti yanked his hand, dragging him toward another small group of partygoers. "I wonder where Max is? He almost never misses these things."

"He told me he works a lot," Sam said, following her.

She re-gripped his hand and pulled harder when he didn't move fast enough. "Maybe he's seeing Abby tonight."

Sam almost stumbled from trying to keep up with her. "Who's that?"

Triniti suddenly stopped and spun back around. "She's his business partner."

Sam came within inches of colliding with her. Their faces were so close he could smell the beer on her breath and a hint of her jasmine perfume. The assets Chet had become obsessed with pressed pleasantly against the front of his shirt. "Oh?"

Her coquettish smile returned as she traced his chin with a long fingernail. "Let's just say they're a lot closer than most business partners." Triniti waggled her eyebrows.

Sam stepped back, putting a little more distance between them. "I feel like I'm getting the inside scoop on a town secret."

"It's hardly a secret," she said, giggling. "They've been together for a couple of years. Actually, now that I think on it, she's out of town at some business conference thing."

Reaching into her small handbag, she pulled out a cell. She started clicking, then scrunched up her face and tossed the phone back into her purse. "Forgot the stupid service is still out. Damned storm. Really? What the hell? They can make mascara that doesn't run when you cry and a carburetor that will go a hundred miles on a gallon of gas, yet something as simple as a few trees falling in the river means I can't send a text message."

"Chaos," Sam said somberly. "The world is falling into utter chaos."

She raised her arms into the air. "Thank you! I pay my bills, well, most of them, yet I'm still deprived of the basic necessities of life." Triniti snatched another woman's hand as she walked by. "Kimberly! I've got someone here I want you to meet."

Sam sighed as the cycle started again.

Monica walked along the shore. Cool sand gushed between her toes with each footfall, while the breaking waves whispered a quiet lullaby.

As a teenager, when the ghosts had haunted her dreams and the demons had mocked her failures, she'd spend hours strolling the beach barefoot, with only the moonlight as a guide and the surf and stars for company.

She had imagined she could see mermaids and waterborne fairies playing in the moonlight. Attracted by the lunar glow, they'd leapt and danced beneath the constellations. These mythological creatures had represented the carefree happiness she could not recall in memory but, nonetheless, still harmonized the melody in her heart's song. She'd longed to join their schools, wanting nothing more than to dart beneath the water and dive among the waves, to be free of the loneliness and relieved of her burdens.

Monica glanced to her side and smiled. Unlike in her youth, when she would walk alone, she now had her reluctant, out-of-joint friend marching beside her. She smiled at the seriousness and determination etched into Angel's face.

Her faithful companion had insisted they "pack heat." As such, Monica wore a tool belt with a screw driver, garden spade, the vampire stake with a blade duct taped to the tip, and, of course, a ball-peen hammer. An accessorizing can of mace dangled on a lanyard around her neck. With each step, the tools rattled like stirrups, as if they were a couple of anachronistic gunslingers preparing for a shootout at Ye Old Home and Garden Expo.

Angel glanced over and caught Monica looking at her. "What are you smirking about? We're in real danger out here."

Monica tried to wipe the expression from her lips but couldn't quite manage it.

Angel sighed. "Just so you are aware, from now on, we aren't going anywhere without packing heat."

Monica's grin grew, and she nodded. "I wouldn't have it any other way. We are so totally badass, only a fool with a death wish would try to mess with us now." She whipped out a small stun gun that looked like a 1960s *Star Trek* phaser and mocked pulling the trigger as imaginary Klingons and Romulans attacked. "Bitcheeeeessss, you wanna fight? Zzzzzzap!"

Angel cocked her head, narrowing her eyes to hard flints. "Really? You need to take this seriously."

Monica holstered the Taser she'd found in the *Home Security* section of the hardware store and pulled the machete from her belt. "How serious is this?" She whipped the blade through the air like a Samurai. The knife's shiny surface and eager-to-slice edge flashed and glinted in moonlight. "Whaaaaaa! Woosh! Woosh!" Grinning at her friend's somber, exasperated face, Monica returned it to its sheath.

"I think you're punch drunk," Angel said as she continued trudging up the beach.

Maybe she was punch drunk or maybe she'd simply gone crazy. Fear and anxiety had been pummeling her for so long that she'd become emotionally numb and mentally exhausted. It probably had been idiotic to go for a moonlit stroll, but somehow the danger had lost its urgency while she was losing her edge. She floated along, no longer an active participant in her own life but an actress reading her lines and simply pretending to be scared.

Monica fell in step beside Angel, letting the quiet spin out so her friend could cool off. After a while, she broke the silence. "You were my savior, you know. When I was a kid, I mean."

"Just as a kid? By my count as an adult too."

Monica chuckled. "Yeah, I suppose so. But that's not what I mean."

"I know," Angel replied.

Monica looked out over the ocean. "I never wanted to go home, so I'd come out here to walk just like this." She brushed the blunt edge of the large knife hanging from her belt as her "spurs" rattled. "Okay, maybe not *exactly* like this."

Angel snorted.

Monica scanned the dark horizon as they continued. "This was my place to think and sometimes cry. Mom was never home. She was always off with some guy. So, after coming here, I'd go to your house."

Angel directed her gaze at Monica. "I don't think I ever told you this, but after your walks on the beach, you usually smelled like sweat and seaweed. I had to wash my sheets all the time because you not only stunk them up but also got sand all over them."

Monica frowned. "I did not... Did I? Wait. Why are you only now telling me this?"

"I figured since we're probably going to die, I'd come clean and tell you all the things I'd always meant to."

Monica's cheeks grew hot.

"Don't be embarrassed." Angel shrugged. "It comes with the high-maintenance Monica territory I signed on for."

Monica folded her arms. "I am not *that* high-maintenance... Am I?"

Angel placed her hands on Monica's shoulders. "Mon, neither that, nor your BO, nor your sleep farts are important right now. We need to focus on staying alive. Erebus is out there."

Monica jolted. "What?"

Angel turned and started walking. "Erebus is out there."

Monica reached out, snagged her friend's arm, and yanked her back. "No, the thing you said about farting in my sleep."

"Mom called them sleep farts once and it kinda stuck."

"Your mom... She heard?"

Angel nodded. "From down the hall."

"What? No, she didn't. You're making that up. You're just mad that I made fun of us packing heat."

Angel peeled Monica's grip from her arm. "See? This is why I don't tell you things. You always say I make stuff up, but every time, you find out I'm not. I think it surprises you that sometimes the C-student knows a thing or two that you don't. Call her and ask her yourself if you want, but right now, we have to focus. Like I said, Erebus is looking for us."

Monica remained rooted in her spot as her friend turned—the barest of grins playing across her lips—and strutted away.

☆☆☆☆

Sam had begun to reach his social and intelligence gathering saturation point. He could catalog and absorb a lot of information, but after such a long day, even he had limits.

And while he could act the part—in this case, the new boy-toy for a well-endowed, self-centered regional surfing champion—the ruse sapped his energy.

Triniti had begun anew one of her sea-taming stories when someone sidled up behind Sam.

"Hey. How's it going, man? Need a break?"

Sam glanced over his shoulder. "Dios! More than you can imagine."

"Are you sure?" He glanced at Sam's date. "I hate to break up this spellbinding conversation."

Triniti paused mid-sentence, her gleaming smile faltering into consternation. "Dios? What's up?"

"I hate drinking alone," he said. "So, I'm going to borrow your new friend for a brew. You don't mind, do ya, Trin?"

Triniti folded her arms. The half dozen or so elaborate bracelets she wore tinkled as they slid on her wrists. "Since when are you *ever* alone?"

Dios smiled and shrugged. "I know. I'm as surprised as anyone, but who can understand the mysteries of the universe?"

Triniti scowled.

"Don't worry," he said, touching her chin and giving her an exaggerated wink. "I won't keep your boyfriend long." He turned, heading off.

Triniti focused on Sam and cocked her head, asking the question without vocalizing it.

Sam shrugged, kissed her cheek, and followed his new best friend.

Dios weaved his way through the crowd. Stopping at the huge cooler, he pulled two beers from the ice. After handing one to Sam, he opened the other. "Man, you looked like your brain was about to crawl out of your skull."

Sam twisted the top off the bottle. "Triniti and her storytelling? Nah. It's okay. She's just...enthusiastic."

"She's so full of her own shit, it's a wonder her eyes aren't brown."

"I'll admit she's a little...self-focused."

"Perhaps not entirely on herself though. Don't look now, but someone's checking you out." Dios indicated to Triniti with a slight nod.

Sam gazed across the small crowd. The surfing champ's dazzling smile had made a miraculous reappearance. She raised her beer as if toasting him and turned back to her latest victim. Her captive had just begun to slip away when the busty chatterbox snared the poor woman once again in a merciless verbal assault.

"I don't think she's really interested in me," Sam said. "She's just showing me around a bit."

Dios' gaze remained fixed on the two women. "Well, you play your cards right and you could be taking that crazy thing for a spin. I know her well enough to know that look. Only, don't get too attached. She's more popular than a carnival ride on Coney Island and has about as many screws loose."

"I'll try and keep my emotional distance."

Dios turned away from the ladies. "Underneath all that babble, she's actually a pretty nice girl. But ya gotta wade through a ton of crap to find her. You two will have some good times, just don't expect her to settle down with kids and a dog."

Sam shook his head. "A house with a white picket fence hadn't even crossed my mind. I did that once. *Never* again."

Dios clicked Sam's beer with his own. "Hear. Hear. Ain't no one tying these *espíritus libres* down. We don't answer to no one but ourselves, and that's just the way we like it."

"I've heard all about Triniti's accomplishments ad nauseum, but what about you? Do you surf?"

"Nah," Dios said. "I've dabbled in it some, of course, but mostly I just stay to the shore, charm the ladies, and look beautiful. Besides, I'm too busy. I own a business, which sucks up most of my free time."

Sam was about to ask about the venture when a small boat, about half a mile offshore, caught his attention. Despite the cool sea air, a cold sweat broke out on his forehead as the vessel cruised through the moon's reflection. "Hey, Dios, what's up with the boat? I'm not a captain or anything, but shouldn't it have its running lights on?"

"Hmmm, looks like a dory," he said, squinting into the darkness. "But I can't make out the name." He turned to the crowd. "Hey, Kyle."

A voice from somewhere in the back answered. "Yeah?"

Dios pointed. "Whose boat is that?"

After a brief pause, the voice floated back. "Not sure. Might be Leonard's."

The small craft continued making its way across the horizon.

Something's not right. Chet's voice, laced with anxiety, hesitated.

Yeah, Sam said. *I feel it too, but what is it?*

Chet shook his head. *I don't know. But get ready.*

Sam stared harder. Though he couldn't be completely sure, it looked like something had been rigged to the mast.

220

He wished he'd brought his night binoculars. The deck suddenly lit up like a flare. The light illuminated the details of the vessel for half a second before the cabin erupted into a fireball.

The conversations on the beach ended in an instant. In the ensuing silence, the flickering whisper of flames drifted over the calm waters.

Dios turned to him. "Damn cell service is still down, so we can't call this in. We need to run into town and let Roo know."

Sam frowned. "Who's Roo?"

"R-U." Dios said, enunciating the syllables. "The Alabaster Cove Beach and Rescue Unit."

"We don't have time to go to town. It'll burn out long before then." Sam thought it over for a second, turned, and sprinted through the crowd.

Triniti's voice followed him as he flew past her. "Hey, where are you going?"

Sam didn't answer or slow down. He ran up the beach to the *Mile 2* marker he'd seen earlier. Below the sign, a small gray box had been strapped to the pole's side. A wire snaked out of the bottom and into the sand. Before cell phones had made them obsolete, he'd seen hundreds of the little units all along the coastline.

Popping open the salt-crusted door, he grabbed the old-fashioned, heavy-duty handset, tucking it in between his cheek and shoulder. The face of the phone had no buttons, so he waited.

The earpiece resonated with a faraway tinny bell. The buzzing stopped, and a deep voice barked into the receiver. "RU."

Sam breathed a sigh of relief. "A dory off the coast of mile two is on fire. I couldn't see if anyone was on board when she went up, but someone thought it might belong to..." Sam searched his memory for the name. "Leonard."

The man yelled something which Sam could not make out. "Okay, thanks. Who is this?"

"My name's Sam Bradford."

"Okay, thanks, Sam. We're on it."

He hung up the phone and returned to the now somber party.

Hands on hips, Triniti stood at the edge of the crowd, waiting for him. "Where'd you go?"

Sam marched past her to where he'd left Dios. "There was a squawk box up the beach. I called RU."

Triniti fell in step beside him. "A what?"

Sam indicated the direction he'd come. "The pole with the gray box on it. Before we had cell phones, we had squawk boxes. They're hardwired phone lines to the local emergency unit."

"Huh." She glanced back in the direction Sam had gone. "I've lived here my whole life and never noticed."

Sam nodded. "Well, you're not alone. They're a little outdated and most of them have been taken down. Guess they hadn't gotten around to that one yet. It's so old, I'm just amazed it still worked."

"That was quick thinking," she said, taking his hand.

Dios waited near the breaker's edge. "Where'd you go? You took off like a *relámpago.*"

"He called RU," Triniti informed him, giving Sam's hand a squeeze.

Multiple sets of lights bounced along the water, approaching the flaming boat. As soon as they pulled up alongside, several people leapt on board. Wielding extinguishers, they dowsed the flames. The team milled about with flashlights until someone shouted and they all focused on the mast.

Dios stared. "What do you think they found?"

"I don't know," Sam said. "Nothing good."

The rescue team climbed back into their own boats, rigged a line to the charred vessel, and began to tow it.

Dread filled Sam's stomach. "Where are they going to take it?"

Dios pointed at a distant string of lights sticking out in the water. "Just before the next pier, there's an RU station about a mile or so south of here. They're probably taking it there."

Sam began to jog toward the station.

"Hey! Where are you going?" Triniti yelled after him.

"I need to go see what was on that boat."

"Why?"

Sam pivoted around and ran backwards for several steps. "I think I saw someone on board just before it went up." He turned, resuming his stride.

She ran up beside him, matching his pace. "Well then, I'm coming with you."

☆☆☆☆

Having broken out of her emotional paralysis, Monica had just started to resume her beach stroll when Angel stopped and pointed to the ocean. "What is that?"

Monica followed Angel's line of sight. In the distance, a flickering rosebud of flames illuminated the black surface of the ocean. "I think it's a boat. But it looks like it's on fire."

A half dozen watercraft approached at high speed. They surrounded the larger vessel and doused the flames.

The hair on the nape of Monica's neck stood on end. *Someone's watching us.* She turned slowly in a circle. While the overwhelming sensation urged her to run, the night around them remained quiet and undisturbed.

Angel frowned. "What is it?"

Monica made another slow circle, scanning the darkness. As she completed the rotation, she stopped and faced her friend. She considered telling Angel about the weird feeling, but what exactly would she say? That it had been a bad idea to go walking in the middle of the night alone because Erebus might be stalking them? Angel would have a few choice words on that particular topic.

Instead of admitting her mistake, Monica said, "I've lived here my whole life and never seen anything like that. You?"

Angel studied the sea for a moment, as if hoping the breakers would provide the answer for her. "No. Nothing like that. But what does that have to do with us? It's probably just a couple guys, drunk off their asses, dropping a cigarette or some other idiocy."

"No. It's Erebus." Monica pointed at the burning wreck. "He did that."

Angel furrowed her brow and slowly nodded. "Yeah, I think you're right. But why?"

"I couldn't begin to fathom why he does anything he does."

The smaller crafts, with the scorched boat in tow, headed toward the *Mile 3* pier.

"But whatever the reason, we need to find out," Monica said. She stepped up her pace, making her way to the pier and, perhaps, to face her worst nightmare.

Chapter Twenty

A series of overhead halogens bathed the RU pier in midday brilliance. Sam arrived just as the rescue workers looped the charred wreck's mooring lines around a pair of dock cleats.

Triniti had jabbered the entire time they'd been jogging down the beach. In almost any other situation, her cardiovascular endurance might have impressed him. But as they'd trekked along the shoreline, Sam had tuned out her verbal musings over which drunken fools had caught the boat on fire.

Fortunately, Triniti didn't want a conversation, just a sounding board. While she talked, Sam had mentally worked through his own theories, which had nothing to do with drinking or foolishness.

As he arrived at the pier, he climbed the steps, transitioning from dry sand to the sea-bleached wooden surface.

A good portion of the beach party attendees had trailed after him. They also crowded onto the platform. The spectacle of destruction was evidently too interesting to pass up.

The rescue team had already begun to sift through the wreckage.

While Triniti hung back, mingling with the crowd, Sam headed toward the boat. Before he made it halfway across the dock, a huge figure in an ACRU baseball cap and a name tag identifying him as *Chief Palmer* stepped in his path. "Sorry, this is a crime scene."

"I'm the one that called it in," Sam said. "I saw what happened."

The man checked a clipboard. "Sam Bradford?"

He nodded.

Chief Palmer flipped to a new page and pulled out a pen. "Okay, tell me what you saw."

Sam switched to police speak where boats become vessels and people become witnesses, perpetrators, or victims. After he provided a succinct description, he added, "At approximately 19:45, there was a flash, like a flare or some other small incendiary device, mid-stern. Almost immediately thereafter, the cabin erupted in flames. It didn't catch fire gradually but all at once."

The man finished jotting down notes. "Okay, I appreciate you reporting this."

Someone from the wreckage yelled up. "Chief, you need to come see this."

"Be right there," he called over his shoulder. To Sam he said, "I need your number for the record and so I can contact you if I have any follow up questions."

Sam rattled off his number. The chief wrote it down and turned to leave.

Sam tried to follow, but the chief stopped him. "Sir, I need you to stay here."

"The flames were instantaneous," Sam replied, disregarding the man's command to not follow him. "I believe an accelerant was used. This was not an accident."

The chief stared at Sam for a few seconds. "I understood the implications of what you told me. But, it's *our* job to make that assessment based on evidence, not by an observer who, as you stated, was about a half mile away. I appreciate your enthusiasm and reporting what you witnessed. But now I need you to step back and leave this in the hands of the professionals."

The chief turned to leave, but Sam stopped him. "I am certain I saw someone on board. There was only a second between the ignition and the detonation, but from my position, it appeared that someone had been tied to the mast. You have a murder on your hands, and you need to treat it as such."

Behind him, a murmur went through the group of partygoers.

"Please, we don't need you starting rumors or causing a panic," the chief replied, ribbons of irritation lacing his voice. "We are only now beginning our investigation. Like I said, I appreciate you reporting it, but I need you to please back away."

Something's up here, Chet said. *You need to get on the boat and figure out what happened.*

Sam considered trying to go around the huge man. However, Chief Palmer would be a formidable obstacle if he chose. Instead, Sam assumed an authoritative demeanor. "I have law enforcement and crime scene investigation training. I also did several tours overseas in the Marines. Let me assist you in the investigation."

The chief's lips narrowed into a hard, thin line, and his eyes brimmed with impatience. "While I appreciate your offer and your service to our country, this is *my* investigation. *My* team is trained in the proper procedures to investigate this incident. When we determine the cause, and if someone has been injured, a statement will be made to the media. You may read about it at that time. Until then, I need you to step back and let us do our jobs."

Behind him a collective gasp rose up from the crowd. Sam tried to ignore the sudden buzz and excited whispers when a female voice called out from behind him. "Peter? Is that you?"

Shit.

Sam had burned the falsified set of identification documents—driver's license, passport, credit card, and such—after completing an assignment under the assumed name of Peter Morrell. As the wind carried away the ashes and The Agency deleted records and scrubbed databases, he'd mentally discarded the fake identity background and personal data.

Within minutes, Peter Morrell never existed.

Only, they couldn't as easily remove the memories—and pain—of the people he'd interacted with. As per regulations, he'd only shared the "Peter" identity with a scant few. And of those, only two would have a reason to come to the Cove.

Sam turned to find both of them—a machete-wearing Monica and a ball-peen hammer-wielding Angel—staring at him with huge round eyes.

Monica gasped. "It *is* you. What are you doing here?"

Sam looked from one to the other. He'd raced here—violating a direct order from his boss—to find and protect these women, but he also needed to figure out why Erebus had torched the boat. "There's been a murder. I'm looking into it."

He tried to ignore the wicked looking blade dangling from Monica's hand.

Chet stared at the large knife. *How exactly did you leave things with her? I can't remember.*

We had a few laughs, took the bike for a spin, spent the night together, and then she asked me to leave.

Chet's attention remained fixed on the weapon. *Yeah, but perhaps you forgot the whole double-crossing her thing where you got her friend killed and almost got her killed. Oh, and you busted through a restaurant window, messed up their dinner, and then you shot her computer. But who knows, maybe she's forgiven you?*

I only did that to save her from Erebus. If I hadn't arrived when I did, he'd have tortured and killed them.

However, Chet shot back, *she wouldn't have needed saving had you done your job and stopped him.*

Chief Palmer tucked the clipboard under a beefy arm. "We don't know that anyone's been hurt. And this is *my* crime scene."

Chet glanced between the chief and Monica. *Oh, that's just great. On top of having to deal with a bitter ex, you've also got the Not-So-Jolly Green Giant breathing down your neck.*

Monica and Angel moved in closer. The tools around their waists clanged and clinked like poorly tuned windchimes. The four of them—the women, plus Sam and the chief—formed a comfy little circle.

"Yes, I know about the murder," Monica said. "I read about it in the paper just like everyone else. And, as you can clearly see, I'm *not* dead. So you and the rest of the baboons can stop looking now."

"Not you," Sam replied. "I know you're still alive." He jerked a thumb back over his shoulder. "Someone else. On the boat."

Chief Palmer growled. "We don't know there's been any foul play."

Sam continued to stare at Monica but directed the conversation to the huge man. "Go talk to your people, Chief. Have them tell you what they found on the mast."

Just when he thought the chief might cooperate, Triniti pushed her way next to Sam, joining the small but growing social circle. His heart sank.

Triniti looked at Monica. "So, the rumors are true."

"They usually are," Monica said. "But we're a little busy here right now, so if you don't mind..." She made a move along gesture with the tip of the blade.

She seems just a little too comfortable with that machete, Chet observed.

Triniti ignored Monica's request to leave. She looked at Sam. "Who's Peter?"

"He is," Angel said, pointing at Sam with the hammer. "His name is Peter Morrell."

Triniti faced Angel and sighed. "Just what we need, the drunk's daughter and her loser tagalong meddling with town business. You two are a joke. We were all so much better off when you were away."

Angel gave Triniti the once over, her gaze pausing briefly on the woman's chest. "Us? Oh, no. Not us, honey. The only joke around here is you and your ridiculous bags of silicone."

Flames of anger ignited in Triniti's eyes, and she snarled. "At least I've made something of myself."

"Yeah, something *artificial*." Angel huffed. "Maybe you should have looked into a brain enhancement. Because if you trust anything this guy says, then it's clear your cup size is larger than your IQ."

The crowd had grown quiet, pressing in closer so they didn't miss a word. They ignored the boat, ignored the potential murder victim, and instead focused on the little melodrama that had unfolded.

As Triniti's gaze dropped to Angel's chest, a mean smirk graced her lips. "Obviously, you have to make fun of me, since... Well, I think we can all see why." Before Angel could respond, Triniti turned to Sam. "What's this Peter nonsense they're talking about?"

Dude, we don't have time for this. Anxiety wove through Chet's words. *You have to get busy.*

Sam started to sweat. His body screamed that he needed to move, to do something. "Look, I will explain later. But this," he indicated toward the boat, "is part of my job, and I need to focus on it right now."

"Wait. What?" Triniti frowned. "I thought you were in finance or something?"

Angel laughed. "Finance? Really? Not only did you buy his story but you're smitten too. I can see it all over your face. Well, before you go jumping into bed with this guy, you should know that right after this bastard seduced my friend, he skipped town."

"Because *she* asked me to go," Sam said.

Angel ignored him. "Not satisfied with just crushing my friend's heart, he helped the mob find her. And they blew up her house."

Triniti, for once, didn't have anything to say.

Monica touched Angel's elbow. "Ang, you know that's not true."

Angel yanked her arm away. "I don't know any such thing." She let out an exasperated breath. "Monica's giving him the benefit of the doubt, saying he's just stupid and incompetent, but *I'm* not convinced he didn't light the dynamite himself. I don't know what he's told you, but he's a con. And he's probably responsible for whoever got murdered on the boat."

The chief growled. "We don't know if anyone's been killed. I want everyone to stop spreading rumors. Now, I need you all to move back."

Angel ignored the chief too. Her attention remained glued to Triniti. "Everyone knows you're as dumb as a bag of gravel, so I'll do you a solid and spell it out in a way that even *you* can understand. Dump this guy before he breaks your heart, destroys your house, shoots your computer, and gets you killed."

Chet glared at him. *I know you're having fun playing tabloid talk show host and all, but you really need to get back to the business at hand. And you need to do it now.*

I know. But I feel like a deer that smells a lion but can't tell where it's at. We need to work this out.

Chet began to pace. *There's a body on board. You know that. Yes.*

It was tied to the mast. Even from a distance you saw that. Yes.

Chet halted mid-stride. *Find out how he was killed.*

Sam turned to the chief. "How was the victim killed?"

The large man blinked, evidently confused by the abrupt shift in conversation. "What? What victim?"

"The person tied to the mast," Sam said, pointing. "Look, we all know it happened, so there's no sense denying it."

When the chief still didn't answer, Sam leaned in, placing emphasis on each word. "We are running out of time. This is important."

"I can neither confirm nor deny that anyone was on board the boat. Part of the reason I can neither confirm nor deny it is because I'm out *here*, dealing with *you*, and not *there*, doing my job."

Though Sam felt the urge to run, to move, he had to focus and keep control of himself. Action without purpose was worse than no action at all. "Ask your people how the person was killed. Do it now."

The two men stared at one another. The chief's face turned bright red, and Sam began to formulate a plan in the event he had to disable the huge man and get the information himself.

Finally, Chief Palmer snorted like a bull and called out without breaking eye contact. "Polly."

A woman's voice floated up from the vessel. "Yes, Chief?"

The crowd had gone completely silent, hanging on every word.

"Was there anyone on board?"

The voice hesitated. "Chief? I don't think it's a good idea..."

The chief glanced over at the boat. "I understand all of that. Just answer the question."

After another brief pause, the woman replied. "Yes, Chief. A man I estimate to be in his late sixties. We have not made an I.D. yet."

The chief glared down at Sam. "Satisfied?"

"How was he killed? I need to know."

Chief Palmer snorted again and called back. "Polly, did you hear the man's question?"

She hesitated again. "His throat was cut."

A low murmur trickled through the crowd.

Who do we know that has an affinity for cutting people up? Chet asked.

Yes, I think you're right. But none of this makes any sense.

Chet resumed his pacing. *Maybe he knows you're here. If so, he knew you'd probably see the boat. And if you saw it, you'd chase it down. He wanted you here. He wanted you to see this.*

But why? Sam's nerves twitched as perplexity and fear gripped his heart. He needed to act, but he still didn't know what needed to be done.

Let's think about this guy's MO, Chet continued. *He's always sliced and diced, but he's recently expanded upon his murdering repertoire to include organ removal and the devil only knows what else. He's trying to get his grubby, nasty fingers on Monica, but you keep getting in the way. He wants more than anything to have his lady fun without the pesky federal agent busting up the party.*

Sam tried to glean a conclusion from his inner conscience's words. *Okay, so he knows I'm here and he wants to kill me to get me out of the way.*

No. He doesn't just want you out of the way. He wants revenge.

Sam thought that over for a second. *He wants to get back at me for shooting him in the face. But why not just kill me? If he knows where I am, why not just slip up behind me and put a knife through my ribs?*

Chet rubbed his temples. *Well, a couple of reasons. First, there's no drama. This guy loves the limelight. Second, killing you quickly won't hurt you like you hurt him. You've taken an oath to protect your country and its citizens. He knows you'll die to carry out your duty. The best way to hurt you is to make you fail.*

Sam stared at Monica and then looked around at all the people watching him. He whipped around to the big man. "Chief, get your people out of the boat. Now!"

A vein in Chief Palmer's forehead began to pulse and his eyes turned to granite. "Huh? What are you talking about? Look, I've had about as much of you as I can——"

Sam got right in the man's face. "Listen to me. I know who did this. If you don't want all your people dead, then you need to get them out!"

Everyone froze, staring at the confrontation. Silence descended once again as the red in the chief's face flamed to purple.

Chief Palmer poked Sam in the chest with a thick finger. "I don't know who you are or what your agenda is, but you'd better be right about this." He turned and barked over his shoulder. "Polly. Get your people out of there."

The woman's voice, authoritative yet calm, echoed across the dock as she gave her orders. "Alright, you heard the man. Everyone out."

Sam turned to the crowd. "All of you, get back!"

The gathering started shuffling toward the beach.

"Don't trample each other, and don't panic. But do move quickly," Sam said, trying to mimic Polly's calm.

Red shirts scrambled from the boat. As the last man hopped out, the vessel erupted into a huge fireball. And the night turned to hell.

Chapter Twenty-One

Sam lay on a cool bed of sand. A meteor shower of flaming wood and fiberglass rained down from an otherwise perfect night sky. Microphone feedback clogged his ears. A plume of smoke, as thick and gray as dryer lint, blurred his vision. He squeezed his eyes shut, trying to relieve the burning cloudiness from his retinas.

Overwhelmingly exhausted, he almost gave himself permission to relax and go to sleep. But cries of pain and pleadings for help pierced the buzz in his ears and began to clear the veil of fog that had blanketed his mind. He needed to move.

Though it felt as if a dozen menacing goblins pounded on his skull with tiny war hammers, he opened his eyes and lifted his head.

Fifty feet in front of him, a man, engulfed in flames, ran in circles on what remained of the dock. He screamed and flailed, beating at the inferno as it devoured his body.

A man had been leaping from the deck of the boat when the explosion ripped apart hull and planks. Sam tried to pair that face with the wailing, tortured soul before him.

The glowing figure leapt off the side of the decimated pier and splashed into the ocean. The sea snuffed the flames and muted his screams. The prone figure struggled for several heartbeats before relaxing into the water, succumbing to his fate.

In the distance, sirens added a layer of soprano shrill to the dissonant choir of tinnitus and cries of the wounded.

Sam had been so focused on the burning man, he hadn't noticed the woman in a red RU shirt lying a few feet away. Groaning with the effort, he forced his lead-filled body to get up. He stumbled his way over to her.

Falling back to his knees, he brushed her long, dark hair away from her face, afraid of what he'd find. Besides grime and soot, only a small cut on her forehead and another on her cheek marred her clear skin. He placed his fingers against her neck and timed the fluttering pulse.

After glancing at her name tag, he gently shook her shoulder. "Polly. Polly, wake up."

When she didn't respond, he leaned next to her mouth, listening for breathing. But the screeching chorus made it impossible. He watched her chest for the telltale movement of respiration, but she remained still.

Sam tilted her head back, pinched her nose, and blew into her mouth.

After several breaths, she gasped, coughing out a cloud of smoke. She rolled over onto her side as a fit of violent hacking bent her in half.

He moved away, giving her space to expel and clear her lungs. The spasms subsided and she opened her watery, vibrant green eyes. She stared at him for a second and started another round of coughing.

"Go." She wheezed. "I'll be fine. Go help someone else."

Sam wobbled to his feet and looked around.

Across a debris-strewn stretch of sand, a man sat leaning against a log. He stared at the large dock cleat—a fragment of the singed, smoking mooring line still looped around it—sticking out of his chest. As if in slow motion, he grasped the heavy sliver of steel.

Sam cried out for the man to stop, but his vocal cords refused to cooperate. His voice croaked a whisper and he began coughing.

The man yanked the cleat out, signing his own death certificate.

Hacking as he went, Sam stumble-crawled as fast as his throbbing head and uncooperative legs would allow, while a river of blood poured from the man's chest.

Sam ripped off his shirt sleeve and fell next to the doomed man. "Hold on. Hold on. Help will be here in a minute." Sam pressed the cloth to the gaping hole. The fabric quickly saturated and began weeping crimson tears.

Desperate, Sam looked about for anyone that could help, but he and the dying man owned this corner of the beach.

The guy turned his eyes up to Sam's face; confusion and fear lurked in their depths. Sam grasped one of the man's hands with his free one. "I'm here. I'm not going anywhere."

The dying man—whom Sam had initially thought to be middle age but in reality couldn't have been old enough to drink—tried to say something. But blood bubbled from his lips, preventing the words from forming.

"It's okay." Sam lied in his most soothing voice. "Everything will be just fine."

The young man gave a final shuddering exhalation. His eyes turned to glass and his hand fell limp.

Sam lay the kid down and gently closed the lids over his sightless gaze. "I'm sorry, my friend," he whispered.

A hundred paces away, an ambulance with elevated suspension and oversized wheels plowed through the sand. As it came to a halt, a half dozen paramedics spilled out, racing in all directions.

After wiping the boy's blood on his pants, Sam got back up on his feet.

Dozens of flaming pieces of dock debris littered the beach. People milled about, stunned by the ferocious, senseless violence. Across the confusion, a woman, her arm dangling and bent at an unnatural angle, wandered toward the ocean.

Sam staggered over to her.

The shredded remains of a light summer dress hung around her hips, leaving her partially scorched torso exposed. Sam removed the remains of his shirt and wrapped it around her shoulders, covering her near-nakedness.

He gently slipped his arm around her waist. Careful not to touch her injured limb, he guided her away from the water. "Come this way. Help is over here." She let him lead her back to the ambulance.

When an EMT ran to them, Sam handed the woman off. "Her arm looks broken and dislocated. She's got burns under the shirt too."

The EMT took Sam's place beside her. "Hello, ma'am. Come this way." As the tech led her away, he called back over his shoulder. "There's a pile of shirts over by the bus."

A heap of clothes and blankets sat near the open doors of the ambulance. Sam had just started to slip on a shirt when a man's voice broke through the chaos. "Over here."

Chief Palmer strained as he tried to move a thick section of the dock, which had folded over onto itself. A leg stuck out from under the rubble.

Sam hobbled over and slipped his fingers under the platform. Together, they lifted, revealing a woman beneath. They tossed the crumpled plane of fragmented planks aside, and a pair of EMTs descended on her.

Sam looked around at the piles of wood and melted boat at the end of the dock. "Anyone else?"

The chief shook his head. "Don't know."

They worked their way down the dock, tossing boards, metal, and fiberglass aside. Sam lifted the edge of a large piece of plywood, revealing a dark-haired man. "Here," he called.

The chief ran over, and they heaved the board aside.

Sam knelt, grasping the man's face in his hands. "Dios. Dios, can you hear me?"

His new friend grimaced. He blinked several times before his gaze focused on Sam's face.

"What the hell happened?" Dios asked, rubbing his forehead with a grimy hand. "One minute you were getting your butt severely kicked by several beautiful women, and the next, we're in a Bruce Willis movie."

Sam started checking his friend over for injuries.

Dios pushed his hands away. "Stop groping me. If I wanted to be fondled, I'd go find a hot nurse."

Relieved, Sam said, "You're gonna be just fine. I think you've just been stunned."

A woman with a soot-infused red shirt, long dark hair, and vibrant green eyes muscled her way next to Dios.

Sam moved aside. "Hey, I just gave you CPR a minute ago. Are you okay? Shouldn't you get to the ambulance and get checked out? I've got this."

She didn't answer as she shined a pen light into Dios' eyes. Unbuttoning his shirt, she pressed a stethoscope against his chest.

Dios grinned weakly up at her. "I knew it. I just knew it. In my final minutes on Earth, God sent His most stunning angel to guide me through the pearly gates. Thank you, Lord, for delivering the beautiful Polly to me. It's unfortunate that only now does she understand the true depths of her feelings."

"Amigo," Dios said, glancing up at Sam. "Promise me you'll comfort her as she mourns the loss of our love. Someday, when she joins me in Heaven, we will finally be able to express our true passion for one another."

"Please shut up," she scolded. "I can't hear over your blather."

Dios' grin never faltered, but he did stop talking.

After a minute, Polly nodded. "You're going to be fine." She glanced over her shoulder. "Chief, he's good to go. Get him to the bus."

Sam and Chief Palmer lifted Dios to his feet and helped him over to an ambulance.

As they walked away, Sam said, "Earlier, I saw someone fall into the ocean."

"Why didn't you say so before?"

Sam headed to the jagged remains of the dock. "It was too late. There were other priorities."

The chief fell in step beside him. "You have seen this before."

"Like I told you, I did three tours in the Middle East." He stopped at the edge of the dock where the burning man had fallen.

Chief Palmer scanned the ocean. After several seconds, he pointed. "There."

Sam slipped into the water, careful of debris that may be lurking beneath the surface. He swam out and guided the body back. After pulling himself up, he and the chief worked together to lay the burned man onto the wooden surface.

Chief Palmer knelt and gently closed his fallen co-worker's eyes. Anger twisted his expression as he stared down at the corpse. He glanced up. "You knew this was going to happen. Who did this?"

Sam removed his sodden shirt, laying it over the dead man's face. "Let's finish up here, then we'll talk."

The chief gave a curt nod. He stood, and they continued their search.

Chapter Twenty-Two

Eye-melting perimeter lights bathed the landscape in a shadowy yellow haze. Deputies picked through dock debris and shredded boat remains, in what could have easily been mistaken as the ground zero of a tornado touchdown.

Chief Palmer and the sheriff stood off to the side, occasionally glancing at Sam while they talked quietly. Wrapping up their conversation, they trudged shoulder to shoulder toward him.

"Evening, Sheriff," Sam said as the two men approached.

The lawman touched the wide brim of his hat by way of greeting. "The chief tells me you were aware that there was a bomb on board that boat. Said you also claimed to know who planted it."

"Yes, I suspected that an explosive had been planted aboard. And I know, with reasonable certainty, who's responsible."

"I see." He paused, as if gathering his thoughts. "Assuming you didn't set it yourself, why, if you had such knowledge, did you let this travesty happen?"

"I didn't *let* anything happen."

He rested his hands on his thick leather belt. "Four of my people are in the morgue and three more had to be airlifted out. There's at least a dozen in the clinic with serious burns, cuts, and who knows what else. All of that could have been prevented had we known in time. Had you told us."

Sam had been prepared for such an accusation. Had he been in the lawman's position, he'd have done the same.

"I'm sorry, Sheriff," Sam said. "If I could have prevented it, I would have, but I didn't figure it out until it was almost too late. As soon as I realized what was going on, I started shouting and moving people away. We tried to get everyone out, but there just wasn't time."

The sheriff's eyes cut to the chief for a second. The larger man nodded. Sheriff Austin lifted the brim of his hat and scratched the top of his head. "Alright. Besides needing to know who's responsible, I also need you to tell me how you came by this—what do you call it? —epiphany."

"I can't tell you how I knew, Sheriff."

"Listen, son," the sheriff said. "We don't just have dead and wounded. The owner of the boat was strung up, carved like a Thanksgiving turkey, torched, and then blown up. My men are scraping pieces of him up with spatulas."

Chief Palmer added, "And one of the people who died was one of mine."

"Before that," the sheriff continued, "a body washed up on shore that looked as though it had been put through a wood chipper. While all of this is going on, you show up. I don't believe in coincidences."

"Neither do I," Sam replied.

"I'm glad we agree on something. Folks are scared. And rightfully so. This kind of shit does *not* happen in my town." Sheriff Austin leaned in closer. "I don't give a rat's ass why you *think* you can't tell me. Right this minute, you are my only suspect. So, you're either going to talk here, or you'll do it from behind bars."

A woman's voice, from over Sam's shoulder, said, "The man who did this is Tyron Erebus."

Everyone turned to see Monica approaching, with Angel in tow.

Chet sighed. *Well, shit. This just keeps getting better and better. Here we go again.*

Monica strolled up to the group. "Remember me, Sheriff? The not-dead girl? Remember how we tried to tell you, but you didn't want to listen?" She held up her hands, indicating the devastation around them. "Well, this is the result."

"I don't have time for sarcasm, girl."

Rage filled Monica's hazel eyes. "No, I don't suppose you do. Now you've got no choice but to believe me, huh? Too bad you didn't have time to put your ego aside earlier. Maybe all of this could have been avoided."

Angel placed a hand on her friend's shoulder. "Mon, he couldn't have stopped it. Don't put this on him."

Monica took a deep breath and touched Angel's fingers. "Fine. Like I said, the man you want is Tyron Erebus. He did this." She gestured across the destruction. "All of this. He killed the girl in the papers too."

The sheriff pulled out a small notebook and began to write.

"He's an assassin hired by a drug lord named Laven Seth Michaels," she continued. "I saw something I shouldn't have and found myself the key witness who would have put him away for life. As you can imagine, he was very motivated to make sure I never made it to the courtroom. Only, Laven's dead now, killed by some other gang. Unfortunately, Tyron didn't get the memo."

The sheriff paused mid-scribble. "You want me to believe the mob hired a hitman to kill you? Darlin', I think you've been watching too much television."

"Seriously, Sheriff," Sam said. "Look around. Does it look like she's making this up?"

The sheriff stared at him. "And what exactly is *your* part in all of this?"

Sam started to reply, but Triniti—her face covered in soot, with an accessorizing blob of motor oil in her hair—marched up. She halted next to Sam. "That's what I want to know."

This shit is getting out of hand, Chet said. *And I don't know if you've noticed, but this scene is starting to look familiar.*

Angel pointed at Sam. "You want to know his part? For starters, he tried to kill Monica in Arizona."

Monica shook her head. "That's not exactly what happened."

"So you keep saying," Angel snapped. "Okay, fine. He's just seriously incompetent and led Erebus and the mob to you."

"We only got away because of him."

Angel's grimace devolved into a scowl. "Why do you keep defending him? Don't forget, he shot your computer too."

Sam ran a sweaty palm across his forehead. "Your computer had been compromised. Every time you logged on, it told him where to find you. *That's* how Erebus knew where you were. I saved both your asses."

Chet cocked his head. *You're not going to tell them that you had Monica in the crosshairs and almost put a bullet in her brain?*

Do you really think that's appropriate right now? I'm trying to get control of the situation.

Chet laughed. *You've not been in control of anything since we got here. What makes you think you can start now?*

Sam ignored his inner conscience, trying to focus instead on the conversation. If he didn't climb on top of this mess and get everyone cooperating, he might as well pour kerosene on the whole town and strike a match himself.

Monica cocked her head. "It did do something weird when I logged onto my email. The screen flickered several times. I thought it was going to crash, but then it stopped."

"Yes," Sam said. "That's probably when the tracker app installed itself."

"Okay, whatever. It doesn't matter how he found me; he just did. And just before that, you showed up. The two things have to be related."

"They were." He hesitated. "I was sent to find you as a possible person of interest in another case."

Buddy, Chet admonished, *that's not even close to the truth, and you——*

I don't care, Sam interrupted. *It's not important right now. In fact, it will never be important.*

Chet didn't reply.

Monica's eyes locked onto his. "What case? Who sent you?"

"I can't tell you that. But I'm here to eliminate Erebus and keep you safe."

Angel barked laughter. "Yeah, you're doing a bang-up job of that."

Monica furrowed her brow. "So, whoever sent you to find me has also sent you to kill Erebus? That's what you're saying, Peter?"

"Not exactly," Sam said, shaking his head. "I'm here on my own. I came because Erebus has to be stopped."

The sheriff broke in. "I thought your name was Sam. Who's Peter?"

"Peter was the cover name I used on my last assignment," Sam informed him.

Sheriff Austin looked unimpressed. "What are you FBI or CIA?"

"No, but something like that. It isn't important." Sam pointed at the lawman. "What is important is the longer we stand around here wasting time, the longer Erebus has to do something else. We need to find him, and in order to do that, I need you to tell me everything your people know."

The sheriff narrowed his eyes. "I don't care who you work for; you have no authority here. I don't have to tell you the time of day. For all I know, you're in cahoots with this Erebus person." Sheriff Austin's gaze lingered on Monica and Angel. "Maybe all of you are in this together."

"What exactly do you think is going on here?" Monica snapped, putting her hands on her hips. "Do you honestly believe I faked my own death and then came back a couple weeks later for some kind of murderous rampage? Do you truly believe that Peter would try and get everyone off the dock if *he* had planted the bomb?"

Aww, you fooled her. She doesn't think you're a murdering psychopath after all, Chet mused.

Shush. I've got enough going on without being distracted by you. Sam gazed over the carnage. The destruction. The pain. He had to fix this. With either his action or inaction, he had somehow made this all happen. And he had to somehow make it all right.

Angel turned to the sheriff. "Look, give the man whatever he needs to help you catch this guy."

Chief Palmer and Sheriff Austin glanced at one another. "What do you think, Sheriff?"

"I'm starting to think I never should have left LA." The lawman sighed. "At least there I understood the crazies."

The sheriff stared at Sam for several heartbeats, then let out a long, exasperated breath. "Fine. I'll help you, Sam, or Peter, or whatever the hell your name is, but only if *you* help *me*. Quid pro quo. You have to tell me what you know. I need to understand his motivations, and I need to know what the hell he's planning to do next."

"I don't know what he's planning," Sam said. He nodded toward Monica. "But I think his ultimate goal is to get her. He's obsessed and won't stop until she's dead."

"That's not very helpful. The dead girl in the ocean already told us that."

"Sheriff," the chief said. "Our records indicate that Leonard Thorsen was the boat's owner. Though we hadn't yet made a positive ID before the explosion, the victim tied to the mast matched Mr. Thorsen's age and physical description."

Sheriff Austin nodded. "I'll send a team to his house to see if our perp is hiding out there."

"If he was," Sam said, "he won't be there anymore. He'll have moved on. Forensics probably won't find anything of value either, but they should still do their due diligence. When I searched April's house, it looked as though it had been wiped clean."

The sheriff frowned. "Who's April?"

Sam took a deep breath. "April Goodman. She was the vic you found washed up on shore a couple weeks ago."

A collective gasp rose from the group.

Huge tears welled up in Triniti's eyes. "This guy killed April? *She* was the one in the paper?"

"Triniti, I'm sorry." Sam took her hand. "I just found out a little bit ago that she was your friend."

She yanked her hand free while violently shaking her head. "No. No. No, that can't be. She can't be gone." The tears rolled down her cheeks.

The sheriff's eyes lingered on the heartbroken woman; they narrowed, growing hard as he focused on Sam. "You should have alerted us as soon as you found out. Instead, you withheld information, tampered with evidence, and compromised a crime scene."

Sam held his gaze. "We don't have time for propriety. We need to collect as much evidence as possible, as quickly as possible, so we can find this guy."

"Propriety? The laws are in place for a reason and you're breaking every one of them. It's no wonder you almost got this young lady killed. I don't care who you work for, I'm taking you in for obstruction—"

The radio clipped to the lawman's belt squawked to life. "Good evening, Sheriff."

Sam's blood went cold. "It's him. It's Erebus."

Monica nodded her assent. "He's right. Be careful, Sheriff."

The sheriff paused, his eyes lingering on Sam. He thumbed the receiver. "Who is this?"

When he released the button, the radio static, which previously had melded seamlessly with the subtle grumble of ocean waves, now blared as ominous as the ringing of the phone at three in the morning.

As the seconds spun out, Sam wondered if the psychopath wouldn't answer.

The buzz broke. "I would have phoned, but you seem to be having...technical difficulties with your cell service. Are you having a little trouble talking to the outside world, Sheriff? I thought by now you'd have gotten it fixed." He tsked. "Modern communication systems are so fragile. One piece goes down and none of it works."

"What's he talking about?" the chief asked.

"After these two," the sheriff nodded toward Angel and Monica, "stopped by my office, I issued an emergency work order to add more crews. I issued another granting the use of the police helicopter to get the internet and cell service restored. It's expensive, and using the Huey adds risk. But I needed to get the coroner's report. Based on her conclusions, I might have had to call the CSI unit back in."

The sheriff glanced at Angel. "I'm not as incompetent as *some* people want to believe." He turned back to the chief. "The crews worked all day and had just strung up the temporary line when some relay overloaded and fried the cell tower's base station. So, until bridge access is restored, we're completely cut off."

Monica's face dropped. "He wants us isolated. It makes us easier to pick off."

The sheriff reached for the radio. "I'd best find out what he wants."

Sam grabbed his wrist. "Let me do it."

"Son, don't you think you've caused enough damage?"

"No, he's right, Sheriff," Angel said. "He's got the training and he knows this guy."

Monica blinked. "You've been arguing the opposite for weeks now."

"I know. But incompetent or not, there isn't anyone else that can stop him."

Monica looked deep into her friend's eyes. "Let him do it, Sheriff."

Skepticism lined the lawman's face as he glanced between the two. Finally, he unclipped the handheld from his belt and handed it to Sam.

All eyes watched as he lifted the radio to his lips. "This is Sam."

Chapter Twenty-Three

G ood evening, Samuel." Tyron Erebus' voice echoed through a dozen police radios all around the beach as though an army of psychopaths were invading by sea.

Sam paused as something nagged at him from the back of his mind. He tried to grab it, but it eluded him. Letting it go for now, he spoke into the handheld. "Hello, asshole. You know you're going to pay for what you did tonight." He had little energy left and even less patience.

A chuckle traveled across the airwaves. "Your generation is so unrefined. Everyday civilities, such as the art of small talk and common pleasantries, are foreign concepts. I blame bad parenting and a failed public school system. But as far as the events that have unfolded, this is only a little preview of what's to come."

Sheriff Austin touched the radio in Sam's hand. "Find out what he wants."

Sam nodded and pressed the button. "What's the point to all of this?"

"My point," Erebus said, "is twofold. First, I want you and everyone else to understand the seriousness of my resolve and the stakes of the game you're playing."

"No one doubts your seriousness. What else?"

"Second—and I'll admit, this would have been more for my own personal pleasure than practicality—since you are always sticking your nose where it doesn't belong, I figured there'd be better than fifty-fifty odds you'd get caught up in my little getting-acquainted present. But just like when we met in St. Louis, Lady Luck seems to carry your fortune."

Sam thumbed the receiver. "That wasn't luck; I kicked your ass in St. Louis."

The reply came immediately. "I'd hardly frame the incident in such vulgar terms." Undertones of anger rippled through Tyron's voice. "What was merely a minor setback for me was probably a major victory for you."

Sam kept pressing on the nerve. "And how's your complexion these days? As I recall, after I shot your face off, I left you lying in a pool of your own blood. Had you not busted the place up—and if you'd died the way everyone had hoped—the restaurant's special of the day would have been Soup de La Asshole."

The crackle of static broke. "Classy. An unfortunate complication, but one of no consequence. And might I remind you that it was *you* who damaged that second-rate eating establishment with your barbaric warmongering. I only disposed of the bargain-basement cook."

"You're getting off topic," the sheriff whispered.

Sam nodded and spoke into the radio. "Tell you what, let's you and me meet someplace. We'll hash this out."

"How very noble of you," Erebus said. "But we aren't going to draw pistols at twenty paces. This isn't the Old West. I don't care about you at all. I was assigned to take care of the girl, and I will complete my task. No one and nothing will get in the way of that."

Sam pressed the radio's transmit button. "That job is over. Your boss is dead. I shouldn't have to be chasing you around the country because you shouldn't even be here."

"Yet, here we are."

"Listen closely." Sam enunciated each word. "Your. Boss. Is. Dead."

Erebus tsked. "Your reasoning says more about you and your lack of work ethics than an entire dissertation on the subject. To alleviate your naiveté, let me explain it to you. Mr. Laven paid me to complete an assignment. Just because he's been disposed of does not negate my obligation."

"How about I give you an assignment? Please pay close attention; write it down if you think it'll help you remember. Ready? Take your gun, stick it in your mouth, and eat a bullet."

The killer's smile echoed in his voice. "Oh, come now. Surely we can settle this like civilized men."

"Civilized men? Do you honestly believe that what you did to April was 'civilized?'"

Erebus' voice took on a professorial tone. "I took that which was severely flawed and made it beautiful. By removing the ugliness of sin, one can create art. I know that you are not a refined man, but surely even you can see that."

"All I see is a rabid dog that needs to be put down," Sam snapped.

Sheriff Austin placed a hand over the radio before Sam could continue. "He's getting into your head. Stop letting him mess with you."

Sam cursed under his breath. The lawman was right.

Until this moment, Sam had believed that the carefully crafted emotional armor he'd forged over the years was flawless and impenetrable. But the corrosive acid of guilt and a puzzling sense of obligation had created soft spots in the metal. By the malignant glow of Erebus' aura, the fatigue along the joints and the rust decaying the seams showed like a tumor on a CT scan. He'd entered into this battle certain of his defensive superiority, but the entire suit—from helmet to the sollerets—offered no more protection than an overactive imagination against an archer's arrows.

Perhaps these vulnerabilities hadn't stemmed from his emotional entanglement with Monica but from a subconscious distrust of the crumbling hierarchy at The Agency. Even if he hadn't been aware of it at the time, the foundation of his world had begun dissolving the second blood money had been exchanged for his services. Forcing him to find his own purpose. His own morality.

Regardless of its source, if he didn't regain control, if he didn't recast the breastplate of indifference and shield of stoicism, he might as well hand himself—and everyone else in town—over to the murderer and be done with it.

Rule #101:
Stay completely emotionally detached.

Emotions skew perceptions, jade conclusions, and distort judgement. Isolate them. Always. To stay objective and remain in control of a situation, emotions of every variety have to be removed from the equation. It is impossible to be effective when angry, sad, happy, frustrated, or joyful. Even something as simple as annoyance will hinder objectivity and prolificacy. Using your opponent's emotions against them is your greatest weapon. Letting them use yours against you is theirs.

—122 Rules of Psychology

Sam took a deep breath. With a sieve of resolve, he filtered out the anger and frustration pounding through his heart. Gathering the impurities from his bloodstream into a mass that would make an oncologist blanch, he locked them away. Sealing them in the emotional vault with everything else that might chink his armor.

Relieved of sentimental burdens, Sam reevaluated. In previous assignments, the considerable resources of The Agency had always provided the advantage of knowing more than his adversaries. But now things were flipped. Erebus had known Sam would see and follow the boat. He'd known Sam would be on the pier when it exploded. He'd known Sam would help with the wounded and that he would answer this call. Each move had been more calculated and strategic than a chess grandmaster foretelling checkmate.

Sam needed to throw Erebus off his game. Instead of replying, he let the minutes slip away.

The static on the radio broke. "Have you calmed yourself?" Erebus asked.

The group stared at Sam, but he still didn't answer.

Another minute went by before the static broke again. "Samuel, did you run away? Maybe I should talk to the sheriff if you're too distracted by your bimbo and Polynesian princess?"

Angel frowned. "What's he talking about?"

"I'm the princess," Triniti said. "Technically, I'm half Samoan, not Polynesian. But, clearly 'bimbo' is a reference to you."

Angel started to say something, but Sam shushed her as he finished silently counting. *One. Two. Three.* "No. I'm here."

"I would like to come to an arrangement," Erebus said. "A truce if you will."

After waiting the full three count, Sam replied, "What did you have in mind?"

"You undoubtedly would like for me to leave. I am exhausted of this ridiculous town. Give me my property, and I will go with no further bloodshed."

One. Two. Three. "And what exactly is it that you think belongs to you?"

"The girl, of course," Erebus replied. "She belongs to me."

"No."

"Are you sure about that? Perhaps you should ask the good sheriff or put it to a vote with a committee? One worthless tramp to save dozens, if not hundreds."

Sam counted. "I've already offered myself. That's the best you're going to get."

Irritation tinged the killer's voice. "I have no interest in you."

"How about a compromise then?"

Static buzzed for several seconds before Erebus replied. "What sort of compromise?"

Sam made Tyron wait. *One. Two. Three.* "If you allow the sheriff to take you into custody, I might be able persuade Monica to come visit you."

The killer's reply almost came on top of Sam's words. "I wish you would be sincere."

Sam spoke into the radio. "I meant what I said."

"No, I don't believe you did." An edge of impatience wove through the tone of Erebus' words. "You have not presented anything that I find acceptable. Didn't they teach you negotiation tactics at The Agency?"

Rule #39:
If what you are doing is predictable, do the unexpected.

—122 Rules of Psychology

Instead of answering, Sam turned his attention to the sheriff. "Can you track him by the handheld?"

"No." He shook his head. "These units don't have transponders."

Sam handed the radio to the sheriff. "In that case then, Sheriff, please order all of your deputies to turn off their radios."

Sheriff Austin arched his eyebrows and pushed back his hat. He stared at Sam for several seconds, and then a slight grin tugged at the corners of his lips. "I can't do that, but I can do the next best thing." He took the device. "Dispatch, this is Sheriff Austin."

A no-nonsense voice squawked from the radio. "Go ahead, Sheriff."

"Whose radio has been compromised?"

A brief pause. "Deputy Adams'."

Though he maintained a professional demeanor, sadness tinged the lawman's eyes. The officer in question had probably died at the hands of the lunatic. "Please disable Deputy Adams' radio."

The dispatcher replied with a ten-four.

The psychopath army snarled over a dozen speakers. "How dare you silence me. You think this is a game? I'll string bodies from here to Canada. I'll spill so much blood, there won't be anyone left to——"

The radio fell silent.

The sheriff sighed. "Dispatch, get a party out to Adams' last ten-twenty."

"Ten-four, Sheriff."

"Why did you do that?" Chief Palmer asked.

Sam started toward the hodgepodge of police and EMT vehicles. "Negotiations have failed. Nothing could be gained by continuing the conversation. Besides, we have another person to save."

The chief called after him. "Who?"

Sam turned back. "Max."

Chapter Twenty-Four

Triniti blinked, confusion and concern clearing away the sadness in her eyes. "Max? What about him?"

Sam refrained from telling her that her friend had almost certainly become another casualty in the one-man war waged by a psychopath who had chosen violence as his hobby and savagery as his occupation. "I think..." Sam tried to find exactly the right words that would keep her from having false hopes but also not crush her heart prematurely. "He's in trouble. We need to get to his shop. Now."

Triniti's eyes glistened, huge and jaundiced in the harsh florescent lights. "What kind of trouble?"

"The Erebus kind. Where's your car, Triniti?"

Chief Palmer picked up his clipboard, shaking the sand off of it. "Do you need me to come? We can take a bus if we need to."

"You need all of your ambulances, Chief," Sam said. "Stay here. Take care of your people and finish your investigation."

The sheriff folded his arms. "You may as well go; this is my investigation now."

Chief Palmer frowned. "Oh no. Those were my people that—"

"Stop," Sam said, looking at each of them in turn. "What we need is interdepartmental cooperation. You two working together will be far more effective than fighting over jurisdiction. Pool your resources. Find out what you can about the explosives and figure out where they came from. It seems unlikely Erebus brought them to town with him. We have to keep him from getting more."

The two men locked eyes, sharing a silent conversation.

The lawman gave a curt nod and turned back to Sam. Exhaustion, anger, and determination filled the sheriff's eyes. The lines on his face had turned from foot paths to canyons since he'd issued Sam the traffic ticket about a thousand years ago.

"Make my job easier," he said, dropping his voice to a whisper. "Put the bastard down. The judge's nephew was one of the casualties tonight. I think the court would be...understanding if this guy never made it to trial."

Sam hadn't been concerned about going to jail, but at least he wouldn't have to contend with an ambitious city prosecutor if he inadvertently removed Erebus from the gene pool without due process. "We'll do our best."

Triniti grabbed Sam's hand and tugged. "Come on. You said we needed to go, so let's go."

He followed her past the *Mile 2* marker, over the dune, and into a small parking lot. Hinges screeched as she yanked open the door of an old orange Volkswagen bus and hopped into the driver's seat. Monica and Angel, who had been silently following them, climbed into the back while Sam took shotgun.

Triniti started the engine, backed out of the space, dropped the transmission into first, and floored the accelerator. The engine revved like a windup car, only with less oomph. Even after Triniti put the pedal to the metal, the vehicle trundled down the road like a sloth on Valium.

Angel leaned forward between the front two seats. "Hey, can you pick it up a little?"

"Well, excuse me, Ms. Danica Patrick," Triniti snapped, "but your pit crew seems to have forgotten to install the turbo booster."

Angel harrumphed and sat back.

I'm with Angel on this one, Chet said. *We could walk faster than this.*

Sam watched the road slide under a windshield roughly the size of a baseball diamond as the vehicle gingerly got up to speed. *Patience. It isn't far. We'll get there. Besides, I'm not sure if it matters.*

Are you prepared to deal with their wrath if what we suspect happened to Max has, in fact, happened? Right now, you have the support of the chief and the sheriff. But if Max is dead, this whole thing could come apart. It's not like they're ever going to give you the key to the city or anything, but if this goes south, you'll lose the few fans you've got.

I don't care about fans. I just want Erebus to die.

Sam rubbed his temples and glanced around at the anxious faces staring out the windshield. He tried to formulate some kind of plan, but exhaustion chewed on his bones like ravenous coyotes, numbing his senses and fogging his mind. He needed to find some way to keep going.

He envisioned the burning man running aimlessly on the dock. His screams had washed over the beach like a tsunami of napalm as the flames consumed his flesh. The scene shifted to the boy with the cleat sticking out of his ribcage. Sam recalled those young and frightened eyes the moment before death removed the disbelief and incomprehension from their depths, replacing it with a dark vacancy.

A spark of anger lit in Sam's soul. As he paraded the images of the senseless, merciless brutality through his imagination, the flame became a roiling, furious inferno. Sam drew strength from the rage. It fueled him, and as it did, his fatigue vanished and his mind cleared. *I just hope Erebus is there. Maybe we can finish this thing tonight.*

Chet folded his arms. *Really? What are you gonna do? Slap him with a surfboard? Throw rocks at him?*

Sam cursed under his breath. *You're right. We have to equalize the playing field.* He turned to Triniti. "Slight detour. Go to my hotel. The Alabaster Inn."

"Seriously?" she said, giving him an uncertain side-eyed glance. "You told me we needed to get to Max. You said he's in trouble."

"Just do it."

She gave him a dirty look but spun the steering wheel sharply, guiding the wobbly vehicle off the main street and down an alley. Two minutes later, they came to a stop with a squeak of the brakes.

"Wait here," Sam said and leapt out. He ran through the sliding glass door of the lobby and tore across the small entryway. Bypassing the elevator, he took the stairs two at a time. Busting through the fire exit, he barreled down the hall and jammed the plastic key into the door's card reader. The LED indicator flashed red and then buzzed unhappily. He cursed and tried again. On the third attempt, the lock clicked.

Chet held up his hands. *Stop. You need to think before you*—

Without letting Chet finish his thought, Sam pushed open the door and raced inside. *What? Why?* He slapped the wall switch as he entered the short hallway. Nothing happened. The room remained concealed in shadows.

As the door behind him closed with a soft *snick*, Sam halted, understanding Chet's warning several seconds too late.

A floor lamp blazed to life, bathing the room in brightness.

"Hello, Mr. Bradford." Erebus sat in the lone wingback chair against the window. With triumph in his grin, he aimed a gun at Sam's chest.

Chet sighed. *That's why. The prick disabled the overhead, and in case you don't recognize it, that's your gun.*

Sam considered leaping at the killer, trying to catch him off guard, but a football field of mangy green carpet lay between the two of them. He wouldn't make it two steps across the abyss before a bullet—one of Sam's own—stopped him cold.

He glanced around the space, looking for an advantage. But Erebus had removed anything that could have been used as a weapon and stacked it in the corner. It looked as though he'd planned to hold a cheap hotel furniture and knickknack yard sale. Everything must go.

Since Sam couldn't go on the offensive, he would have to wait for an opportunity. It would come.

He stared the murderer in the eyes. "You've been busy."

Erebus gave a slight shrug. "You know what they say. Idle hands are the devil's workshop."

Chet motioned toward Tyron. *You'd better do something and do it quick because right now, he's holding all the cards.*

Sam studied the man with the gun for a heartbeat. *Not all of them.*

Instead of addressing Erebus, he turned, casually strolled past the madman, and walked into the bathroom. After closing the door, he unzipped his fly and took a long, slow leak, letting the splash make as much noise as possible. He flushed the toilet and took his time washing his hands.

When he came out, he removed his bloodstained shirt and started rummaging around in his duffle. Sam muttered, "I can't find anything in this mess." Shaking his head in disgust, he upended the bag, dumping the contents onto the bed. He began to hum quietly as he folded each of the garments, stacking them in neat piles. Selecting a clean shirt, he put it on, buttoned it, and then checked his reflection in the mirror.

Erebus hadn't said a word during this series of events, but a little of the smugness in his eyes had given way to indignity.

We need to go, Chet urged.

Sam's taut nerves began to fray with anxiety. *Yes, I know, but I've got a little situation here in case you haven't forgotten.*

Well, this isn't Project Runway, and you aren't in a modeling competition. Get on with it.

Picking up his wallet and the keycard from the dresser where he'd deposited them before using the bathroom, Sam headed toward the door.

As he reached for the handle, Erebus leapt up from his chair as though the seat cushion had come to life and slapped his bottom. "You so much as lay a finger on that knob and I'll blow it off."

Sam glanced into the full-length mirror hung on the back of the door, pleased to see that the killer's face had turned an amusing shade of red.

"I figured you'd want to go somewhere else to, you know." Sam nodded toward the gun in the mirror.

"Now why would you figure that?" Erebus asked, his gaze narrowing with suspicion. "Why wouldn't I just kill you here?"

Sam slowly spun around. "Because if that was your plan, then you would have already done it. Besides, you may be a sadistic bastard, but you aren't stupid. You know that about thirty seconds after you shoot me, you'll have the sheriff and his posse of deputies crawling up your ass like a bad case of hemorrhoids. Who, just so you're aware, told me not to bother making sure you get your day in court, if you catch my drift. And even *if* you manage to evade the police, after your little stunt with the boat, pretty much everyone in town is hoping to rip off a large chunk of your ass. Not even you can take on a mob of angry citizens by yourself. But if you're so inclined, then go ahead. Shoot me."

Erebus' cheeks turned crimson.

"It just seems," Sam mused, "like getting killed might cramp your style. It would be especially irksome to die for someone you said you weren't even interested in." *Come on, try it. Come get me.*

Though the killer's posture remained tense and alert, a slow smile slinked across his lips. "You're right. Killing you here would cause unnecessary complications. It would also deny me the pleasure of shooting off little pieces of you, one at a time."

Sam turned and grabbed the door handle. "See? That's the spirit." When he pulled it toward him, he kept the man in the mirror in his peripheral vision. If Erebus stayed far enough behind, Sam might be able to use the door as a barrier. He'd have to time it just right though.

"Use the stopper to prop it open," Erebus said. "Don't let it close."

Doing as instructed, Sam led the way to the elevator and pressed the down arrow. The close proximity inside the small car would allow him to attack while minimizing the chance of getting shot.

Erebus shook his head. "No. The stairs."

"But I'm tired."

Erebus smiled as though a small child had just tried to play a silly—and obvious—prank on him. He gestured with the gun toward the fire exit.

Sam continued along the hallway. He pulled open the door and waltzed down the stairs, his senses alert for any distraction that might capture the killer's attention. He only needed a half a second, but they had this section of the building to themselves. He pushed through the emergency exit on the ground floor and walked across the deserted lobby.

The sliding glass entrance whooshed open, and they left the building. Sam hadn't seen another soul, which was for the best because his grumpy new traveling companion probably would have put a bullet in any potential witnesses.

Sam needed to draw him away from Triniti and the girls waiting in the bus. He couldn't protect them while also disabling Erebus. If the murderer tried to shoot one or all of them, Sam might not be able stop him. Best to keep him distracted.

Sam headed in the opposite direction of the rumbling VW. Stretching and yawning, he made a great show of enjoying the cool night air. "Where too?"

"Brown car in the back of the lot."

"Graduated to grand theft auto, I see. You're the curdled cream of the crop, Erebus. Your momma must be so proud."

"You can stop now, Mr. Bradford. As I told you on the radio, you've had your victory. That was a gift. You won't get another by goading me."

Sam shrugged and smiled meekly. "Can't fool you, can I, E? Well, you can't blame a guy for trying."

Erebus didn't reply as he followed Sam to the rear of the parking lot and away from the VW.

Chapter Twenty-Five

The drumming of Triniti's fingernails against the steering wheel drizzled grains of chafing sand into every wrinkle of Monica's brain. She could barely resist snapping off the surfer's press-ons and tossing them out the window.

"What the hell is taking so long?" Triniti groused. "We're supposed to be in a hurry."

Monica gritted her teeth. Triniti's reputation for being a powder keg with a volatile temper and an abysmally short fuse preceded her. She might have stopped with the damned drumming if asked, or—most likely—she would explode, making the situation even worse. "I have long ago given up trying to understand this guy."

On the seat next to Monica, half-hunched and arms folded, Angel glowered at Triniti. "You really should reconsider getting involved with this guy."

Triniti turned around to face her. "Seriously? *You're* giving *me* dating advice?" Her gaze traveled the length of Angel's lithe body, a smile as warm and inviting as a frosty glass of formaldehyde forming on her full lips. "You're nothing but a surly, lowlife grocery clerk with no future, no social skills, and a surprising ability to repel any man with a pulse."

"And you're a has-been surfer wannabe who has to turn tricks for tips because she's the worst waitress on the planet."

Triniti's fake smile flattened. "I happen to be the reigning regional female surfing champion. I've tamed waves all up and down the West Coast."

"That's not all you've tamed up and down the West Coast."

Triniti narrowed her eyes and bared her teeth. "Listen—"

Despite the danger of getting caught in the crossfire, Monica leaned between the would-be combatants before hostilities escalated out of control. "Not now." She gave each of them a withering glare.

Angel raised her hand at Triniti. "If she wants to go there, I'll take her."

"With so much crap to worry about?" Monica snapped. "We don't need to add to it by fighting amongst ourselves."

Angel and Triniti each huffed and turned away, staring out their respective windows.

"We have to get moving," Angel said, continuing to gaze out the side pane of glass. "We should be doing something besides sitting on our asses while this idiot's boyfriend takes his sweet time having brunch with the queen, or whatever he's doing. I say we go in after him."

"Sam said to wait here," Triniti replied, not looking Angel's way. "He's trained in Special Ops or something. Maybe even Delta Force. We do what he says."

Angel barked out a harsh laugh. "You're shitting me. Sister, you watch way too much TV. You have no idea who he is or what he's done, but I can tell you he sure as shit isn't Delta Force. Tell ya what, you wait here for just as long as you want, but I'm going in." She popped open the side door.

Monica turned to stop her when movement caught the corner of her eye. She peered deep into the gloom of the parking lot. Two figures emerged from the shadows. As they walked under a puddle of illumination, cast by an overhead lamp, her blood turned to liquid nitrogen. Satan's lackey held a gun to Sam's back as they walked away from the hotel.

Monica put a hand on Angel's shoulder. "Hold on." She pointed. "Look."

They all craned their necks, staring out the pizza box rear window of the bus.

Triniti frowned. "That's Sam, but who's the other guy?"

"Your worst nightmare," Angel replied.

"Where are they going?"

Angel slid her door shut. "I don't know, but I'm not going to let them get there." She turned to Triniti. "Move over."

Triniti blinked, consternation and confusion written across her face. "Wha——?"

"Now!" Angel grabbed the regional surfing champion by the arm, hauled her up, and tossed her into the passenger seat. Shoving past Triniti, Angel climbed behind the steering wheel. She released the emergency brake and pressed the accelerator. The engine revved, but the vehicle did not move.

275

Swiping her hair out of her face, Triniti sat up straight. She crossed her arms and pouted from the passenger seat. "It's a manual transmission, dummy. You need to put it in gear first."

Angel pressed the clutch and wrestled the stick shift into first. The van lurched and stalled, rocking all three of them forward in their seats. Cursing, she smacked the steering wheel. When she turned the ignition, something in the back of the bus ground unhappily.

Triniti glared. "What are you doing? You're going to ruin my Volksie!"

Angel ignored her as she tried again. This time, the engine roared to life like an enraged meerkat. As she eased up on the clutch, Angel growled low in her throat, and the bus started to roll.

☆☆☆☆

Sam continued leading Erebus away from the VW, to the opposite side of the parking lot. "I really am amazed that you're still on the case, seeing as how your boss is dead and all." He subtly picked up his pace as he jabbered.

Erebus matched his cadence but did not comment on the increase in tempo. "I have an infallible work ethic. My boss paid for a job to be done. As I said, the change in his situation does not relieve me of my duty."

"I guess not, but this feels like it's more than a job to you. It seems personal."

In the distance, the VW's engine died.

What are they doing? Sam asked his inner conscience.

Chet grimaced at the unmistakable grinding of gears. *I don't know, but if they don't hold it down, your friend here is going to notice.*

"There's something bigger at stake," Erebus said, seemingly oblivious to the chaos ensuing on the other side of the parking lot. "Something you couldn't possibly comprehend."

The engine whined and immediately dropped in RPMs as the driver engaged the transmission.

Sam expected the sound to diminish as they drove away. Instead, it seemed to be getting louder, as if they were getting closer. Confused, he glanced back over his shoulder at the killer, hoping to spot the vehicle in his peripheral vision. "Really? Why don't you enlighten me then?"

I don't know what they're planning, but get ready, Chet warned.

I think I know what they're up to, but I have to keep him distracted to pull it off.

Sam lifted his hands away from his sides and stopped.

Erebus bumped him in the back with the gun. He must have thought better of being so close while brandishing a firearm and moved several steps away.

Slowly, Sam turned around. "You know what, I've changed my mind. I don't care about your big picture stakes nonsense. I don't care what your goals are or what motivates you. In fact, I don't care about you at all."

Erebus stared at him. "Tell me then, Mr. Bradford, what do you care about? What is it you want?"

Sam closed the distance between them until the weapon pressed against his abdomen. "You really want to know?"

"More than anything."

"I want you to drop the gun. I want to finish what we started in St. Louis."

After seeming to consider the offer, Erebus cocked the hammer and raised the gun, pressing the barrel against Sam's heart. "I don't know what kind of game you're trying to play, Mr. Bradford. But I don't have the time nor the patience for it."

Sam glared at him. "Oh, I'm not playing." He leaned harder against the weapon. "I'm in this for keeps."

☆☆☆☆

Monica tensed as Angel circled the van around.

Triniti huffed and sat back in her seat. "Congratulations. You can drive. What's your plan now, Einstein?"

Nostrils flaring, Angel spun the wheel, straightening the vehicle and aiming for the men.

The killer had his gun pressed to Sam's chest, and they appeared to be arguing. Neither paid attention as Angel narrowed the distance.

The engine revved harder—the infuriated meerkat raging—and the vehicle slowly picked up speed.

Monica stared, waiting for the explosion and smoke of the killer's gun. "Come on. Come on," she muttered, willing the bus to move faster. She held on tight to the back of Angel's seat as they sailed to an unlikely rescue.

☆☆☆☆

The knocking of the engine grew louder as it ricocheted around the parking lot, making it difficult for Sam to triangulate its position.

Here they come, Chet warned.

Sam stared into Erebus' eyes. "I'm not playing games. You are. You're the one killing innocents all in the name of completing some lame mission. Surely Laven must have insisted you keep a low profile, but instead, you're blowing up boats and skinning girls alive. Your name is on the lips of every person in town, and about four government agencies are out hunting for you. That doesn't seem very low profile to me."

Chet tensed. *Ready...*

"Oh, come now, Mr..." Erebus' words trailed off as he glanced over his shoulder and into the blinding headlights of the oncoming bus.

Chet shouted. *Now!*

Sam leapt back while simultaneously plucking the gun from Erebus' outstretched hand. When he landed, Sam's feet tangled and he tripped, falling heavily onto the dark asphalt between two parked cars.

The VW flew past. The murderer grunted as the bus collided with him.

Tires squealed. Metal crunched with metal.

He rolled to his feet and darted toward the stalled Volkswagen, which had collided into a parked car several spaces away. As he ran, Sam caught a glimpse of the killer's unmoving legs on the far side of the accident. He silently prayed that the part of Erebus he couldn't see had been crushed in the wreckage.

A man ran out of the lobby and yelled. "What happened?"

Sam called back, "Get the sheriff. There's been an accident."

The man nodded and sprinted back into the building.

Sam tried the passenger door, but it had buckled in the impact. He ran around to the driver's side. Angel leaned against the steering wheel; blood oozed from a gash above her eye.

Pulling open the door, he checked her pulse. Steady and strong. From the passenger compartment, Triniti groaned as she rubbed her forehead and grimaced.

In the back seat, Monica slowly sat up. "What happened?"

Sam popped open her door and gently touched her scalp, looking for blood. "You killed the bad guy."

"Did we?" She burped as she stared vacantly ahead. "Go us." Monica leaned her head between her knees and vomited onto the floor.

Triniti glanced around. "What's that awful smell?" She looked at the mess Monica had made. "This is exactly why I don't let other people drive my Volksie." She closed her eyes and leaned back. "I suppose that Angel is still alive too."

Sam pulled a rag from behind the seat and handed it to Monica. "Yes, everyone seems to be okay."

"This night just gets better and better," Triniti said. "At least tell me we got the bastard."

"You did. Hit him good."

"Were you fighting with Erebus?" Triniti asked. "It looked like he was about to shoot you."

"He was waiting for me in my hotel room. I was trying to keep him distracted so he didn't notice the three of you in the car."

Triniti stared at Sam for several heartbeats, and then her face hardened. "Okay, well it looks like we're all fine here, so maybe you should go arrest him or something before he gets up and walks away."

Chet laughed. *Even she knows your job better than you do.*

Sam looked over the three women once again before he skirted the end of the vehicle. As he rounded the bumper, he froze. He'd expected a gory mess of serial killer pulp, but instead only twisted metal and broken glass awaited him. He pulled out his gun and went around to the far side of the parked car. No one lay battered and bruised in the shadows. *Shit.*

Chet shook his head. *You can say that again.*

Sam scoured the immediate area and trampled through the nearby bushes, but the killer appeared to have vanished.

A police cruiser pulled up and Sheriff Austin emerged, looking tired and ragged. "I'm assuming that you found him and that this," he indicated the damaged vehicles, "is a result of that encounter."

Sam nodded. "The ladies in the van are banged up, but I think they're going to be okay. We need to get an EMT here to check them over though, just in case."

The sheriff's exhausted eyes flared. "Oh, well, let me just round up a couple of extra medics. Oh, wait, I can't because they're all cleaning up the *other* mess he created earlier tonight." In spite of his words, he thumbed the CB radio clipped to his shoulder and called in the accident.

"Roger that," squawked the voice on the other end of the receiver.

Sam began poking through the bushes again.

"What are you looking for?" the sheriff asked.

Sam moved aside a thick clump of branches. "Erebus surprised me in my hotel room. The ladies ran him down with the car and now I'm looking for his body."

The sheriff pulled out a large Magnum flashlight and shined it around.

While they searched, the EMTs arrived and began attending to the women.

Monica hobbled over, a thick blanket draped across her narrow shoulders. "He's not here, is he?"

Sam stopped and looked around, trying to determine which direction Erebus would have gone. "No, he's not."

Even in the subdued lighting of the parking lot, Sam could see the disappointment in her eyes.

She turned and trudged back to the bus.

"What now, James Bond?" the sheriff asked.

Sam took in the small parking lot. "We need to form a perimeter around this area. He just got hit by a car, so he couldn't have gotten far."

"My men are already stretched thin, but I'll see if there's anyone left that can be spared." He scratched his head and glanced at Monica. "That girl's right. It's too late. Hit by a car or not, he's gone."

Sam locked eyes with the lawman's and nodded. Somehow, the killer had slipped through his fingers. Again.

Chapter Twenty-Six

Sam walked around the VW, inspecting the smashed headlight, caved-in grill, and twisted bumper. While cosmetically displeasing, it looked as though the damage wouldn't be debilitating.

He climbed into the driver's seat and turned the ignition. Despite his mechanical diagnosis of "dented but functional," he half expected the vehicle not to start; but the engine cranked, burbling like a fat baby blowing bubbles.

Angel, who'd been sitting on a curb next to a blanket-wrapped Monica, said something. They stood, making their way to the bus.

Triniti jumped up from the back of the ambulance, surprising the EMT bandaging a gash on her arm, and half-stumbled across the parking lot. "Hey! What are you doing?"

Sam rolled down the window. "I'm going to Max's."

"Well, I'm coming too." Before Sam could reply, she limped around to the passenger side and yanked on the door handle. The bus rocked slightly, but the door didn't budge.

As Monica and Angel pulled open the back slider and plopped onto the bench seat, Triniti heaved and grunted without success. Giving up, she followed the others to the side door. She started to get in but stopped halfway, wrinkling her nose in disgust. Triniti grabbed the puke-covered floor mat and tossed it onto the parking lot.

Cursing under her breath about losers and idiots trying to destroy her baby, Triniti slid onto the backseat, knocking Angel aside with the bump of a curvy hip.

Angel scowled and grunted as she collided with Monica.

Sam turned around to face them. "I know you want to see this through, but my advice is for you all to stay here. It's too risky."

"Seriously?" Angel laughed humorlessly. "He can't be *that* dangerous. We just ran him down with the car."

Triniti rolled her eyes. "How many times do I have to say it? It's not a *car*; it's a Volksie. But the point is true enough. Danica Patrick here smashed the bastard good. If he's still alive, he's hurt bad."

Sam needed to deal with Erebus on a level playing field, and he would be severely handicapped if he had to be a nursemaid for three bystanders. "Hurt or not, I don't think you understand just how dangerous he really is."

Three pairs of furious eyes glared at him. Sam began to wonder if it had actually been safer for him back in the hotel with the psychopath pointing a gun at his chest.

Angel reached past Triniti and pulled the door closed. She fell back into the seat. "Your 'concern' over our well-being is so stupid I'm not even sure it warrants a response, but I'll try. We just hit the lunatic with the car. You thought he was pissed before...now he probably wants to shish kebab us all. Not to mention that he could be *anywhere*. Max's, my apartment, your hotel, the damned grocery store. Since you claim you want to keep us safe, I'm not sure how abandoning us to fend for ourselves, when we are just as likely to run into him walking down the street as you are at Max's, helps you achieve that goal. But I'm going to chalk up your idiocy to exhaustion."

Sam started to protest, but Angel placed a finger on his lips. "No. No more talking. No more advice. No more anything." She pointed out the front window. "Drive."

He stared at her for a heartbeat and, without replying, turned around and dropped the gearshift into reverse. When he let up on the clutch, the bus resisted, still hung up on the parked car. Sam applied a little more gas, and, with an indignant squawk of metal, they jolted backwards. Sliding the VW into first gear, he headed to the exit.

In the rearview mirror, Saw watched as the sheriff got out of his patrol car. The lawman's gaze followed them as they rumbled out of the parking lot.

In LA, the police would have arrested Sam for fleeing the scene of a crime and driving away evidence. But Sheriff Austin made no move to stop them. Sam gave a silent thanks to small-town rule bending.

Thick anticipation, like the electrified humidity preceding an oncoming tornado, filled the interior of the vehicle as Sam navigated the empty city streets. He had less than ten minutes to come up with a plan and about a thousand contingencies. He needed to—

Triniti leaned up between the front seats, breaking the silence and his train of thought. "You never told us why you think Max is in trouble."

"I don't think, I *know* Erebus has Max."

"Okay, how do you *know?*"

Irritated by the interruption, Sam tried to keep his mind focused on what he would do when they arrived while also carrying on a conversation about something that could clearly be put off until later. "Because I went to his shop this afternoon to check out a board."

Angel leaned in next to Triniti. "Are you purposefully trying to be cryptic, or is it just your nature to aggravate everyone around you?"

"I'm not trying to be aggravating or cryptic; I'm just distracted," he said as he turned down a side street. Internally, he sighed, giving up, for the moment, on devising a strategy. "The board I picked has a mural of a hula girl on it."

"I thought you said you weren't trying to be cryptic," Triniti snapped. "Are you implying that he doesn't like Max's art or something?"

Sam glanced at her in the rearview mirror. "If you'd let me finish..."

Though Triniti's exasperated eyes told him she longed to argue, she flapped her hand at him. "Go ahead."

But before he continued, Angel answered for him. "It's not you. At least not the way you think it is."

Triniti looked at her. "What's not who?"

"You," Angel said, looking at Triniti.

The surfing champion huffed a long breath through clenched teeth. "Someone had better start making a little sense before I blow a gasket. *What's* not me?"

"The Polynesian princess," Angel replied, a slight smile tugging at the corners of her lips. "Erebus said Sam was distracted by a Polynesian princess and a bimbo. The princess is the girl on the surfboard. Which makes you..."

Sam glanced in the mirror as Triniti glared at Angel. With the hostility level between the two of them already at DEFCON 2, he refrained from verbally confirming Angel's interpretation of the bimbo comment. "Erebus could only know about the board if he saw me and Max together this afternoon."

A whole range of emotions seemed to pass over Triniti's face. Anger, disbelief, then finally denial. She shook her head. "That seems like a leap. It's too convenient."

"Perhaps," Sam said. "But remember on the radio? Erebus called me 'Samuel.'"

Trinity shrugged. "So what?"

"There are just two people in town who know my full name—Sheriff Austin because he gave me the gift of a moving violation on the day I arrived and Max because he copied my driver's license onto the rental receipt."

"He could have guessed," Triniti offered weakly, though based on the lack of conviction in her voice, Sam didn't think she held out any real hope.

Silence descended on the bus for a moment, then Angel asked, "Did you also put your room number on the receipt?"

Angel had made a well-reasoned, though unfortunate, leap in logic. She had intuited more tragedy at the hands of the madman. "No." Sam tried to keep his voice neutral. "When I got to the hotel and when we came downstairs, the lobby was deserted. I suppose it's possible the desk jockey was on a smoke break, but I'm guessing Erebus used his *influence* to find out my room number."

"Any idea who had the night shift at the hotel tonight?" Monica directed her question at Triniti.

Triniti shook her head. "Abby's the owner. I'd call her, but the damned phones are down. Maybe after we get Max, we could come back and—"

"Either Erebus did or didn't get to him," Sam said. "Either way, there's nothing we can do."

For several seconds, the bus remained silent, save for the ba-ba-ba of the engine.

Triniti leaned back in her seat. "It's possible Erebus heard the sheriff or one of his deputies talking down at the diner. Or maybe he hacked the city computer. Or maybe he really thinks I'm a Polynesian princess..." She sniffed and wiped her eyes. "I don't know. I'm just saying, there are other ways he could've found out."

Sam didn't contradict her false optimism, but in the rearview mirror, he could see a tear running down her check.

He wished he could hop on board her happiness train and cruise down Pollyanna Avenue with her. Maybe, just maybe, her friend had been away from his shop when the killer had broken in. Maybe Max was home right now, sleeping in his bed or knocking back a cold one after a platter of cheesy enchiladas.

But false hopes and wishful thinking only postponed inevitable heartache. On occasion, the truth dawdled, allowing daydreamers time to mask common sense with their desires. For them to believe that good things actually happened to good people. But when reality did finally storm the fort, trumpets blowing and guns blazing, the bitch took no prisoners and made no concessions.

The vehicle's one working headlamp flashed onto the miniature surfboard jutting out over the entrance of the shop. *The Board Wake, Epic Fayl Designs.*

Time to find Max.

Chapter Twenty-Seven

With nothing more than a bare outline of a plan in mind, Sam guided the bus into a parking space and turned off the ignition. He left the sad little headlight on to shine through the big picture windows.

They piled out and Sam slipped his gun from his waistband, leading the way to the front door. Their exaggerated shadows dove and leapt among the boards and surfing paraphernalia, as if a hoard of demons had stopped in to play a rambunctious game of hide-and-go-seek.

He tried the handle. Locked. "Is there another way in?" he whispered.

Triniti motioned with her chin. "Yeah, there's a workers' entrance around back."

Sam led the group around the side of the building and down a narrow alley. The further they crept, the more the darkness didn't so much hide them as envelop them. Feeling along the wall, Sam stopped when his fingers found the rear corner. Nothing disturbed the silence except the distant, rhythmic crashing of waves.

He peeked around the edge. As desolate as a fading star on the edge of the universe, a small light mounted halfway up the cinderblock fought valiantly against the pitiless sea of blackness. Beneath the lonesome island of illumination, a service entrance broke the monotonous plane.

"Stay here," he whispered. Leading with his gun, he slipped around the corner.

Sam crept along the exterior and then pressed his ear to the door. If something waited for him beyond the entrance, it made no more noise than a phantom wandering among a garden of tombstones. He gently twisted the knob and eased open the entrance a couple of inches to peek through the small gap.

The dark inside rivaled that of the alleyway, but the external bare bulb sliced through the inkiness with a serrated edge of light.

He stared, scanning for threats among the random shadows.

Though the madman had gotten a head start, it seemed unlikely Erebus could have made it back to the shop before them, especially after being struck by the VW. Still, Sam kept underestimating the psychopath, and just this evening, he'd found himself at the wrong end of his own gun in his own hotel room. If he failed this time, no one would come blazing out of the night in a surfer's hooptie to save his bacon.

He gingerly pulled opened the entrance and slipped inside. The *snick* of the door closing behind him echoed as loud as a cymbal crash in the silent workspace. Dropping to the floor, he froze, waiting and listening.

A slight shuffling and a low thump emanated from the cool, dark tomb, then became still once more.

Someone was here.

The soft hush of the door and the brief flash of light had most certainly alerted the lurker to his presence. Since Sam hadn't been pulverized in a hailstorm of bullets, his unseen adversary probably didn't brandish something as practical as an automatic weapon. However, the lack of gunfire might mean the madman had elected stealth over noisy, sheriff-summoning convenience, choosing instead to arm himself with an ax or a scythe.

Rather than stepping into the room and thus risking becoming an Ichabod Crane doppelganger, Sam sat up and ran his hand along the wall next to the entrance. At first, his fingers only brushed over the prickled flatness of rough wood before stumbling upon an electrical switch. He tensed, gun held at the ready, and flipped on the lights.

He almost reflexively fired off a shot when, instead of the blinding flash of overheads, an industrial-sized vacuum system roared to life.

Having given away his position as effectively as igniting a road flare, he tucked and rolled to the side. Popping up in a crouch, he swept his gun across the space he'd just vacated, staring in the utter blackness for an attacker and straining to hear the telltale thump of approaching footsteps beneath the bellow of machinery.

Nothing.

Instead of turning the vacuum off, he used it to mask the sounds of his own movements and ran toward what vaguely resembled a stack of wood. Halfway across the floor, his legs tangled, and he fell, his face colliding with a pair of sneaker-clad feet.

"Ow!" A male voice screamed loud enough to over-power the heavy-duty system.

The legs, belonging to a pair of pissed off feet, began bucking and kicking with the exuberance one normally reserved for a line dance competition. A knee smacked Sam in the face before he could get his arm up to protect his head. Rolling, he dug his elbow into the soft tissue of the assailant's stomach. The man grunted, and Sam rolled again, pressing his gun into the side of the man's head. "Don't move."

An angry bark replied from the dark. "And where would I go?"

Even through the vacuum's roar, Sam recognized the voice. "Max? Is that you?"

"Who else would it be?" Max grunted. "Man, get off me."

Sam stumbled to his knees, aiming his gun into the blackness, his eyes seeking, but not finding, a threat.

"Ow!" Max yelled again. "Get off my arm."

Sam had knelt on something hard, which he'd pre-sumed to be a board. "Sorry." He slid to the side.

"Dude, you're killing me. Ow! Ow! Ow! Now you're on my hand."

Sam continued to slide until his butt made contact with the floor. Though distracted by Max's protests, he still searched the shadows. "Are you hurt? Where's Erebus?"

"If you mean the asshole that tried to mug me, he's gone." Max's voice sounded strained and pained, and Sam wondered why the surfer was lying in the middle of the floor.

"When?"

"Man, I don't know. A couple hours ago, at least. Are we going to sit here all night playing Twenty Questions, or are you gonna help me?"

Sam hesitated before slipping the gun into the waistband of his pants. He made his way back to the door and turned off the vacuum. Merciful silence descended like a shroud upon the workshop as the system's motor spun down.

Ears still ringing with the machine's throaty bellow, Sam patted the perimeter of the service entrance. He found another switch and flipped it. This time, the lights came on with a blinding glare.

Squinting against the brilliance, Sam returned to Max's side.

The surfer still lay on the floor, and Sam suddenly understood why the other man hadn't gotten up. Nails. Nails had been driven into his hands, anchoring him to the floor.

The back door flew open and the three women filed inside. One after the other, their eyes widened as each, in turn, took in the scene.

"Oh my god! Oh my god!" Triniti shrieked. She ran over and knelt next to her friend, touching his face. "Max! Are you alive? Max!" She trailed her fingers down his arm.

When she touched his hand, he screamed. "Ow! I am, but I'm pretty sure you guys are trying to kill me."

She looked up at Sam. "We need to go get the sheriff."

"No," Max said. "Just get me off the damned floor."

"Don't you think it would be best for us to call in the——"

"For the love of Mike and all his saints," Max snapped. "Please help me up."

Perplexity crossed Triniti's face. "Mike?"

"Trin, just do as I ask. Please?"

Sam began rummaging through the organized drawers of a large toolbox. Finding a long crowbar, he returned to Max's side. "This is going to hurt. A lot."

"It already hurts. A lot. Just do it."

Sam placed a small wedge of wood on the floor so he wouldn't smash Max's hand when he levered up. He set the curl of the crowbar on the wood and slid the claw slot under the nail head. "Are you ready?"

Max visibly tensed and gave a curt nod.

Sam levered the bar.

As the long nail came out, Max hissed. Though the stake no longer stuck to the floor, it still remained in his hand, which had followed the arch of the crowbar.

Triniti's gaze zeroed in on the impaled palm. She screamed and fell onto her butt as the color drained from her face. When a drop of blood oozed out of the wound and dropped to the floor, her pale cheeks turned pallid, her eyes rolled back, and she passed out, landing in a thick pile of sawdust.

"Drama queen," Angel scoffed. She grabbed a bottle of water from a shelf and dumped it over Triniti's head.

The surfing champion woke with a start, sputtering and gasping. "Wha? What happened? Why am I all wet?"

Sam moved to Max's other hand and repeated the process.

Though revulsion marred her face, this time, Triniti remained conscious.

Sam dropped the tool and helped Max up onto a bench.

Max plopped down. Breathing hard, he grabbed the head of the nail impaling his right hand and yanked the stake from his palm. He hissed again but then grasped the other nail and pulled it out too.

Monica got some rags and a thick roll of tape from a nearby shelf, knelt in front of him, and wrapped his bleeding hands.

After she'd finished, Max flexed his fingers, rolling his knuckles and his wrists, grimacing as he did so. He looked up at the group watching him. "I'm going to be okay."

Triniti got to her feet, wiping water from her forehead. "We need to get you to the clinic."

Monica stood. "I agree. You were nailed to the floor. That seems medical worthy."

Max glared at them. "I am *very* aware of what's medical worthy and what isn't. I've been lying here for hours thinking about it. Compared to when the bastard held the nail gun to my forehead and pulled the trigger, this hardly ranks."

Angel's mouth fell open. "He did not!"

"He did," Max retorted. "But the gun jammed. It's been doing that on and off for the last couple of weeks, and I'd been meaning to take it in and get it fixed." He shook his head. "I'm glad I hadn't gotten to it yet."

Sam glanced around the group. "We've been dealing with this guy all evening. He's killed a lot of people. I don't understand why he didn't...well, you know."

Max's bloodshot eyes found Sam's. "You mean, why didn't he bash my head in? Yeah, I don't understand either. When the gun didn't fire, I thought he was going to crush my skull, but he said something about not arguing with the Fates. Then he kicked me in the face. I must have blacked out because when I woke up, he was gone."

Max paused. "The thing that really pisses me off is that I had him. The bastard snuck in and tried to club me, but he didn't know how hard my head is. When the board bounced off, I turned the sander on him." He pointed at the large electric disk sander lying on the floor a few feet away. "Had the guy dead to rights, pinned down. All I had to do was pull the trigger and he'd have been nothing but spray. Instead, I tried to call the police, but I dropped the phone. The next thing I know, I'm nailed to the floor." He shook his head.

"It isn't your fault, Max," Sam said. "This guy seems to have nine lives. I thought I'd killed him in St. Louis."

Angel touched Max's shoulder. "We've beaten him up. Twice. But it's like he's got some kind of protective demon in his back pocket."

Max looked her and Monica over, as though noticing them for the first time. He blinked several times as recognition dawned in his eyes. "Monica? But the paper said that you were..." His shoulders drooped, and he swallowed. "Ah, shit. The nail gun didn't misfire. I'm dead, aren't I?" He looked around. "He got you too, Trin? Bastard."

"I'm *not* dead," Monica said, putting her hands on her hips. "The sheriff got it wrong, and the paper ran with it."

Max scratched his head, grimacing as he did so, and grunted. "Yeah, I can believe that. I know the guy that prints that garbage. Getting his facts straight isn't exactly his first priority." He scanned his gaze over their tool belts and various screw drivers, knives, and hammers. "So, what's up with the stakes and stuff? You look like Xena warriors who robbed a hardware store."

Angel held up the Taser. "These are for protection."

"We don't go anywhere unless we're packing heat," Monica said, slipping out a machete.

A painful smile played at the corners of Max's lips. "Against what? A disgruntled Home Depot employee?"

Angel cocked her head. "Seriously? We're protecting ourselves from the same effer that staked you to the floor as if you were the son of God. And as for our weapons of choice, didn't you just tell us that you almost took him out with your sander thingy?"

Max gave her a half-smile. "Touché."

"Come on," Sam said. "We need to get you to the hospital."

"No." He shook his head. "Home. I'm really tired. I just want to clean my hands, take a leak, and sleep for like three days."

Triniti knelt in front of him, her eyes imploring. "I really think you should—"

Max gently touched her cheek with his fingertips. "No, I'm fine. A buddy of mine did the same thing to himself when he was roofing. The doc said that as long as he can do this..." He rolled his fingers. "Then the bones aren't broken. The holes just need to be cleaned."

Her gaze lingered on his rag-wrapped palms. "What about tetanus? I still think—"

"Had a shot last year."

"I—"

He held her gaze. "I'm fine, Trin. Now, did you bring Charlie, or do I need to walk?"

She huffed. "Fine. Come on." She stood and, grabbing his forearm, helped him to his feet. Together, they slogged to the door, the group trailing after them.

As they rounded the front of the building, Max stopped in front of the bus. "What happened? The van's a mess."

"Please, don't remind me," she said. "It's just part of the fun we've been having tonight."

He stooped to get a closer look at the caved-in grill. "Did someone hit you?"

She grimaced. "Not exactly. Look, I really don't want to talk about it right now." Triniti wrapped her fingers around his bicep and pulled him to his feet. "Come on. It's been a long day. Let's regroup tomorrow, and we'll make a plan then."

"No," Sam said. "There is no 'we.' Erebus is way too dangerous. *I* will deal with him."

Angel put her hands on her hips. "You did *not* just say that."

Chet flinched. *Oh, now you're in for it.*

Sam stood his ground. "Yes, I did. He's a professional killer. I have training. You do not."

The woman's eyes narrowed to slits of molten granite. "Peter, or Sam, or whatever your name is, I don't even know where to start. You've had your chance. You should have killed this guy in Arizona before this whole thing got out of hand. But you failed. You had another chance in St. Louis, but again, you failed. You followed the bastard here to the Cove, supposedly to save Monica, but instead, you got half the town blown up. Your incompetence has not only destroyed a lot of my hometown but almost gotten Max killed too. I don't know where you got this 'training' you're bragging about, but maybe you need to go back and take a refresher course or two."

Ouch! Chet said. *That's gotta hurt. It's pretty much what I've been telling you for years, but still, that's gotta sting a bit.*

Though Angel had spoken out of anger, she'd also spoken out of ignorance. She'd borne witness to some of Erebus' destructiveness but couldn't possibly understand his true capacity for evil. She wanted to protect the people she loved, even if that meant improvising with a leather belt and half the tools from a hardware store.

Sam took a deep breath. He'd been tracking down enemies of the state without fail for over a decade. Being trounced by this lunatic again and again perplexed him. Until now, he'd never experienced failure. Perhaps he'd finally cashed in all his chips and the gods were simply calling in their markers.

His methodologies, philosophies, and strategies had never worked on Erebus. The rules that so easily manipulated everyone else came up short when the perp in question didn't follow any societal or humanistic guidelines himself.

The time had come for Sam to change the rules.

Rule #122:
Throw out the Rules.

There are times and situations where the *122 Rules of Psychology* do not apply or cease to be effective, thus failing to fulfill the required goal. In these rare cases, throw them out. A generous dollop of creativity, ingenuity, flexibility, and un-predictability sometimes serves better.

——122 Rules of Psychology

Though grimy and haggard, each of the faces watching him looked determined and willing.

I know what you're thinking, Chet said. *You cannot ask them to help. Without the proper training, they'll be slaughtered.*

They're already being slaughtered.

"All right," Sam said to the group. "You want to be involved? You want to help? Then you need to follow me and do as I say. *All* of you."

Monica said, "*You're* offering *us* your protection and guidance?"

Sam ignored the sarcasm. "Yes. We don't know what Erebus knows. He could have found out where you've been hiding and be waiting for you. We need to stay together."

"If that were true," she replied, "we'd already be dead. He wouldn't have bothered with Max and the boat, none of it."

Chet sighed. *She's got you there, Chief. Who's the agent again? Sometimes I forget.*

"I'm ready to go home." Monica glanced at Angel. "How about you?" She turned back to Sam. "We'll see you tomorrow."

"Can we meet at your place?" Sam asked Triniti. "We need to regroup, but we shouldn't be out in public."

She nodded.

He faced the two women glaring at him. "Tomorrow at noon."

"Fine," Angel snapped. "Come on, Mon. Let's go." They pivoted and started marching down the street, the tools on their belts clanking and clinking with each step.

Triniti called after them. "Do you want a ride in case Erebus is around?"

"I'd love it if he came at us," Angel shot back. She pulled a hammer from her belt, brandishing it like a sword. "We'd bash his head in, rip out his spleen with our bare hands, and then feed it to him."

Max's eyes lingered on the duo as they stormed off. "I don't doubt it."

"*You* were hired to protect *them*?" Triniti asked.

Sam frowned. "Right? Come on, we need to get Max home."

They piled into the van. Triniti drove the busted-up vehicle, its one headlight illuminating their way like a bright-eyed cyclops. No one spoke as she pulled into the driveway of a small single-story house.

She put the bus in park. "Max, do you want us to come in and help you?"

"No, I can take care of myself," he said, climbing out of the van.

She touched Sam's arm and whispered, "Stay here."

"You're going to tell him about April?" he asked, keeping his voice low. "Do you want me to come too?"

She shook her head. "He barely knows you. It should come from me." She took a long breath, got out, put on a fake smile, and walked over to Max. "Are you going to call Abby? She'll make Angel look like Gandhi on weed if you don't tell her what happened."

He returned her smile. "I'll call her in the morning, but—"

"No buts. It *is* morning."

"But the phone lines."

Her shoulders fell. "Oh, right."

Max looked at Sam through the open passenger window. "Good night. Thanks for...well, you know." He held up one of his bandaged hands. "Everything."

Sam returned the gesture. "See you in the morning."

Triniti, her eyes shiny with tears, looped her arm through Max's. "Come on. I'll walk you. I need to tell you something."

They strolled side by side up to the entrance and then paused in front of the door. Touching his cheek, Triniti began to talk. Max stared at her as a range of emotions crossed his face—disbelief, incomprehension, sadness.

Finally, Triniti pulled him into her arms, and as he laid his head on her shoulder, they cried together. After a few minutes, he straightened and glanced over at Sam, grim determination set in his expression. He turned back to Triniti and said something.

This time, Sam could read Triniti's lips, "I promise."

He asked her something else. She nodded and wrapped him in another long hug. Max broke the embrace, opened the door, and disappeared into the house.

Triniti lingered on the porch for a minute, wiping her cheeks before trudging back to the bus. "He's coming over tomorrow to help," she said, reclaiming the driver's seat.

Sam didn't reply; he'd expected as much.

They remained quiet as Triniti dropped the van into gear and backed out onto the street. Instead of driving to Sam's hotel, she turned in the opposite direction.

When she pulled up in front of a large beach house with giant windows and cedar siding, she shut off the engine. "This is my place, and I do *not* want to be alone." She climbed out of the bus.

Sam followed her up the walkway and into the house. He closed and locked the door behind them.

Chapter Twenty-Eight

E rebus peered between the tall, cotton-topped reeds of pampas grass as a cruiser raced by. The car's tires chewed up the blacktop while its amplified siren screamed in self-aggrandizing pomposity. The blaring shrill shredded the stillness of the otherwise tranquil environment, yet another victim to the albatross of civic and societal duty.

The rank and file uniformity of these Neanderthals, strutting about in their ridiculous police costumes, was nothing more than the full-on realization of a little boy's cops and robbers fantasy, complete with guns, bulletproof vests, and fast cars slathered in blazing lights. Delusional egomaniacs exhibiting their self-proclaimed superiority under the guise of law and order.

But these supposed "authoritarians" were no better, no stronger, no smarter than those they claimed to be protecting or pursuing. In fact, in his experience, Erebus found the opposite to be true. They were often only marginally better equipped, moralistically guided, and intellectually superior than man's simpleton grandfathers who burned witches at the stake and pursued monsters with torches and pitchforks.

Another clown car of arrogant and misguided cretins flew down the road.

Despite pretending otherwise, the police's arsenals were still governed by the same limiting laws of physics as their forefathers' weaponized garden tools. Their psyches were just as culpable and their flesh just as fragile and prone to bleeding as any other man's.

Distant, urgent voices floated through the air. These idiots were no more intimidating than a marauding squad of toy soldiers wielded by a five-year-old's imagination and chubby fingers.

You can look all you want, but I'm not there. And the more time that passes, the more I'm not there.

Erebus slowly made his way along the bottom of the dry, gently sloping floodway. The huge clumps of pampas and European Beach Grass grew well along the canal's hard-packed silt edges, effectively rendering him invisible to passersby on the road.

A large, box-shaped vehicle approached, orange lights flashing and siren screaming. He didn't bother to duck down. The vegetation and a bad case of tunnel vision would prevent the simpletons from noticing anything except their own destination.

It had been a productive night. But despite his many successes, he had not yet been able to kill Agent Sam Bradford who, frustratingly, kept preventing him from reaching the bitch. He'd even gotten the drop on the man. A bullet through the brain—while not as satisfying as gutting the agent and leaving him to bleed to death—would have, nevertheless, been quite effective.

But events hadn't gone the way he had anticipated.

The Fates had taught him yet another lesson this evening. Like the police, Erebus too occasionally suffered from bouts of arrogance. He had thought that he was about to conquer the man via a quick, neat execution on the far side of the hotel parking lot. This would have cleared the path for Erebus to capture the ladies, remove their many flaws, and complete his own ascension.

But he had been so astonished by the unanticipated presence of the vehicle bearing down on him that it had jammed his cognitive processes. Self-preservation instincts should have kicked in with sufficient time to avoid the collision, but the searing headlights and the glacial pace of the unlikely orange-blazed loaf had so enraptured him, it hadn't been until just before being struck that his seized muscles and synapses fired.

Understanding the futility—and possible fatality—of trying to jump out of the way, he'd instead leapt straight up and in the same direction of the approaching vehicle. At the instant of impact, he had assisted the vectors of force and momentum to hold him in place by grabbing hold of a windshield wiper while his feet found purchase on the bumper.

For one fleeting moment, he'd stared through the huge window at the driver. Her wide eyes locking with his.

Perhaps because she had been watching him, she hadn't been paying attention to where she was going. In the reflection of the glass, he saw as they approached the parked car. Again, leaping the instant before the inevitable collision, he'd rolled over the hood of the sedan and onto the pavement.

Other than being stunned for a few minutes, he hadn't sustained any serious injuries. Rather than try and regain the strategic advantage, he'd chosen to retreat, regroup, and form a new plan.

In the distance, he detected the distinct rumbling of the bus as it coughed to life. He stopped to watch it amble past.

As the engine faded into the distance and the squawk of police radios waned, blurring into obscurity, he tried to prepare his next move. But an uncertain disquiet settled over his nerves as he reached for plans that refused to materialize. He needed to remove ego from his actions—another lesson the Fates had delivered unto him this evening. Only the unpretentious would prevail.

He gazed up at the moon, offering himself in servitude. Bathing in its lunar caress, he allowed it to enfold and swaddle him. Erebus connected with the cosmos, melding with it at an atomic level. The cells of his being harmoniously and seamlessly interwove into the unending fabric of the universe, quilting all matter into a single, eternal tapestry.

An unknown time later, he lowered his head and dropped his eyes as the answers he sought were provided. He digested the information and began to move once more.

Though his body followed a man-made canal, his soul would forever travel on an eternal conduit engineered by the gods. He understood what he must do to be worthy of the deities' favor. He didn't mind the work. In fact, he relished it.

As he looked off into the distance and the components of his plan fused together like primitive elements bonding to form a new and fantastically destructive acid, Tyron Erebus smiled.

This was going to be fun.

Chapter Twenty-Nine

As soon as Sam closed the door behind them, Triniti whirled on him. "Why is this happening?"

He'd been anticipating her emotional explosion—the clenched steering wheel, the set jaw, and the narrowed eyes. Triniti looked like a box of TNT in a room full of hot ignition coils.

Even though he'd been gearing up to try and help her, he didn't *want* to want to help. He didn't *want* to care about Monica, Angel, or Max either. He didn't *want* to care about anything or anyone. Caring implied an obligation to protect them. Saving the souls of this town didn't benefit his country, and it didn't help further The Agency's cause.

Even worse, caring didn't come alone. It toted a travel trunk, bulging with so much moralistic muck that it could suck the most stoic of hearts and the most apathetic of spirits into a quagmire of neediness and melodrama. His foundation—built upon the rock-solid soil of logic, reasoning, apathy, and planning—hadn't been shored up against the destructive flood of uncertainty battering him like an angry sea breaching its levees. The sodden emotional ground beneath his feet was quickly turning not just to sand but to quicksand, and as it devoured him, it twisted the straight lines and skewed the right angles of his saltbox universe.

He studied Triniti's face as she waited for him to help her make sense of her unhappy reality. With her cheeks flushed red and the veins in her neck sticking out like high tension cables, she appeared on the verge of hysteria. And why wouldn't she be? For her entire life, she'd been isolated in this little city, protected from the specters that lurked in the shadows. But a demon had invaded her dreams, and the monster had done as monsters do—tossed out nightmares like candy at a Fourth of July parade.

One of the objectives of the Rules was to trigger the mourning process, either by the betrayal or loss of a loved one. In this vulnerable state, Sam could easily manipulate and deceive his target. By twisting his victim's perceptions and controlling their emotions, he or she could be turned against their strongest commitments and waiver on their most sacred relationships.

By properly channeling that rage, Sam had destroyed families, crushed lifelong friendships, made brothers murder brothers, and convinced mothers to disown their children. Usually it took Sam weeks, sometimes months, to bring someone like Triniti to that point, but Erebus had managed to do it in just a few hours.

Standing in the middle of this stranger's house in the darkest hours of the morning, Sam found himself trying to figure out how to defuse—rather than ignite—the additional crates of emotional dynamite stacked up along the already vulnerable walls of her heart and crumbling borders protecting her spirit. But even without damaging it further, trying to reassemble her decimated world would be like trying to piece together the fragments of a shattered mirror. No matter how good of a job he did, the reflected image would always be distorted and scarred.

Destruction could be wielded like a hammer, but salvation must be delivered by a dove.

Triniti paced the small living room. "That bastard killed my friend. April was like my sister. She never hurt anyone. She painted and loved. That's it. I don't care if he's sick or if his mommy didn't hold him enough. There's no excuse. No explaining what that abomination did to her."

"This isn't the first person he's done it to either," Sam said. "There've been more. A lot more."

"And Max," she snarled, continuing to pace. "He nailed him to the floor like some kind of insect. And then when Max couldn't fight back, he tried to put a stake in his skull. If the gun hadn't jammed, my friend would be dead. Dead! He's one of the kindest people... No, he *is* the kindest person I've ever known."

"He needed something, and Max was in the way."

She stopped pacing. Glaring at him with huge, wet eyes, she flared her nostrils like a stampeding mare. "Angel and Monica keep saying you failed. That all of this is happening because of you. Angel's an idiot. If it was just her, I'd ignore it. Monica's always been a bit of a drama queen, but she's no slouch in the brains department. So, despite her choice in friends, I trust her opinions."

She paused studying his face. "So, Sam, explain to me why they are accusing you of this. What did you do? Also, who are *you* exactly? You aren't in finance, that's obvious. And you aren't some workaholic who looked our town up and decided to come here on vacation."

More out of habit than from a conscious decision, Sam prepared to recite the background of one of his many fake identities. The rehearsed tale would sound plausible enough and might even stand up under scrutiny, but he just couldn't bring himself to lie to her again.

"I was on assignment. My job was to kill Monica," he admitted.

Triniti wiped her eyes with the back of her hand. "That makes no sense whatsoever. Are you trying to tell me you're some kind of mercenary?"

"No. I work for a government...organization, and I was told she was an enemy of our country. That she was involved in the mob and with drugs. But to be quite honest, the details of her real background and the fake one are all starting to blur together in my head."

Triniti rubbed the back of her neck. "You still aren't making sense. What does that have to do with this Erebus guy?"

Sam explained the corruption surrounding the Laven Michael's case, Erebus' obsession with finishing the job he'd started, and his own efforts to save Monica.

A tear, as fat and shiny as a trust fund baby's diamond, slid down Triniti's cheek. "He blew up the dock and killed all of those people because he's trying to get to Monica? He murdered and hurt *my* friends because he has some vendetta? Who did you say he was?"

"An assassin. The cruelest I've ever met," Sam replied.

"And you're what? A cop? FBI?" She implored him with red-rimmed eyes. "You never really answered that question."

"No, I didn't. It's something like that, but it doesn't really matter."

As the remaining anger bled from her voice, her entire demeanor seemed to implode under the weight of her pain and sadness. "But he didn't have to kill my friend."

"I know."

"Those people on the dock..." She got a faraway look, as though she could still see her friends on fire, smell the charred flesh, and hear the cries of pain.

Sam walked over and touched her hand.

She hesitated for a second before falling into him, burying her face in his chest.

He wrapped his arms around her, and she began to sob.

"He didn't have to do that," she murmured. "He didn't have to do that." She shook her head against him as her tears soaked his shirt.

Sam let her weep. Let the pain flow from her until she hiccupped and her breathing calmed, and then he guided her down the hall to her room. He folded back the blankets, and Triniti—still coated in sweat, dirt, and grime—crawled into bed, curling up into a small ball.

Sam kicked off his shoes and lay down next to her. At first, she didn't move, but when she rolled over, he pulled her into his arms.

Triniti wrapped herself around him. She shook, and her crying began anew. Her tears formed a small puddle beneath her cheek as the sobs racked her body.

Sam stroked her hair until she drifted off to sleep.

Sam stared out the window. Sleep, in all its glorious annoyance, mocked him but refused to visit.

The moon gazed down through thin curtains, bathing the room in a soft glow. The ancient Greeks believed that when their warriors ventured out at night, Artemis, the goddess of the moon and the hunt, traveled with them. That she helped find and capture prey by illuminating their path with her stellar brilliance.

Sam could use a little illumination and brilliance right about now because none of his experience nor his training applied to this situation. He had been tracking people for more than a decade. No one had been his equal. But Erebus had proven to be vastly different than anyone he'd ever dealt with before.

Sam had always been the pursuer, using his skills and intuition to unearth and eliminate his targets. These marks had shown themselves to be enemies of his country, a danger to freedom, or threats to the structure and foundation that formed the basis of society. In normal circumstances, the legal system would eventually remove such evildoers. But for those too elusive, too dangerous, or too politically untouchable for the usual processes of trial and prosecution, agents like Sam delivered justice.

He wasn't above the law, but instead, he strode along beside it. Assisting it when it stumbled and compensating for its shortcomings. He was the man behind the curtain who helped a well-intentioned but cumbersome system. Though known by almost no one, Sam, Josha, and the entire Agency had become an integral component of the democratic republic's undercarriage. Like the gears of a vehicle, never seen but necessary to propel their burdens forward. They were the unsung heroes who slipped around the red tape and did the deeds no one wanted to admit needed to be done.

But the chaser-chasee relationship had been flipped, and this non-case had gotten complicated in ways he'd never imagined. Sam found himself in the impossible position of both predator and prey. He had to keep safe a town, which had inadvertently found itself a target, while he too had crosshairs on his back.

Sam had never encountered a foe so unpredictable and dogmatic, nor one so willing to kill on the off chance of getting the upper hand. The psychopath's murderous rampage had gained considerable momentum, and if it continued unchecked, it would destroy the entire town. Only Sam could stop him.

He glanced at the woman lying beside him. Triniti had oscillated between terror, anger, and grief. Nothing in her years as a boardhead had prepared her for such senseless violence and death.

He needed to protect her. He needed to protect them all.

Chapter Thirty

The mountains began to glow like a midwinter hearth, and the moon faded to the transparency of wet tissue paper. Sam's mind whirled, forming and discarding plans until the sun peaked over the mountain tops and he succumbed to exhaustion. His eyelids drooped shut, and a temporary peace overtook him.

Triniti's scream tore him from slumber's embrace.

His heart hammering, Sam rolled out of bed and snatched the gun from the side table in one quick movement. He crouched, scanning for a target. "What? What is it?"

Triniti touched his back. "Sam, everything's okay. I had a dream. I'm sorry I scared you."

He glanced back.

Her mussed hair and bloodshot eyes accentuated her pallor. Triniti looked like she'd gone a couple rounds with a debilitating disease. Only the sickness she'd been battling hadn't been caused by traditional bacteria or a flesh-eating virus but by something far more sadistic and ruthless.

Sam let out a long breath. Though he'd been asleep, and fatigue permeated every cell of his body, the adrenaline pumping through his veins would prevent him from getting any more rest. He plopped down onto the edge of the bed.

Triniti looked up at him. "I appreciate that you are so, um...capable, but would you mind checking the house?"

He considered telling her that thumb-bolts and window latches wouldn't keep the murderer at bay. That if Erebus had wanted to get in, he would have already. But he couldn't crush the small light of faith in her large, expectant eyes, so he nodded.

Triniti wrapped the sheets around her near-nakedness and lay back. "Thank you."

He made a good show of examining the lock on the bedroom window, then strode down the hall, tugging and turning each doorknob and pulling on all the windows. He looked in the closets, poked his head up into the attic, and searched behind the couch.

Erebusssss. Chet called. *Come out, come out wherever you are.*

Sam pulled open a linen closet door. *He's not here.*

I know. But he's not far.

Sam stood in the middle of the living room, examining it for hiding places and vulnerabilities. After repeating the process in the kitchen and spare room, he returned to the bedroom and closed the door behind him. "The house is secure."

Triniti watched him with huge, dark eyes. "I didn't hear any gunshots or my house being torn apart, so I figured."

He stood awkwardly, not sure what to do. Triniti gave him a weak smile and pulled back the covers. She patted the space beside her. The sheets were smudged with the grime they'd been too tired to wash off the night before. "Come. We have a few hours before everyone gets here."

Chet sighed. *Really? With all of this going on? And, might I add, you're both a little ripe if you know what I mean.*

Sam smirked at his inner conscience. *The lady needs some comfort, and I'm the one to give it to her.* Though he talked big to Chet, in truth, exhaustion dogged him. He wanted sleep and a plan, not to start something up with a local he'd just met.

Chet rubbed his neck. *The lady needs therapy if she thinks you're going to give her anything but grief.*

Sam put his gun in the nightstand drawer and lay down.

Triniti pulled the covers over them and kissed him gently on the cheek. "Thank you for keeping me safe." She wrapped her arm around his waist, nuzzling her face into his chest. Sam stroked her hair.

Triniti burrowed deep into him, sighed, and began to snore.

☆☆☆☆

Sam looked around at the motley crew gathered in the kitchen. Though they appeared presentably clean, matching dark crescents hung under everyone's eyes, as if they'd all joined the same sleep deprivation gang. They watched him, waiting for answers he didn't have.

"Okay, Mr. FBI, what's the plan?" Angel asked, crossing her arms.

"First of all, I don't work for the FBI."

A flash of anger lit her eyes. "Right. Whatever. Look, no one else seems to be willing to actually take this dirtbag down, but we are. Monica and I have played his game.

We know how he thinks. I say we form groups and begin searching from one end of the city to the other. We can handle him."

When Sam had left his apartment a few days before, he'd set out with the solitary goal of protecting Monica. But Erebus, who didn't play by the rules, had upped the ante by about a million. Things had gotten very complicated very quickly, and Sam was having trouble formulating the right course of action. Too many people with too many opinions, trying to react to too many unknowns.

Sam met Monica's gaze. Though she held fast, uncertainty lurked in those hazel depths. The only way to save Monica was to save them all. The unfamiliar, overwhelming weight of responsibility—and the lurking consequences of failure—pressed on his heart.

"No, you can't," Sam finally answered her, focusing on Angel once more. "You think you can, but you have no way to predict what he'll do. Plus, you've never actually killed anyone." He pointed at her tool belt. "You've got hammers and bad attitudes, but that's all."

"And you think you're so much better?" she scoffed. "As I recall, he was holding you at gunpoint, when we," she motioned to herself, Monica, and Triniti, "used our 'bad attitudes' to save you."

"Angel, I——"

She didn't let him continue. "What about Max? Just look at his hands. A fluke saved his life, not you. You're supposed to be some kind of supersecret, trained something or other, but each time you've had the chance to

320

take this guy out, you've failed. You talk a big game. If you don't like my idea, what do you suggest we do?"

Despite Angel's berating, Sam had the inkling of a plan. "Max, is there a general meeting place? Somewhere large and open."

Max blinked as if he'd just tuned into the conversation.

Come on, Sam silently urged. *You wanted to be part of this. I need you to move past April for now and focus.*

After a couple seconds Max replied, "The Central Park gazebo is where we hold concerts, picnics, town functions, that sort of thing. It's right in the middle of downtown."

Good man. "That'll work. Spread the word that we're having a meeting there this afternoon."

Max nodded slowly, grim determination replacing the dazed look in his eyes. "The phone lines are down, so we can't call. But the local net is still up. We could post it on the town's web page. I know the guy that runs the site; he can take care of it." He paused. "The dock's going to be busy today. The place is a disaster. I could go down and let everyone know. Are you planning to give a speech?"

Sam pointed at him. "No, you are."

Max held up his bandaged hands. "What? No, no, no. Man, I'm in no shape to talk to anyone. Besides, I'm just a simple surfer, not a politician. I don't do public speaking. Why don't *you* do it? This is your show."

"Because I've got other things that I'll be doing while you're talking. Besides, no one knows me from Adam. You not only survived a one-on-one encounter with Erebus but, like a lot of people in town, you've lost someone to this lunatic."

Triniti touched his arm. "Sam's right. You should be the one talking. People will listen to you."

Max studied her face, then let out a long breath. "Fine. Okay. I'll do it. You need to tell me what I need to say though."

"Trin," Sam continued, "do you know anyone who can print up a few hundred flyers?"

She thought it over. "Yeah. I know a guy down at the Gazette who can do it."

"Okay, here." He pulled a thumb drive from his pocket. "I've downloaded some pictures and typed up the gist of what to say. Can you head over there now?"

She frowned. "Right now?"

"Yes. It might take a little while."

Triniti looked around, consternation on her face.

Max gave her a half-hearted smile. "Don't worry. We won't steal your silverware, and I promise to lock up when we leave."

"Fine. By the way, the clinic will be really busy. There were a lot of people hurt last night. I'll go talk to Polly about posting a flyer. I'm sure she'll be more than willing to talk to her patients too."

"That's great thinking, Trin." Sam said, smiling at her.

She returned his smile with a meek one of her own, shouldered her purse, and left.

Angel clasped her hands in front of her. "Are you serious about this? I kept waiting for the punch line, but *this* is your grand plan. Gather everyone in one place so we're like mice in a cage waiting for the cat? You know what he's capable of. He's *escalating*. Each thing he does is more grandiose, more destructive, than the last. He's confident that we'll never be able to touch him."

She glared at him. "And he's going to be there, armed to the teeth and ready to mow everyone down."

Sam locked eyes with her. "That's exactly what I'm counting on."

Chapter Thirty-One

S am adjusted the riflescope. He slid the crosshairs from face to anxious face as the crowd milled about in front of the gazebo.

So far, Erebus had not made an appearance.

The volume of trees around the plaza had limited Sam's options, making the sweltering city hall rooftop the only viable vantage point with an unobstructed view of the park.

Unprotected from the afternoon sun, he roasted like an arsonist's Thanksgiving turkey. The gasping breeze, no more forceful than the final exhalation of a dead man, offered no relief from the feverish onslaught. He'd grown accustomed to scorching temperatures during his three tours in Afghanistan, but the combination of humidity and undulating rays of heat simmering off the hot tar pushed the limits of what he could tolerate.

Squinting through the scope, Sam absently wiped sweat from his eyes and brow. He took a deep pull of Jacuzzi-warm water from his thermos and picked up the walkie-talkie. "Team, check."

As each member reported in, Sam grew more anxious. More concerned. A pregnant pause of anticipation hung like a dark cloud. The eerie quiet seemed to be whispering the same premonitions of pain, suffering, and loss promised by Death to the residents of an oncology ward.

After the last lookout radioed in, Max's strained voice squawked over the little device. "Still no sign of Erebus. I was really hoping we'd have him in cuffs or a body bag by now."

"We can't delay any longer," Sam replied. "It's time to get going. You'll be fine. We've been all over the gazebo. There's nothing there, and there's no place for him to hide. We've got people stationed around the park. If he shows up, he'll be spotted, and I'll take care of him. No judge and no jury."

Max paused for several seconds before his voice came back over the tinny little speaker. "I'll tape the transmit button now so you can hear us."

"Remember..." Sam said. "Once you do, I won't be able to contact you. So, if you need me, just yell."

The radio stuttered with static. "Got it."

Sam looked through the scope again, examining the crowd. *Where the hell are you?*

This isn't going to work, Chet said. *Erebus is not stupid, and he's not reckless.*

I know he's not, but he won't be able to resist the crowd.

Chet shook his head. *He doesn't want the crowd. He wants Monica.*

Max stepped up on the bench under the gazebo and raised his bandaged hands. The crowd turned and faced him, growing quiet. "Hey, everyone." Max's voice carried through the small handset.

Sam ran the crosshairs over the gatherers' faces. *Maybe he's in disguise?*

If he is, it's a good one. Chet said. *I haven't seen anyone that even looks remotely like him. And with those scars... No matter how good of a disguise he has, he'd stand out. Besides, that's not his style.*

Movement in the corner of the park caught Sam's attention and his focus shifted from the crowd to a sobbing woman stumbling her way across the lawn. He zoomed in on her.

Battered face. Swollen eye. She looked as though she'd barely survived a car accident.

The first of Death's cold premonitions filled Sam's stomach, sour and as thick as the tar on city hall's roof. "Oh damn."

He jumped up and ran across the top of the building. Flinging open the door, Sam pounded down the stairs. He burst through the entrance at the bottom and sprinted toward the gazebo.

☆☆☆☆

As Sam bolted across the field, Max held up Erebus' picture and began addressing the crowd.

The crying woman slogged her way to the back of the group and began weaving through the townspeople.

Sam thought he heard Max say, "Rachel?"

Max stepped down from the podium, meeting her in the middle of the small throng. As he took her hand and pulled her into his arms, the concern on his face transformed to one of confusion.

Sam tried to yell as he ran. "Get back! Get away from her!"

But due to his impromptu sprint and ragged breathing, he simply couldn't get enough air into his lungs, and his words came out in a hoarse gasp. Giving up, he pushed harder.

With the same subtlety of a metal band at a monastery, he slammed into the back of the crowd. He blazed a trail through the assemblage as though plowing through a field of wheat. When he reached the couple in the center, instead of slowing, he lowered his shoulders and charged.

Knocking Max to the side with the sweep of his arm, Sam barreled into the woman.

"Hey!" Max yelled as Sam yanked her from his embrace and fireman-carried her out of the crowd and into the side of the park. When they reached a deserted expanse of grass, Sam set her down.

Several people trailed after them, but Sam spun around. "Get back. All of you. Now."

The onlookers froze.

He pointed at her. "She's got a bomb."

Max, who'd also followed, hesitated only a second before he started pushing people away. "It's true. I felt it when I hugged her. Get back."

Disbelief kept the gawkers from moving.

"We don't have time for this," Max yelled. "You saw what happened down at the dock. Now move."

This seemed to get through to the stunned group, and the crowd took several collective steps back.

Sam touched the sobbing woman's shoulder. "What's your name?"

"Ra-Ra-Rachel."

He took her hand. "I'm Sam. I'm going to help you. I won't leave your side until you are safe. Okay?"

She nodded as more tears cascaded down her cheeks.

Sam took a deep breath and nodded toward her stomach. "Okay, let's see it."

She unbuttoned the front of her loose summer dress, revealing the hodgepodge of wires and a red stick of dynamite strapped to her waist.

A shadow fell over her ashen face as Max stepped next to them and stared. "Can you take it off?"

Being careful not to touch any of the electronics, Sam moved aside the seam of Rachel's dress so he could get a better view. A small box, with two lights on the front—one yellow, the other dark—had been affixed to a simple belt. A set of wires ran to either end of the dynamite. "I think so."

Rachel touched his hand. "On my back. There's a radio. The man who did this said to tell you that he wants to talk to you."

Sam and Max exchanged a glance.

He looked up into Rachel's face. "I'm going to reach into your dress and get it, okay?"

She nodded.

Sam tensed as his fingers brushed her thin waist, then snaked around to the back of the belt. He traced a rectangular box with his fingertips. It felt like a radio.

Gingerly, he unclipped it and pulled it out. The large handheld looked like the same kind used by the police, only it seemed far heavier than he remembered.

The gig is up. He's been monitoring us all day. We weren't going to surprise him. Chet's mournful tone reflected Sam's dread. As usual, Erebus had been two steps ahead of them.

Sam said into the radio, "Hey, asshole. Are you there?"

He dropped the radio into the grass, turning his attention back to the bomb.

In the military, he'd learned how to disable the most rudimentary of explosives, but those classes were years ago. Though the specifics of the teachings remained fuzzy, this design looked like it had come straight out of the textbooks. A small glimmer of hope sparked in Sam's soul as the deactivation steps began to return to him.

He needed time though. He had to stall Erebus without appearing to stall. "Max, see if anyone has a pocket knife."

Max turned to leave, but Sam caught his arm. "Keep it quiet. I don't know where Erebus is. He could be watching us."

Max glanced around the park, nodded, and returned to the crowd.

The radio crackled. "Mr. Bradford, after all we've been through, I thought you'd take me seriously by now."

Sam picked up the walkie. "What do you want, Erebus?"

The static broke. "You've got something—well, some-one—I want, and I'm not going to stop until I get her."

"Tell ya what, why don't you come here, and we'll discuss it?" Sam replied.

Max reappeared and handed Sam a Swiss Army knife.

Sam dropped the radio, pulled out the Phillips attachment, and began to remove the screws holding the box's lid.

"I thought we could be reasonable," Erebus said. "After all, we both want the same thing."

Sam reached down and pressed the talk button. "You want you dead too? Well, why didn't you say so?"

"Tsk. Tsk. Tsk. Mr. Bradford, you disappoint me. We both want me to leave this godforsaken town. I don't want to be here any more than you want me here."

Sam removed the lid. After gently pulling the wires free, he started tracing the leads.

Max grabbed the radio. "You'll *never* get what you came for. I'd as soon see you in Hell first."

"Mr. Fayl, I presume." An obvious smile added a lilt to Erebus' voice. "Good to know that your friends were able to free you after your unfortunate accident. Tell me, how are your hands?"

"Strong enough to choke the life out of you."

A mild chuckle clucked through the device. "Is that what you plan to do? Send me to Hell by asphyxiation? You should add to your website that you're not only religious but a fire and brimstone man. It'll make the church types come flocking. Tell me, did you find it a little surreal to be nailed to a slab of timber like your false god? Perhaps He saved you?"

Max ground his teeth. "What? I'm not religious. Listen, you little—"

Sam put his hand over the speaker. "Don't. He's trying to rile you."

Max hesitated, then lowered the radio to his side.

Sam turned his attention back to the wires. Pulling out a blade from the knife, he pinched the wire that should disable the bomb. He slid the edge in the loop and glanced up at Rachel's strained face.

She watched him with wide, terrified eyes.

Sam took a deep breath and pulled.

For a second, nothing happened, then the yellow light winked out. He let out his pent-up breath and relaxed.

As he cut the belt free, Rachel started to cry again. When the bomb fell to the ground, she wrapped her arms around him. "Thank you."

He held her for a few seconds before passing her off to Max, who took her into his arms. Sam picked up the radio and was about to press the *transmit* button when it came to life.

"I don't need you to give me what I want. I will get that on my own."

Sam frowned. "Really? Yet, we seem to be stopping you at every turn. The little gift you just sent us? That's no longer going to help you. Sorry, you'll have to do better."

A short laugh erupted from the tinny speaker. "Your ego really seems to get in the way of you seeing the bigger picture, doesn't it, Mr. Bradford? Tell me, did it not seem a little convenient that you knew *exactly* how to handle such a device. *Almost* as if the design had come from the very class in which you studied."

The relief Sam had felt only seconds before fled as his stomach twisted into a knot. Suddenly, he had the urge to run. To take action. Except he didn't know where to direct his efforts.

Erebus continued. "Believe it or not, you are about to exit this world, but before you go, I want you to understand just how fully you have failed."

Sam tried to look in every direction at once. "What do you mean?"

The madman's voice crackled over the little speaker. "Instead of standing there, spinning in circles like a five-year-old, focus on where you were hiding until I sent in my little diversion."

Sam and Max looked up to the top of city hall.

Rachel followed their gaze and gasped. "Mike? Oh my god! Mike!" She turned to Sam, her expression pleading. "That's my husband."

A man stood at the edge of the roof. With his hands tied behind his back, he wore a blindfold and a noose around his neck.

"What are you doing?" Sam asked. "You don't need to——"

A shot rang out and the man fell forward.

Rachel shrieked.

The rope caught and he dangled. His feet kicked. Once. Twice. Then he became still.

A collective scream rose from the crowd. Some ran toward city hall while others sought cover.

The radio squawked with feedback. "Goodbye, Mr. Bradford. I'd like to say that it's been a pleasure, but it has not."

Throw the radio! Throw it now! Chet yelled.

Sam didn't hesitate. He yanked back his arm and pitched the radio into the nearby pond. Shoving Rachel and Max to the ground, he covered them with his body. Behind him, the walkie exploded. Muddy water and dirt rained down around them.

Sam sat up and stared as the ripples across the pond faded.

Rachel lifted her gaze to the man hanging by the rope and burst into tears.

Max stood and tried to help her up, but she shoved him away. She stumbled to her feet and started running toward city hall. She had only managed a few awkward steps before she stopped, her shoulders sagging in defeat. Slowly, she turned back around, staring at Sam with vacant, pain-filled eyes. "I wish you had just let him kill me."

The new widow took a long, hitched breath and started plodding across the lawn to where her dead husband dangled in the breezeless afternoon sunshine.

Chapter Thirty-Two

From behind a dumpster, Tyron smiled as the crowd ran to city hall. The curious little beavers were all eager to catch a glimpse of the man hanging from its rafter. People were so predictable. As mindless as sheep, he could herd them, corral them, and even slaughter them at will.

He had expected Sam to recognize the woman's state of distress. The most compact explosive, embedded in the smallest of designs, could have easily been hidden under a loose garment—a sundress, for instance. But even if he'd melded it to the woman's body, blending it as seamlessly as a chameleon's camouflage, he couldn't have hidden the terror in her eyes, even if he'd wanted to.

Death does not discriminate. It looks the same on every face, of every race, on the planet. The ex-military man had seen it, and it had sent him running to her rescue.

Erebus had also expected that Sam would discover the bomb hidden in the radio. In fact, he'd wanted the federal agent to think that he'd foiled yet another plan. Believing Erebus could be thwarted increased the man's faith in his own abilities. But misplaced overconfidence would make Sam sloppy, reckless, and easier to control.

Whether or not Sam died was of little consequence. Erebus only needed the distraction. Max, Sam, and the rest of the town would be focused on the dead man, like monkeys circling a monolith, allowing Tyron the freedom to do what he wanted.

He threw Sam's rifle and the extra clips he'd retrieved from the city hall rooftop into the dumpster. The missing gun would have them too busy watching their own asses to fully focus on him. Erebus smiled at the mental image of the agent and his brood, ducking behind cars and slinking into alleyways while waiting for the blast of the rifle.

Sam's rifle.

Tyron stood and began casually making his way in the opposite direction of the flowing crowd. He pulled his hat low as he walked through the racing people, all of whom were looking at city hall...as he knew they would be. Even with the flyers of his face being plastered all over town, no one gave him a second glance, such was the intensity of their focus.

He sidled up to the side of the hardware store and waited for the street to empty. Without the cover of darkness, he needed the town preoccupied.

After the last of the monkeys scampered by, he skirted around to the back of the building. He slipped out his pick tools and disengaged the rear door's deadbolt. Inside, the bitch and mongrel would be waiting for word of his capture.

He gently pushed open the door and slipped across the threshold. Closing it behind him, he remained in the shadows while his eyes adjusted to the gloom.

The mongrel's muffled voice floated through the stuffy stillness. "Where did everyone go?"

"I don't know. Should we go see?" The bitch's words sent ripples of happy goosebumps over his entire body, soothing his nerves like cool water on scorched flesh.

He closed his eyes, inhaling deeply. Below the aroma of old wood, plastic, and dust, the scent of her hair and skin caressed his olfactory senses like the tender touch of a new lover. He imagined the smoothness of her lips and the sweet saltiness of her sweat and tears. Felt the heat of her blood as it flowed unhindered and free between his fingers.

Erebus' body began to tingle in anticipation.

He opened his eyes. Sliding along the back wall to the end of the last aisle, he peered around a row of paint cans and display of brushes. The bitch and mongrel stood on either side of the big picture window, staring out.

"No," the mongrel said, shaking her head. "We're supposed to wait here. That's what your boyfriend told us to do."

"He's not my boyfriend, and I wish you'd stop calling him that."

The mongrel glanced up and down the street. "Well, you did go out on a date, and you spent the night with him. Not that I blame you, he's pretty hot in an incompetent, let's-get-everyone-killed sort of way."

The news slammed into Tyron like a block of ice. Bradford and the bitch had been intimate. His blood got so hot it threatened to pressure cook his brain.

Erebus had been toying with the ex-military man. While he'd found their simple game amusing, it posed no more of a threat to him or his destiny than rain to the ocean. But this. This changed everything. No more games. No more latitude. No more anything. The next time he had the chance, he would put the agent down like a stray dog.

Tyron stared at the whoring bitch through a new prism of understanding. He would have to work that much harder to cleanse her of her flaws. Redeeming her would take even *longer* and require so much more effort than he'd anticipated. He clenched his fists in rage. The nails pressed into the flesh of his palm until drops of blood began seeping between his fingers, falling to the floor like a spring rain.

"There's nothing going on right now," the mongrel reported. "Nature's calling. I'm going to go find the bathroom." Abandoning her post, she strolled down the front aisle and out of sight.

Erebus took a deep cleansing breath. He had to let go of his anger for now and focus on the task at hand. His jagged nerves calmed and his shaking subsided. He crept forward, his sneakers soundless on the old wood.

The closer he got, the more his senses drew her in. Temporarily forgetting her heathenistic sins, he bathed in her scent, lavishing in the warmth of her aura. Just a few feet from her, he paused. The anticipation of being this close was so delicious he couldn't help but stop and savor the moment.

"Hey, psycho boy." The words from behind him broke his reverence. He turned just as a shovel, wielded by the mongrel, made its arch toward his head. As he completed the rotation, he caught the brunt of the gardening tool's momentum full on in the face.

His nose crunched, and Tyron Erebus' world went black.

☆☆☆☆

Tyron floated back on an inky sea of semiconsciousness, awakening to the bitch's angry voice. "We need to get Sam. He can deal with this bastard."

"He's been trying to kill you for months," the mongrel snapped. "Don't you want to get a little revenge first? Besides, I don't trust anyone else. Your boyfriend, the police, and the FBI have had more than their fair share of chances and they keep failing. I say we do it ourselves."

Of course the mongrel would want to slaughter him. That would be her instinct. Kill or be killed, such was the way of animals.

Erebus remained still, keeping his eyes closed and his breathing shallow while assessing his body and surroundings.

He lay on the floor, but he couldn't have been out for more than a few seconds since they hadn't tied him up yet. His face throbbed, and the scars stung as though a thousand angry hornets had descended upon him. Blood seeped from his broken nose, dripped into his mouth, and pooled beneath his cheek. His ears rang as if an exuberant bell choir had taken up residence in his skull.

Otherwise, he seemed to be okay.

Tyron cracked open one of his eyes just enough to see the two women standing over him. The bitch explained she didn't feel right about killing anyone, not even someone who had tried to kill her.

The mongrel threw her hands up and turned away. "Ugh! You're impossible sometimes."

"I just can't do it, Ang. I vowed to protect those that couldn't protect themselves and to put those who deserved it behind bars. There's a system for dealing with these low-lifes. I should know because I'm part of it. Besides, I think Sam's right. Neither of us has killed anyone before, and I don't think this is the time to start."

Though the bitch had argued for due process, he knew that subconsciously she longed to be one with him. She'd fought him and, by all appearances, had struggled for her own survival. However, on some level, whether she acknowledged it or not, she knew that their destinies intertwined. Her desire to be purified—to become part of something larger, more substantial, more stellar—was what drove her sentimental and seemingly foolish defense of him. She desired him just as much as he desired her.

Tyron had to keep himself from smiling.

The mongrel stared at her, exasperated, and shook her head. "Fine, have it your way." She ripped open a package of zip ties. "You can call the police, send him to jail, or whatever makes it so you can sleep at night, but in the meantime, I'm tying him up. There's no way I'm giving him the chance to hurt us again."

When she grabbed Erebus' hands, he seized her arms, flipped her over, and punched her in the face in one smooth movement.

The bitch screamed and leapt on his back. She wrapped her hands around his head and tried to dig her nails into his eyes.

He flung her off, and she crashed into a rack of paint brushes. The machete strapped to her hip, skittered across the floor. Its blade stuck fast under a display of gardening gloves, spades, and flower seeds.

The mongrel grabbed a ball-peen hammer from her tool belt and took a swing at his head.

Tyron ducked and narrowly missed getting pinged in the temple as the steel head whizzed by his face. He slapped the tool from her hand, grabbed her wrists, and threw her to the floor. Pinning her down with one hand, he wrapped the other around her throat and began to squeeze.

"You will not stop us from fulfilling our destiny," he snarled.

She bucked and twisted, but her fight faded quickly.

Just as her eyes rolled up into her head, pain so severe it seemed as though someone had stuck a lightning rod through his calf muscle ripped up his leg. The crack-snap of electricity permeated the air, accompanied by the aroma of fried ozone and seared flesh.

He fell off the mongrel, clutching his injured leg.

The bitch aimed a Taser at his hip as she dove after him.

He backhanded her across the face before she could reestablish contact and electrocute him again.

Her head whipped to the side with such force that she collided with a display case. The rack crashed to the floor, sending smoke detectors rolling in every direction.

He tried to stand, but spasms jerked and twisted his muscles into knots. Instead, he bellycrawled to where the bitch had already gotten up onto her hands and knees. She glared at him as he approached and reached for her toolbelt with a trembling hand.

Just as her fingers graced the handle of a long screwdriver, Erebus punched her in the face.

She went down, falling into an ungraceful heap among the smoke alarms and fire safety paraphernalia. One of the pamphlets fluttered open to a cartoon sketch demonstrating the stop, drop, and roll technique.

Tyron hoisted himself onto a five-gallon bucket and massaged his seizing muscles until the worst of the pain passed. Gingerly getting to his feet, he hobbled across the store to a row of fully assembled wheelbarrows. He yanked one out and parked it next to the bitch.

Fighting cramps and spasms, he lifted her up and dumped her into the tub. He grabbed a tarp off a nearby shelf and draped it over the woman, tucking it neatly under her feet. If someone spotted them, they might not recognize a body in the open barrel.

The mongrel had begun to moan as Tyron pushed the unconscious girl toward the front door.

He loved the symmetry of using her own hammer to end her pathetic existence. But as he bent to retrieve the tool, his calf muscle seized again, and he feared the effort would cause his leg to begin another round of disabling convulsions.

He settled for kicking the prone girl in the head as he walked past. As her body jerked, he stumbled but caught himself before falling to the floor.

As satisfying as it would have been to put the mongrel down, he would have to be content with killing the one person she cared about most.

Tyron unlatched the thumb-bolt and pulled open the door. Squinting against the bright but sinking sun, he scanned both directions. The boardwalk and beyond remained deserted. He pushed the wheelbarrow across the threshold and toward their destiny.

Chapter Thirty-Three

Sam ran toward city hall.

Erebus isn't there, Chet informed him.

Sam didn't slow until he slid to a stop at the roof's stairwell entrance. He tried the knob, but it refused to turn. "Keys. Who's got the keys?"

Max ran up beside him, panting for breath. "The door's locked? I don't understand; we unlocked it earlier. How did it get locked again?"

Sam considered trying to break the door down, but the reinforced steel frame, handle, and casing would resist all efforts short of explosives.

"We need to find the janitor," Max said as he led the way to the front door.

Sam followed him into the building.

They checked each of the offices but found them locked as well.

Sam shook his head. "There's no one here."

Max held up a finger. "Wait, there's one other place." He opened a side door and flipped a switch, bathing a downward staircase in light. He descended into the basement but froze halfway.

Sam ducked beneath the ceiling to see, but he already had a good idea of what he'd find. In the corner, propped up against the wall, a man in coveralls stared sightlessly. A bloom of red had blossomed across the front of his work shirt.

Max closed his eyes and looked away. "Mr. Delphini. He's worked here since about forever ago."

Sam slipped past him on the stairs and knelt next to the dead man. "I'm sorry, Max. But we don't have time to mourn right now." He began to search the janitor's pockets but found nothing. "No keys."

Max looked one more time, turned, and headed back to the stairs. "There should be another set in the office. I'll call in Mrs. Finley; she's the head secretary." In the atrium, Max picked up a wall phone, listened for a second, and then slammed the receiver back into its cradle. "Of course. The phones are out. I'll get someone to run over to her house and get them."

Sam led the way back outside. "Get someone you trust to check things on the roof. I left my rifle up there. So make sure they are smart enough to handle a gun. He may—"

That's gone, Chet interrupted. *Erebus took it. It's probably what he used to kill the husband. Remember the shot that we heard right before the poor schmuck fell over the ledge?*

Sam stopped on the steps of the building. *But why? Why, for god's sake?*

This is all a distraction. He's slowing you down.

The radios. He heard us. He knows where Monica is.

Max looked at him expectantly. "He may what?"

Sam shook his head. "Never mind about the gun. I think Erebus has it."

"What?"

Sam began down the steps again. "We need to get to the hardware store. I'll bet that's where Erebus is headed, if he's not already there."

Max followed, but Sam stopped him. "Wait. I need you to finish what you started. Get the flyers out, get people looking for him, and get the keys. Then join me." Sam turned and began running across the park.

It's too late, Chet said. *We took too long to figure it out. He's got her.*

Though he agreed with his inner conscience, Sam had to remain open to any scenario. *You never know. There's two of them. They've defeated him before.*

They got lucky before. He won't underestimate them again.

Sam ran faster.

Sam made it to Alabaster Cove Hardware in record time. With his back to the side of the building, he tried to listen. But if there was anything going on inside, he couldn't hear it over the chugging of his own breath and the freight train gallop of his heart.

Sliding his Sig Sauer from the waistband of his jeans, he chambered a round. Sam tried to glance in through the big picture window, but without cupping his hand around his face to cut down on the glare—making him a very visible target to anyone inside—he couldn't see anything except his own reflection.

He jogged down the alleyway, glanced around the corner, and made his way to the service entrance.

The second he opened the door, he would be a backlit target. He closed his eyes—allowing his pupils to become accustomed to the dark—hunched low, flung open the door, and rolled inside. As he popped up into a crouch, he swept his gun back and forth.

Nothing moved, and no one shouted.

Staying low, he began making his way around the perimeter of the store. He had to step around random racks, tools, smoke detectors, and paper littering the floor. No Erebus and no girls, but something had happened. It looked as if the place had been ransacked.

Maybe if he could have tapped into the sheriff's resources, he could have surrounded Monica with a dozen armed men waiting for Erebus to make his move. But the police were busy tearing apart April's house and cleaning up the destruction the madman had left in his wake. With only a handful of untrained volunteers, Sam had been forced to hide the women and use the little manpower he had at his disposal to keep vigil on the park.

Cursing under his breath, he continued searching. Down the back aisle, a figure lay sprawled out on the floor. Too small to be a man. One of the girls.

He sidled down the row, expecting a trap, but hearing nothing, he knelt. Angel. Remaining alert, he reached down and touched her neck. Her skin was warm and her heartbeat strong and steady.

"Angel," he whispered, while trying to watch both ends of the aisle at the same time. "Angel."

She didn't move. He needed to finish securing the building, then he'd try and wake her.

Sam made his way to the back office, up the stairs, through the remaining aisles, and into the storeroom. Nothing. He holstered his weapon.

Returning to the woman, he pulled out a small flashlight and shined it over her face. Dark purple bruises lined her eyes, and a ligature-like ring circled her neck. Erebus had beaten her up and choked her, yet he'd left her alive. Somehow, she had survived another encounter with the madman.

He scooped Angel up in his arms. She needed to go to the hospital. She may have had internal bleeding or a concussion. Plus, he needed the doctors to wake her up so he could find out what had happened.

Marching to the door, he had just reached for the knob when it flew open, crashing into him. Sam stumbled and fell. Angel's body landed on his chest, knocking the wind out of him. He struggled, trying to get out from under the unconscious girl.

Someone grabbed him by the shirt and hauled him up.

"Max, it's me," Sam wheezed.

"Huh? Oh, Sam." Max released him, and Sam fell back to the floor. Angel once again rolled on top of him.

The little bit of air still remaining in Sam's lungs went out in a rush. "Get Angel off me."

"Sorry, sorry," Max said, scrambling to get his arms under her. "It's really dark in here."

When the weight came off, Sam got to his feet.

"You guys are killing me," Angel muttered. "Put me down, Max."

Crouching, Max set her on the floor. "Are you okay?"

She rubbed her forehead. "I was doing a whole lot better before you two extras from *Morons Gone Wild* came to 'help' me. Actually, calling you morons is an insult to morons." She touched her swollen cheek. "Damn, my face and throat hurt."

Max tried to brush some hair off of her forehead, but she smacked his hand away. "What did I just say? I'm hurt. That means, don't touch."

"Sorry, sorry."

Angel sat up, wincing. She rubbed her stomach, winced even harder, and then scooted back so she could lean against the counter.

"So, ah, Angel," Max said. "What happened?"

"What do you mean what happened?" she snapped. "Erebus happened. That's what. Are you his idiotic backup team that's here to ask me a bunch of stupid questions until I take my own life?"

"Did he take Monica?"

She rolled her eyes. "And the hits keep on coming. You think she went for ice cream?" She swallowed, cringing. "We really have no chance with the two of you in charge. I should have known this plan was a bust."

Max opened his mouth, but Sam cut him off. "Did he say anything that might have tipped you off as to what he was planning to do with her?"

"Finally, a question that makes a *little* sense. But, no. While he was choking me, he said something about me not preventing him from fulfilling his destiny, but that's all."

She paused as she seemed to reconsider. "No, that's not quite right. He said I wouldn't prevent *us* from fulfilling *our* destiny. 'Our,' plural."

Max frowned. "When he nailed me to the floor, he'd mentioned the Fates. Did he say anything more about that?"

Angel shook her head. "No. Just 'our' destiny."

"I don't know what any of that means," Max said.

Sam sat down next to her. "Don't take this the wrong way, but I don't understand why you are still alive." He looked at Max. "Each of you survived run-ins with Erebus."

She held up her fingers. "This is my third rodeo with the bastard, and to be quite honest, I'm really getting tired of it."

"I'll bet. Do you think you can walk? We need to get you to the hospital."

Angel sighed. "Probably. But we don't have time for doctors; we have to go find Monica. I don't think he's got an afternoon of pizza and a movie in mind."

"I know how to find them," Sam said. "Let's get someone to look at you, and then Max and I will go round up the troops."

She furrowed her brow. "What do you mean you know how to find them? Since when did you become telepathic?"

"Not telepathy," Sam said, shaking his head. "Technology." He reached for her hand. "Come on, let's get you to the doctor."

Angel smacked it away. "Hold on there, cowboy. What do you mean 'technology?'"

She's not going to like this one bit, Chet warned him.

"A bug," Sam admitted. "I slipped a tracking device into her pocket this morning in case something went wrong."

Angel's face contorted with rage. "You what?" Her eyes blazed. "You *let* him take her."

Sam held up his hands. "No. I—"

"I can't believe it," she interrupted. "I knew you were an asshole, but I didn't know you were an asshole's asshole." She glared so hard that Sam could swear his skin was beginning to blister.

"You used her as bait, and now he has my friend." Angel's hand snaked out cobra-quick, grabbed Sam's ear, twisted, and yanked.

Before he'd had a chance to process what she was doing, he found himself facedown against the floor. Excruciating pain exploded from the side of his head. Angel got onto his back and ground his cheek into the pine board. "You used her as bait," she hissed.

"I didn't use her as bait," he wheezed. "The tracking device was a backup plan in case something went wrong. That's all."

Her breath, hot against his face, almost burnt his skin with its venom. "You *let* something go wrong, and now he's got her."

Max paced, watching them. "Angel, I was there. Erebus took us by surprise. No one saw it coming."

She twisted Sam's ear harder. "Well, Mr. FBI here *should* have seen it coming. That's what he's supposed to be trained to do. Or do you only seduce and abandon helpless women?"

Sam considered explaining that Monica, who was anything but helpless, had asked him to leave after their one and only date. Not the other way around. But he had a feeling she already knew this, yet still blamed him, so it seemed pointless to argue. "Angel, we have to get to my gear and get the tracker. We don't have time for this. If you want to kill me, do it after we save Monica."

Angel grunted, gave his ear one more hard twist, and got off of him.

Sam slowly stood up. The side of his head felt as though he'd stopped a speeding truck by dragging his ear against the asphalt.

Angel marched to the door, flung it open, and stormed out into the evening sunshine.

Max watched her go but made no move to follow. "I guess she's okay."

Sam rubbed his ear. "Yeah, I don't think there's a doctor in town I'd wish that hot mess on. I just hope your friend was able to get the keys. The tracker is in my bag, which is still on the roof of city hall."

Max looked at the door Angel had just vacated, then turned back to Sam. "Well, if not, I'm sure Angel could just gnaw the door down with her bare teeth."

Once they were sure the coast was clear, they followed her out and headed back to the center of town.

Chapter Thirty-Four

Sam, Max, and Angel arrived at city hall just as a tiny, gray-haired woman pulled up in an aging Prius.

"Hello, Mrs. Finley," Max said as she got out of her car.

She closed and locked the door, then made her way to the bottom of the side stairwell. "I don't understand all of this fuss. Why are you dragging me out on Sunday afternoon? I have a casserole in the oven, and now I'm missing the Super mo... mov..." She stopped mid-stride, her gaze riveted on the man hanging by his neck in the deepening twilight.

From behind thick lenses, her eyes grew impossibly huge, the red veins wrapping around the whites like barber poles.

She put one hand to her wrinkled lips and gasped. "Oh my." She glanced around at the faces surrounding her. "What happened? Why is that man...oh my. That's why you needed my..." She began to fumble in her purse. A thick ring of keys tumbled from her quaking fingers and clattered to the sidewalk. She started to bend over to get them.

Sam moved forward to help her, but Angel beat him.

She put a hand on the gray-haired woman's shoulder. "I'll get them, Mrs. Finley." Angel retrieved the keys and handed them to Sam. She looped her arm through Mrs. Finley's, stabilizing the secretary as she began to sway on her feet. "I've got you," Angel said. "Can you tell me which one opens the outside stairwell door?"

Mrs. Finley continued to gawk at the man hanging by his neck. "The um... The um... The brass one. With the blue handle."

Sam flipped through the keys until he found one that matched the description. He slid it into the knob and the lock turned. After removing the key from the loop, he handed the ring back to Angel, who slid it into the secretary's purse.

Mrs. Finley looked at Angel. "I know that man. It's Mike. Mike Sutlan. He and his wife, Rachel, run the little garden store over on Third. He's a really nice man. He comes in once in a while to talk to the mayor about the layout in the park. He does the plants. He's a really nice man."

She glanced around the group again. "Why would anyone want to hurt him?"

"I don't know, Mrs. Finley," Angel replied, holding onto the woman's arm.

A big tear slid down her wrinkled cheek. "He's a really nice man. Why would anyone hurt him?" she asked again.

Angel's expression softened. "We're going to find the person responsible for this. Okay? Right now, one of these gentlemen will take you home."

A man in his mid-twenties stepped forward. "Come with me, Mrs. Finley."

The aging secretary took the man's offered arm. She glanced up once more at the figure hanging by the rope, and then allowed herself to be led away. "Henry, I don't know why anyone would hurt Mike. He was such a nice man."

The couple slowly continued down the sidewalk and back to her car.

Angel turned to Sam, a glaring accusation in her gaze, but she held her tongue.

Sam opened the stairwell door.

Both Angel and Max tried to precede him, but he held up a hand, stopping them. "Me first. If Erebus set a trap, I want to be the one to find it."

"Then, please. Lead the way," Angel said, sweeping her arm toward the entrance.

Sam entered the stifling, fully enclosed stairwell. Light bulbs, anchored to the wall like small caged animals, did little to chase away the shadows. He pulled out his phone and turned on the flashlight, waving the small beam over every surface—walls, ceiling, floor—before moving up to the next step.

The utilitarian passageway, continuous flowing concrete steps and walls, contained no place to conceal traps or any protrusions from which to string wire. Sam moved quickly, but since he'd underestimated Erebus before, he remained vigilant. Nothing hid in the shadows, and he reached the final step without incident.

Before opening the closed door at the end of the top flight, he ran the light over every inch of the frame, searching for telltale imperfections that might indicate a rigged explosive. But other than the usual scuffmarks of a well-used entrance, he found nothing.

Angel and Max had followed close behind, watching him but saying nothing.

He turned to them. "Get back. If the door is rigged, I don't want it taking all of us out."

They glanced at one another and then retreated to the next lower landing. Their luminous eyes shone bright in the gloom as they stared up at him.

Sam returned his attention to the door.

This is taking too much time, Chet complained. *Erebus is getting further away with every passing minute.*

Sam peered around the edge of the frame one more time. *I know, but he's kind of been into explosives lately, and I don't want to be the next recipient of his latest hobby. We have to be careful.*

Chet remained quiet for a moment. *There's nothing here. He didn't have time.*

Are you sure?

Yes, but if your bag is still there, check it for anything he might have tossed inside. There could be a nasty surprise waiting for us.

Sam grasped the doorknob, turned, and pushed.

Other than the high-pitched squeak of the hinges, wailing like a cat in heat, nothing happened.

Chet laughed. *You winced.*

Searching for trip wires as he went, Sam made his way around the perimeter of the roof, stopping on the far side where he'd spent the afternoon waiting for the madman to make his move. The duffle remained where he'd left it. Though, as Chet suspected, Sam's rifle was gone.

Max and Angel poked their heads through the door.

Sam held up his hand. "Hold on. I need to check my bag first. Once I've verified it's secure, you can let everyone know it's safe to come up."

"What about your gun?" Max asked.

Sam shook his head.

Max's face went pale.

Sam knelt next to the satchel. He cursed himself for leaving it, but at the time, it had seemed more important to stop Rachel from blowing up half the citizens of town. Gently, he pulled back each pocket. The Velcro fasteners sounded like exploding grenades in his ears, and it took every ounce of will to keep from flinching each time he ripped one open.

As he pulled one of the fasteners apart, the glint of metal froze his galloping heart as though it had been dropped into liquid nitrogen. When he didn't immediately explode, he took another look, and his blood began pumping again as he recognized the extra clip for his Sig Sauer.

Frigging bag has more pockets than a herd of kangaroos, Chet complained.

Sam paused as he took a breath. *Tell me about it. We get through this and I'm dumping this thing. Okay, it's clean on the outside. Let's see if he messed with the peanut butter in our Reese's.*

Sam slowly unzipped the bag until the central opening stared at him like an infected eye. *I don't see anything.*

Chet shook his head. *It isn't what he left, but what he took. Do you see what's missing?*

Sam opened the bag wider. *Damn.* He poked around, less careful now. But nothing else appeared out of place. He turned to the anxious couple watching him. "Okay, you can let everyone come up now."

Max gave the all clear, then came over to him. "You didn't find anything in your bag?"

"On the contrary. The extra clips for the rifle are gone."

Max and Angel, matching expressions of horror on their faces, glanced around at the surrounding buildings.

"Well, that's just great," Angel growled. "Please tell me you at least have the transmitter?"

Sam pulled out the small device and flicked it on. It hesitated, then a green light blipped on its black screen, the pulse steady and strong. He turned it around so they could see. "We've got him."

With Angel and Max on his heels, Sam charged down the stairs and followed the small green blip on the transponder screen. When he reached the other side of the park, he stopped, studied the small device, and then pointed at a narrow road heading toward the beach. "That way."

Max looked over Sam's shoulder. "It's hard to tell how far away it is, but I'm guessing it's one of the houses either on Oak or Maple."

As they jogged down the sidewalk, Sam glanced up a dead-end street at April Goodman's house. Yellow crime scene tape now barred the door.

They turned down Maple Avenue. Sam tried to not think about what Erebus could be doing to Monica or that the killer had a military-grade rifle. The psycho could, right now, be cutting her to pieces or lining them up in the gun's crosshairs.

Sam followed the transponder to the side of a simple, single-story bungalow with washed-out trim, a failing gutter system, and weed-choked yard. "This is it." He shut the tracker down and pulled out his gun.

Angel started up the front steps.

"What are you doing?" Max stage-whispered.

She turned on him, pointing back at the house. "I'm going in there and getting my friend. Let that bastard come at me."

Sam would be less effective trying to stop her than he would be trying to bend a steel spoon with his mind, but he could at least take the point position. "I'm going in first." Once again under Angel's withering glare, he marched up the porch steps.

Protocol dictated that he go in low and sweep for targets. *Screw protocol.*

Sam smashed open the door with his foot. The door-frame exploded, sending tinkling wood shrapnel flying in every direction. As he charged into the living room, the putrid aroma of decaying flesh clubbed him over the head as though delivered by the business end of Thor's hammer.

Max gagged as he and Angel followed Sam into the house.

A head covered in white hair poked out above the top of an old leather recliner. The television blared the Sunday Super movie that Mrs. Finley had been so anxious to watch.

The figure didn't move as Sam circled him, gun extended. When Sam came around the front of the overstuffed chair, he lowered his weapon.

An old man had been strapped into the worn recliner. Dry, sunken eyes with milky irises stared at the blathering TV. Gore from a gaping slash in his neck coated his shirt. His purple and black mottled skin sagged, and various fluids leaked from his eyes, nose, and mouth.

Max and Angel started to follow him, but Sam held up his hand. "You don't need to see this." He kept his breathing shallow in a vain attempt to inhale as little of the dead man as possible. "We should search the rest of the house."

She's not here, Chet informed him. *Nobody is.*

Sam moved down the hallway, his gun pointed at one of the two closed doors. *I don't think so either, but we have to do our due diligence.*

One's a bedroom and the other's a bath. There's probably nothing in the bathroom, so clear that first.

Sam kicked in the door at the end of the hall. True to Chet's prediction, a toilet, shower, and sink lay on the other side, but no one waited for them in the closet-sized space. Sam turned his attention to the second door. He kicked it in as well and swept the room with his gun. Nothing jumped out at him, and no bullets flew in his direction. Moving to the closet, he pulled aside the clothes, then checked under the bed.

Max and Angel stood in the entrance, staring at the simple mattress on the Hollywood bedframe. Covered in a thick, black substance that could only be old blood, the comforter and sheets looked as cold and hard as lava rock from an ancient eruption.

"Where is she?" Angel asked. "I thought your gizmo said she was here?"

Confused, Sam shook his head. He flipped on the transponder. "It says she's right here. We're practically standing on top of her."

"Guys," Max said from the corner.

Sam and Angel looked up.

Max held up a pile of clothes.

"No!" Angel ran over and grabbed a shirt from the stack.

Sam frowned. "What is it?"

Angel unfolded the garment to reveal a picture of the Eiffel Tower in glowing pink sequins. "I bought this in Paris."

Max shook his head. "What? Are you saying Erebus raided your closet?"

"No, dummy," Angel snapped. "Monica borrowed it from me. She was wearing it when that bastard grabbed her this afternoon."

Sam stared as the ramifications of this information sank in. The trail had just run cold.

Chapter Thirty-Five

S o, let me see if I have this straight." Sheriff Austin said, lifting up the brim of his hat and scratching his head. "This Erebus fella strolled into town, killed April Goodman then Elon Wick, the owner of this house." He jerked a thumb over his shoulder.

The sheriff continued, "He hung out for a couple weeks, then blew up the dock and strapped a bomb to Rachel Sutlan's stomach. And while you were busy disarming said bomb, he shot Rachel's husband, Mike Sutlan, with *your* gun and hung him from the roof of city hall."

The lawman pointed at Angel. "Even though you hit him in the face with a shovel, he beat you up and kidnapped Monica, the girl who had been reported dead but wasn't? Do I have that about right?"

Angel held up one of Max's hands. "You missed that he nailed Max to the floor of his own shop and tried to put a stake in his forehead."

"Oh, and he was holding Sam at gunpoint until we hit him with the car," Angel said.

"And that he put a bomb in Sam's radio," Max added.

The sheriff harrumphed while scribbling on his clipboard.

"I think that's everything...in this town," Sam said. "There's more of course, but it's not relevant to us finding him."

That's quite an impressive resume, Chet said. *Come on, Sheriff,* he urged. *Say it. I dare you.*

Sam frowned at his inner conscience. *He's not going to say it. Now, can you let me concentrate?*

The sheriff ran his finger down the list. "That's an impressive resume."

Chet did a touchdown victory dance. *Booyah! Who's your daddy?*

Angel pushed the sheriff's clipboard down. "We don't have time for paperwork. We need to find Monica. *Now.*"

Sheriff Austin tugged the clipboard out of her grasp. "Thank you so much for your insightful suggestion. I wouldn't have known to look for a missing, kidnapped girl if you hadn't told me."

Angel opened her mouth to give, no doubt, an unpleasant retort, but Sam stopped her.

"Look, Sheriff," Sam said. "We aren't trying to tell you how to do your job. But this guy is out of control and we need to find him. If he hasn't already killed Monica, he will. After he killed Elon, I think he hid here while you and your men canvassed the area. I'd suggest another canvass. This time, if no one answers, you go in and check yourselves."

Sheriff Austin looped a thick thumb through a beltloop on his khakis. "Are you suggesting breaking and entering? I'm as desperate to find this guy as the rest of you, but we are still a law-abiding community. If the police start ignoring the law, then things fall into chaos."

Sam let out a frustrated breath. "I'm not talking about ignoring anything; I'm talking about being thorough. Make sure that Erebus has no place to hide. If a house is locked up, find someone who has the key. This is more than protecting your citizens' rights; this is about keeping them alive."

The sheriff studied Sam so long that he wondered if maybe the lawman intended to arrest him instead.

Finally, Austin beckoned to one of his deputies. "Get every available officer and do a sweep of the whole town. Start on the south end, create a line, but do not let any house go unsearched. Do you have that? None." He turned to Sam. "Satisfied?"

"I'll only be satisfied when this bastard is dead," Angel replied.

Sheriff Austin regarded her. "I understand that you're planning to go into law enforcement yourself?"

Angel stood taller, staring him in the eyes. "Yes. So what?"

"Here's your first lesson," he said, pushing back the brim of his hat. "Sometimes things don't go the way you want them to. Sometimes you don't stop the bad guys before they do bad things." He looked at each of them in turn. "I've given you freedom and leeway because it seemed like the best course of action. But things have gotten out of hand. We are no closer to catching this guy than we were yesterday, and more good people have died because of it."

Angel started to argue, but the sheriff held up his hand. "I don't want to see any of you out there helping or taking the law into your own hands. You've made a mess, and now the cleanup crew is here to straighten things out. Do I make myself clear?"

Instead of backing down, Angel leaned in. "If it comes to me or him, I will put him down like a dog. Do I make *myself* clear?"

The sheriff stared at her a moment longer before shaking his head. "Just stay out of our way."

She stared back. "Don't worry. You won't even know I'm there."

"Okay, it's going to be another long night." The lawman turned to his deputies. "Let's get moving." He and his officers loaded up into their cars and drove away.

Chapter Thirty-Six

Monica awoke to blinding, harsh lights drenching her like acid rain. She tried covering her eyes but couldn't move her arm. She tugged again, with the same result. Still dazed and semiconscious, she blinked against the glare as she strained to see why. Heavy straps bound her wrists, securing her to the top of a table.

Not good.

Craning her neck, she looked above her head, hoping someone might be nearby to help. As soon as she did, she regretted making the effort. A wicked array of knives, scalpels, scissors, hooks, needles, and other nastiness gleamed menacingly on a silver tray.

Really not good.

She shivered and suddenly realized that her bare back and legs were pressed uncomfortably against the cool wooden surface. Looking down at her body, she discovered that her clothes, save her panties and bra, had been removed.

Yet more not good.

Who would strap her down, remove her clothes, and delude himself into thinking he was a surgeon? Then, through her murky headache, she remembered the hardware store. Erebus.

The worst.

Monica tugged against her wrist bindings. When that failed, she attempted to swing her body from side to side. Her efforts only seemed to be making the straps tighter and, perplexingly, the room smaller. Her lungs began to billow as they desperately tried to sustain her on air that suddenly lacked the necessary elements. Primal, self-preservation instinct kicked in, pushing her to flee.

Get away. At all costs, run. Now.

The vulturous mantra circled around and around, dive-bombing her mind and fragmenting her thoughts. Monica twisted and yanked, pulling so hard a tiny voice in her head squeaked a warning that she might snap her bones or shred her tendons. Even if she ripped her arms and legs from their sockets and tore her body to pieces, she didn't care. She just wanted to be free from the straps. Free from this block of wood. Free from this place. Free from Erebus.

Nothing else mattered.

After several minutes of futile struggling, she screamed in frustration and collapsed back against the table while the express train of her heart thundered wildly against her sternum. She lay spent as her evaporating sweat turned to steam and drifted away on currents of deoxygenated air. Monica's chest heaved and her muscles twitched. Her efforts not only hadn't loosened her bonds but had left her skin chafed and raw as if she'd exfoliated it with a cheese grater.

She needed to think. She needed a plan. She needed a knife...or better yet, her machete.

Monica looked around. To her left, a wall rack held several sharp-edged tools. Any one of those would probably work, except she had no way to reach them. A tall red and silver tool chest parked at the end of a long workbench also lay beyond her grasp. To her right, a large boxy machine—maybe a vacuum system or something—took up a sizeable portion of the wall yet offered her no means of escape.

A workshop. She was in a workshop. But which one? Though the adrenaline pumping through her system had begun to clear her mind, she still struggled, wading through a Scotland-worthy haze.

She looked down at the long, dark space beyond her feet. A helter-skelter of surfboards and woodworking supplies littered the floor.

Max's. I'm in Max's shop.

At least she knew where she was. Now, if she could just get loose. She twisted her wrists, trying to gain a little slack in the bindings.

"Hello, bitch." The familiar voice echoed in the cavernous space.

She froze as a wave of electrified tremors radiated through every nerve in her body.

"You won't get loose," Erebus informed her. "Those are industrial-strength nylon ties and custom rachets. I've waited a very long time for this, and I didn't want to take any chances that you'd get away."

"You bastard. Let me go. You know that my friends are looking for me. When they find you, you're dead."

Erebus laughed humorlessly. "I seriously doubt they have time for you. They are too busy chasing ghosts and waiting for me to gun them down."

"What are you talking about?"

"It's not important. Let's just say it's been a rather amusing afternoon."

She looked along the wall, trying to see past the bright overheads. Twisting her neck painfully, she scanned the shop. On the second sweep, she found the silhouette standing in the doorway that led into the back of the store.

Though unimpressive in mass, Erebus projected the presence of a much larger man. As if his flesh contained not a soul but a rancorous demon who would, at any second, explode from his body in a spray of bone, skin, and blood.

She glared. "Amusing for you maybe. How many people have you killed trying to get me? And for what? I'm nothing, a nobody, just another job. But here's a newsflash for you; your boss is dead. The job has been cancelled."

"You don't get it," the silhouette said, shaking his head.

Monica could almost see the horns, wings, and claws of the beast waiting to be free of Erebus' body.

That monster had touched her. He'd carried her here, removed her clothes, and the Lord only knew what else while she'd been unconscious. Monica shivered in revulsion. Even if she took a hundred bleach baths, she didn't know if she'd ever feel clean again. As if the infection of him had penetrated her skin, infiltrated her bloodstream, and now fed upon the marrow in her bones.

"You are everything," he said. "You are the path to the next level."

She let her head fall back to the table. "The next what? Level? I don't even know what that means."

Erebus closed the door and glided over to the table. He put his hand on top of her head, stroking her hair.

She wanted to scream in disgust and slink away from his touch, but the damned bindings made that impossible. Instead, she pretended to not notice. Refusing to give him the satisfaction.

"I know you don't understand," he continued. "So let me lay it out for you. In order for me to ascend and become one with the other, I need the right partner. You are that person. Why do you think you've been so hard to catch? The gods would never make it easy to become one of them."

Completely mystified, Monica stared up at his scarred face and glimmering yellow eyes.

It doesn't matter how insane he sounds. Show no fear.

"The reason it wasn't easy to catch me isn't because the gods are testing you; it's because you are highly incompetent," she scoffed. "We've kicked your ass so many times I'm surprised you don't walk funny."

He tsked and shook his head. "That's what someone like you would think, but the gods *wanted* you to test me. You've helped prove my worth. They've known all along that you were the path to my enlightenment, but for me to be allowed to ascend, I had to have the fortitude, the tenacity, the wisdom, and the insight to catch you."

She rolled her head on the hard wood surface. "You're completely crazy and delusional."

Erebus wandered over to the tray and picked up a scalpel, its lethal edge flashing in the overhead light. "You're lucky, you know."

"Are you freaking serious?"

He spun the little blade in his fingers while his eyes found hers. Had they changed color? She'd thought they were yellow, but now they glimmered red, as if the irises had been replaced by picture windows overlooking the firepits in Hell.

"Oh yes," he said. "You see, even though you are undeserving and a nonbeliever, you will get to ascend with me. I will save you. I will redeem you. After tonight, our souls will intermingle, and we will forever be one."

She choked back the terror, keeping it from overwhelming her. Though he made no sense, Erebus believed every bit of his blathering. Instead of arguing with him, she turned his own words against him, hoping to find his deepest— though utterly crazy—fears. "You can rape me, kill me, whatever you want, but I'll *never* be with you. You think that the gods were testing you?" She forced a bark of laughter. "They were *mocking* you, Erebus. You'll never walk among them. In fact, you'll soon be dead. And when you die, there won't be an ascension. Just pain, suffering, and blackness."

But the man she'd been fighting for so long wasn't listening. Rather than reply, he replaced the blade on the tray, closed his eyes, and began to chant softly.

Well, that didn't work.

Monica looked around the room. There had to be some way out of this fix. Her gaze landed on the scalpel. If she could get it, she might be able to get free.

370

She had no idea how long the psychopath would stand there whispering his gibberish to whatever donkey ghoul he imagined wanted him to prove himself, but she wouldn't waste a second of it.

Monica began methodically twisting and bending her restraints, searching for a weakness.

Sam absently watched Triniti and Angel pace the kitchen. Back and forth, they passed one another. Max sat on the counter, drinking a beer.

Angel groused as she stomped a path in the bright, floral linoleum. "This waiting around is killing me. We should be out there looking for her."

"I want to find her too," Max replied, taking a pull off his beer. "But you heard what the sheriff said. We are supposed to stay out of the way. We won't do anyone any good if we're arrested."

Angel growled, "I want to do something." She looked over at Sam. "What are you doing, Mr. FBI? You're sitting there all quiet."

Sam had only been half-listening and tuned in to the conversation. "I'm trying to review the case in my head. There has to be a clue someplace. Something we missed."

"Do you care to share with the rest of the group?" Triniti asked, stopping to look at him.

Chet glanced around the ragtag collection of wannabe heroes. *Usually you just have me to contend with. Now you're going to have to interact with other human beings. Granted, they aren't as awesome as I am, but I'll bet they'll have better insights than you.*

They do know the town. Maybe...

Try them. Perhaps trusting someone else for once will be good for you.

Sam examined the expectant faces watching him. Taking a deep breath, he started at the beginning, summarizing the Laven Michaels case, Erebus' attempts to kill Monica, Sam's efforts to stop him, and ending with how Sam figured the psychopath had slipped past them and kidnapped Monica. "From the hardware store, he brought her back to Elon's, undressed her, then he must have loaded her up in Elon's car and driven away."

Triniti raised her hand. "Am I the only one confused by her being naked?"

"Actually," Sam said. "It makes perfect sense. When I chased him across the country, I used a tracker app on his phone. He probably thought I'd do something like that again. He didn't want to take the time to search her, so he removed her clothes, thus he——"

"Got rid of any tracking devices you may have planted on her," Triniti finished for him.

"Exactly. And he did it at Elon's because he doesn't need that hideout anymore, and he probably thought we'd waste more time there searching."

"But where would he go?" she asked.

That's the question, Chief, Chet commented. *You've got everyone's attention; you've almost brought it home. Can you put it together?*

Sam frowned at his inner conscience. *I don't know where he took her. It could be anywhere. The beach, the woods, someone's basement.*

He needs time alone with her. A lot of it. In fact, probably most of the night.

Sam glanced around at the expectant faces. "Let's assume Erebus knows we're canvassing the town. Where can he go that he'll be alone that's not in a neighborhood? Is there an abandoned store or a warehouse or something?"

Max shook his head. "I don't know, man. There's no place like that around. Most of the businesses will be too close in proximity to houses to... Oh, shit. I know where he went."

The three of them waited.

Max raised his eyebrows. "Come on. It's totally obvious. Where's the one place in town that's sound-insulated because its owner has heavy equipment and works late at night? Where's the one place in town not near a neighborhood that has a private workshop in the back? Whose owner is injured," Max held up his hands, "so he probably won't be showing up to interrupt Erebus' fun..."

The pieces clicked into place and Sam nodded. "Yes."

Max set down his beer and headed to the door. "Grab your keys, Trin. It's time to go to the office."

Chapter Thirty-Seven

While Erebus continued his rambling chant, Monica pushed and pulled against her restraints until she'd chafed her skin raw.

She had been about to try and shift her efforts to the strap holding her legs when a cool breeze washed over her bare skin. She paused, wondering if the air conditioner had kicked in, but aside from the rhythmical blathering of the lunatic standing over her, the room remained as still and lifeless as the inside of a mausoleum.

In an instant, the temperature plummeted. Her body shook and her teeth chattered. In the harsh lights, her exhalations turned to frost, as if she had been transported to the middle of a frozen lake deep in the heart of Alaska.

A sulfurish, moldyish—like burning rotten seaweed in a smoldering car tire—smell drifted through the air. Like the frigidity, she couldn't identify the source of the odor. Perplexingly, she realized that, while the rest of her body was practically hypothermic, the bottoms of her feet had grown uncomfortably warm.

Just great. The damned place is on fire. I'm chained up like some dog and frigging Erebus is touring the outer planets.

She stared down past her body, trying to identify the source of the heat. But the room appeared to be as vacant and motionless as it had a few minutes before.

No flames illuminated the space. No glowing embers. No smoke.

The tendrils of heat slinked up her calves. It washed over her thighs, stomach, and breasts, then wrapped around her neck like an electric blanket set on broil. Erebus had made no move to touch her, yet phantom fingers ran themselves through her hair and along her cheeks.

She began to sweat, but her exhalations still became plumes of frozen fog just inches above her face.

Monica yanked and tugged some more, swallowing a scream that would surely wake her psychopathic companion. She pulled until the muscles in her arms bulged, but the stubborn straps held firm.

Erebus' eyes snapped open and his relentless chanting halted mid-syllable, the caressing fingers ceased, and the room returned to its normal temperature.

As Monica stared, her heart paused and then began to gallop. Erebus' irises—which had previously been yellow, then had turned red—were now black. As if the laws of light and refraction had been altered, she could now see into an eternity of darkness so deep that, if she gazed too long, would hungrily drink the essence of her soul.

She no longer just feared for her safety but for whatever comprised her spirit. This man, this thing, might just take more than her life; he might also take her salvation.

She focused on freeing her arm, pulling at the restraint with everything in her. The strap dug deeply, splitting the skin. Blood, hot and wet, ran down her hand and dripped onto the floor.

Erebus cocked his head, watching her struggle with the same affection a man might have as he gazed upon his new bride the first time they made love. With long, elaborate strokes, he brushed her hair. His callused palm felt diseased, as if he could somehow infect the follicles on her head with the oil from his skin. "Do not fear. I will purify you. I will cleanse you of your flaws, and you will be redeemed. We will be joined. We will be together forever."

Monica screamed.

The blow to her abdomen knocked the wind from her lungs and the words from her lips. A hard slap across the mouth and her world swam in and out of focus.

A wavy, slightly blurry Erebus waggled a finger in her face. "Now, now. If we get interrupted, we won't be together in the afterlife. We won't get to ascend."

He picked up the scalpel. "Now, shall we begin?"

☆☆☆☆

"Faster, Triniti. Faster." Max urged from the back seat of the bus.

White-knuckling the steering wheel, Triniti navigated the empty streets. As she tore around a corner, the bus leaned precariously to the side.

Sam glanced out the window. The asphalt seemed to be coming up to greet them, and he wondered if the old VW would just tip over, killing them all.

"I'm doing the best I can," Triniti shot back as she righted the vehicle. "Now stop distracting me. You're going to make me wreck."

Too much time had passed. Dread, cold and sorrowful, filled Sam's gut. By the time they'd figured out where to look, Erebus had already been alone with Monica for a couple of hours.

In his mind's eye, he saw the "art" from April's house. Skin painted on canvases and a heart pinned to the wall, rivers of blood and lakes of gore saturating the bed and pooling on the floorboards. The girl's body mangled and floating on the sea.

Though only three miles separated Triniti's house and the surf shop, it felt like hundreds.

Sam checked his watch and shook his head. Whatever they found at Max's store, it would be too late. His efforts to save Monica had been a total failure.

Finally, Triniti guided the bus into a parking spot in front of the surf shop and came to a stop. She hadn't even had time to set the brake before the doors flew open and everyone piled out.

As the group beelined for the entrance, Sam got in front and held up a hand, stopping them. "Hold on. I need you two to stay here."

Angel stuck out her jaw and put her hands on her hips. "What do you mean, 'Stay here?' Um, no. That's not going to happen."

Sam faced her. "Max and I will disable Erebus by whatever means necessary, then you and Triniti come in and get Monica. If something——"

Angel's nostrils flared as she cut him off. "And you're thinking that Max, with holes in his hands, will be better in a fight than us?"

Triniti came over and stood next to Angel. The duo glared at him in unlikely solidarity.

He shook his head. "No, that's not what I think at all. Max is coming because it's his shop. He knows the layout and not only what Erebus could turn into a weapon to use against us but what we could use against him."

"Angel's right," Triniti said. "I spend a lot of time here. We either all go in, or I should be the one that——"

"No," Sam interrupted. "If something happens, we'll need you to go get the sheriff. No one should be alone, so it's absolutely imperative that you both stay here and wait."

The two women glanced at each other. The rage in their eyes for once not directed at one another.

Finally, Angel turned to him. "And exactly how are we supposed to know when to come in?"

"One of us will come out and get you," Sam said. "Or if we're too busy, Max will flash the store lights. Either way, you'll know. If neither of those things happen, go get help."

Angel ground her teeth. Sam prepared to argue with her some more, but she crossed her arms and harrumphed. "Fine. Go be the hero."

Relieved, Sam took a deep breath. He had to keep Max safe, but at least he wouldn't have to worry about Triniti and Angel too.

Max hesitated, then stuck his key in the door and undid the lock.

Sam nodded and slipped inside with Max on his heels.

☆☆☆☆

Erebus ran the blade along the flesh of Monica's thigh. Though he hadn't sliced her skin yet, she cringed in anticipation. He traced the tip of cold steel slowly up her bare belly, over the contours of her bra, and along the curve of her neck. The edge of the blade paused at the base of her throat, gently pressing against the carotid artery.

Her heart almost exploded in fear as she waited for him to cut her open.

The black abyss of his eyes grew deeper. Colder. Impossibly more vacant. "I can feel the life that's flowing through you," he hissed. He lingered, keeping the blade pressed firmly against her skin. "Delicious," he said, as though on the brink of orgasm.

Orgasmically delicious? Not exactly what she'd been thinking.

"Erebus," she began. "I—"

The pressure against her throat suddenly abated. Though she had no idea what she'd been about to say, surprise cut her off mid-sentence.

Erebus cocked his head and appeared to be listening to something she could not hear.

More voices?

After a few seconds, a hyena smile slinked across his lips. "Your friends are here. I knew we couldn't really begin until they'd arrived and been dealt with."

He ran the back of his hand along her cheek. "Do not worry, my love. Soon, we will be together." He pulled a rag from his back pocket. Though she fought him, he gripped her cheeks, forced her jaw open, and shoved the cloth into her mouth.

He held a finger to his lips. "Ssshhh."

When he kissed her forehead, his hot, poisonous breath washed over her, and she had to swallow hard to keep from retching against the gag.

He walked away. Something clicked. The room plummeted into darkness.

☆☆☆☆

Standing in the back of the shadowy showroom, Sam quietly grasped the workshop doorknob. As he prepared to dive through, gun blazing, the mat of light spilling under the doorjamb went dark.

He and Max looked at each other.

"What does that mean?" Max whispered.

Sam shook his head. He didn't know, but this turn of events gave him pause. If he charged in, a bullet could be waiting for him. "Where's the light switch?"

"It's to the left about hip height," Max said, touching the spot on the wall.

Sam nodded. "Okay, I'm going to go in, hit the switch, and blow away anything that moves, so stay behind me."

Max frowned. "What about Monica?"

"We're running out of time. I'll just have to watch for her. Ready?"

Max gave a curt nod.

Sam took a deep breath, twisted the handle, and rolled across the threshold. He flipped the light switch, but nothing happened.

Behind him, Max cried out and the door between the shop and the sales floor slammed shut.

Sam spun, grabbed the handle, and twisted, but it refused to turn. Someone had just locked him in the workshop.

The thick door separating the sales floor from the back room, heavy enough to keep power tool noise from disturbing the patrons, also prevented Sam from just breaking it down. With no way to return to the front of the building without going outside and around, he began banging on the thick door. "Max!"

With a reverberating thud, something—or some-one—smashed into the wall. Then stillness.

The killer hadn't been waiting for them in the workshop as Sam had anticipated. In a severe case of tunnel vision, Sam, focused on the light, must have walked right past Erebus on the way to the rear of the store and fallen into the madman's trap.

He cursed. They'd underestimated Erebus. Again.

Chapter Thirty-Eight

Sam had instructed the women to stay in the bus with the intent of keeping them safe. Except now, staring around the utter blackness of the workshop, he wondered how smart it had been to sideline half of his team. Angel may not be formally trained, but she made up for it in enthusiasm and ferocity.

"Monica," he whispered into the darkness. He detected movement someplace ahead. Keeping his gun raised, he slowly shuffled forward. "Monica," he whispered again. More movement and what sounded like muffled screaming.

He continued sliding forward until his foot collided with something. A clang resounded, as loud as a clap of thunder. Sam jumped and aimed his gun at things he could not see.

A large drop of sweat ran down his forehead and into his eyes. As he wiped it away with the sleeve of his shirt, a glacially cold draft breezed over his skin. Before his mind had a chance to digest the significance of the chill, something solid and heavy collided with him, sending him sprawling.

The gun flew out of his hand, lost in the inkiness. He fumbled, trying to find purchase on whoever sat on him. The squatter grabbed his hair and drove his head into the floor. Once. Twice. A third time. Exploding stars dazzled Sam's vision.

Before he had a chance to recover, his assailant flipped him over, pinning his arms. The unmistakable zing and cinching bite of a zip tie encircled his wrists. He weakly tugged, but his hands remained secure behind his back.

Hot breath blew in his ear as Tyron Erebus whispered, "Gotcha."

Grabbing his hair again, the psycho slammed the side of Sam's head into the floor one more time. The world blitzed into a kaleidoscope of fireworks. Then his universe faded, and Sam saw nothing at all.

☆☆☆☆

The lights blazed to life and Monica had to blink back tears as her eyes adjusted. At first, she'd hoped that her friends had arrived to save her, but as her vision cleared, her heart sank. Sam lay on the floor, his hands bound behind his back, head bleeding.

Erebus stood next to the fuse panel on the far side of the room, the cobra smile still on his lips. He walked over and touched her chin. "Now that we won't be interrupted, we can continue." He pulled the rag out of her mouth.

"You'll never get away with this." Monica spat in between bouts of coughing.

Erebus looked at her as though she were the most pitiful creature on Earth. "Away with it? I don't want to get *away* at all. That's not the goal. Don't you understand that?"

Monica glared at him. "The only thing I understand is that you'll be dead soon. More people will come, and they will put an end to your pathetic existence." While she'd tried to sound brave and confident, her groundless threat sounded weak even to her own ears.

He shook his head. "No one else is coming. And as soon you truly understand my gift of redemption, you won't want them to."

"Well," she said resignedly. "You might be right; perhaps no one else is coming."

"There. You are finally beginning to see—"

"But it doesn't matter because I can take care of myself." She whipped her hand out from under the side of the table. The wicked blade of the scalpel in her palm flashed and glinted in the bright light as it arched through the air toward Erebus' throat.

His eyes grew wide as he dodged.

Unable to adjust the path of the weapon in time, she buried the knife into his shoulder.

Erebus snarled and reached for it. But as he grasped the handle, a blurry figure flew across the room and collided into the madman's stomach, driving him into a large pile of paint cans.

"Max!" Monica yelled in surprise.

Having only been able to free her wrist, she remained a hostage on the workbench and could only watch frustratingly, infuriatingly helpless as the two men punched and pounded one another.

Triniti and Angel stormed through the showroom door and ran to Monica's side.

Angel's face hovered above her. "Are you okay? Oh my god, your hand is bleeding."

Relief flooded Monica's veins. "Yes, yes, I'm fine. Hurry, cut me loose. We need to help Max."

Triniti grabbed a pair of scissors from the little silver tray at Monica's head and snipped the strap on her wrist and the other one binding her legs. "We saw the bastard come around the side of the store and we thought he was trying to get away. But when he went back inside through the front door, we kinda figured things hadn't gone..." Her eyes went wide as she held the long, sinister blades up to the light. "Was he going to use these on you?"

Monica nodded. "Pretty sure that was his plan."

Fury etched lines around Angel's eyes and in the set of her mouth. She grabbed the scissors from Triniti, marched over to where Erebus pounded Max's face, and raised her hand above her head.

Max must have looked at her, giving away her element of surprise, because as her arm came down, Erebus reached up, caught her wrist, twisted it, and flipped her over.

The scissors fell from her hand and Angel cried out as she too landed in the pile of cans.

Erebus hit Max one more time and then stood.

Free at last, Monica sat up, preparing to take on the madman as he turned toward her. But to her utter shock, Triniti stepped between them. "To get to her, you'll have to go through me."

Laughing, Erebus grabbed Triniti by the throat. The large veins in his forearm bulged thick as baby vipers as he squeezed.

Howling with rage, Monica leapt off the table. She jumped on him, screaming and tearing at him like a feral cat. Though she drew blood, he kept on choking Triniti.

"Hey, asshole."

Both Monica and Erebus looked down just as Max pressed the nail gun to the top of Erebus' boot and pulled the trigger.

Erebus roared and let go of Triniti, who fell to the floor in a heap. He tried to push Monica off of him. At first, she kept on scratching his face and tearing at his eyes. But when he shoved her harder, she lost her grip and landed on the floor next to Triniti. A loose plank dug painfully into her hip.

The nail gun jerked as Max put another metal spike through Erebus' other boot.

Erebus screamed louder and tried to pull free, but the wooden floor held him in place.

"Triniti," Max wheezed. "Here." He slid the scissors across the floor. "Get Sam."

She caught them and began crawling toward Sam.

Bellowing, Erebus grabbed for the nail gun.

Instead of trying to yank away, Max pushed forward while pulling the trigger. The safety head released, and the tool barked, driving a nail into Erebus' palm.

He cursed, lost his balance, and fell forward onto Max, knocking the gun to the side. Erebus grabbed the gun's hydraulic air hose and began pulling it back to him.

"Oh no, you don't," Monica snarled. Despite the pain in her hip, she stumbled to her feet and leapt on him again.

"Bitch," Erebus growled and shoved her off once more. Monica flew through the air and collided with the workbench, driving the air from her lungs.

The madman grabbed the handle of the tool, pushed Max to the floor, and pressed the tip against his forehead.

"No!" Monica wheezed.

A deafening roar filled the room as a puckered hole appeared in the back of Erebus' shirt. For a heartbeat, the world froze. The spot began to weep crimson, and Erebus slowly turned. With anger and disbelief in his eyes, he glared at Sam, who kept the barrel of the smoking gun aimed at him.

The pneumatic tool clattered from Erebus' hand as he fell to the side. Twisted awkwardly with his feet still stuck to the floor, he stared up at the ceiling.

The fathomless color of his irises muted, losing their depth and intensity. As the madman bled out onto the cold wood floor, his eyes changed from black to red, then finally faded to yellow.

☆☆☆☆

Tyron Erebus felt the blood soaking the back of his shirt as the life force drained from his body. When the other started to drift away, Erebus pleaded with the deity he'd spent his whole life worshipping.

Take me with you.

The other swirled around him, trying to leave, but Erebus grabbed it, pulling it back. He didn't know he could do that until just now. If only he'd known before, things might have turned out differently.

The spirit flared with angry heat. It cursed and condemned him as it lashed out, striking him again and again with electrified fury. He lost his grip and the other whipped him once more before vanishing.

Erebus floated in a void of nothingness. Alone. Lost. He'd just begun to wonder if he'd spend eternity drifting through an icy vacuum of desolation—not ruling the gods as had been preordained—when a streak of lightning tore through the blackness. Instead of fading, the bolt grew, widening into a chasm that seemed to rip the fabric of the universe in two.

Rage, beautiful in its pureness, poured out, enveloping him and filling his entire being with agony.

Staring in awe and wonder, he whispered, "It's beautiful. Such pure hatred. Such anger."

The chasm erupted. The force of the blast exploded all of the windows of *The Board Wake*. Glass flung so violently in every direction that large shards stuck into the surrounding structures, burying themselves deep into nearby trees and shattering the windshield of Triniti's beloved bus parked out front.

The chasm collapsed with the man inside of it, and Tyron Erebus was no more.

Chapter Thirty-Nine

Lights flashed and winked from half a dozen cruisers parked in front of the surf shop. From the back of an ambulance, Sam watched the deputies and CSI team methodically take statements and tag evidence. He and Max—who sat next to him—sported matching ice packs pressed to their heads.

Monica had been given a set of scrubs to cover her near-nakedness. She, Angel, and Triniti sat huddled together in the rear of another ambulance. An EMT tried to examine Angel's bruised and battered face, but Angel kept waving the poor woman away. The two exchanged words, which Sam could not hear at this distance. Finally, the tech gave up and turned her focus to Monica.

Sam smirked. "That'll teach her to mess with Angel."

Max nodded.

Night had given way to early morning. The two men sat in companionable silence while they waited for the women to finish up and the sheriff to give them the green light to leave.

"That thing we saw," Max said quietly, without looking at Sam. "The thing we *felt*. The cold and then the heat and the...pressure."

"What about it?"

"You had us tell the police that Erebus set off a bomb."

Sam didn't reply.

Max, still not looking at him, said, "But we all know that's not what happened. Whatever did that, whatever that was...it wasn't from here. It wasn't natural."

"Maybe, maybe not. Are you wondering if we should have told the police the truth?"

Max forced a chuckle. "Hardly. I can only imagine what the good sheriff's reaction would've been had we said that a seriously pissed off demon, or poltergeist, or whatever had busted up the shop."

"Then what?" Sam asked.

Max was quiet for several seconds. "I'm thinking that what we told the police, about the bomb, needs to be the truth."

Sam nodded slowly.

"He must have set up the explosives before we arrived. Maybe had them on a trigger. I'm not a pyromaniac, so I wouldn't know." Max paused again. "I've never killed anyone before."

"And you still haven't. I did that. I shot him."

"I know, but I was part of it. I helped. I'm an accessory."

"You did what you had to do," Sam said. "You saved us all." He added, "There's no reason for you to feel guilty."

"I don't feel guilty. Not even a little. We killed the man who murdered my sister and a lot of other people. That's completely justifiable in my book. I won't lose a single minute of sleep over it. It's just that..."

"...you're not sure you want to consider a world where something else, something not from here, is possible," Sam finished for him.

Max shivered. Reaching behind him, he grabbed a blanket, unfolded it, and wrapped it around his shoulders. No breeze stirred the early morning air or whispered secrets through the branches of the palm trees lining the street. The mercury in the thermostat hovered in the mid-seventies, as it did most nights in towns so near the equator. But something—a notion, a thought, or a phantom—must have put a chill in his bones.

"I'm just a boardhead," Max said, "from a backwater town. I run my business, worship the ocean, hang with my friends, and love my girl. That's it. The possibility that there are other...things that we can't see doesn't fit."

"Speaking of your girl, what are you going to tell her?" Sam asked.

Max shrugged. "The truth. I always tell Abs everything. There are no half-truths or white lies between us."

Sam digested this. He wondered what it would be like to live so simply and honestly, to be free of the burdens of deceit, manipulation, and ulterior motives. He stared up at the moon, listened to the waves cresting and crashing, and briefly imagined giving it all up. The money he'd stockpiled could easily see him drift off into the sunset. With all that had happened in The Agency—the corruption and backroom deals—what was he really fighting for anyway?

Before he had a chance to contemplate further, Angel and Monica, recently released by their medic, strolled over, hand in hand.

"Here's trouble if I ever saw it," Max said with a half-cocked smile.

Angel glanced at him before turning to Sam. "Well, you finally managed to do your job. Glad to see that only a couple dozen people had to die, a town had to be traumatized, and Max's shop had to get blown up for you to get it done. Hope you're proud of yourself."

"Hey, I..." he began, but then he noticed the wisp of a grin playing at the corners of her lips. He shook his head. "You need a better poker face."

Angel pointed at him. "You fell for it, Mr. FBI. I saw it."

"Please stop calling me that." To Monica, he said, "You're finally free. For real this time. So, what's next?"

"School." She nodded sideways at Angel. "For both of us actually. Law for me and criminology for her."

Angel said, "We had a plan, and we're sticking to it. What about you guys?"

"I've got to fix the store." Max nodded toward the building with the busted-out windows. "It's kind of a disaster right now."

"How are you going to explain it to Abby?"

Max frowned and glanced around the group. "Why does everyone keep asking me that? She's not a tyrant."

Angel raised her eyebrows. "She's got a vested interest in your business. When she sees the bills, she'll make Erebus look like a Buddhist monk."

"Nah," Max said. "She'll be cool."

Monica's eyes found Sam's. "So, what's next on the agenda for you, Peter-Sam?"

"I really haven't given it a lot of thought." He paused. "I think I'll stay around here for a while. Max could use some help putting the shop back together. I still feel like I should have been able to stop the bastard before he caused so much damage."

Angel raised her hand. "I second that notion."

Sam ignored her. "I think I'm finally due some vacation time. Once we're done with the shop, I'm going to give hula girl a ride."

"I told you you'd dream about her," Max said.

Monica glanced over her shoulder at Triniti, who had a blanket wrapped around her shoulders and was still with the EMT. "I think there's someone that's going to be really glad to hear you're staying."

Sam followed her gaze.

Triniti caught them looking at her and smiled.

He nodded and returned the smile, though it felt disingenuous on his lips. He'd been playing Triniti, using her to gather information. But now, he worried that she might have actual—or at least have the beginnings of—feelings for him. Normally, he'd just ride out of town and not worry about the emotional debris he'd left in his wake.

Sheriff Austin joined the group. "Alright, looks like we're done here. We need the bus for evidence, but we should be finished with the shop in the morning."

Max nodded. "Fine by me, but you'll have to talk to the lady over there about her beloved Charlie. I don't know if she's going to take the news so well."

The sheriff lifted the brim of his hat and scratched his forehead. "Yeah, I reckon not. A couple of the deputies have offered to take you home if you're ready."

"Are we ever," Monica and Angel said in unison.

The sheriff went back to his car.

Angel started to turn away, but she paused. To Sam she said, "For someone I loathe, you're actually not too bad."

Monica leaned in and kissed him on the cheek. "Thanks for everything." She pulled back, holding his gaze. In her eyes, he glimpsed a lifetime of unjustified loneliness, pain, and suffering. But he also recognized an uncanny strength and resolve to persevere.

The women turned and walked away. Just before Monica followed Angel into one of the squad cars, she stopped. Her eyes locked on his for a heartbeat, and then she ducked inside and closed the door.

"They're going to be alright," Sam said, more to himself than anyone.

Max nodded. "Yep, I know. It's time for me to go too. Abs was planning to come home tomorrow. I just hope they have the bridge put back together by then. It's going to take a week to tell her all of what happened."

Sam offered his hand. "Good luck with that."

Instead of shaking, Max grabbed Sam's palm, pulled him into a bear hug, and thumped him on the back.

Surprised by Max's easy affection, Sam froze. It must have been about as comfortable as hugging a telephone pole, yet Max didn't seem to care. Nor did he let go. After a second—though he felt conspicuous as hell—Sam awkwardly returned the embrace.

To his relief, Max *finally* released him and grinned as if reading Sam's distress. "Guess I'll see you in the morning."

Max slid into another squad car. The cruiser's lights flared to life and it drove off.

Sam went to Triniti, just as the medic finished putting away the field kit.

"Are you ready to go home?" he asked.

"Am I ever!"

"The sheriff said they're taking the bus for evidence."

She shrugged. "I figured. But it looks like the deputies are giving everyone rides."

He took her hand and led her to one of the waiting squad cars. Sam opened the rear door.

Triniti hesitated, studying his face. "You aren't coming with me. Are you?"

He smiled at her as he shook his head.

She inhaled deeply and let out a long, slow breath. Returning his smile with a sad one of her own, she dabbed at her eyes with the corner of her blanket. Triniti leaned over and kissed him on the cheek, in the exact same spot Monica had just a minute earlier. Without another word, she got into the back seat.

Sam closed her door and watched as the car drove away. He gazed up at the starry sky and the moon peaking over the mountain crests. A loon called in the distance. Then, serenaded by the soft overture of ocean waves, he headed off into the night.

The End

Acknowledgements

First and foremost, I want to thank my readers. As I mentioned in the dedication, some of you have been waiting over three years for the concluding half of the Monica Sable case. Gracious alive, y'all are a patient lot.

Thank you to my street team: Jessica Calla and Chrissy Lessey, both great writers who agreed to step out of their normal genres to read *Redemption*. Nobody gives it to you straighter than another author, and you two did not disappoint. Your insights were invaluable and your efforts appreciated. Thank you for lending me your expertise.

Becky, aka Guido. Sister friend, you rock. I don't know if your hawk eyes for catching typos was learned or inherited, but I'm grateful to you for digging through the rocks and rooting out those slippery little buggers that everyone else missed. For the record, my book is never complete until it has Guido's stamp of approval on it.

To my father, who was the first one to point out in *122 Rules* (when my characters tended to have potty mouths) that foul language is like chili powder: a little bit goes a very long way. Thank you for that lesson and for always providing your insights into my books.

To José: Thank you for teaching me a bit of slang, Española style.

My beta team: Nicole and Jason. Y'all are awesome!

To my editor, Erin Rhew. Thank you for lending your amazing editorial skills. Your talents and efforts have not only made this book a zillion times better, you've made me a much better writer. You are the best in the business, and I'm incredibly lucky to have you as my editor.

To my bride, Erin Rhew. From 3,000 miles away, you stole my heart and every day since you've shown me the true meaning of partnership. Thank you for your love, your support, and your unending patience. I adore you more than there are words in the English language to describe.

About the Author

Deek did not set out to be a writer. Originally, he wanted to follow his father's path as a career military man and fly for the Air Force. So, Deek spent two years in high school preparing for the ROTC. During a routine check-in, his recruiter asked about any handicaps, to which Deek jokingly replied he was colorblind. The recruiter got a funny look on his face and informed Deek that the closest he'd ever get to the pilot's seat was from the scheduling office. Ummm...no.

After that, Deek focused on his love for music—touring with a local rock band and majoring in art in college. Unfortunately, he didn't enjoy the life of a pauper, so he started secondary school over. Ten years later, he walked across the stage with a computer science degree. He now slings web code during the day to support his seven day a week writing habit.

Though he loves his job and the people he works with, Deek has been enthralled by the written word and storytelling since he picked up his first Stephen King novel, *It*. On his way to work one day, a scene so vivid flashed through his mind that he felt compelled to pull over and put it to paper. Having neither quill nor parchment in which to document the image, he laboriously pecked out the first chapter of *122 Rules* on his phone.

A transplant from a rainy pocket in the Pacific Northwest, Deek now lives in a sultry corner of the US of A where the sun shines bright, the sweet tea flows, and the hush puppies are hot and delicious. He and his brilliant, but stunning author bride, Erin Rhew, live a simple life with their writing assistant, a fat tabby named Trinity. They enjoy lingering in the mornings, and often late into the night, caught up Erin's fantastic fantasy worlds of noble princes and knights and entwined in Deek's dark underworld of the FBI and drug lords.

He and Erin love to share books by reading aloud to one another. In addition, they enjoy spending time with friends, running, boxing, lifting weights, and adventuring.

Thank you for purchasing this copy of *122 Rules - Redemption*, Book Two in the 122 Rules Series. If you enjoyed this book by Deek, please let him know by posting a short review. If you purchased this book through Amazon, it is eligible for a free Kindle Match.

One of my favorite things about being a writer is building relationships with readers.
I occasionally send out newsletters with details on new releases, information on how to become part of my advanced reader team, as well as subscriber-only material.

If you sign up to the mailing list, you'll get a Tenacious Books Starter kit which includes two **free**, award-winning novels.

You can get both books for free by scanning the above QR code with your smartphone.

Alternately, you can register at:
www.DeekRhewBooks.com/contact.html

Thank you for being a
Tenacious Books Reader!

Made in the USA
Coppell, TX
03 December 2022

87717692R00236